# YOU
# CAN
# HIDE

## Also by Rebecca Zanetti

# YOU
# CAN
# HIDE

## REBECCA
## ZANETTI

## ZEBRA BOOKS
### Kensington Publishing Corp.
www.kensingtonbooks.com

First Printing: December 2022
ISBN-13: 978-1-4201-5434-4
ISBN-13: 978-1-4201-5435-1 (eBook)

10 9 8 7 6 5 4 3 2 1
Printed in the United States of America

*This one is dedicated to the English and writing teachers I was lucky enough to learn from through the years, and while I've forgotten many names, these still stand out: Dr. Ken Waters, who taught me to trust my instincts when it came to writing, Eileen Bieber, who taught me to structure my writing, Mike Ruskovich, who taught me to let my imagination run wild when writing, Ardyce Plumley, who taught me to stop and enjoy the process of writing, and Ms. Wright, who taught me to diagram sentences and the importance of doing so. Thank you for sharing your love of both reading and writing.*

# Acknowledgments

Thank you to Tony Zanetti for his patience, humor, and ability to magically find lost pieces of paper throughout the house where I've left ideas for a book. Thank you to Gabe Zanetti for calling at the best times and right when I need a synonym for green, and thank you to Karlina Zanetti for being so creative and inspiring with her own stories;

Thank you to my agent, Caitlin Blasdell, for knowing exactly what extra element to add to a story to make it have the magic and for working with me to balance my schedule after arm surgery. Thank you for just talking me through the stress and brainstorming ideas for both my schedule and for my stories;

Thank you to my editor, Alicia Condon, for knowing exactly how to find the right tension to balance a thriller and for being so understanding and proactive in creating a successful schedule for my several series as I healed after arm surgery;

Thank you to the rest of the Kensington gang: Alexandra Nicolajsen, Steven Zacharias, Adam Zacharias, Ross Plotkin, Lynn Cully,

Vida Engstrand, Jane Nutter, Lauren Jernigan, Kimberly Richardson, and Rebecca Cremonese;

A special thank you to Pam Joplin for the absolutely phenomenal copy edits;

Thank you to Anissa Beatty, my assistant and social media expert who often texts at midnight with awesome ideas and who is always up for trying something fun and zany;

Thank you to Leanna Feazel, Madison Fairbanks, Julie Elkin, and Katy Nielsen for your friendship, support, and all-around great times via Zoom and the Rebels. You have no idea how much I love seeing and talking with you online;

Thank you to Rebels Jessica Mobbs, Heather Frost, Kimberly Frost, Madison Fairbanks, Suzi Zuber, Asmaa Nada Qayyum, Amanda Larsen, Karen Clementi, and Karen Fisher for their assistance with this book;

Thank you also to my constant support system: Gail and Jim English, Kathy and Herb Zanetti, Debbie and Travis Smith, Stephanie and Don West, Jessica and Jonah Namson, Steve and Liz Berry, Jillian and Benji Stein, and the entire Younker family.

# Prologue

He didn't feel late January's bite, even though he sank to his knees in the thick snow. Instead, the sparking thrill of anticipation poured through his veins with the heat of a first love. Oh, the woman in the desolate cabin was neither his love nor his first, but for now, she was his purpose.

For weeks, she'd been his sole focus, and now he could wait no longer. Dreaming about her wasn't enough. He knew how to calm the rage inside him. Finally, he'd learned, and it was all so clear. He had been shown the way.

Now he knew his purpose and could be whole.

Another siren's song whispered on the frigid wind, and he'd already left her his calling card, which meant a new project had begun. Although he did like to have one or two projects going at a time, it was time to end this one.

She'd cheated him out of what he needed, and she had to pay for that. She'd completely deserted him and the life they could've had. She hadn't even said good-bye. Out in the middle of nowhere, she'd thought she could hide from him? Avoid the roles they both needed to play? The lover's presents he'd planned to shower upon her had been irrelevant to her—and she must have known he'd made plans.

He had meant nothing to her.

He'd found her hiding place, and then he'd played a little. Leaving her an oddity here, a scary sign there. Just enough to have her catching her breath and then convincing herself that she was imagining things in the middle of nowhere. He was smarter than she was, and it was time she realized that fact. Not only smarter, but more powerful.

Life was about power, was it not? He'd learned that the hard way.

Darkness hung heavily above the mountains as another winter storm punished the trees. Brutal snow pummeled the over-loaded branches and assaulted the ice shielding the creek. His woman, for right now she was his, always emerged about this time to trudge around a series of rocks to the primitive outhouse. He had opened the door one night and poured water on the hinges.

How she'd struggled to shut the door the following morning.

He'd watched from a vantage point across the creek, nearly doubling over with silent laughter. When she'd given up the fight and just used the toilet, he'd snapped pictures with his long-range lens. His groin tightened at the memory.

It was amusing she thought she could hide from him. Oh, she was smart enough to cower where she couldn't be traced—unless somebody had put a tracker on her vehicle. When she'd left her compact to drive an enclosed side-by-side with tracks from the deserted public boat launch, he'd been on her tail already, easily following her trail to this hideaway.

He wasn't a god, but to her, he might as well be.

His gaze caught on an ax beneath an eave near a covered pile of wood.

That would do.

# Chapter One

The victim's hands had been removed—most likely with the ax left leaning against an ice-covered pine tree. Her wrists were bloody stumps resting on cut logs, which the killer must've used to position the flesh for his strike. Perfectly preserved, burgundy-colored flowers littered the ground in every direction around the body, several petals frozen solid to rocks at the edge of the ice-encrusted river. Their stark color leeched into the white snow, creating icy pools of frozen blood.

The victim was female and naked, her flesh frozen to a grayish-blue hue, her facial structure shattered beyond recognition. Blood marred the snow all around her. The techs had worked all morning to gently uncover her and the surrounding area without causing damage.

Laurel Snow crouched on the craggy bank of Witch Creek, a hidden tributary of the Sauk River in northern Washington State. Icy snow clung to her knit hat and pinged off her snow boots. "There's not enough blood here. The mutilations happened post-mortem," she murmured, looking up at FBI Agent Walter Smudgeon, who had bent to study the ax.

He straightened. "Not much blood on the ax." He

turned, his wide cheeks ruddy, his belly hanging over his belt. "Broken face and stolen hands. Somebody definitely wanted to keep her from being identified."

Laurel scrutinized the ligature marks around the woman's neck. "She was strangled. We'll know more after the autopsy." She studied the woman's hair, which was black with a clear demarcation of gray—maybe three or even four weeks' worth. "She was due for a hair appointment."

"What does that mean?" Walter wheezed.

Laurel stood. "I'm not sure." Her phone buzzed from her pocket, and she ignored the caller. Again.

"What's with the flowers?" Walter asked.

"It's interesting," Laurel said, the wind burning the exposed skin on her face and ears. "I think these are black dahlias."

"Black? Those are red," Walter said, pulling his winter coat lower to cover his wide belly, his jowls moving as he spoke.

"They're burgundy colored, and I believe they're black dahlias," Laurel repeated, a sense of isolation cutting through her, even as state crime scene personnel worked efficiently around her. She tilted her head toward Captain Monty Buckley, who was photographing the petals closer to the creek. "Did you find the personal locator beacon?"

The victim had activated the PLB, which sent a distress call through satellite to emergency services around midnight the night before, but searchers had to wait until light because of the devastating snowstorm that had only just abated. The second search team had found the body, which had already been mostly covered with snow and ice, except for her feet, which lay in the moving creek, shoved carelessly beneath a jagged layer of ice.

Monty looked up, his eyes blue and his hair a silvery

gray that was turning more white from his recent cancer treatments. "Not yet." He surveyed the snow still gently falling to cover the earth in every direction. "It's a long shot that we'll find it at all." He grimaced at the flowers. "What's up with the red petals? Some symbolic thing?"

"I believe they symbolize betrayal," Laurel said, clicking through her memory of a book she'd read years ago. "We can conduct more research later."

A tall figure walked between two trees, kicking snow out of the way and creating a trail with his size fourteen boots.

"Huck," Laurel said, taken aback. "Where did you come from?"

"Monty called me. There's an old forest service trail to the north, and I drove my snowmobile along that route. I've cut a trail from there. You're going to want to see this," Huck Rivers said, his eyes a whiskey brown, his whiskers a day past needing a shave, and his hat partially covering his thick black hair. His Karelian bear dog, Aeneas, bounded behind him, tail wagging and tongue out.

Laurel blinked. She and Walter had ridden in Fish and Wildlife UTVs from the Sauk River to the creek to reach the scene, and she hadn't realized Huck would be out there. It had been more than a month since they'd worked together, since they'd seen each other, and she'd wondered about him. Had he spent Christmas and then most of January alone in his cabin? She'd been in DC for much of January working on another case and had only been back in town for a couple of days. "All right," she said coolly, stepping carefully over icy rocks and slippery snow to reach him. "Lead on, Captain."

His gaze inscrutable, he turned, his broad shoulders blocking the trail he'd created. "Follow me."

She'd forgotten how tall he stood and walked close to

him so he could break the brutal wind. Her hands were chilled through the rubber gloves, but she kept them outside her pockets to avoid picking up trace evidence, although the snow continued to land and then melt on her.

They walked for about ten minutes, around bushes, under boughs, and over icy brush, with snow piled on either side of the makeshift trail. Her legs ached, and the biting wind sliced to her bones, weakening her muscles.

Huck paused and partially turned to the right. In profile, his features were more rugged than the brutal mountains around them. "If you look there, the victim's footprints are still visible in the snow because of the tree covering above them. I've taken pictures, because they're going to disappear within the hour."

Laurel squinted to see through the thick trees at the smaller prints, followed by much larger ones. "Are those yours?"

"No. Mine are a yard beyond those prints. I paralleled the trail as I took pictures." He made a hand gesture, and the black-and-white dog sat obediently. "From the spacing of the steps, they were running, and both broke several branches on the way." He pointed farther down the snowy trail. "She fell twice but got back up and kept running."

Laurel could imagine the woman's terror. "Where did she come from?"

"This way." He turned again.

Aeneas sat in place, one ear up as if he wanted to ask her a question.

She couldn't pet him and get fur on her gloves, so she smiled. "Hi, Aeneas. Miss me?"

Did Huck's shoulders square at that question? They'd shared one intimate night together, and then nothing. She'd thought they might be becoming friends, but then he'd disappeared. The dog yipped and flipped around to follow his master.

Laurel trudged behind the two males, stepping gingerly over the exposed root of a tree that rose high out of the deep snow. The pine would probably fall over in the howling wind. She turned at a bend and stopped upon spotting a dark structure that nearly disappeared into the rock wall behind it. "Incredible."

Huck nodded. "Yeah. It's an old forestry cabin that was abandoned about ten years ago, according to my office. Nobody knew anyone was staying out here."

Weathered wooden logs created a square-shaped cabin built against a solid rock wall. A crumbled stack of planks showed what had once been a porch, leaving the door two feet above the ground, now iced over with snow. A tarp partially covered a battered old side-by-side utility terrain vehicle beneath two mature blue spruce trees to the right of the cabin.

"I removed part of the tarp to see what was secured under there," Huck explained.

Laurel looked around. Her phone buzzed again and she ignored it. "I take it UTVs are the only way to access this area?"

"Or snowmobile, during the winter." Huck pointed to his black snowmobile with a Fish and Wildlife designation on the side. "I guess somebody could hike in during summer months. I took that old forest division trail, while you all drove along the river and then cut east along the creek."

A branch broke over by the tarp, the ice and wind having triumphed over the slim wood.

Laurel jumped as ice and pinecones rained down. "Is that how the killer or killers reached this place? We didn't see any tracks on our way in."

Huck wiped snow off his cheekbone. "The snowstorm eliminated any possible tracks out here, so we don't even know which way the killer came."

Laurel looked around and shivered. "What a lonely place to hide."

"Hide?"

"Yes." Laurel moved beyond him, following his trail to the front door, which she nudged open. The cabin was one room with a blow-up mattress covered by several blankets, a fireplace with kindling and neatly stacked logs next to it, and a kitchen shelf holding a battery-operated hot plate, a plate, and a cup. Cans and more cans sat on the shelf. Noodles, soup, beans, veggies, and fruit. Even something that said turkey on it. Along with several gallon bottles of vodka and gin. Enough for months of self-numbing.

She walked to the unmade bed and lifted a tablet from it, scrolling through pages of books. "How—"

"Small portable generator," Huck said, pointing to the one window above the kitchen shelf. "It's right outside with gas not too far from it. She was able to charge her tablet, heating pad, hot plate, and it looks like a burner phone." He gestured to a basket near the bed. "She has enough gas out there for probably another month."

It wasn't even February yet. "So she'd need to traverse the forest again in that UTV, and the conditions will probably be even worse next month," Laurel noted. "From what I can tell, she was more prepared than that."

"Maybe she didn't know how much gas she'd need," Huck mused. "Beyond the gas containers is a very old and rough outhouse. Yards away is an area of rock where she left the empty food cans, after washing them thoroughly with either water from the river or melted snow, from what I can tell."

So no animals would come sniffing around.

Laurel spotted a cabinet barely visible next to the low bed. She removed her flashlight from her pocket and inched closer, shining it inside. "There's something . . ." Tugging open the cabinet, she took inventory.

Huck whistled behind her.

This close, his body heat flushed along her back, even through her jacket.

"SIG Sauer," Huck mused, leaning over her shoulder for a better look. "And what looks like plenty of ammo."

Laurel turned and looked at the door. "She didn't get a chance to use her gun. So he surprised her outside with his attack?"

"The footprints in the snow come from the outhouse area," Huck said.

Laurel tried to imagine the night and how terrified the woman would've been. "So she took her PLB with her to the outhouse but not a weapon? I don't think so. She must've had another weapon." She leaned in to study the bullets.

Huck pursed his lips. "You're right. We'll search the area, and I'll scout the way she ran again. Chances are he surprised her and got the gun but didn't see the PLB before she pressed the button."

"If she was in hiding, she would've used that device to call for help as a last resort," Laurel agreed. "We have to identify her." She held the tablet in her hand. "This should help."

Her phone buzzed again.

Huck's left eyebrow rose. "Somebody is being persistent."

Laurel drew an evidence bag out of her other pocket and slid the tablet into it, before handing the bag to him. "Yes." Giving in, she tugged her phone free, seeing Dr. Abigail Caine's name on the screen. "What is it, Dr. Caine?" she asked by way of answer.

"Now, Laurel, is that any way to talk to your sister?" Abigail bit out, her slight British accent emerging to make her sound more than a little peeved. "You returned to town a full two days ago, and you haven't answered my calls."

Laurel shut her eyes and centered herself. She would not ask about Abigail's familiarity with her schedule. "I'm in the middle of a case right now. We'll have to chat another time."

"No," Abigail snapped. "We will speak now. I am in danger, and as my sister, you are going to help me."

"Half sister," Laurel returned, unwilling to deal with this right now. "I will call you later, Abigail."

"No. Somebody is harassing me, and it has to stop. I returned late last night from a retreat to find flowers scattered all across my front lawn this morning, some already frozen and some still breezing along. It's weird."

Laurel stilled. She cut Huck a look; he was watching her carefully. "Flowers? What variety of flowers?"

Abigail sighed. "They're black dahlias. A substantial number of them."

# Chapter Two

The high-end subdivision where Abigail Caine resided was quiet in the overcast afternoon. Angled rooftops and tall windows predominated in the wood, brick, and stone homes as Laurel drove past several mansions to the far cul-de-sac where Abigail lived, with forest on one side and another vacant-looking house on the other, a good distance away. Trees and landscaped yards made each home private, so it was quite possible the inhabitants hadn't seen anything unusual happening at Abigail's.

Laurel drove down Abigail's icy drive, noting the many blackish-red petals covering the portion of the yard closest to the house. Snow and ice had crusted over them, showing they'd been there for at least a couple of nights.

She cut off the engine of her new, rented Nissan Rogue, which she'd picked up just yesterday. Since she wasn't certain she'd be staying in town, purchasing a vehicle didn't make sense. Then she sat as silence descended, heavier than an anxiety blanket. Unlike many of the other homes, Abigail's had light shining through the flimsy curtains on the massive floor-to-ceiling windows.

Snow fell lazily from a darkened sky, covering Laurel's

windshield. Cold almost instantly seeped into her SUV, and she shivered.

The front door opened.

She exited the car and shut the door, studying the iced-over petals. There was no discernible pattern, and the snow had obliterated any possible footprints. These flowers had been scattered *before* the ones around the body found near the river. Odd.

"Laurel? Come in. There's no pattern to the flowers or petals," Abigail called, her breath puffing in the cold air.

Laurel turned and made her way along the freshly plowed driveway to the walk, meeting her half sister at the porch.

Abigail partly blocked the way inside, her head cocked, her eyes—one green, one blue—scrutinizing Laurel. "I swear, it's like looking in a mirror. Don't you think?"

Laurel shook her head. "No. We both have reddish hair and different-colored eyes, but our bone structure is different, as is our skin tone." Well, at least to somebody who'd seen the same face in the mirror for almost three decades. To anybody else, they might look like twins. But she wouldn't admit that to Abigail. She couldn't.

Abigail scoffed and pulled Laurel inside the home, where starkness reined in opposition to the warmth blowing through the space. The surfaces were hard concrete or stone, and all white or a light gray. Even the pillows on the new black leather sofa were a glaring white. Her original sofa had been barraged by bullets during the Snowblood Peak case. "We have more than red hair in common and you know it. Genuine red hair is found in only ten percent of the population, and ours is auburn. A true auburn with brown and red. What percentage has that color?"

"Minuscule," Laurel agreed, brushing snow off her unfortunately rare hair color. She shrugged out of her coat and let Abigail hang it in the nearby closet before kicking off her boots on a mat near the door. "I'm not saying we lack rare genes." Considering they had the exact same heterochromatic eyes, one blue, one green, and a burst of green in the blue one, they were definitely unusual, which was a much nicer description than what she'd been called many a time by a cruel classmate or two.

Of course, that had been back when she was growing up and didn't know Abigail or even that she had a half sister. The truth had emerged during Laurel's first case in Genesis Valley, when she'd been shocked to discover she had a half sister from a father she'd never known. Her mother had always refused to give Laurel the name of her father. Her mom had been underage and her father a pastor at the church, and there was no consent. Her mother still had nightmares about it. "Tell me about the flowers on your front lawn."

Abigail gestured to the high-end leather sofa fronting a gas fireplace. "I'll ignite this. You must be chilly." She hustled over and flicked on a button, roaring the fire to life.

Laurel sat, even though she would've preferred to talk at the dining table or even the bar separating the kitchen from the great room. This was too casual. She glanced at the rear wide floor-to-ceiling windows, seeing the jagged, snow-covered mountains in the distance. Those windows lacked any covering, perfectly framing the freezing world outside. "The dahlias?" she prodded.

Abigail paused. "Could I get you anything to drink? How about coffee with a splash of Baileys? You look positively frigid."

"I'm fine." Laurel gestured to the matching leather chair. "This is official business, Abigail. I need to know everything about those flowers and now."

Abigail rolled her eyes and took the chair, sitting gracefully in it with the mountains behind her. The weak light poured inside the windows, caressing her reddish-brown hair, which she'd bluntly cut to fall at her shoulders, just like Laurel's. Her features were delicate and her skin more cream than peaches, making her unique eyes stand out even more. Today she wore black slacks and a green sweater that probably cost as much as Laurel's entire wardrobe. "I returned late last night from a retreat, didn't see the flowers, and only noticed them when I woke up. They've obviously been there for days."

Laurel sat back and watched for any nuances in Abigail's expression. She had an eidetic memory and didn't need to take notes, but she would write down the entire conversation later. "Your neighbor's house looks vacant. Any chance they saw anything?"

"No." Abigail studied Laurel as intensely as she was being studied. "The Northertons are snowbirds. They move to Arizona in October and don't return until May or June. Like most people around here."

"Are they retired?" Laurel asked.

"Yes. He worked in Silicon Valley and she owns a chain of eye clinics across the country. They retired here three years ago because their children, two of them, live in Genesis Valley. They see the kids here in the summer and then have them all visit Arizona in the winter." Abigail picked a piece of lint off her dark pants. "How predictable, right?"

"That life might sound ideal to many people," Laurel murmured. "Why would anybody leave flowers scattered over your lawn?"

Abigail threw up her hands. She wore silver rings on both, one with a stunning ruby in the center. "I don't know. Black dahlias, as I'm sure you're aware, symbolize betrayal."

"Who have you betrayed?"

Abigail stilled. "I'd watch my tone, were I you, sister." Her warning held a muted British accent left over from attending school for years in Great Britain.

"Why is that?" Laurel asked, keeping her tone mild.

"You really do not want to hurt my feelings." Abigail leaned forward. "Speaking of feelings, how is our Captain Huck Rivers?"

Huck had worked on the case that revealed Abigail's half brother, not related to Laurel, had been a serial killer in the area, one Abigail had killed to protect Laurel. Her brother had murdered young blondes and thrown them off Snowblood Peak to the valley below, and concurrent jurisdiction had worked for both agencies. "I have no idea," Laurel said.

Abigail smiled, flashing white teeth. "Oh, sister. We both know you and that mouth-breathing hottie with the hard ass rolled around in the sheets last year, as they say. Surely you've kept in touch."

"Who thinks you betrayed them, Abigail? This isn't a joke—you might be in danger."

Abigail stared at her, brilliance shining in her eyes. "You have ignored all of my calls and texts since my brother's funeral, which you were kind enough to attend before the holidays. I'm rather astounded you're taking this seriously. That you don't think I threw flowers and petals all over my lawn to gain attention from you. Why is that, Laurel?"

"I can't discuss that with you. Now, either you cooperate with me, or I will send somebody else to take your statement." Laurel pushed her damp hair off her shoulder.

Abigail's chin lowered a fraction. "Fine. I haven't betrayed anybody. In addition, I checked the cameras and have downloaded the applicable video for you. He walked down my driveway, which explains how he gained entrance beyond the gate to the subdivision. He couldn't have driven. It was a dark night with plenty of snowfall, and it's impossible to see his features, probably because he's wearing a damn mask. The figure looks like a man, though." She reached into her pants pocket and drew out a USB. "Here you go."

"Thank you." Laurel accepted the drive. "Have there been any other signs that somebody wants to frighten you? Any letters, calls, strange occurrences?"

"No. Nothing, and you know I'd remember if there were," Abigail said. "Why are you taking this so seriously?"

Laurel twisted the thumb drive in her hand. She didn't even have a description of the dead woman in the woods because her face had been destroyed. There was also no way Abigail could've known about the victim, because the body had just been discovered this morning. Plus, the flowers on her lawn had been left before the victim had been killed. "You may be in danger. I can't tell you anything more than that right now, but you need to be careful, and you need to start compiling a list of anybody who'd want to hurt you. Anybody who might feel betrayed by you, or anybody who has been too present in your life, too interested in you."

Abigail blinked. "I work at a university in a field mostly inhabited by men. I'm intelligent and beautiful while seemingly aloof, when actually I'm just bored by most people. They don't know that. The list would be too long to be useful."

There was a lot of truth in that statement. "I can put you in an FBI safe house if you want," Laurel said, needing to distance herself from this woman. "If not, I can ask the local police force to keep an eye on your house, but I doubt they have the manpower to put protection on you full time."

"What has happened?" Abigail asked.

"I can't discuss it yet," Laurel said. "What's it to be?"

Abigail shook her head. "How about you stay here?"

"No."

Abigail sighed, her eyes widening and her jaw slackening. "But I need help. You're trained. I'm scared."

"No, you're not," Laurel murmured.

Abigail lost the fake vulnerable look. "No, I'm not. But most people would be, and you have a duty to protect me. Not only because of your job but because I protected you once. Against my own brother, no less."

Yes, Abigail had killed her brother to protect Laurel. While Laurel appreciated being alive, her sister seemed to have a secondary motive for every action. "I've offered you protection. Say the word, and I'll secure you at a safe house in Seattle." It would only be a couple hours away, so Laurel could still reach her if necessary.

"So I'm in certain danger," Abigail mused. "Interesting. You've seen this before. Women stalked or women killed?"

Laurel stood. "Safe house?"

"No."

Laurel wasn't surprised. "Very well. I'll ask the locals to keep an eye on the subdivision. Please contact me when you have that list, and make sure you engage your alarm system at all times, even when you're at home." She paused. "Why were you on a week's retreat? Didn't you have classes to teach at the university?" Abigail taught several science classes at the premiere institution.

"Yes, but I took this week off." Abigail also stood. "My

vacation was scheduled, and I had my students working on either labs or papers all week."

"Where did you go?"

Abigail lifted one eyebrow. "You know where I went. I invited you."

"Oh." Laurel would have to look back through the texts from her sister. She hadn't opened many of them. She padded in her thick socks to the door and slipped her feet into her snow boots.

"I find your lack of interest in our sisterhood rather insulting." Abigail fetched Laurel's coat from the closet and held it open. Her tone held a hint of warning.

Laurel had no choice but to slip her arms into the sleeves and allow Abigail to assist her. "I have no desire to insult you." She turned toward her sister and zipped up her thick parka.

"You just don't want me involved in your down-home Hallmark movie of a life?" Real emotion flashed in her eyes this time.

Laurel sighed. "My life isn't perfect, and I don't know you. What we share isn't good."

Abigail grimaced. "Our asshole of a father who's been missing for years? You've never even met him. You only know he's a reprobate because of what you've been told by me and probably by your mother. We don't share him. Only I knew him, and I'll take that burden for us both. We're our own people, Laurel, but I am your sister."

Laurel reached in her pocket for her phone, a lump in her stomach that made her want to gag. "I can't prove it, but I know you tried to cover your brother's crimes before you realized we were half sisters. I'm an FBI agent, Abigail." She opened the outside door and stepped into the protection provided by the eaves before turning to face her sister.

Abigail was several inches taller, even in her bare feet. "I did not help him. If I did anything that assisted Robert with his heinous murders, then I'm very sorry."

"No, you're not," Laurel murmured.

Abigail's nostrils flared. "No, I'm not. But since I didn't do anything to help my brother, you must let this go. Besides, what would you do to protect *your* mother? Your Zen-loving, peaceful, flighty mother?"

"Good-bye, Abigail." Laurel turned and walked carefully down the walkway, pausing to snap several photographs of the lawn and mostly buried flowers before returning to her vehicle. Once inside, she dialed Captain Monty Buckley's number.

"Buckley," he answered over the sound of a printer grinding in the background.

"Hi, Captain," Laurel said, watching Abigail watch her from the open doorway. "Did you get jurisdiction settled?" They'd reached an agreement easily at the scene by the river, but it still had to be approved.

"Yeah," Monty said. "FBI has primary because the body was found on federal land, but we'll correspond and assist since Fish and Wildlife knows the area the best. We're coordinating now with the locals to tie them in."

"Good." In Washington State, Fish and Wildlife were fully commissioned officers. "I have a second crime scene I need processed, as well as an entire subdivision to canvass. Please have the state process and the locals canvass." She started her engine, her gaze still caught by her sister's. "Let's also see if we can get Dr. Ortega to conduct the autopsy and hopefully identify the victim. He did a good job last time."

"You've got it. Also, you should know, I'm having Huck take the lead on this for Fish and Wildlife. I have radiation treatments every day and might not be up to par."

Laurel paused. She'd learned weeks ago that Monty had prostate cancer. "I hope you feel better. If I can do anything, let me know."

"Just catch this psycho before he kills anybody else," Monty said grimly. "Unless you think this was a one-time thing and the guy was just after this poor woman?"

Laurel tore her gaze free to look at the frozen black dahlias beneath the ice. "No. This is just the beginning."

# Chapter Three

Shaking off the odd interaction with Abigail, Laurel arrived at her office and slid into a parking spot, impacting the curb with her front tires. Sighing, she backed up so she wouldn't block any part of the sidewalk. A large sign, partially covered with snow, read STAGGERS ICE CREAMERY across the front of the entire building. The ice cream shop took up the center of the first floor with the FBI office above it. Fish and Wildlife encompassed the two floors to the right, and a beauty school took residence to the left.

She jumped out of the Nissan and made her way to open a thick wooden door, which led to a small vestibule. To her right, a sign above the door to the Fish and Wildlife office said PARK AND WILDLIFE. It was handmade and rough, and she'd never asked about the mistake. Obviously sentimentality trumped fact.

Shrugging off snow, she stomped her boots across the rubber mat to clear the ice before pulling open a door that revealed stairs to the second floor. She climbed the steps, no longer noticing the wallpaper featuring half-naked dancers on the walls. At the top, she pushed her damp hair away from her face as she was greeted by her assistant from behind a glass pastry display case, angled against the far right corner of the landing area.

"Howdy," Kate Vuittron said, shuffling piles of papers into place on the glass.

"Hi. I thought you were acquiring a new desk." Laurel noted that Kate had placed file folders inside the case. They'd most likely smell like cinnamon cones for the next month.

Kate shrugged. "Since we might be temporary, no desk for me." She smiled, her unlined skin and shoulder-length, sandy-blond hair making her look much younger than her early forties. "The only furniture we've been able to secure so far is that awesome FBI-confiscated conference table and chairs from a government auction in Seattle. That stuff looks like it belongs in a high-end magazine conference room. Like *People* or *Cosmopolitan*. Right?"

"I'll take your word for it." Laurel moved beyond Kate to the open doorway in the middle of the wall.

Kate cleared her throat. "Is there a chance this office will become permanent? I thought after the Snowblood killer case that you were going to head up a new unit based out of Genesis Valley."

Laurel breathed out. Kate had a right to know the plans, such as they were. "Honestly, I don't know. I was successful in helping to wrap up the DC firewood murders after the holidays, and now George is having second thoughts about stationing me in the Pacific Northwest."

"George?"

"Yes. Sorry. Deputy Director George McCromby. He's a mentor to me." The firewood killer had been bludgeoning elderly men with pieces of split wood, and she'd successfully analyzed his behavior at the crime scene to lead to a suspect and then arrest. She could most likely sway her boss's decision, but she was uncertain about returning home permanently.

"Just let me know when you do, okay? If I need to look for a new job, I'd like to get on it." Kate reached for a pen.

That was more than fair. "For now, while I'm here, we have a new case, and I'd like to schedule a meeting about it in an hour or so. Where is Walter?"

"He went to grab us all a late lunch and should be back any minute." Kate typed efficiently on a laptop. "What kind of case?"

"Murder, probably ritualistic." Laurel paused. "Would you please invite Captain Rivers? We're going to coordinate with Fish and Wildlife on this one."

Kate reached for an older-looking office phone. "Of course." She kept her voice professional. "It'll be nice to work with Captain Sexy again. Why is a grumpy man with a chiseled jaw so appealing?"

That was one mystery Laurel didn't have any interest in solving. "Thanks, Kate." She strode down the center hall, flanked by offices, a conference room, and a computer room, to reach her office at the rear. The entire floor was quiet. If the unit became permanent, they'd need to hire staff besides Walter and Kate. Although Kate's three teenagers were always happy to help out, they'd just started another semester at school and no doubt had better things to do.

She paused at the sight of two stylish white rolling chairs on the closest side of her desk, with another one behind it. "Kate?"

"Four extra chairs were sent with that spectacular conference table, so I put three in your office. They're better than the ice cream stools you've been using," Kate yelled back. "I'm going to use the fourth but haven't rolled it this way yet."

Laurel set down her laptop bag and hung her coat on a nail protruding from the wall. The high-end chairs looked comical surrounding her desk, which was an old, weathered door plopped over cinder blocks. While she didn't mind using the old door, it would be nice to have a drawer or two. She sat and inserted the USB into her laptop, pausing at the sound of heavy footsteps in the entryway and then the rumble of a low voice.

Her heart sped up.

"Go on back," Kate called a little loudly, no doubt to alert Laurel of Huck's presence.

Long strides brought the man to her doorway within seconds.

"Captain Rivers," Laurel said, sitting straighter in her chair and once again regretting the fact that she'd attended college during her early teens, when she should've been learning how to navigate social situations and deal with the opposite sex. "What can I do for you?"

"Huck. The formality is irritating considering we've seen each other naked." He stood in the doorway, filling the entire space, his body long and lean with a barrel of muscular chest.

She schooled her expression. What was the appropriate reaction? Irritation, embarrassment, humor? She didn't know. "Why are you here?"

Stubble from a couple of days covered his jaw, snow dotted the black hair that curled beneath his ears, and nothing dimmed the topaz glint of his deep brown eyes. A pair of black gloves peeked out from his jacket pocket. "Monty passed this case to me, so I thought we'd get a handle on it fast. Is it going to go south?"

"Yes." She gestured to one of the white chairs on the other side of the desk.

One of his dark eyebrows rose and he walked to take

the chair, his bulk more than filling it. He wore faded jeans, a black shirt, and a F&W green jacket. "Dr. Ortega promised to prioritize the autopsy and should have preliminary findings to us by tomorrow morning. I don't think that man sleeps."

"Good." Laurel turned the laptop so they could both see it. "If we don't find this killer quickly, none of us are going to sleep for quite some time." The words rang through her and she shivered. "This video is from the security cameras around Dr. Abigail Caine's home."

Huck frowned. "What does this have to do with our case?"

Laurel pushed play.

The screen filled with a night scene captured by a camera that must've been mounted near Abigail's garage, pointed toward the walkway and lawn. Snow drizzled down, mixing with rain. A figure moved smoothly along the walk and then onto the snowy grass, a dark backpack over one shoulder.

"Not a great picture," Huck muttered.

The infrared wasn't bad but the snow made the video blurry. "Broad shoulders," Laurel said, squinting to see better. "About five foot ten or eleven, maybe?" A stocking mask covered the figure's head and face, and bulky clothing, gloves, and thick boots shielded the rest of the body.

"Could be a woman," Huck said, watching closely. "Best guess is male though."

"Agreed." Laurel sat back as the figure took objects out of the pack and placed them around the front lawn, almost gleefully throwing them in every direction.

Huck breathed out loudly. "Don't tell me. Those are black dahlias?"

"Yes. This video was taken three nights ago, and the flowers are still visible beneath the snow and ice on her lawn." The video ended with the figure finishing up and walking out of camera range. "Would you have your team search all CCTV in the area to see if we can catch sight of him again?"

Huck nodded. "No problem. This is a coincidence I don't like."

"Me either." She tapped her fingers on the old door and studied him. "Do you mind walking me through the facts? Sometimes it helps to hear facts instead of writing them down."

He flattened his broad hands on his jean-clad thighs. "Two women, both gifted with black dahlia flowers. One after death and one before. I don't like that to start with, and I really don't like that your recently discovered sister is one of the women. You're the new profiler in town, your sister is involved in your second case after also being very involved in your first? What are the chances?"

Laurel shook her head. "I don't know. Much of this depends on the identity of the victim we found. Did she know my sister? If so, it's more likely that Abigail also knows the killer. If not, then what? Could Abigail have killed this other woman and made herself a victim to . . . what?"

"To get your attention?" Huck asked. "She's a malignant narcissist, or a psychopath, or a sociopath, or one of those many labels that just don't make any sense anyway. Is she that nuts?"

"I can't answer that question," Laurel said, her mind spinning and her stomach cramping. "She might suffer from one, none, or all of those conditions. I don't know her." It would take years to counsel and study a person to make that determination, and with somebody as brilliant as Abigail, even longer. Abigail would know how to answer test questions to fit any condition or label she wanted.

Including perfectly sane. "I don't see her as having killed the woman in the woods merely to gain my attention."

"Why not?"

Laurel breathed deep. "Because there was so much . . . rage. The way the victim's face was obliterated. That was ferocious."

"It also prevented us from identifying the body easily. That was strategic." Huck scratched the stubble over his chin.

"No." Laurel shook her head. "It was more than that. To keep hitting a face, a body, after death . . . that's pure fury. Primal hatred."

Huck looked at the worn door serving as a desk. "Do you mind working with me on this?"

She stilled. "No. Why would I?" It was an important case and he'd be very helpful.

His smile was slightly lopsided and unintentionally charming. "Why would you? Okay. I forgot that about you."

Curiosity had her head tilting. "What about me?"

"That you don't play games and are unbearably logical." His broad shoulders visibly relaxed.

"Unbearably?" What in the world did he mean by that? Logic was crucial in finding killers.

He sighed. "To the ego, Laurel. Just to the ego. Don't worry about it."

She wouldn't, mainly because she had no clue what he was talking about, and it didn't seem relevant to the case. "All right. So we know black dahlias symbolize betrayal, but we shouldn't assume the killer knows the same. It might mean something else entirely to him."

Huck shifted his weight on the white chair and swiveled to the side. "Why do your guest chairs have rollers?"

"Why not?" She tapped her finger on her lip. "Where

would somebody purchase black dahlias at this time of year?"

"I'll put an officer on answering that question." Huck looked over his shoulder at the quiet hallway. "Shouldn't you be hiring agents now that you're a permanent team?"

She did need more people to do legwork but she liked the team she'd put together. Small and easy to manage. "It depends if this unit becomes permanent or not. The FBI deputy director has had second thoughts about it."

His eyebrows rose. "Sounds like you were too successful working that case in DC."

So he'd known of her activities during the last month. "Apparently so. If the unit becomes permanent, the FBI will assign additional agents. But for right now, I'll need to rely on state agencies as well as my federal colleagues."

"Well, keep me in the loop about your plans." Huck rolled back his chair and stood, looming over her desk. "When you started to handle serial murders in the Pacific Northwest, did you have any idea there would be so many close to your home?"

"I assumed more crimes would be committed in Seattle or even Everett, but serial murders often happen in places like this. Cold and remote with easy pickings." She'd heard the expression from an agent at Quantico years ago. "Let's keep in mind that we might not have a serial killer in this case. Assuming anything would be a mistake." The killer might've just wanted the current victim dead. "Leaving flowers at Abigail's home might be an attempt to distract us. We have to identify that victim."

Huck walked toward the doorway, turning at the opening to stare at her. "You said something that got under my skin."

Her breath heated. "How so?"

"About your sister."

That breath cooled. Of course. "What did I say?"

"You said that the victim by the river was beaten with rage that someone like Dr. Caine wouldn't feel."

Laurel nodded. "I stand by that assessment."

He cocked his head. "If she is a sociopath or a malignant narcissist or whatever, she still has emotions, right?"

"Yes. In fact, her feelings might be stronger than most, if not understandable by the rest of us."

Huck grunted.

Laurel lifted an eyebrow. "Why do you ask?"

"If she feels, you're the only person in the world she probably experiences true emotion about." He zipped up his jacket. "If she were to feel rage, aren't you the person she'd feel it for?"

One lonely chill shivered down Laurel's back. "Yes."

# Chapter Four

Laurel called the deputy director from her phone while driving home after work. Snow fell almost lazily to dot the vehicle, as if trying to lull the world into relaxation before another winter storm hit. She kept her hands on the wheel and let the Bluetooth do its thing.

"George McCromby," the deputy director answered, sounding distracted.

"We have a new case, sir," Laurel said, slowing down when she saw two deer on the side of the road.

He sighed. "I'm doing well, Agent Snow. How are you doing on this fine evening?"

She frowned, keeping an eye on the closest doe in case the animal decided to dash across the road. "I'm driving in the snow. How are you doing?" Sometimes she forgot the niceties.

"It's so very nice of you to ask," George said. "I'm knee deep in budget negotiations right now, and my wife wants me to attend the opera."

"I thought you didn't enjoy the opera." Laurel picked up her speed. Nor did he often employ sarcasm, so apparently he was experiencing stress at the moment.

A slam of a hand on a stapler echoed through the line. "Why don't they make bigger damn staplers?"

"I think they do, sir." She slowed to turn a corner, appreciating the lack of traffic on the country road. The only movement around her involved clumps of snow periodically falling from the boughs of pine and fir trees. Why were they talking about operas and staplers?

"Tell me about your case."

She relaxed into talk of murders and statistics, explaining that they knew nothing. "We should have the Tempest County Medical Examiner's report tomorrow morning, and hopefully the ME can identify the victim in some manner. Her dental records are of no value because her teeth were fractured and scattered in the snow. It's doubtful the techs could find many of them, but Dr. Ortega is very discerning."

"Lovely," McCromby said. "Good job on handling jurisdiction and getting everybody on board. Maybe I *should* assign you permanently to lead the Pacific Northwest Violent Crimes Unit, since you have absolutely no ego about it."

What did ego have to do with anything? "I just want to find the maniac that obliterated this woman's face." Laurel turned down the heat on her seat. "Have you made a decision on whether or not to sign the paperwork?"

"No. I'm awaiting reports from three other units across the country where you might be of more use, and I'm also waiting for you to make a request. Where do you want to be stationed?"

She usually made rapid decisions based on empirical data. "I don't know," she admitted.

His laugh was a short bark. "There's nothing like family to screw with logic, right?"

An unfortunately true statement. She enjoyed being close to her mother and uncles, and she'd made friends already, which was difficult for her to do. But living near Abigail wasn't appealing, and Laurel hadn't yet discerned the best way to keep her family outside Abigail's focus. The woman would have no problem harassing Laurel's mother or uncles to gain attention. "I'll make a request soon and hope that you and I reach the same conclusion. For now, I'm focusing on finding a killer."

"Good. Before I forget, I assigned you a computer tech for the duration of this case. Guy's name is Nester Lewis. He's from your neck of the woods and is a fresh graduate of Quantico after earning degrees at the Tech school you have out there. The kid can pretty much write his own ticket, and he wants to go home, apparently."

Excellent. She needed a computer guru. "When does he arrive?"

"He's scheduled to start work tomorrow. I haven't met him, but the guy seems a bit like you, which I figured would be good."

"Like me?"

"Yeah. Frighteningly smart," George said.

Laurel didn't find her intelligence frightening, but it was intriguing that some people apparently did. "Does he need a ride from the airport?"

"No. He negotiated a month off before starting work, and I think he's been home for the holiday season. His family lives somewhere outside of Everett, probably close to Genesis Valley." A chair creaked loudly. "So, tell me. What's the average height of the people to whom you've spoken directly during the last thirty days? And don't give me a national average this time. It has to be people you've said real words to during the month."

She sped up while traversing a straight part of the country road, even though it was icy. "The most accurate guess would be five foot nine." Interesting. That was taller than the national average. "I surmise that people are tall around here."

Ice clinked in a glass over the line. "How many of them wore pink shoes?"

"Do boots count?"

"Yes."

A lot of children had pink boots, and she'd spoken to an entire elementary class right after their holiday break while she'd been in DC. "Nineteen."

He snorted. "Did you talk to a bunch of kids?"

"Affirmative." She sped up the windshield wipers as the snow fell more quickly. "I counted fuchsia as a pink, by the way."

"Fair enough. Did the kids' eyes glaze over when you talked?"

She grimaced. "Yes, but then I showed them my badge and they reengaged. They asked questions and the situation improved greatly."

"I can only imagine their questions. How many blondes did you see in the last week?"

"True blondes or does that include bottle blondes?" she asked absently, her mind returning to the recent murder. How in the world was the victim by the river connected to Abigail Caine? This killing felt too close to home.

"Both."

She would have to interview Abigail again as soon as they had an identification of the victim. "Forty-seven if you count three women with blondish-gray hair. I haven't attended any gatherings lately and remained close to my mother's farm during the holidays." She cleared her throat.

"I require additional agents to work this case, and I'd prefer an agent with tracking experience." Then she wouldn't have to rely on Huck Rivers.

"I'll see what I can do, but from what I understand, you're already working with the best of the best." He sipped loudly at his drink. "You definitely need more muscle on the team. Smudgeon is on his last legs, according to his latest physical."

She'd have to see about that. While Walter had had some issues during his last assignment in Portland, he'd been helpful during the Snowblood Peak case. "Walter is a good addition to the team. He has experience and knowledge, and he is well versed in procedure." Was there a way to institute an exercise regimen for the team? Walter wouldn't like it. "Let me know about possible new hires."

"I will. I also wanted to give you a heads up about a potential political issue."

Laurel groaned. "Also send me somebody who can deal with potential political issues. That is not my forte."

"I'm well aware. The head of the Seattle field office is making waves because I'm thinking about creating this unit in Genesis Valley, and I might appoint you the lead. He wanted the new unit to run out of Seattle, under his command. His problem is that the last case was too close to you, considering your half sister and all. So as long as she's not involved in any other cases and you keep it all professional, we're good."

Laurel's chin dropped. "Well, since you mentioned Abigail . . ."

Laurel slipped across the icy porch with its myriad of wind chimes freezing beneath the eaves and stepped into her mother's warm home. "Mom? I'm home."

"Dinner is almost ready. I hope you're hungry," Deidre called from the kitchen.

"I had a late lunch but could eat again." Laurel shook off her outerwear and padded in her thick socks through the living room to the kitchen, which was the hub of her mom's quaint farmhouse. "Something smells delicious. Crock-Pot chili?"

"Yes." Deidre turned from stirring the fragrant brew to study her daughter. She wore a black yoga outfit with a bright blue jacket, her short blond hair ruffled and her cheeks rosy. "I heard there was a body found by the river today. Is that your case?"

"I take it the media has already caught the story?" Laurel walked to the cupboard to remove water and wine glasses. When her mother didn't answer, she set the table. "Yes, that's my case. I don't know the identity of the victim as of yet, but she was definitely murdered." It was unnecessary at this juncture to worry her mother by telling her that Abigail Caine might be involved. Again.

Her mom ladled chili into ceramic bowls. "Toppings?"

"Cheese and sour cream," Laurel said, reaching for a bottle of Opus One Cabernet. Her mom might love clipping coupons and saving money, but she had expensive taste in wine.

"Sure. I'll throw in green onions and my spinach dip just to keep you balanced," Deidre said, doing just that. She brought the steaming bowls to the round country-style kitchen table and sat. "The news said that Fish and Wildlife was on the scene with the body. You're not having to work with that Huck Rivers again, are you?"

Laurel sat and sipped her wine, humming at the rich taste as it slid down her throat. "The captain is a good officer, Mom."

"Huh." Her mom sampled the chili and then smiled.

"Right. I know you had a night with him, and I know he didn't call you afterward."

"I didn't call him either." Laurel ate some of the chili and let her stomach warm. The spinach dip mellowed out the spices nicely. "He was shot protecting me from a bullet, so I'd think you'd like him a marginal amount."

Her mom sipped the wine, her green eyes thoughtful. "That's a good point. I guess taking a bullet for you gives him some cred, even though he hasn't called. Why haven't you called him?"

Laurel shrugged. "What would I say?" She truly had no idea. They'd worked a case together, had one night of excellent sex, and then he'd gotten shot as they'd closed the case. She'd spent some time visiting him in the hospital, and they'd seemed to be starting a friendship, but then things had fizzled out. Or rather, she'd headed back to DC to work another case, and he'd disappeared into his lonely cabin in the woods with his dog. "We're just work colleagues."

Deidre nodded. "That's a good thing. No offense, but that man needs saving, and you have no clue how to save a man."

Laurel chuckled. "No offense taken. Speaking of saving, I saw another dividend was deposited into my account earlier. The holiday sales for your teas must've been better then we'd projected." Laurel had assisted her mother in creating a tea company with a subscription service and owned twenty percent of the business.

"Yes, it was wonderful," Deidre said happily. "We had a ten percent increase in new subscriptions for the new year. I think the monthly theme of interesting locations and their teas was a great idea. We've almost sold out of the extra supply for February, which is a warm turmeric-centered brew based on Zermatt, Switzerland and its excellent skiing mountains."

Laurel ate more of the spicy chili. "I saw the Switzerland label for the apothecary jars. It's beautiful."

"I had Kate's middle daughter create it. The girl is only fourteen but is incredibly talented." Deidre finished off her wine. "March's offering is based on love and Paris, and you should see her mockups."

Laurel smiled as she remembered the drawings in Val's notebooks when the kids had worked at the FBI office to help out during the Snowblood murders. "Val is very creative. I'm glad you hired her."

"Me, too." Deidre finished her chili. "Also, I've been waiting for a good time to talk to you about perhaps finding a permanent place for you to live here on the ranch." She set her hands on her lap and her eyes sparkled. "I mean, where you could have some privacy but still be close to family. The ranch is a massive property, as you know."

Laurel pushed her napkin onto the table. "I don't understand." She still hadn't made a decision as to where she wanted to work, and neither had the FBI, so why make plans?

Hope brightened Deidre's pixie-like face. "Just work with me on this. Remember the old barn over by Rascal Creek? I've been thinking of remodeling it and creating a barndominium."

"A barndominium?"

"Yes. You can help design it, and if you end up not wanting the place, I can use it as a rental for people on retreat. You know. Authors, artists, burned-out lawyers."

Laurel mulled it over. It was surely her mom's way of getting her to stay in town, and that was sweet. Deidre suffered from extreme anxiety and worried too much over Laurel, but she'd been managing her condition with yoga and other coping mechanisms she'd learned through the years. "I don't have concrete plans yet."

Her mom smiled. "I know, but it's a smart business decision either way. I do hope you're not planning to move to Everett or Seattle, though. There's no reason for you to live in a big city."

Excitement thrilled through Laurel. "I would enjoy the challenge of remodeling that barn." While it was approximately ten acres away, there were plenty of trees and terrain to provide privacy. "If I am stationed in Genesis Valley, it'd be the perfect place to live, and if I'm stationed elsewhere, it'd be a peaceful place to stay when I visited." The barn had been abandoned by the family when the cattle had been moved to another part of their sprawling ranch, and it was starting to crumble, but the structure had been built strong. "The surroundings are very peaceful."

Deidre's light eyebrows arched. "Peaceful? You're looking for peaceful?"

"Who isn't?" Heat filtered into Laurel's cheeks. "The farm is lovely." Both of her uncles lived on the farm, acres away. They farmed cattle, pumpkins, apples, and hay as well as other vegetables. Deidre's tea factory, if it could be called such, was also located farther down the lane from her home. "In fact, why don't we go into a partnership? If I am stationed here, I'll buy you out. If we use it for business, then we'll split the profits." She had to make a decision on where she wanted to live and work. Why was it so difficult this time?

"I love that idea." Deidre patted her hand. "That barn is going to take creativity to make into a home."

"We did just receive some large dividends," Laurel mused. Her phone buzzed and she tugged it out of her pocket, glancing at the face. "I need to take this. Excuse me." She stood and hurried into the living room to answer. "Hi, Huck. What's going on?" She kept her voice low.

His was lower. Much. "We found the hands."

# Chapter Five

The morning sky was a startling blue, cold and expansive. A weak sun shone down and sparkled on the icy snow as if too tired to attempt melting the mass.

Laurel readjusted her seatbelt in Huck's truck after they met in the office parking lot. They'd decided to carpool to the Tempest County ME's office, where the doctor should have results for them any moment. Huck had placed two coffees in the holders between them, and she paused, staring down.

"The one in front is yours. Chai latte with almond milk," he said, turning onto Main Street.

She swallowed. He'd remembered her drink. That was nice. "Thank you." She reached for the cup and then partially turned to see the dog in his crate in the back seat. "Hi, Aeneas."

The Karelian bear dog's ears perked up. A distinctive white hourglass shape marked his face with black fur on either side. His chest and paws were white as well. When he wasn't chasing bears from residential areas, he was searching for and rescuing people. She couldn't reach around to pet him, so she settled back into her seat and sipped her latte. "I wonder. Does he miss chasing bears during the winter?"

"Yes. It's in his blood, but he's good at searching as well." Huck drove easily down the icy roads, his profile harsh in the soft morning light.

She'd like to see the animal herd a bear away from people. For now, she had a murderer to find. "Tell me about the hands."

He turned left to go toward Everett. "They were found on a tree stump about three miles away from the crime scene, down the trail I cut in yesterday."

Laurel watched the snowy world fly by outside. "How were they placed?"

Huck dug his phone from his back pocket and handed it over.

She pressed the icon for photographs, and the two hands appeared. They'd been left palms down with the thumbs just touching each other. They were mottled and purple, no doubt frozen solid.

"What does that mean?" he asked.

"I'm uncertain," she murmured, setting her latte back in the holder and using two fingers to widen the picture. "One theory was that her hands were taken to postpone identification of the body, but if the killer placed her hands where we could find them, then that hypothesis is disproven."

He reached for his coffee and took a deep drink. "Then why cut off her hands?"

Laurel shook her head. "Good question." She could spend all day creating theories and postulating concepts, but they didn't know enough about this killer to even begin.

The silence stretched during the drive, not comfortable, but not awkward, either. Maybe she should try some sort of small talk. The weather didn't interest her, and it probably didn't interest Huck. They'd already talked about the dog. She racked her brain for something interesting. "Did you read that the scientists at CERN have found unusual data from a B meson that might open a new area of physics?"

He blinked and looked at her for a second before turning back to the road. "Does that have something to do with the frozen hands?"

"Um, no." So that wasn't interesting. It was to her, but that was just because she liked mysteries that could be solved. "Probably not." So much for that topic.

He turned down the heat in the cab. "I didn't think physics was one of your degrees."

"It isn't."

He nodded. "What are your degrees again?"

Was that small talk? Maybe. "I have degrees in bioinformatics and integrative genomics, data science, organizational behavior, psychology with an emphasis in abnormal psychology, game theory, and mathematics."

"Right." Huck drank more of his coffee. "I guess physics would be in some of those disciplines. So tell me why somebody would stalk a woman until she hid in the woods and then find her, smash in her face, and cut off her hands."

"Anything I said would be conjecture at this point." Laurel took a drink of the latte. Staggers used excellent chai—it was just spicy enough. "At first glance, it appeared the killer wanted to hide the victim's identity, which means he could be tied to her somehow. Then with the flowers at Abigail's house, he created more than one possible crime scene and way to track him. To find the hands of the victim just waiting on a tree stump is . . . odd."

"What could it signify?" He glanced in the back at his dog and then returned his focus to the snowy road.

That was an excellent question. "He has a problem with hands? He wanted to confound us?" She thought back to the crime scene. "There were no hesitation marks, but with an ax, there probably wouldn't be. This might've been his first kill." Laurel settled more comfortably in the seat. "He didn't want her hands and didn't care if we found them. So why take her hands in the first place?" There were a few reasons she could think of immediately, but psychopaths didn't think linearly. "Perhaps she fought him and got in a good punch, so he took her hands. Or maybe he has a fetish for hands or severed wrists. I have no way of knowing."

"Any idea why Dr. Ortega wants to meet us in person instead of giving us his report over the phone?"

Laurel started. "No. Why?"

"Because he was emphatic about it and said that you had to be present." Huck cut her a look, his eyes a deep sepia in the morning light. "Care to explain?"

The hair sprang up on the back of her neck. Instinct whispered that this was one of those proverbial land mines, and she'd never been able to navigate them. Yet it was a noticeable improvement that she even recognized it as such. "I don't have an explanation, and your tone lowered two decibels when you asked the question, so I surmise there's a hidden meaning or question there. Would you please clarify that for me?"

He shot her a look from the corner of his eye. With his dark hair falling over his ears, he looked like a dangerous mountain man. The kind of male Kate would call a hot badass. "My voice did not lower."

"Yes, it did." She tilted her head, trying to dig deep into his. What was this about?

His chest filled and then he slowly exhaled. "I just need

to know if there's anything going on that will screw up my investigation. Anything between you and Ortega."

She blinked. "We worked with Dr. Ortega on the Snowblood Peak killings, Huck." Had he somehow forgotten that? "Have you sustained a head injury since we last worked together?" That would explain why he hadn't bothered to call.

The look he shot her this time wasn't veiled. Irritation with a hint of amusement lifted his upper lip. She'd studied facial expressions and emotions *ad nauseam* through the years, trying to learn how to relate to people. It appeared she was finally becoming proficient at it.

"Are you being a smartass?" he asked.

"No," she said honestly.

He shook his head. "Forget about it."

"I don't forget anything." She was missing something, an understanding just out of her reach. Like something fluttering slightly beyond her line of vision. Her mind mulled it over. "You and I had one night together. You said it was a 'one-off,' I agreed, and I thought we were becoming friends."

She chewed on her lip, not needing him to respond. "Yet you dislike the idea that a relationship might have begun between Dr. Ortega and me." Her mind knitted connections together faster than her hands could piece a quilt. "So you don't want the case compromised, you're concerned that he's much older and married, or you don't like me being intimate with another man just because I had sex with you one night?" Triumph filled her. "Am I close?"

He looked fully her way. "Are you fucking with me?"

"No." Her shoulders fell.

"It was more than once."

Warmth filtered through her. "That's factual. One

night." Three times in one night. The captain had stamina. "Am I misinterpreting your words?"

He studied her and then looked back out the front window. "You are an odd one, Laurel Snow."

"This is not the first time I've heard that statement," she said, taking another drink of her latte. She could talk to Kate later about the entire conversation. The woman was admirably insightful.

"Fine. It's probably all three of those things," Huck said, not looking at her. "I don't want my case messed up, I don't like the idea of Ortega cheating on his wife, who is a very nice person, and I don't enjoy the image of you sleeping with him. Happy now?"

Happy wasn't exactly her state of being, but she was definitely intrigued. "How do you know his wife?"

"I've lived here awhile, Agent Snow," Huck muttered. "I get out once in a while, you know."

"I didn't know," she mused, finishing off her drink. "The last time I spoke with Dr. Ortega was during the Snowblood Peak murders, and I have no personal relationship with him. I don't know why he insisted I accompany you today or why he refused to relay the results over the phone." More importantly, she didn't understand why Huck would care if she became intimate with the medical examiner. "You and I do not have a personal relationship. Correct?"

"Right."

"I thought we were becoming friends," she mumbled, turning to look out her window. Had she misunderstood? She crossed her arms over her ribcage.

He set his cup back in the holder. "I'm not a very good friend."

"Oh." She hadn't considered that he was the one who'd miscalculated. When it came to relationships, it was usually her error that ended them. She didn't understand most people. "I don't know what makes a good friend."

He slowed down to drive around a curve in the road. "Everyone knows what makes a good friend. Loyalty, honesty, trust, and I guess spending time together. Maybe protectiveness as well."

She mulled over his words. "During the time we worked the Snowblood Peak cases, I found you to be loyal to your dog and the Fish and Wildlife organization, honest to the point the local sheriff almost punched you in the face, and someone I could trust with not only my life but that of anybody in trouble. In addition, you have a protective streak that belongs in one of those romance television shows." She stretched her chilled hands toward the heating vents. "So your failing as a friend lies in the fact that you prefer being alone with your dog and not spending time with people?"

"One of those romance television shows?"

"You know, streaming every episode. Even the mysteries or thrillers usually have a hero with a protective edge. You have perfectly symmetrical bone structure and impressive muscle mass like they do." There was no question he'd been gifted in the bone structure department.

He shook his head. "If I didn't know you better, I'd really think you were messing with my head."

"I get that a lot."

He chuckled. "You are such a brainiac."

"I get that a lot as well." She smiled, her shoulders lifting. Apparently she hadn't ruined another friendship.

"At least you used the term 'sleep with' and not 'engage in coitus' when denying a relationship with Ortega." Humor tilted Huck's tone.

She sat back, her hands now toasty warm. "I'm not a complete dork."

"Huh."

She laughed. "How about we create our own definition

of friendship that doesn't involve you having to leave your cabin and dog?" It was surprising how badly she wanted to be his friend. She'd talk it over with her mother later, although Deidre was wary of Huck Rivers. But Deidre would understand Huck's need to spend a lot of time alone.

He turned down a busy street and parked in front of the ME's office, which was attached to the county hospital. "All right, Laurel Snow. I guess we're friends." He smiled. "You're not going to pressure me for more, are you?" His smile seemed teasing.

"For more of what?" She frowned.

He barked out a laugh. "Forget it. Friends it is, then."

# Chapter Six

Dr. Ortega met them in his office, which had been decorated with a precision that must have involved many levels and rulers. Framed diplomas and other certificates, all with exactly the same black wooden frame and cream-colored matte were hung precisely behind his desk. Twin inlaid bookshelves bracketed the wall and held photographs, signed baseballs in protective glass containers, and bowling trophies on shelves. There were three items on each shelf, and their height and width balanced the opposing shelf exactly.

"Take a seat," Dr. Ortega said from behind his desk, which held three piles of salmon-colored file folders, a monitor, and a keyboard. Today the doctor wore a black shirt and slacks beneath his unbuttoned white lab coat.

Laurel and Huck sat in the brown leather seats that matched the one in which the doctor sat, except the back of his was taller.

"Thank you for coming in person," the doctor said, reaching for the top case file.

"No problem," Huck said, unzipping his Fish and Wildlife parka.

Dr. Ortega smiled at Laurel. His hair was black with

gray heavy at his temples and above his ears. He had to be in his early sixties, and his brown eyes were intelligent and slightly bloodshot. "Sorry to pull you out on such a cold day."

"I'm sorry you had to work through the night," Laurel said. "What did you discover with the autopsy?"

He flipped open the file folder. "Your victim had breast implants, so I was able to trace the serial numbers and get you an ID." He removed a photograph and pushed it across the desk. "Printed this off the Internet. Her name was Charlene Rox. She was a thirty-eight-year-old psychiatrist with a practice outside of Seattle."

Laurel studied the photograph. Charlene had symmetrical bone structure, short black hair, dark eyes, and full lips. In the picture, she wore a red blazer, black shell, and a thick silver necklace. Her earrings were silver and dangled a little, exhibiting a bit of whimsy. "She was a doctor?"

"Yes," Dr. Ortega said.

Like Abigail. There was one tie between them already. "What did you determine to be the cause of death, Dr. Ortega?" Laurel asked.

"Blunt force trauma. She was beaten so badly her skull was fractured along with every bone in her face," he said. "And please call me Pedro. I have a feeling we're going to see more of each other if you're going to be leading the Pacific Northwest Violent Crimes Unit." His smile was charming.

"Pedro," Laurel agreed. "But the position has not been formally filled as of today. I may be assigned to a unit in the DC area." She needed to focus them all on this case. "About the autopsy. Was she raped?"

"Yes," Dr. Ortega said.

Huck exhaled loudly. "The guy managed to rape her in

subzero temperatures?" His jaw hardened. "That takes a serious compulsion. Tell me you got DNA."

"None," Dr. Ortega said. "Traces of a condom, but no DNA on her. My guess is that he wore gloves and kept on as much clothing as possible. Even so, he spent more time bashing in her head than raping her. He had to have."

"Maybe he couldn't finish the rape," Laurel said. "Could be what led to the anger. Or part of the rage, anyway." They had to find this monster.

Huck lifted the photograph and looked at the woman. "Anything else?"

"Stomach contents showed she ate a meal of stew the night before. Other than that, she did have a tumor on her left ovary that had to have been causing her problems, and severe gout, which is rare in women. I didn't find any evidence of medication in her blood, so she wasn't treating it right now. There weren't any pain killers, either."

Huck shook his head. "How terrified did she have to be to freeze in the middle of nowhere without medication and experiencing that kind of pain? Who was she hiding from? Did she have any clue?"

"That part is your job," Dr. Ortega said. "Also, she had surgery to repair a torn ACL, probably in her teens. There was remodeling on her right wrist from a fracture, also in her late teens. She might've been an athlete in her youth. Besides everything I've mentioned, she was in good health. That's all I have." He handed over the second file folder. "Copies of everything for you."

"Sounds good." Huck accepted the file and stood.

Dr. Ortega cleared his throat. "Agent Snow? Could I speak with you for a moment?" A light flush spread across his oval face, visible even beneath his gray goatee. "Privately?"

Laurel paused. "Of course."

Huck looked at Laurel, his brows lowering. "I'll wait for you in the truck. I need to feed Aeneas a treat, anyway." The truck had a special heater for the dog's crate so he stayed warm when he had to remain in the truck, where he also had water and food. Huck shut the office door after he left.

Laurel sat back in her chair. "What can I help you with, Dr. Ortega?"

"Pedro. This is awkward." The doctor shifted uneasily in his chair. "Do you think criminals are always criminals? Or that there is a criminal mind?"

Laurel tilted her head. "I need more information than that."

He sighed. "Last year my wife and I took in our youngest niece after my brother and his wife died in a car accident. She's seventeen and a little wild but very smart and very kind. She's dating a young man that I think might be a bad influence on her."

This was way out of Laurel's field of expertise, and she still didn't have enough facts to be helpful. But she truly did want to assist him. "I don't know much about teenage dating. I was in graduate school by my teens."

Dr. Ortega smiled. "I figured. Even so, this young man has spent time in juvenile detention for underage drinking, vandalism, voyeurism, and I don't know what else. He's from a prominent family in Genesis Valley, and I'm concerned he's done worse, but the mayor has buried any records."

"The mayor?"

"Yes. This new boyfriend is Tommy Bearing, the mayor's youngest son. He's back at school now, and I don't like that he's dating my niece, but Joley seems enamored with him."

While the concern was understandable, Laurel didn't

have insight to offer. "The voyeurism is concerning, but we don't know the details. Sometimes, especially when something is newsworthy like the mayor's son getting in trouble, facts get distorted. Why don't you just ask the young man what he did? If he's learned his lesson?"

The doctor sighed. "I haven't had much of a chance to talk to him. I adore my niece. Joley's top of her class and has a mathematical mind like you wouldn't believe. She even attended space camp last year, which only accepts the best and brightest."

"That's true," Laurel said.

"And this Tommy has that smug look rich kids get. You know? The one where they're polite to your face while they have drugs in their pockets. Or plans that include breaking the law."

Laurel couldn't answer that. She didn't know what that expression looked like.

He threw up his hands. "She has missed curfew twice, and I think she had been drinking the other night when she came home. She's even doodling his name on her physics notebook."

"Doodling is a sign of teenage interest," Laurel said lamely. She'd been so much younger than everyone in college that she'd never doodled anybody's name.

He sighed. "Why do smart girls like bad boys?"

Laurel winced. "Probably because smart girls think they can heal bad boys." At least that's what she'd learned by observing young adults in college when she'd just been thirteen. By the lifting of the doctor's bushy eyebrows, his question had been rhetorical. "I think the best strategy would be to speak with both kids."

"I was thinking that maybe, I mean with your connections, that you could perhaps conduct a background search? The FBI can get into anybody's records, even a juvenile's, right?" Dr. Ortega set his file atop the others and carefully patted it into place, not looking at her.

She waited until he did meet her gaze. "That would take a warrant, and we don't have grounds for a warrant." Surely the doctor wasn't asking her to break the law or circumvent the judicial process. The man appeared to be ethical and accomplished at his job, but it was possible his concern for family was clouding his judgment. She could sympathize but wasn't going to break procedure.

He flushed more deeply. "You're right. Of course, you're correct." Standing, he gestured toward the door. "I hope we can forget this entire conversation."

Laurel stood and scooted around the chair toward the exit. "I don't forget anything, Dr. Ortega. But I will keep this confidential, if that's what you meant." She opened the door and walked out into the quiet hallway with its perfectly mopped tiles. "Thank you for the expedient results on the autopsy."

He followed her. "Do you think this is a serial? I mean, with the symbolism of the black dahlias and such?"

"I don't know yet." But the ache in her solar plexus was one of instinct and experience, and everything inside her knew they had to find this killer and fast. She wouldn't confirm the truth out loud, but even statistics told her that this was only the beginning, and he'd strike again.

Probably soon.


Back at her office, Laurel shed her coat and snowy outerwear before trudging past Kate, who was arguing with somebody on the phone about what sounded like more office equipment. She walked down the center aisle, stopping as a young man emerged from the makeshift computer room. "Hi."

"Hi." He held out a hand. "I'm Agent Nester Lewis. You must be Special Agent in Charge Laurel Snow." His shake was brief and professional.

"Laurel. Please." She studied him. He had to be around twenty-four, not much younger than she. He stood to about five nine or ten with a bald head, light brown eyes, an engaging smile, and russet-colored skin. For his first day on the job, he'd dressed in gray slacks, a cream-colored shirt, and a green silk tie. Then she looked beyond him to the room. "You managed to bring new computer equipment." Although it was still perched on old doors set on cinder blocks.

"Yeah. I'm trying to order a desk or two, and I could use a couple more monitors. But I probably can't requisition more equipment until we know if this unit will be based here or in Seattle." He rubbed his bald head. "I have the entire system up and ready to go, however. Anything you need."

She handed him the case file. "The victim's name is Dr. Charlene Rox, and I need to know everything there is about her."

His eyes gleamed. "No problem."

"I also need your personnel file." She turned back toward her office.

"It's already on your desk," he called back, disappearing into the computer room.

She already liked the young agent. Almost reaching her office, she paused as the door to Kate's reception area opened. Turning, she watched Walter Smudgeon wipe sweat off his brow and lumber toward her, his face ruddy and his belly hanging over his belt. "Hi, Walter."

"Hi." He coughed several times. "The local sheriff called and wanted an update, so I popped by his office after lunch. Even though the locals don't have jurisdiction on this one, I thought we should play nice and at least attempt to keep him in the loop. He's still an ass."

That situation wasn't likely to change. "Are you feeling all right?" She didn't like the hue of his skin.

"Yeah. Just fighting something." Reaching the computer room, he waved at Nester and then kept walking toward her. "Do we have an ID on the victim?"

"Yes," Laurel said. Apparently the two men had met earlier. Good. "Nester has the file. Walter, please go ahead and start preparing a warrant to search her home, vehicles, and office once we have locations. I'll sign the affidavit once you've prepared it."

He nodded. "Now that we have an ID, I'll also call the sheriff and see if he has any records regarding the victim." He hitched away, his breath labored.

Laurel moved into her office and sat behind her desk, rapidly working through paperwork she'd been avoiding.

Around five, Nester approached her office, a pile of papers in his hands. "Boss? I have the research you wanted as well as the affidavit for you to sign."

She looked up from taking notes on an unrelated case DC had asked her to review and gestured him inside to one of the new chairs. "Come on in. What did you find?"

Nester sat and handed over the papers. "Dr. Rox lived east of Genesis Valley in a high-end condominium development and commuted to her practice in Seattle."

"Did anybody report her missing?"

"No. I called her office, and the answering machine said that she had gone on sabbatical and wouldn't be back for a couple of months. She gave the names and numbers of colleagues that her patients could contact for assistance." Nester's eyes gleamed. "She's been married three times, and all three ex-husbands live in the state. I've found them in Seattle, Tacoma, and over in Spokane by the border."

He gestured toward the papers. "All information about them has been printed out."

Laurel glanced at the stack. "Did you discover any hint of violence in her life or any protection orders taken out by her?"

"Not against the husbands." Nester tugged a sheet from the bottom and handed it over. "More recently, she made several local police reports about being harassed or stalked, but she didn't have any idea who was doing it. Everything from somebody slashing her tires to cutting her electricity to possibly breaking into her home. All of the reports are in the stack."

"Do the reports mention any flowers left for her?"

"Yeah. Black dahlias left on her balcony. The interesting part is that she lives on the fourth floor, so either the stalker went through her condo to get to the balcony or somehow climbed up from the ground. We need to take a look at the place." Nester straightened the remaining papers.

Interesting. Laurel craned her neck. "Walter?"

"Yeah?" he bellowed back from his office.

"Did you speak with Sheriff York and give him the identification of the victim?"

"Sure did."

Good. "Did he mention that our victim had filed complaints about a possible stalker?"

Walter huffed as he crossed into the doorway. "Nope. Didn't say a thing about that and if there are any, apparently he didn't look for me. I even asked if he'd met her, and he said that he had not."

"It's possible he hasn't," Laurel said, glancing at the reports for an officer's name. "Officer Frank Zello. On all three reports. We'll need to speak with him." She looked at her computer. "Walter, please deliver these and get a judge to sign off on the search warrants for Dr. Rox's home and office, and then let's finish work for the day. We'll convene first thing tomorrow." They both left her office.

She lifted her phone to her ear and dialed Huck.

"Rivers," he answered. It was quiet in the background.

"Hi, Huck. I should have signed search warrants for our victim's home and office by tomorrow morning. I'll ask the FBI Seattle field office to search her office, but do you want to meet and go through her place after the crime scene techs finish?"

Aeneas barked once in the background. "Sure. I'll call the state team and tell them to be ready early. Also, another storm is moving in right now. I'll follow you along Birch Tree Road until my turnoff. The road to your farm gets better after that, anyway."

Her chest warmed. "I don't need backup, Huck."

"Meet you outside in fifteen minutes. That's what friends do." He clicked off.

It was?

# Chapter Seven

After a night during which Aeneas barked erratically at invisible ghosts outside, Huck kept his hands easy on the wheel as morning brought more lightly drifting snow. Laurel sat quietly in his passenger side seat as they drove away from their office building, her gaze out the window, her eyes shadowed.

She secured the back of one gold earring. "The Seattle team didn't find anything interesting in a search of Dr. Rox's office outside of Seattle. She was a solo practitioner in a small house turned commercial venture, and one of her colleagues had already picked up the patient records pursuant to state law."

Huck sighed. "Damn, I'd love to get my hands on those patient records."

Laurel nodded. "As would I, but HIPAA laws prevent that. The colleague will make the necessary notifications to patients and then follow the law as to storage. There's no way for us to see those, unfortunately."

She sighed. "Nester is continuing his investigation into her life but hasn't found any safety deposit boxes or anything else of interest."

Huck nodded. "I'll have someone from my team reach

out to her colleagues. Maybe they know why she was hiding in the woods. We'll find out who to call when we get the phone dump." He glanced her way. "You okay?" he asked.

She started and turned toward him. "Yes."

Okay. He was learning that she was as literal as a street sign. "Let me rephrase. You have shadows beneath your eyes and look like you didn't sleep well last night. Did you have difficulty sleeping?" One of Laurel's good characteristics, and she seemed to have many, was that she wouldn't find any hidden meanings in his question. Many a woman would be insulted that he mentioned she looked tired. She'd take him at his word.

"Yes." She clasped her hands in her lap. "I had nightmares last night, which I suffer from sometimes."

Not for the first time, he wondered who comforted her. He'd met her mother, who was fiercely defensive of her daughter. But there were some serious demons in that woman's eyes. "We're friends, right?"

"Yes." Laurel tilted her head in that way she had as if she were trying to decipher some sort of code or language she didn't understand. "Why do you ask?"

"Because friends talk to each other." He was the last person in the entire world who should be giving advice or trying to connect, but she drew him in a way even he couldn't fight. Probably because she wasn't trying to attract him in any manner. "I read somewhere that talking about nightmares helps people to overcome them." Actually, a shrink who'd once treated him for PTSD had told him that.

"Nightmares aren't axiomatically detrimental," she murmured. "They can be a way to deal with stress and fear. I don't necessarily want to overcome mine."

Was there an answer for that? He wasn't sure. Even so,

he watched her from his peripheral vision. In the gray light, the deep red hue of her cabernet-colored hair shone like some symbol of strength. While her hair was interesting, her eyes were fucking captivating. One blue, one green, with a star of green in the blue one. She was a torch of color on a dismal day. "Tell me about your dream anyway."

She shrugged. "Okay. I was walking barefoot in the snow by Witch Creek, and birds were flapping high above me, squawking in a way that wasn't natural." She wrapped her arms around her waist as if chilled.

He flicked the heater up higher in the truck.

She looked back out the window. "My feet started to freeze and I couldn't move. All of a sudden, frozen black dahlias began to fall from the sky, hitting me in the head and knocking me to the ground. I knew somebody was coming, and I knew they had a hammer and were going to hit me. There was no way to get free." Her voice trailed off at the end.

He fought every instinct in his body to keep from taking her hand. They weren't that kind of friends. "Sounds like a pretty normal dream after the scene we witnessed yesterday." Her vulnerability and naïveté was such a contrast to her devastating intelligence that he wanted to know more. Wanted to get inside her head. It was a fascinating place. "You're a woman, a professional woman like the victim, so it isn't a surprise you'd identify with her."

"Thank goodness," she whispered.

He jolted. "What?"

A light pink filtered beneath her smooth skin. "I'm always afraid I'll identify with the killer."

Whoa. Not what he'd expected. He glanced into the back seat to see if Aeneas had caught the anxiety in her voice, but the dog was snoozing happily. "The killer has to be some sort of psychopath, right? You're not a psychopath."

"We don't know if the killer is a psychopath or not," she countered, her voice stronger now. "But we both know I'm unusually intelligent, and brilliance and insanity are but one click away on the clock of life." She still didn't look at him.

What the hell? "You think you might go insane?"

"No." Finally, she smiled. "But you won't find many people who've been categorized as a genius who haven't thought about it."

Her smile was natural and pure. She was correct that she brought out a protectiveness in him he thought he'd abandoned after leaving the service. But he'd seen her survive a car crash and jump out into the snow to fire at her attacker. She had an impressive strength. "What's your IQ, anyway?" Was it rude to ask?

"I don't know the number." She hunched her shoulders. "I was tested when I was young, and my mother always destroyed the results, figuring that my knowing the number would influence my decisions. Looking back, she was correct. I don't think an IQ can be truly measured, and a number would just be arbitrary. While I'm curious about many things, an indiscriminate number that's supposed to define me is not one of them."

"Genius must be inheritable, right? Considering you and your half sister are both prodigies."

She stiffened. "I suppose so, but I've never met our biological father, so I can't say."

"Are you still searching for him?"

"Yes." Her chin firmed and her eyes sparked. Her father had been the preacher at a local church, but he'd disappeared on a walkabout a few years ago. "The FBI has an active file on him since the current preacher filed a missing person's report."

This was none of Huck's business, unless the man had met with foul play. "Do you think he's alive?"

She reached forward and turned down the heat. "I don't know if he's alive or not. I do know that he met with my half sister when she returned to town and then left shortly afterward. If she feels anything toward him like I do, I'm not certain she'd let him live."

Huck swallowed. "I didn't know you had bad feelings."

"I do. Very." She paused as if trying to decide how much detail a friend should be given. "He raped my mom when she was seventeen, and she had me. My uncle Carl fought him and sustained a head injury that still plagues him to this day."

"I'm sorry."

She shrugged. "Me, too. In the span of one month, I discovered the identity of my father, who needs to be held accountable for his crimes, and the existence of a half sister who's at least as intelligent as I am, if not more."

Huck nodded. "I know we can't prove it, but I think she helped cover for her brother's crimes until she shot him to save you." He sighed. "Based on her past—being taken from her father, who's apparently a bad guy, then being thrown into college at a young age by herself—I can see her wanting to protect family."

"Yes. She didn't have the security and love that I did."

"You feel sorry for Dr. Caine?" He liked to keep Abigail in the doctor category because every instinct in his body told him she was dangerous.

"Yes. I often wonder who I'd be if I'd grown up alone like she did," Laurel said softly.

He glanced her way. "You'd be exactly who you are. You fight evil, Laurel. That matters."

She fiddled with her earring again. "Don't you wonder

why I chose this field? I do, and I haven't delved deep enough to really understand my motivations, if they can even be understood." For a second, she sounded lost.

The bewildering complexity of the woman made him feel relieved that they'd decided to just be friends, but he sympathized with her unease about Abigail and the pastor. Both were the kind of brilliant that could lead to crazy. He pulled to a stop in the parking lot of a luxury condominium complex. They'd have to continue this discussion later.

Laurel scrutinized the messy kitchen in the condominium. "She left in a hurry." Cupboards had been left open and their contents spread over the countertop.

Huck kept his gloves in place as he snapped pictures with his phone. "The crime scene techs did a good job cleaning up after themselves. They caught some prints but nothing very interesting, from the sounds of it."

"Agreed." Laurel moved to a partially open drawer and pulled it out. Just wine corks. A lot of them. Her gloves in place, she opened the cupboard door beneath the sink to find a garbage can smelling like wine, gin, and vodka. The scent of red wine wafted up. "It looks like Dr. Rox enjoyed her alcohol." Or perhaps she was self-medicating because she was terrified of her stalker.

"Maybe." Huck looked at the open-concept area, standing in the kitchen and studying the living room. "She liked calm, soothing colors."

Laurel nodded. The entire place was decorated in muted tan, white, and light purple. She looked from the front door to the balcony, then walked that way and opened the door. About a foot of snow covered the area, and ice crusted the black railing. "According to one police report,

Dr. Rox found black dahlias up here. The stalker must've reached the balcony through the condo, right?" The rear of the building looked over an open field that bordered forested land, and deer browsed for food through the snow. She craned her neck to look over the railing and below but couldn't see without stepping onto the balcony. "There are no footprints. I'm going to walk through the snow."

"All right." He was suddenly at her back, snapping pictures of the pristine area. It was vacant, save for the snow. "Go ahead. I photographed the scene."

"Thanks." She kicked a small trail straight to the railing, pausing and looking down. "I don't see how he could've come up this way."

Huck appeared at her side, leaning over. His sheer size took her aback for a moment. The man had such a calm demeanor, she forgot he was at least a foot taller, much broader, and more muscled than she. He probably outweighed her by a hundred pounds. "The balconies are positioned on top of each other. I could jump from one railing to the other and pull myself up each time." He cocked his head. "But that'd be a risk because anybody inside the affected condominium would probably hear me." He made a note on his phone.

"If the stalker lifted himself up to each balcony, he's athletic," Laurel murmured, the cold wind slapping against her face. She shivered. "I'll search the master bedroom and you take the office next to it."

"Okay." He waited for her to step back inside before following her and shutting the door. "I called in a team to start canvassing the other condo owners, and I'll make sure they ask about the railings and the possibility of someone climbing up. We have a new investigative team within the Fish and Wildlife office here, and they're ready to get to work."

She paused. "I'm surprised you wanted to expand the local office."

"I didn't. Monty did. He used the juice from our solving the Snowblood Peak murders to make it happen." Huck shrugged. "It's fine with me since Monty will be back in charge come late spring, once he's healed up." They were of the same rank, but Huck was a loner who only interacted with the team for search and rescue operations or for the bear program.

She moved past the office to the master bedroom to see the bed unmade and clothing strewn about. "You know, it's possible she didn't do this. That somebody searched her place afterward." Yet an unmade bed wasn't proof. Laurel methodically went through each drawer, finding nothing of interest.

After about ten minutes, Huck appeared in the doorway. "Her office is surprisingly sparse, and there's no laptop. I didn't find anything to help with the case."

"Neither have I." She glanced up at him. In the early morning, with dark stubble on his chin, he looked both dangerous and competent, and she felt safer with him as her partner. The different golds and browns in his eyes created an intriguing pattern as well, and it was odd she'd noticed that fact.

"What?" he asked, one dark eyebrow lifting.

"Nothing." She looked under the bed to just find dust. Straightening, she fought a sneeze. "We're going to need some luck to find this killer." Statistics told Laurel the murderer was almost certainly male.

Plus, to fracture a skull like that took a lot of strength.

And rage. Incredible rage. Was it focused only on this

victim? Was it personal? Were they about to find more bodies?

Huck gestured toward the door. "How about we grab lunch?"

She stood and stretched her back, pausing as she considered the work she needed to complete. Then she moved toward the doorway. While it was early for lunch, she was hungry. So this was what friendship was like for Huck. He pressed his hand to her lower back, walking behind her. At his touch, her skin warmed and her breath caught. She knew just how good he could be with those hands.

Clearing her throat, she stepped around a pile of shoes in the foyer. "Lunch would be good." Did she sound casual?

Yes. She sounded casual.

Probably.

# Chapter Eight

After a long day of work, Laurel stood outside the old, weathered barn on the family farm, up to her knees in snow. The wind ripped right through her coat, freezing her to her bones. Shaking her head, she kicked a trail from her SUV to the human-size door next to the large tractor door. Grunting, she shoved it open just as a farm truck slid to a stop next to her vehicle.

She stepped inside the darkened interior and turned to watch her uncle Blake jump out and stomp her way, using her trail. Blake was her mom's older brother who managed the farm. He had green eyes like her mom, rapidly graying hair, and a lumberjack frame. He reminded her of the dad on that old show *The Walton's*, but she'd never told him so.

"Hi." He took off his gloves and slapped them on his jeans, stepping inside and turning on the industrial-sized flashlight he'd brought. "We're going to make a barn-dominium, huh?"

She grinned. "It's Mom's way of tempting me to stay." It figured her uncle had heard of barns being turned into homes. "Some of my best memories are of spending time in here with you, figuring out how tractors work." How many hours had she spent learning all about engines?

About tires, wheels, and belts? She looked around the wide space, smelling motor oil and leather. Good smells that grounded her with the sense of home. Of family and of love. The middle of the structure was wide and two stories high, while one-story wings extended on either side. "What do you think?"

He looked down at her, his eyes twinkling. "You have money?"

"Mom and I both do. We're partners in this venture." She rubbed her hands together. "What's the first step?"

"Making sure you have money." His chuckle was deep. "Then we need to get plumbing out here. Good news is that you already have electricity." He rubbed snow off his hair. "You'll need an architect. Carl and I can definitely help with the labor, but you're going to need a licensed architect to sign off on the plan I know you have. Tell me about it."

She felt eight years old again and full of excitement. Carl was Blake and Deidre's older brother, her "odd" uncle, and she adored him as well. "Okay. Double-door entrance into a vestibule with the kitchen on the left and a circular staircase to the right. Great room with fireplace and wide windows straight ahead. Beyond the kitchen, a guest room with bath and a powder room. To the right, past the entrance to the garage, a knitting room next to a small workout and yoga room." She knitted little outfits for premature babies and had started a nonprofit that was doing well across the country. "I figure the knitting room would work for any artist or author who might rent the space if that's what we do here."

He looked at the dirt floor and weathered boards on the walls. "Exposed beams?"

"Everywhere. For the second floor, a large master bedroom, bathroom, and closet next to an office." She could visualize it so clearly. "I'd like to keep the character of the barn with weathered wood, a stone fireplace, and the exposed beams. What do you think?" She held her breath.

He grinned. "I think it sounds awesome."

"Good." Relief calmed her nerves. "What architect do you like?"

He frowned. "Harvey Brewerston, but he had a heart attack and died a while back. The kid who took over for him changed the business name to something green sounding, and I doubt he has the experience to take on a job like this. Let me ask around and see who my friends are using these days." He kicked at the hard dirt beneath his boot. "We'll need to pour cement to start. I have a couple of old barns on the northern side I've been meaning to bring down. I can reclaim the wood from those for you. I assume you'll want barn boards on the walls. What kind of floor are you thinking?"

"Either limestone or a different wood," she mused. "Maybe use the wood for the floor, structure, and beams and something lighter for the walls to brighten the place." She could feel herself building something that would last. With her job, she was always arriving places after somebody had been killed. While seeking justice for the harmed was her passion, so far she hadn't built much that would last should she disappear. Well, except for the nonprofit she'd started, which might last beyond her life.

"Sure. Hopefully this means you'll stick around." He slung a heavy arm over her shoulders and tugged her close in a half hug. "I heard there was a murder out by Witch Creek. You on that?"

"Yes." She slid an arm around his thick waist. Blake was the closest thing she'd ever had to a father, and she would like to spend more time with him and her aunt Betty. "With my job, I'm never certain where I'll be working, but I agree that this is a good investment regardless." The wind scattered ice against the door, whistling sharply through the trees. "I don't suppose we can start right now?"

"Let's get an architect first." He drew her through the doorway and out into the blistering cold. "For now, let's go see what your aunt Betty has on for Friday night supper. I think she was planning on cooking her cheesy chicken casserole. We can call your mom and pick her up on the way. I'll shoot Carl a text, but he's probably lost his phone again."

She staggered as the wind assaulted her. "I'll follow you to Mom's and pick her up." She had the oddest urge to invite Huck to dinner, but that would seem more like a date and not like a friend situation. Probably. She wasn't certain.

If she did stick around, as Uncle Blake put it, did she want to just be friends with Huck?

Huck fetched the microwave mac and cheese out of the microwave, singeing his fingers. "Damn it." Grabbing a kitchen towel, he secured the side of the carton and dumped the contents onto a plate. A fire crackled cozily across the living room, and he snagged a fork before heading to his well-worn sofa. Aeneas snored softly by the fire, content to be inside, where the wind couldn't pierce the secured windows. It was well after midnight, but it had taken Huck so long to plow out his long driveway and shop area, and then shovel the walkway, that he'd missed dinner. He'd also shoveled the back deck and around the hot tub, knowing his aching muscles would need it in the morning.

Sitting, he extended his legs to the coffee table, noting his left sock had two holes. Shrugging, he stirred his dinner around to cool it, wondering about Dr. Rox and how she'd survived by herself for three weeks out in that freezing cabin. The woman must've been absolutely terrified to have lived that way.

His phone buzzed and he reached for it on the sofa table, setting his plate on the cushion. "Rivers." He eyed the still-cooling dinner.

"Hi, Huck. I hope it's okay I called." A female voice came clearly over the line.

He looked up at the ceiling. Why hadn't he glanced to see who was calling? "What do you want at midnight?" He and Rachel Raprenzi had stopped dating a long time ago.

"I knew you'd probably be up, as am I. Besides, is that any way to talk to your ex-fiancée?" she asked, both humor and charm in her voice.

He pulled the plate onto his lap and set his phone on speaker, putting it on the cold leather. "Not gonna ask again." Then he dug into his dinner, instantly burning his tongue. Only pure stubbornness kept him from swearing out loud.

"I'm in Washington State and thought maybe we could get together for dinner or even just a drink. You know. Like friends."

Friends. What was up with everyone wanting to be his friend lately? "No."

"It's Friday night and we're both home alone. That's sad." Rachel sighed. "Come on. I said I was sorry. You were drifting away, and I knew it was probably over, and I was just trying to . . ."

"Exploit my downward spiral for your own gain?" He took another bite and once again wondered if he should learn how to actually cook.

"No. Trying to figure out what was happening, and I may have used the wrong approach."

The wrong approach? He'd lost a kid in a case, and

she'd used that failure to propel her journalism career and write articles and do podcasts about him and the case. She had even guest hosted the nightly news in Portland. "To find out what was happening, all you had to do was ask. Me. Not other experts." He continued eating his gooey dinner. It was pretty good. Who needed to cook?

"I asked you," she exploded. "You wouldn't talk to me."

His gut started to ache and not from the food. "I lifted a dead kid out of a river. One I did not save." Although he'd caught the killer, he'd failed that one child. He probably hadn't been the nicest guy to be around for a while. "I'm sorry if I hurt you." It was the first time he'd said that.

By her sudden and unusual silence, she agreed. "Um. Well, thank you. I'm sorry for everything I did that hurt you, too."

A feeling of stress he hadn't realized he still held wafted away. "We're good, then."

"Good." Her tone brightened. "So dinner?"

"No." He'd moved on. "That chapter of my life is over. You're part of that chapter." It wasn't kind, but it was honest. It was the best he could do for her. "I left Oregon and am never returning." He liked it here in the mountains of Washington State, and he was finally feeling whole again.

She cleared her throat.

His instincts started to hum.

"About that. Well, I've been transferred to Everett. We're expanding our streaming news service, and I'm going to head up the Everett division, just a teensy car ride from Genesis Valley and you. I almost got Seattle but missed out to that jackass Larry with the perfect comb-over."

Huck blinked. Wait a minute. "Rachel?"

"Yeah, I'm working the Witch Creek Murder. Isn't that the best name for a case?"

His ears rang. Name for a case? He bit his lip to keep from snapping that the case was about a raped and brutally beaten woman, not some catchy name. "No comment."

"I figured," she said. "But can you get me an introduction to the lead on the case? Laurel Snow is big news, especially after the two of you closed that Snowblood Peak murder case. I swear, the names of the places around here just ask for a murder, right? That might be a decent lead-in, actually." Her voice trailed off thoughtfully.

"You'll have to go through official channels to get a comment on this one," he said, stabbing his fork into the food.

"What? The petite FBI agent can't handle the press?" Rachel challenged.

Huck had no doubt Laurel could handle anything, although there was a naïveté to her brilliance that made him want to shield her. "No comment."

"Is there something between the two of you? She is intriguing looking. Really weird with that hair and the bizarre eyes."

Intriguing? Yeah, that was it. Laurel was also purely and naturally beautiful. There was nothing weird about her looks. "You know I don't mix business with anything else, ever." In fact, when he'd started dating Rachel, she'd been a freelance travel writer. Why had they even gotten engaged? It had seemed like a good idea at the moment, but now he couldn't remember why he'd agreed. "I have nothing for you on this case, Rachel."

"Well, I might have a thing or two for you. I'm good at my job. I'll trade you for information."

He stiffened. If he remembered correctly, she was great at digging up leads. Maybe she did know something about the case. "It's late. I'll think about dinner and let you know. Right now, I have to go." He clicked off and looked at his unfinished noodles. So much for his appetite.

His phone buzzed again and his temper awoke. Then he caught sight of the caller. "Laurel?"

"Hi, Huck." He could hear the rustle of clothing. "We have another body. It's the mayor's sister-in-law."

# Chapter Nine

Laurel drank the extra strong coffee she'd brought from home as Huck drove an hour up into the mountains to the far reaches of Genesis Valley near Scottish Lake. Heat blasted from the vents, and her seat warmer was on high, nicely warming her glutes. "You don't always have to drive." Although tonight, he did. She'd had several glasses of wine with dinner, and while it had been a few hours, her head wasn't clear yet.

"I prefer to drive." He navigated around another bend, his truck heavy on the snow. His dog snoozed quietly in his crate in the back.

The man appeared to have control issues, but he was also an experienced winter driver. "I had no idea the city of Genesis Valley extended so far into the mountains." Which meant that Sheriff York had jurisdiction for now. Unfortunately. "Tell me about Scottish Lake. I remember seeing it on a map, but I don't know much about it."

He ducked his head to look up at the dark sky. "It's two hours from Everett and three from Seattle. It's where rich people go to spend leisure time and unplug during the summer months. No motors are allowed on the lake, so no boats or jet skis."

"Sail boats?" She took another drink and the potent brew hit her stomach.

"The lake isn't that big. Well, it probably is, but sailing across it would be boring after the first run. In the summer, you'd see kayaks, fishing boats with no motors, and paddle boards." The snow fell in front of the bright headlights shining on the road. "There are two large lodges on either side of the lake where corporate folks have retreats every year."

She set her coffee aside, not willing to risk the lining of her stomach any more than she already had. "Does Fish and Wildlife stock the lake?"

"Every summer by helicopter," he said. "It's fun. Next summer, I'll bring you along."

She blinked. That was a kind offer. She'd never seen fish fall from a helicopter before. "I would enjoy that."

"Good. For now, tell me what you know about this latest death." He flicked the wipers on faster. "I'm surprised you got the call from our friendly sheriff."

"I didn't. Dr. Ortega was called to the scene, and he phoned me on his way out there. He should have just arrived a few minutes ago, I think." She tightened the ponytail holder she'd put into place to secure her hair as she'd rushed to get ready. "Flowers were left around the body, apparently."

"Black dahlias?"

Laurel shrugged. "Dr. Ortega didn't know yet and said the sheriff hadn't said." If the sheriff tried to assert jurisdiction, and it looked like the cases were related, she'd have to take it from him. "Perhaps you should take lead on the scene. The Genesis Valley Sheriff didn't like me during our last case."

"He didn't like me, either," Huck said grimly, passing a silent, dark cabin that looked as if it had been shut down for the winter. "I'd like to think he didn't respect you because you're a Fed and not because you're a woman, but I'm not sure."

"I'd rather he didn't disrespect me either way."

Huck snorted. "Good point. All right, I'll deal with him if need be."

"It's not needed," she hastened to add. "I just don't want anything to interfere with the case and finding justice for the victims."

"I know you can handle yourself, Laurel," Huck said, turning down a drive that had been marked with a flare on the snowy road.

"Thanks." She leaned forward to peer at the wooden cabin up ahead. Two patrol cars lit the area with blue and red swirls next to a champagne-colored luxury SUV, a green Jeep Wrangler, an ambulance, and the ME's van. "Apparently, we're the last to arrive." No doubt the sheriff had called everyone else but her.

"Do we have any details?" Huck rolled to a stop next to the ME's van and cut the engine.

"There's a dead woman surrounded by flowers who happens to be the mayor's sister-in-law." Laurel released her seatbelt and shoved open the heavy door to climb out.

"Great." Huck followed suit and gestured her in front of him toward the cabin.

She tromped along a now well-worn trail in her snow boots, eyeing the rustic-looking cabin. Lights blazed from the wide windows of the two-storied, log-sided structure. Thick wooden columns stood tall, flanking the steps, and the wide front door had a metal *B* engraved in the center. She opened the door and walked into the warm interior with Huck on her heels. Aeneas, well trained by Huck, stayed back far enough to remain outside the scene.

"Hi," Dr. Ortega said, gloves on his hands and his bag

on the floor. "I've already done a preliminary and wouldn't let them move the body until you arrived." His hair was mussed around his face and his pants wrinkled as if he'd hurriedly dressed in yesterday's clothing. "I'm glad you're here."

It was nice to have an ally. "Thank you for making sure we were called," Laurel said, pulling gloves from her pocket. She looked around the main room, which had been decorated in western style, from the cowboy paintings on the walls to the checked blankets on the leather chairs. "Where is she?"

"This way." Dr. Ortega turned and led them into a spacious kitchen, where state crime techs were at work cataloging the contents of the refrigerator. He kept moving to a sliding glass door that opened to a covered deck.

Floodlights had already been set up along the perimeter of the home. Sheriff York stood near an empty hot tub snapping pictures of the scene with his phone. Several flashlights flickered through the trees and bounced off the frozen surface of the darkened lake many yards away.

Laurel walked out far enough to allow Huck room to see and then paused, staring down at the dead woman. Even though she was somewhat protected by the eaves covering the deck, she was frozen over with ice and a skim of snow. Her skin was gray and her eyes a light blue, wide open in death. The rest of her face and part of her skull were battered nearly beyond recognition. Brain matter had frozen to the side of her mangled ear. Her long hair appeared to be a light brown strewn with blood, and it was impossible to tell her age. She was naked, and her hands had been removed. In addition, black dahlias had been scattered across the entire deck and down the stairs toward the lake, all of the flowers frozen solid beneath ice and snow. "She's been dead a while," Laurel said, taking in the scene.

Dr. Ortega nodded from within the cabin. "I'd guess a week or two but won't know until I get her back to my lab."

Laurel looked at Huck. "She was killed before Dr. Rox." Just how many victims were already out there? Were they all in remote locations and out of touch with people who were supposed to know them?

Huck focused on the sheriff. "Have we found the hands?"

"Not yet," Sheriff York said, hitching his belt up. Snow had fallen on his receding hairline and then melted down the side of his face to mush in his thick mustache. His gaze flicked to Laurel. "This like the other body you found?"

"This is very similar," Laurel said, crouching to study the cut marks on the wrists. "Have you found an ax?"

"Yes. Already bagged it, and it has blood on it," the sheriff said. "We'll get it examined for fingerprints."

This guy didn't leave any prints. Laurel stood and spotted firewood neatly stacked at the far end of the porch beneath the eaves. "We don't know if he needs to use an ax or has only used them out of opportunity so far."

"Does that matter?" the sheriff snorted. "He cuts off their damn hands. That's what matters."

Laurel focused on Dr. Ortega. "Who found the body?"

"Her sister," Sheriff York answered. "Mrs. Bearing was worried when she hadn't heard from her sister, so she came up here and found her. Called me."

Laurel angled her head to look inside. "Where is Mrs. Bearing?"

"I sent her home."

Huck frowned. "You did what?"

The sheriff straightened to his full five foot ten, which was still about six inches shorter than Huck. "She was understandably upset, so I had a uniformed officer take her home after interviewing her. She didn't know anything except that her sister was up here for a couple of weeks working and should've been home earlier this afternoon. That's all."

What an imbecile. Laurel kept her voice level. "Working on what?"

"I don't know. She's some sort of hobby writer." The sheriff flipped open his small notebook. "Name was Dr. Sharon Lamber. She was a published author and apparently had a doctorate in botany, which she taught at the Genesis Valley Community College. Also guest lectured across the country, according to her sister. Right now, she was taking a semester off to work on her writing."

Wait a minute. Dr. Sharon Lamber? "The poet?" Laurel asked.

York shrugged.

"You've heard of her?" Huck asked.

She nodded. "Yes. If this is the same woman, she's won several poetry awards. I've read her. She was incredibly insightful and often wrote about the earth and flowers. Makes sense with her botany background." The poems had been beautiful and intelligent at the same time. They'd been striking to a person who normally missed subtext. Such was Lamber's talent. Was Lamber up here hiding from a stalker? Or had she just been working? "We'll need to talk to her sister. Was Dr. Lamber married? Did she have any other relatives?"

The sheriff rolled his eyes. "Yes, she's married, but supposedly she and her husband are separated. Mrs. Bearing didn't know why."

More likely the sheriff hadn't pushed for answers. Laurel didn't want to work with this man again, but she also didn't see a way out at the moment, unless she wanted to pull rank. She did not as of yet. "I assume the luxury SUV out front is hers?" At the sheriff's nod, she glanced back at Huck. "Let's get warrants for her vehicle, home, and office at the college. We can speak with her sister first thing in the morning, and we need to find the husband."

Huck nodded, already texting on his phone. "If we're awake, might as well get everyone else up. Except Monty. He needs sleep."

The sheriff shoved his notebook back into his jacket. "Don't tell me. You want to create another task force and get your face in the newspaper again?"

"That's not necessary," Laurel said smoothly. "We'll just keep everybody in the loop this time." She liked that particular colloquium.

"This is my case," he said.

Laurel sighed. "I would like to work with you on this, Sheriff."

"That's fantastic, so long as you realize I take the lead. I will loop *you* in when I think you need to be involved. As of right now, you don't have a reason to be here, except that Ortega wouldn't take the body until you saw everything firsthand. For some reason." His eyebrows rose.

For some reason? "I assume it's because I caught the first case and saw the other victim." Laurel tilted her head. "What other reason could there be?"

The sheriff met her gaze, his chin lowering. "You tell me. In my years of working this city, I've never had the county ME insist we call in the feds. What's so special about you?"

Was he being literal? "This is exactly the kind of case

the Pacific Northwest Violent Crimes Unit was created to handle." Surely he knew that fact.

"Uh huh." His gaze traveled from her face down her body and then back up.

"Oh," she said, finally catching on. "You're making a sexual innuendo that Dr. Ortega called me because he finds me attractive." At least now she understood what he was trying to say. "Are you serious about that or are you just trying to be insulting?" She really didn't know.

His mouth opened partially and his eyes squinted.

Huck coughed and almost covered a laugh.

She cleared her throat. "If you're serious that there has been a breach of protocol, then you should file a report through proper channels. If you're merely trying to insult me, you failed. I care nothing about your opinion." Perhaps now that they had that out of the way, they could get back to the case. She glanced toward Dr. Ortega. "Why did you call me?"

"For professional reasons only," the doctor said, a small smile playing beneath his goatee.

"That's what I thought." She looked again at the frozen body. "Let's focus on the poor woman who was brutally murdered."

The sheriff took a step toward her. "Listen, you—"

"I wouldn't." Huck moved toward him, his voice holding such a strong threat of harm that even Laurel caught it.

She looked from one to the other, pausing. What in the world was happening? They had a victim on the ground in front of them, naked, violated, and frozen. It wasn't a time for egos or anything but rational thought. "We're in the middle of a crime scene. Let's get this done."

The sheriff flushed a deep red. "I don't need your help. This murder occurred within my city limits, which gives me jurisdiction. It was a mistake to call you." He gestured toward the doorway. "Get out of my crime scene."

This was exactly what she'd wanted to avoid. What had she done wrong? Hadn't she been polite? "I'm sorry, Sheriff, but 28 U.S.C. §540B grants the FBI the right to investigate serial killings, and I believe this one is connected to our victim out at the creek."

His eyes gleamed. "Only if the state officials request FBI involvement. I am not requesting your help."

"I am," Huck said mildly. "As a state officer, I have the authority to request FBI assistance, and I'm doing so right now."

Laurel waited, wondering how smart the sheriff actually might be.

His smile gave her one hint. "Fine. However, 'serial' is defined as three or more killings within the United States Code, and we only have two. So fuck off."

Huck took another step toward the sheriff, and Laurel pivoted slightly, putting her hip against his thigh.

He remained in place and his words were clipped. "I'm taking the case, Sheriff. You don't have the resources to solve a murder in the city, so it's a state matter. The state has decided to coordinate efforts with the FBI. We're done now."

Laurel once again looked at the frozen body. The woman deserved better than to have investigators fighting over her case. They should all be trying to find her killer. "She's frozen solid to the wood planks beneath her, Dr. Ortega. This is going to be difficult." Crouching again, she studied bone fragments poking out of the woman's shredded face. "Fury and rage belong on another plane, not within the human heart," she murmured.

"Who said that?" Huck asked.

"She did. In one of her poems." Laurel stood, her lungs feeling heavy. Who would do something like this?

A shout came from down by the lake.

"Sounds like we found the hands," the sheriff drawled.

# Chapter Ten

After another night beset by gruesome dreams, Laurel sat on top of the new conference table and studied the glass boards now mounted to the wall. She'd placed pictures of both victims as well as one of Abigail on a board, making notations below them. The women looked nothing alike. That was interesting.

"Hi." Huck filled the doorway, carrying two steaming drinks from Staggers. He looked at the boards. "The victims aren't similar." Moving inside, he handed over one drink. Aeneas bounded in behind him, no doubt having received love from Kate on his way. Laurel had called Kate and Nester in to work a half day, even though it was Saturday. Walter was stricken with a bad cold, and she'd told him to remain at home and recuperate.

"Thank you." Laurel took the drink. Perhaps she should start taking him warm drinks, if this friendship was to be two ways. "They don't look similar. Charlene Rox had short black hair, dark brown eyes, and darker skin. Sharon Lamber was very tall with light brown hair, blue eyes, and very pale skin. Abigail has mahogany hair and heterochromatic eyes." So appearance wasn't what drew the killer. "All three are successful professional women, and they each have at least one doctorate." That was the only similarity so far. "I have Nester performing extensive background checks on all three, and we have warrants to dump the phones of the two deceased victims." She'd need Abigail's permission to gain her records.

Huck drew out a white leather chair and sat. "Nice stuff you have here."

"FBI raid," she murmured, remaining on the glass top, which was reinforced with copper-colored metal in a circular design.

He cleared his throat. "Are we certain your sister should be on the board?"

"The black dahlias all over her yard tie her to the victims," Laurel said, looking at the picture that could double as her own driver's license photograph.

"Is there any way she could've heard about the victim and then somehow created a similar situation at her home?" Huck shrugged. "She's over-the-top brilliant and could probably do something like that, right?"

Laurel bit the inside of her cheek, thinking. "I don't see how. The flowers at Abigail's were left before the ones with the body by the river, so Abigail would've had to have known there would be a murder, and I don't see how that could be possible. In addition, we have the video of the person leaving flowers at Abigail's house, and it isn't her." She scratched her neck. "Plus, her alibi checks out—she was at a spa." She'd gotten that info already from a team she'd contacted in DC.

Huck nodded. "Then it follows she's one of the victims, which means we should put her into protective custody."

"She refused," Laurel said, trying to find any further resemblance between the victims. There was none. She'd have to tie them together in another way to find this murderer. "I don't believe she feels fear like most people do."

Did Laurel herself? Sure, she was afraid sometimes, but her intellect often took over, allowing her to act when others might freeze. She shifted on the hard glass, uneasy at the thought that she and Abigail shared traits beyond the physical.

Huck twirled his disposable cup on the table. "You were quiet on the ride back to your place last night. Were you mad at me?"

She turned her head to meet his gaze. "I was thinking about the new victim. Why would I be angry with you?"

"Because of the whole thing with the dumbass sheriff." Huck rolled his neck and something quietly popped. "I wanted to hit him."

"Oh. Well, he is a dumbass." She took a sip of the drink. "I'm not angry." In fact, it was rather nice that Huck had stepped in to defend her, even though she could defend herself fairly well. "I understand that you're protective of people in general but most especially women, even cops. It stems from your abandonment by your mother at an early age as well as your time learning to protect and defend in the military. Plus, it just might be you and how you're made. Life is both nature and nurture, and such traits could be inherent in DNA. It's entirely possible."

His jaw went slack. "Could you please not profile me at every turn?"

Oh. She blanched. Normally she kept her thoughts to herself, but apparently she was becoming much too relaxed around Huck Rivers. "I apologize." She shouldn't have said all that, even if it was the truth. "I will do my best not to profile you." The term was inaccurate, but they both understood what it meant to him, so she made the promise. "Either way, I don't mind your natural inclination to protect me in the field."

"Gee. That's great," he said.

She nodded. It was nice to be back on the same page. "Although I am trained and can fight." Sort of. While her mind was quick, her reflexes were merely average. Perhaps she could not win a fight with the sheriff, who was built like a wrestler and had supposedly been quite successful at the sport in high school and college. "Do you think I could take the sheriff hand to hand?"

"No."

Her eyebrows rose and laughter bubbled up her chest. "You could stop and ponder the question for a moment."

Huck smiled. "Sorry. I know you're trained, but so is he. With his wrestling experience, he'd have you on the ground fast, and that's where you're at a disadvantage with your size and strength. However, you're a zillion times smarter than he, so perhaps you'd kick his ass in the end."

True. Not that she was going to physically grapple with the sheriff any time soon. Or ever. "Nice save."

"Thanks." His phone buzzed and he glanced at the face. "We can speak with the sister now at the mayor's house."

Laurel jumped off the table, careful to keep from spilling her drink. "I'd rather interview her alone without her family around her."

"I tried and not a chance. Not only will Mayor Bearing be there, but his oldest son will as well."

Laurel tugged on her earring. "Mrs. Bearing wants a lawyer to speak about her sister?" That was odd. She'd interviewed Steve Bearing as part of the investigation into the Snowblood Peak killings, and he'd asked her on a date. The attorney was charming and seemed intelligent, but a cloak of ambition clung to him so obviously even she could see it. As the mayor's eldest son, he no doubt felt pressure to achieve.

Huck shrugged. "Who knows. He is her kid and most likely wants to be there for her. But it isn't ideal as far as we're concerned." He snapped his fingers at the dog, who happily trotted into the hallway. "Although we want to interview him about his aunt, too, so we might as well take advantage of the moment. Seeing all three of them in the family home might give us insight."

"Agreed. I'd also like to get a read on the mayor and see what he thought of his sister-in-law." Laurel stopped by the computer room.

She introduced Huck and Nester. "While we're gone, would you continue conducting background searches into the lives of all three women and buy me a copy of Dr. Lamber's poetry books?" She stopped. "Also, let's run a background check on the husband. We need to know more about him before we call him in."

"Sure thing. I already started looking into Morris Lamber, and he's as boring as you'd think an accounting professor would be. I'll have more concrete information for you in an hour or so," Nester said, country music playing in the background. "How long do you want us in today? I have a date tonight."

"Must be nice," Huck said. "Where are you going?"

Nester tapped his hands on the old door. "Kenny Chesney concert."

Huck grinned. "Sounds like fun."

"Yep." Nester turned back to his computer, typing rapidly. "My date actually got the tickets and asked me. She's in marketing for the arena and has decent connections as well as eyes the color of a summer sky."

Huck chuckled. "A computer guru with a romantic streak. It's nice to meet you, Nester."

"You, too." Nester didn't look up from his monitor.

Laurel walked down the hallway. "You're a Chesney fan, Huck?"

"Definitely." Huck followed her past the old pastry case,

pausing to smile at Kate, who also had a Staggers latte in front of her. "How are the girls, Kate?"

"Busy. Very, very, very busy," Kate said, writing on a legal pad. "My oldest is dating a guy who mumbles. Can't understand a thing he says. I just want to smack him on the top of his head." She looked up, seeing Laurel put on her coat. "Do you need me for the rest of the day?"

"Oh, no. It looks like Nester will work for a few more hours, and I don't know when Huck and I will return today." Perhaps Laurel shouldn't have called her in. While she'd been helpful, she had her hands full with three teenagers. It appeared as if the girls' father wasn't cooperative, but Laurel didn't want to pry. "You can head out if you'd like. Stacks of work will still be here on Monday." Probably more if she managed to glean useful information from Mrs. Bearing. "Thanks for coming in."

"Sure." Kate crouched down to rub her hands through Aeneas's fur. "Who's a good dog? Who's the best dog?" she crooned. Then she looked up. "After spending time with this cutie a few weeks ago, my girls all want a dog now. I'm probably going to give in and get one, but who has time to train one?" She stood, brushing off her jeans.

Laurel smiled. "The girls would help, I'm sure." She buttoned up her wool coat. "I'm thinking of turning a barn into a house." She knew she should also share personal information, since she and Kate were friends. In fact, she'd almost lost her mind when Kate had been kidnapped during the last case, and that was rare for her.

Kate blinked. "A barn into a house?"

"Yes." Laurel tugged her gloves from her pockets. "There's a nice old barn that used to hold tractors, and I think it'd make a great home if remodeled correctly. Even if I don't stay in town, I could always use it as a rental for people who want to get away. It's right up against a creek and quite lovely and secluded. You wouldn't know a good architect, would you?"

"No," Kate said.

Huck waited at the top of the stairs, looking odd against the cancan dancers cavorting on the wallpaper. "I have a guy. He did a good job on my shop a couple of years ago. His place is now called Greenfield Architecture and Landscaping. I think they also do snow removal."

Kate perked up. "I need their contact info, too. For the snow removal. Are the rates okay?"

"Yeah. I'll text you the info."

Laurel walked down the stairs, her boots thudding softly. "My uncle plows our road and all of the driveways." She should probably buy him something as a thank you. It had been a while since she'd knitted an adult's hat. Perhaps she also could knit something blue and green for Huck in lieu of buying him coffee.

"Good luck with the mayor's wife," Kate called out. "She's friends with my ex-husband's bimbo and has snarled at me a couple of times."

Laurel winced. "Does she know we work together?" She paused at the landing.

"Yep. She knows we're friends," Kate confirmed.

Laurel sighed. Stupendous.

# Chapter Eleven

The mayor lived in a stately, red brick home on Royal Drive and had a phenomenal view of the mountains from the rear. Huck dutifully removed his coat and boots in the foyer as Laurel did the same, hoping he'd worn socks without holes in them today. A quick glance down confirmed that he had. Good.

He glanced at Laurel's socks. Light pink with peacocks on them. They had to be her mother's. He stifled a grin and followed Steve Bearing into a surprisingly comfortable living room, with Aeneas at his heels. "Are you sure you don't mind the dog?"

"Just keep him off the furniture," Steve said. While Huck and Laurel both wore jeans for this Saturday meeting, the eldest Bearing kid wore creased khaki pants and a blue polo shirt. It was surprising the guy hadn't had his law firm name embroidered across his chest. He might as well have opened the door and declared himself an attorney.

"Please, have a seat. My parents will be in shortly." Steve took a plush, flowered chair and gestured to the matching sofa. His thick blond hair was swept up with a generous amount of mousse, and round black glasses gave his blue eyes a studious look. "My mother is understandably upset."

"How about you?" Huck asked.

Steve blinked. "Very. Aunt Sharon has been a constant in my life since the beginning. She never missed a baseball game or a school recital." His voice broke.

Laurel wasn't tall enough to sit all the way back on the sofa and unobtrusively moved a mocha-colored pillow behind her back. "Do you have any idea who would want to harm your aunt?"

"No." Steve rubbed his clean-shaven jaw. "I've been busy with my law practice and haven't spent much time with her the last few years."

The mayor and his wife walked in from what looked like the kitchen, both dressed nicely. Mayor Bearing was around six feet tall with silver gray hair, pale blue eyes, and smooth movements from playing baseball most of his life. For the meeting, he wore pressed gray slacks and a yellow polo shirt with a Hawaiian golf course logo above the pocket.

Teri Bearing wore light pink linen pants and a flowered sweater with a silver cross necklace and small silver hoops at her ears. Her hair was blond and feathery, her eyes green, and her posture perfect.

Huck stood as they entered the room. "We're very sorry for your loss." The mayor had lines extending from his eyes, and Mrs. Bearing's nose was red and her eyes swollen as if she'd been crying.

"Thank you," the mayor answered, leading his wife to the chair adjacent to her son and then sitting on an ottoman near the brick fireplace.

Huck introduced Laurel and himself, giving their job descriptions. "We're very sorry to bother you at this time, but we need to gather facts while they're fresh in your minds."

Mrs. Bearing clasped her hands together in her lap,

showing one gold band on her ring finger and light pink fingernails. "We understand." Her voice was soft but powerful.

Laurel studied them both. "Would you run us through the events of last night, Mrs. Bearing?"

"Teri. Call me Teri." She sat straighter and her gaze moved up and to the right as if to remember. "My sister asked to stay at our cabin to work on a new book of poetry and went up there, about two weeks ago?" She looked to her husband, who nodded.

"Is that usual?" Laurel asked. "That she'd leave town for weeks and use your cabin?"

"Yes," the mayor answered. "She has always secluded herself somewhere when really digging down to work, and she has often used our cabin, even for a girls' retreat for her college friends one week every summer."

Laurel nodded. "All right. Please continue."

Teri's hands fluttered. "Sharon was supposed to be home yesterday afternoon, because last night we had our first meeting to plan the Spring Tempest Youth Ranch auction, and she co-chairs it with me. We raise money for the organization, which houses and counsels troubled teens." Her eyes teared. "When she missed the meeting and wasn't answering her calls, I knew something was wrong. So I drove up to the cabin."

"By yourself?" Huck asked.

"I was in Billings at a Pacific Northwest mayoral conference," the mayor said. "I caught the first flight home this morning."

Huck nodded. "I need a list of people who can confirm that. Thanks." Then he waited, watching for a reaction.

"Sure," the mayor said wearily, leaning against the brick fireplace.

Not that it mattered, considering Sharon Lamber had

been dead for at least a week, if not two. "Go on, Mrs. Bearing," he said.

She shook her head. "I arrived at the cabin, saw her car, and thought she'd just gotten lost in writing. I was so relieved to see her car." She looked down at her cream-colored boots. "Then I went inside, didn't see her, and kept looking. I found her on the outside porch." Her voice broke at the end, and she pressed a hand to her mouth. "Who would do such a thing?"

The front door opened before they could answer, and two teenagers stomped inside, kicking off snow gear.

"Dad? I hope you're finally happy. We finished shoveling out Mrs. McCloskly's driveway, and she sent a casserole because of Aunt Sharon." The first boy was a younger version of Steve Bearing, and the other had black hair, dark eyes, and a little pudge around his round face along with a slight belly. Was probably about to hit a growth spurt. They both paused at seeing Huck and Laurel.

"Come in." The mayor gestured them inside. "This is our son Tommy and his friend Davie Tate."

Both kids nodded.

Huck smiled. "Tommy? How well did you know your aunt?"

The kid shrugged, his sweatshirt moving over his wiry body. "Aunt Sharon was always around. She's family." He shifted the casserole dish in his hands. "Can I put this in the fridge?"

"Sure," his mom said. "Thanks for finally doing that driveway."

Tommy almost kept from rolling his eyes but not quite.

Laurel had turned her head to view the kids. "Greenfield Architecture?" She read both of their worn sweatshirts. "You two work there?"

"Yeah," Davie said, brushing snow off dark hair that

reached his shoulders. "Old man Harvey hired us a few years back to pull weeds and shovel snow." He sighed. "We're gonna miss him."

Huck's eyebrow rose. "Miss him?"

"Yeah. He died of a massive heart attack last year," Tommy said. "Like his entire heart just blew up."

"Tommy," his mother admonished. "Show respect."

Tommy sobered but his eyes still gleamed. "Yeah, sorry. It's kind of scary because he and Dad have the same cardiologist, right?"

The mayor sighed. "Right, and my heart is fine now, so stop worrying about it."

Tommy shrugged. "Anyway, I guess Jason's doing an okay job trying to take over."

Davie snorted. "Yeah, but without Haylee, he'd be bankrupt."

"You just like Haylee," Tommy scoffed. "Older women for you, dude."

"She's like, I don't know, twenty-two? Maybe? That's not older. I'm seventeen," Davie protested, his hands flexing.

Laurel craned her neck. "My uncle Blake mentioned your company to me when we were discussing turning a barn into a home. Are you taking new clients?"

Huck didn't outwardly react, but it was an odd question from her at any time, much less during an interview.

Tommy shrugged. "No clue, but I know Jason needs money. Give him a call." He studied her face. "Your eyes are very cool." His buddy nodded.

"Thank you," she said.

Davie smiled. "Are they your real eyes or contacts? Totally sick."

"They're mine," she said. "Tommy? Are you dating Dr. Ortega's niece?"

Okay. This had turned odd now. Huck remained quiet to see where she was headed with this.

Tommy shrugged. "Kind of. We hang out sometimes, but that's all. It's nothing serious."

"I see." Laurel turned back around to face the mayor.

The mayor cleared his throat. "Why don't you put the casserole in the fridge and grab something to eat?" It was phrased as a question but most certainly was not.

The boys cleared out.

Teri shook her head. "I'm sorry about the interruption. Are there any other questions for me? I'm rather tired."

"Yes," Laurel said. "We're almost finished. I just need a little more information. Was there any indication that your sister was frightened of anybody?"

The mayor frowned. "No."

"Yes," his wife said instantly. She held up a hand as if to stop the mayor from speaking. "She was, Saul. She'd been getting hang-up phone calls, and she was certain somebody was following her. In addition, little things at her house were misplaced, as if somebody had been inside her home when she wasn't there. I told her to install a security system, and I know she'd planned to do so after her writer's retreat."

The mayor sighed and shook his head. "Teri. Your sister was a very talented writer, which means she had an extremely active imagination. You know that. She's always had issues."

"Issues?" Huck asked.

Teri shot her husband a glare. "Not issues. As a kid, she had imaginary friends. Once in a while, when we were growing up, she'd think somebody around us was guilty of a crime. Just normal stuff for sensitive artist types. Lately, it was different. She was certain somebody had been in both her office and her home, just moving things around slightly. And she was sure somebody had taken a lace panty and bra set from her drawer."

The mayor shook his head. "She was high-strung, Teri. You know it."

"Anything else?" Huck asked.

Teri scrunched up her face, and no wrinkles appeared on her forehead. Botox? "There were flowers. All over her backyard one day. They were kind of reddish purple."

The mayor snorted. "Flowers? That neighborhood has tons of wildflowers all the time. Seriously."

"In the winter?" his wife retorted. "I don't think so."

Huck leaned forward. "Did she take pictures of the flowers?"

"Yes." Teri drew her phone from her pocket and scrolled through, handing it over. "She said they were black dahlias and that they're difficult to grow in the winter, even in a greenhouse. But that it is possible, and she had no idea where they came from."

Huck looked at the photograph and then handed it to Laurel.

"Yes, those are black dahlias," she affirmed.

He fought the urge to go through more of the pictures on the woman's phone. "When did this happen?"

"About a week before she left to write her poems," Teri said.

Laurel widened the picture with two fingers. "Did she file a police report?"

"No. Saul convinced her it was just a coincidence or some goofy prank by her students," Teri said, her tone accusatory. "So she didn't. I mean, we wouldn't want to draw any attention to the mayor's family, would we?"

Huck watched the interplay, not wanting to interrupt in case things got interesting.

"Mom," Steve interjected. "You're upset." He stood. "I think it's time we ended this interview for now. Obviously, my mother needs rest."

Laurel didn't move. "It's our understanding that your sister was estranged from her husband."

"Oh, for goodness sake," the mayor muttered. "Morris and Sharon were never a good match. They fell in love on a cruise and got married on the spur of the moment. It's shocking the marriage lasted the three years that it did. He's a decent man, a little slow, and would never have hurt her. You're barking up the wrong tree there."

"Tell me about Morris," Laurel said, watching Teri intently.

Steve retook his seat, his gaze turning stormy and his collar appearing too tight. The guy even looked like a lawyer sitting in his parents' house in casual clothing.

Teri shrugged. "Morris is a nice guy. Teaches at the college with Sharon, and they didn't meet on that cruise. They'd worked at the same place for a couple of years, and then a bunch of faculty took a two week cruise to the Bahamas, and apparently they fell in love and did something spontaneous by getting married. They were friends before, and my sister has always followed her emotions. Her taste in men has always been . . . eclectic."

"How long have they been separated?" Huck asked.

"Two months," Steve Bearing said.

His mother focused on her son. "That long? I thought it was only a few weeks."

Steve sighed. "She came to me two months ago to begin divorce proceedings. The papers are drawn, and I was about to have Morris served, but Aunt Sharon popped by the office and asked me to hold off until she returned from her writer's retreat. I figured you knew."

"I knew she wanted a divorce but also thought she might change her mind," Teri whispered.

Steve nodded. "She did. Several times, and I have no clue what she might've decided while at the cabin writing."

"When did you last speak with her?" Laurel asked.

"She dropped by my office on her way out of town two weeks ago," Steve said. "That was the last time I spoke with her."

Aeneas stretched from his post by Huck's feet, and Huck let him wander. He sniffed the mayor's legs, and the mayor leaned over to pat him on the head. Then he moved to Mrs. Bearing, and she shifted her pants away from his fur. Almost seeming to shrug, the dog trotted over to Steve, who was watching Huck.

Steve bent over and scratched the dog's ears. "Cute dog."

"Isn't he, though?" Laurel asked, watching everyone carefully.

Steve stood again. "If you have any other questions for my family, please call me first. I guess I'm representing everyone."

Laurel stood. "Do any of you know a Dr. Charlene Rox? She's a psychiatrist."

All three of them shook their heads in the negative. The mayor frowned. "No. Is that the woman who was killed by Witch Creek?"

It wasn't a surprise the man already knew about Dr. Rox. "Yes." Huck stood. "Mrs. Bearing, is there anything else you'd like to tell us? No matter how small, it might help."

She stood to face him. "No. If I think of anything, I'll call you."

Huck handed her a business card. "Anytime, day or night. Even if it seems inconsequential, it might help."

"All right." She slipped the card into her pocket.

"I'd appreciate it if you both kept my office updated." The mayor turned. "In fact, I insist upon it."

# Chapter Twelve

A search of Sharon Lamber's home revealed that the woman was neat and meticulous with organized drawers and clean sheets. There were two pictures of her during her wedding ceremony on the cruise, and other than that, there was no sign that she was married. No men's clothing in the closet or shoes in the rack by the door. She had a small greenhouse off the main house with some flowers and many spices and plants.

No dahlias.

Laurel returned to Huck's truck and texted Nester. "It looks like Sharon lived here alone and Morris had already moved out. We need to ascertain where he's living."

Aeneas sneezed from his warm crate in the back seat.

Huck looked up at the darkened clouds. "There's a storm moving in, and the community college is closed, so how about we search her office on Monday and also catch Morris at work?" He glanced at his watch. "We haven't eaten all day, and I'm meeting a . . . well . . . friend for dinner."

Friend? He'd said that in an odd way. "All right. Just drop me off at the office, and we can meet up first thing

Monday." She fastened her seatbelt and had Siri find a number for her.

Huck shifted his weight on his seat and started the engine. Heat instantly blew from the vents.

Laurel lifted the phone to her ear just as a chipper voice answered, "Greenfield Architecture and Landscaping, this is Haylee."

"Hi. This is Laurel Snow, and I'm interested in converting an old barn into a home. Your business has been recommended to me." She tapped her fingers on her leg.

"Oh. We don't usually have architecture calls during the winter, but it's smart to get ahead on drawing up plans. Let's see. How about you give me the address, and we can see you as early as tomorrow, if you'd like." Papers rustled. "Go ahead and let me know what time you'd like to meet up. We prefer to see the site before sitting down and discussing plans."

Laurel rattled off the address. The company must be looking for work if they were willing to meet on a Sunday. Good. She'd love to have the place ready by spring, either for herself or to rent. "I am free around noon."

"Sounds good. See you then." Haylee ended the call.

Excellent. Laurel could already see the dimensions of a potential home office in her head.

Huck drove through the rapidly darkening day as the purplish clouds rolled over the mountains and covered them. "That was odd."

Laurel set her phone in her pocket. "How so?"

"You. I figured you'd want to interview five architecture firms, pare them down to three, and then make a decision based on house plans."

She pulled the seatbelt off her neck. "You're not wrong. That's normally how I'd conduct this. However,

I'd like to spend some time with Tommy Bearing, and hiring Greenfield is an easy way to do that."

Huck cut her a look. "For the case. That's smart."

"Yes, for the case." She tugged her jacket more closely around her body. "Also, I'm trying to be a good friend." She peered at him across the cab. "We're friends, and I figure we're friends with Dr. Ortega. Or just friendly." She tapped a bit of snow off her left boot. "Or colleagues who look out for each other. I'm uncertain."

"You've lost me."

Her stomach rumbled; she'd had nothing but coffee all day. "Dr. Ortega expressed concern to me about his niece dating Tommy Bearing, and I thought I could get to know him a little better during this process." In fact, she could probably conduct background checks on all of the Bearing men as part of the case.

"So that's why Ortega wanted to speak to you alone the other day? He wanted your take on his niece's guy?" Huck frowned. "I'm not sure that's cool."

"Probably not, but as neither of us are raising teenagers, I'm choosing not to judge." She watched an older truck slide on the road ahead of them and held her breath until the driver regained control and slowed down. "Dr. Ortega mentioned that Tommy has a juvenile record that might include vandalism and voyeurism."

Huck pursed his lips. "Interesting. Isn't voyeurism one of those precursor crimes you FBI behavior science gurus look to in determining future sex crimes?"

"Yes." Not exactly but close enough. "We should investigate Tommy and see if he has any connection to Dr. Rox or Abigail." To rule the young man out, if nothing else.

"Hmm. The kid looks to be in shape and could make the trek through the woods to Witch Creek, and I suppose with enough rage, he could cause the injuries to the victims that we've seen." Huck drove around the slow-moving truck, his hands sure on the steering wheel. "But where would a kid that age find black dahlia flowers this time of year?"

"That's a crucial question. You have people researching that, correct?"

Huck nodded. "I think that's the key. If somebody has ordered all of those flowers, we should be able to track the financial records." He pulled into their office parking lot and rolled to a stop next to her SUV. "I have officers searching for in-state greenhouses that sell dahlias as well. Maybe we'll get lucky."

Laurel sighed. "When do we ever get lucky?"

"Good point."


This was a mistake. Huck knew it the second he sat down at the table with Rachel across from him while soft music played in the background. He'd tried to choose a neutral place, but Alberto's on the River apparently went for romance on Saturday nights. The lights were dim, the candles lit, and the wine flowing.

Rachel smiled. "Shall we order wine?"

"No." The waiter sidled to the side of their table, and Huck ordered a beer. Rachel ordered wine, and then they both ordered the special, which was chicken piccata.

Rachel's blond hair had grown even longer, and she looked pretty in a bright red dress with a tie at the side. "Reminds me of old times."

He munched on a breadstick. "What do you have for my case? You said you had some information."

She rolled her eyes, her blue gaze sparkling in the candlelight. "You never were much for foreplay."

He nearly choked on the bread. That wasn't true. He could remember spending hours one night just kissing her.

Why did that seem so long ago? Like decades instead of just years. There was no way he was going to rise to that bait, so he finished chewing and swallowed. "Let's keep it professional." Although the ambiance of the place wasn't helping any.

She flattened her hand on the table. A hand that had once held his ring—he'd let her keep it when he'd broken off the engagement. What else was he going to do with the diamond? "Don't you miss us? We had some fun."

They'd had a whirlwind romance and he'd liked her, but his focus had been on his job. Until that last case had broken him. "I'm not sure we really knew each other." Oh, they'd been good in the sack, and they'd had some fun at a couple of her podcast fundraisers, but he hadn't realized what made her tick. That ambition and getting her face on television would trump anything they might've created. "I'm not looking backward, Rachel."

"Neither am I. But forward might be a good way to go." She smiled, and he had to admit she looked lovely.

Yet her beauty no longer moved him. "What do you have for my case?" As the waiter brought their drinks, Huck leaned back and took a sip of the local lager.

"You first." She twirled the rosé in her glass, watching the liquid catch the light.

What could he tell her that wouldn't be too much? "What do you know?"

"Come on, Huck." When he didn't relent, she sighed. "Fine. I know you have two victims, both professional women, with their faces smashed in beyond recognition. In addition, flowers were found around both bodies. What kind of flowers?" She had decent sources, but they'd kept the type of flower out of all reports. So it wasn't anybody on the scene who was feeding her information.

"Hell if I know," he said. "I'm not a flower type of guy."

"I remember." She chuckled. "But you're also not stupid, and you know what kind of flower. Does it matter?"

He'd forgotten how smart she was. "Not really, but again, not my focus." He wouldn't tell her about the black dahlias. However, no doubt she'd either charm somebody at the Genesis Valley police station or file a public information request soon, so he might as well give her something she'd find out anyway. He leaned forward, lowering his voice and noting how her breath caught. "All right. Both victims were stalked for a period of time before being killed. Dr. Rox had apparently fled to the middle of nowhere, and the guy found her anyway."

Rachel's mouth slightly parted and her color heightened. "That's a good angle."

What in the hell had he ever seen in her?

"All right." She took a sip of her wine and murmured with approval. "I have a source who claims that Dr. Sharon Lamber was having an affair, and that's why her marriage broke up." Her eyes crinkled with what looked like delight. "The source thinks it might even be the mayor, her brother-in-law, but could not confirm that fact."

Huck kept his expression neutral. "The guy was sleeping with his wife's sister?" He hadn't gotten that vibe from the mayor, but again, the man was an experienced politician.

Rachel held up one hand. "My source was guessing and had no concrete facts. But I'm sure you're dumping the victims' phones?"

Huck nodded.

"When I heard that, I looked for any connection between the mayor and Dr. Rox."

Huck took a bigger drink of his beer. The last thing he wanted was to owe Rachel, but she'd uncovered a connection that he hadn't. "And?"

"I haven't found one yet, but if you do, you have to let

me know. You owe me now." Her eyes gleamed the way they always had when she was on a good story. "I feel something big here."

Huck was saved from answering when the waiter brought the delicious-smelling piccata. He put his napkin on his lap, and the hair at his nape tingled. Slowly, he looked up to scan the interior of the restaurant, his gaze catching on Laurel Snow and her mother as the hostess escorted them to a table. "Laurel?"

She paused and strode toward him, her gaze moving to Rachel and then back. "Huck."

Why did he feel as if he'd just been caught with his hand in a cookie jar? "Hi."

Rachel was already extending a hand. "Special Agent Snow, I recognize you from that interview you gave during the Snowblood case. It's nice to meet you. I'm Rachel Raprenzi from *The Killing Hour*. It's a new podcast that streams through Everett channels."

Laurel shook hands and then stepped back. For her night out, she'd changed into black slacks and a green sweater that made the green in her one eye nearly glow.

Her mother hovered at her side, even though she was several inches taller than her petite daughter. "Hi, Officer."

"Hi, Ms. Snow," Huck said. Would the woman ever like him? Was it just him or all men? After what she'd been through, he couldn't blame her if it was the entire male species.

Rachel set her napkin on the table. "Besides catching up—you know we used to be engaged—we were just discussing the Witch Creek Killer. I mean, the flowers left around the body. The roses?"

Huck's breath sucked in.

Laurel was too smart to take the bait. "I don't discuss ongoing cases, Ms. Raprenzi." She dismissed them both and grasped her mother's arm. "Enjoy your dinner." They moved quickly away.

Rachel's smile was sharp. "You are so sleeping with her."

"We just work together, Rachel. Don't create something out of nothing." But even as he said the words, he wanted to go apologize to Laurel. He should've stayed home tonight with his dog.

# Chapter Thirteen

At exactly noon on Sunday, Laurel waited inside the silent barn, the chill creeping up from the packed-dirt floor, through her boots, and into her bones. The wind whistled outside at a higher note than usual, and the temperature had dropped again. A vehicle rumbled loudly and came to a stop, and she hustled to open the door. Outside, a Chevy truck built in the nineties, faded red and white, was parked near her SUV.

A man jumped out and leaned back in, pulling out a dirty-blond-haired woman in a blue parka whom he hoisted up on his back. He was grinning as he did so and then caught Laurel's eye and strode through the snowy trail to reach her. Tommy Bearing and Davie Tate leaped out of the back seat, both carrying backpacks and wearing gloves and hats.

"Hi. I'm Jason Abbott, and my backpack is called Haylee Johnson." He reached out a gloved hand and shook. He stood about six feet tall and had thick brown hair, dark blue eyes, and a close-cut beard. "She's from Arizona and hasn't figured out how to dress for the weather here yet."

Haylee snorted, her arms wrapped securely around his

neck. "Maybe I just like my fiancé carrying me around." When he twisted and set her down inside the barn next to Laurel, she stretched to regain her balance. "Hi." She held out a white-fluffy-mitten-covered hand. "I'm Haylee, and I'm in charge of scheduling as well as outside land-scaping." She viewed the surrounding trees. "You could have a nice lawn with flowers in front of the barn. Native ones that will spread naturally."

Jason looked at the kids. "You guys take measurements outside first and then come inside to do the same. Double check and do it twice." He turned and looked inside. "Oh, this place is awesome."

Laurel moved back to allow him inside. "Thank you." She studied the young couple. "My uncle mentioned that you took over Mr. Brewerston's business last year after he died?"

Jason nodded, moving along the wall and looking up to the rafters. "Yeah. I worked with Harvey for only a year before his heart gave out. Prior to that, I commuted from here and worked with Smith and Lertin out of Seattle, but I didn't like the big city." He kept moving, tapping the weathered boards as he moved. "I've only lived in Genesis Valley for three years, but I attended school in Minnesota, and we know snow there. And how to design a structure for this climate." He glanced her way. "I can send you refer-ences if you like."

"I would appreciate that," Laurel said, listening to the kids argue about who got to take the first measurements outside. "It's nice of you all to come out on a Sunday."

Haylee rocked back on her slim boots. "We're happy to be here. It's been tough since Harvey passed on, and we're in a rebuilding phase." She giggled. "Pun intended."

Jason snorted. "You are such a dork."

"You love a dork," she retorted, walking to the middle

of the barn and looking around. "This is such a large space. Just think what you can do with it." Her voice echoed softly in the area.

Jason drew a notebook from his backpack and strode to the middle. "What are you thinking?"

Laurel pictured the ideal layout in her head and spelled it out clearly, watching Jason quickly sketch on paper. He had talent. For drawing, anyway. Hopefully he'd be good at the architecture as well.

He nodded. "Space wise, what's more important? The closet or the office?"

"The office." There was no question on that one. "But I do want the three rooms upstairs to each have big windows with a view of the creek outside. For the bathroom, I'd like a claw foot tub against the window."

Jason altered his sketch, scribbling out a line.

As Laurel described her thoughts for the office, something hit the outside of the barn.

Jason sighed and his voice rose loud enough to be heard outside. "Knock it off, you morons. Get the job done, and we'll have a snowball fight back at the office. Haylee and me against you." He winced. "Sorry about that. They're usually more professional."

Haylee snorted. "No, they're not. We're barely grownups in this business. Now *I* can't wait for the snowball fight."

Laurel kicked a rock out of her way. "It's kind of you to hire them."

"I need them," Jason said, looking toward the back of the barn and sketching out a double door opening to what appeared to be a deck. "We added the snowplowing part of the business last year just to keep us afloat, and they do a good job shoveling out the areas I can't reach with the plow. Plus, they're willing to work on weekends."

Laurel scrutinized boards high above that would probably

need to be replaced. "I've heard that Tommy has exhibited behavioral problems."

Jason's eyebrow rose. "Stupid rumors in a small town. You can't believe them." He flipped the page over and kept sketching. "Being the mayor's kid can't be easy, either."

Haylee slapped his arm. "Don't say that. The mayor and his wife have been great about sending us clients, and they've all but taken in Davie, who's a sweetheart."

Laurel paused. "They've taken in Davie?"

"No," Jason said, continuing to draw. "Davie's mom works for a housekeeping service in Seattle and has been trying to find work here but not having much luck. She's overworked but seems like a kind lady. The kids spend a lot of time with each other. They're in high school, Haylee. That's normal."

Haylee nodded.

Laurel mulled over the situation. "Do either of you know a Dr. Charlene Rox or Dr. Sharon Lamber?"

Haylee stilled. "Those are the two dead women."

Laurel swiveled to face her. "How do you know that?"

"I subscribe to *The Killing Hour*, as part of the streaming news," the young woman said, her eyes wide. "They had a big story on earlier this morning. It sounds like we have a serial killer here again. I remember seeing you on the news after the Snowblood Peak murders. Are you investigating another serial murderer?"

"Two murders don't make a serial," Laurel said. Apparently Huck's ex had run with her story after their dinner the night before. What had he told her? How could he trust her after she'd betrayed him? "Did you know the victims?" How close had Tommy been to either woman?

"I was working in my office but did hear part of the podcast." Jason shook his head. "I never met the mayor's sister, but we remodeled Dr. Rox's office last year after

Harvey died. She hired him but allowed us to complete the job. She's the shrink, right?"

"That's correct," Laurel said. "Did Tommy work on that job?"

Jason sighed. "Both Tommy and Davie assisted with the demolition of the former office, as did I. We work with several contractors, and they often need help, and we've needed money for the business. But you're barking up the wrong tree with Tommy. He's a good kid."

"He really is," Haylee said. "Very helpful and always polite. Whatever you've heard about him, if it's bad, isn't true."

Laurel's mind started drawing connections. "What about Dr. Abigail Caine? Have you done any work for her?" She'd need to speak with her half sister later.

"Never heard of her," Haylee said. "Is she another victim? Are there actually three instead of two?"

"No. I was just curious," Laurel said, brushing snow off her jeans.

The door opened and the snow-covered boys stomped inside. "Got the measurements outside," Tommy said, a notebook in his hand. "We'll do the inside now, if that's okay." His cheek was red as if he'd been hit with a snowball.

Davie wiped snow off his face, and more chunks fell off his jacket. "Then we'll take you two on. No mercy, man."

Tommy snorted and moved toward the far corner. "Definitely no mercy."

Late that afternoon, Laurel pulled to a stop in Abigail's driveway; she'd learned the subdivision's gate code the previous month so hadn't needed to call ahead. The wind had finally abated, leaving the sky a cyan blue and the sun a mellow yellow that sparkled off the mounds of snow. The driveway and walkway had been shoveled, so she easily approached the front door and rang the bell. It echoed hollowly through the angles and open spaces of the expansive home.

The door opened. "Laurel." Abigail stood in a yoga outfit with a zippered jacket. "What are you doing here?" Her reddish-brown hair was piled on her head.

"I had a couple of questions for you." Laurel had wanted to catch her sister by surprise. "I hope I'm not interrupting."

"You could care less about interrupting," Abigail said without heat. "Come in." She opened the door and allowed Laurel inside.

Laurel looked out the wide wall of windows showcasing Snowblood Peak in the background and then removed her jacket and boots. "Did you shovel your walk?"

"No. The homeowners association takes care of it." Abigail hung up Laurel's wool coat. "Why did you ask?"

"Just wondering." She'd contact the association later.

Abigail rolled her eyes and walked across the hard white tiles to the sparkling clean kitchen. "We use Philips Snow Removal, and a very nice man named Brutus does my driveway and walk once a day. He's around sixty and brings me homemade wine, whether I want him to or not. Philips Snow Removal is owned by Brutus and his three brothers, Joe, Jake, and John. Apparently, Brutus was a surprise years later, and his enterprising mama decided to throw caution to the wind and not use a *J* for his name." She reached into a cupboard and brought out a bottle of red wine. "Does that tell you everything you need to know about my walkway?"

Actually, it did. "Have you or your neighbors ever used

either Greenfield Architecture and Landscaping or Harvey Brewerston to plow your roads or shovel your drive?"

"Not in the years that I've lived here," Abigail said, opening the bottle.

So much for that idea. "I don't need wine."

"Nobody *needs* wine." Abigail drew out two large wine glasses and poured generously. "Wine is a desire. This is a Leonetti Cabernet, and it costs more than you make in a week. Please at least enjoy it."

The cabernet was fragrant and enticing. Laurel sighed and drew out a silver stool at the tall granite bar counter that fronted the kitchen. "I'm here on a case, Abigail." Even so, she accepted the glass and sniffed in appreciation. One thing she'd learned about Abigail was that the woman did appreciate good wine. Really good wine. She took a sip and the potent brew detonated on her tongue. Her gaze caught on a high-end silver kettle next to an apothecary jar containing her mother's tea.

Abigail followed her gaze. "I subscribe to the monthly club. The destination city theme this year is a smart marketing idea. Yours?"

"No." Laurel took another drink.

"Oh. Well, have you found the killer who is now stalking me?"

Laurel set down the glass. "No. Tell me how you've been stalked, besides the flowers on your front lawn."

Abigail sighed. "I can't explain it, really. Which as you know, is something of a new experience for me. I can explain almost anything." She took a generous drink of the wine. "The flowers were an obvious sign. But the others, I don't know. It's as if I feel somebody watching me sometimes, and other times, things are off. Like the snow is brushed off my car before I get to it at school, or the bulletin board outside my office is slightly rearranged."

"Any threats?"

"No. Also, no phone calls or hang-ups, which would be common, I think." Abigail looked across her living room to the cold fireplace. "I don't think anybody can break into my house, and I haven't noticed anything here. But my office at work . . . I'm not sure. One day I felt as if things had been rearranged. Or not." She shrugged. "Again, I can't be certain."

Laurel couldn't help but take another drink of the wine. "Think hard. Did you have any relationship with either Dr. Charlene Rox or Dr. Sharon Lamber?"

Abigail stretched her shoulders back. "We're all doctors." She swirled her wine in the glass. "I've never met Charlene Rox, but I have met Sharon Lamber. She co-chairs the Tempest Youth Ranch charity auction every year with the mayor's wife, and I've coordinated donations from Northern Washington Technical Institute. So, I've met her in passing but know Teri Bearing much better."

Laurel frowned. "That doesn't sound like you."

Abigail rolled her eyes. "One of the faculty requirements at Tech is to work on two committees a year, and I've found the charitable committee takes up less of my time than the others. Universities are much more used to money flowing their way than the opposite, so it's an easy gig. I assist with the charity auction and the holiday charity drive every year, and that's it."

Laurel sipped thoughtfully. "Have you met the mayor or his kids?"

Abigail shrugged. "Maybe during the setup for the auction last year. Also, Steven Bearing drew up the contracts for the Deep Green Grower's Company for me and my partners. Well, now I just have one partner because, well, you know."

"Yes. I know." One of Abigail's partners in the lucrative marijuana growing business was now dead; he'd been her half brother, and she'd shot him.

Abigail leaned toward her. "Why do you want to know? Please tell me the mayor is your serial killer. How delicious that would be. Politics and violence—they do go hand in hand."

"Doubtful." But she would need to check the mayor's alibi once she received his sister-in-law's phone records. Was it possible they had been having an affair? Even so, why would he also kill Dr. Rox? "You do need some protection, Abigail. More than the drive-bys by local patrol cars. You should let me put you in a safe house."

Abigail shook her head. "I'm armed, and I can take care of myself. Unless you want to move in with me?"

"No."

"Fine." Abigail finished her wine. "I was wondering, since you've clearly stated you have no interest in Captain Rivers, would you mind if I asked him out?"

"Again?" The woman really was a narcissist. But what else was she?

Abigail smiled, her gaze intense. "Yes. Again. I do like his shoulders."

"Go ahead, but I believe he might be seeing somebody." Laurel kept her voice level with effort. She'd apparently grown attached to Huck and hadn't liked seeing him with his ex the other night. She especially didn't like that they'd been discussing her case and that facts had ended up in the news.

"Oh, my." Abigail's eyes gleamed. "Is that jealousy I see in your perfect eyes?"

They had the same eyes. "I don't think so." Laurel frowned. "I want him to be happy, and he says he wants to be alone, so I guess I should be concerned for him?"

"Maybe he just doesn't want to be with you," Abigail drawled. "That's the logical conclusion, no?"

Apparently so.

# Chapter Fourteen

Huck strode toward Laurel's office, a coffee carrier in his hand and file folders tucked beneath his arm. He paused at the darkened computer room. "Happy Monday morning. I didn't know what you liked, so I got you the special. Honey-oat latte." He handed the cup to Nester as Aeneas padded past him to dive into the conference room.

The kid grinned and took the coffee while some sort of program ran on the monitor behind him. "Thanks, man. I like any latte so long as it isn't peppermint." He shuddered. "Worst ever. Who drinks that?"

Pretty much everybody. "How was the concert?"

Nester took a drink. "Excellent."

"Good." Huck moved on down the hall to the conference room, where Laurel was once again perched on the glass table staring at pictures on the wall. She'd added the mayor, both his kids, and the neighbor kid as suspects. There was another man, this one with bushy red hair and green eyes, also posted. "Morris Lamber?" The picture had been printed out from what looked like the college directory.

"Yes." Her tone was curt.

He handed her the chai latte. "I want to explain about Saturday night." Although he didn't owe her an explanation.

"You don't owe me an explanation." She kept her gaze on the pictures and picked up the latte. "It's not right, is it?"

He looked at the board. "None of this is right."

"We don't have enough." She sighed. Today she wore black slacks and sweater over a white button-down shirt, looking professional and smart. Her earrings were blue butterflies, though.

"Nice earrings." Why did he even notice something like that? He took a gulp of his triple cappuccino.

She didn't smile. "Thank you. My mother gave them to me. They're supposed to create light and protection."

Of course they were. "I met with Rachel because she had information on the case. Her source told her that Sharon Lamber was having an affair—quite possibly with her brother-in-law. Our good ole mayor."

Laurel sipped her drink. "I'm surprised you'd trust Rachel again after she used the tragedy of that drowned child and your breakdown to further her career."

The statement felt like a punch to the balls. "I don't trust her, but I will use her to get information."

Laurel looked up, her unusual eyes veiled. "Then how did she gain the information for her podcast?"

"I had to give her something," he said, his temper stirring. "Is this a thing? I mean, you're jealous of my ex?" Even as he said the words, he knew he was making a colossal mistake, but anger still ticked through him.

Laurel blinked. "Jealous? No. But I think you're showing a lack of judgment to give a hungry reporter anything, and maybe your emotions overruled your mind."

Irritation blew right to anger. "Enough. I don't need your opinion on either my personal or my professional life. Let's stick with the case."

"Very well." Laurel flipped open a file folder next to her to reveal the police reports filed by Charlene Rox. "So Dr. Rox reported several hang-ups from untraceable phones. Threats were written in the snow on her car, and she was sure somebody had broken into her house and taken a pair of panties."

He struggled to focus on the case and not pursue the fight he felt coming. "If both Charlene and Sharon thought lingerie had been taken and somebody had broken into their homes, then he wasn't hiding his activities."

"No. He wanted to scare them. It's part of the thrill for him." She closed the file. "Dr. Ortega called and said the cause of death for Sharon Lamber was blunt force trauma, and there were signs of sexual assault but no semen. Same as Charlene Rox. Also, he lists time of death for Sharon Lamber at approximately two weeks ago, most likely Saturday or Sunday, but he can't be certain. The fact that the body was frozen actually helped him narrow it down."

Huck looked at the faces on the board. Ones he couldn't save. "Sharon first and then Charlene, but we found them in opposite order. Sharon and Charlene, both doctors. Their names sound alike?"

"Yes, but if you factor in Abigail, her name sounds dissimilar." Laurel tapped her fingers on the table in a soft pattern. "Although we should look at the case with her both factored in and out. Just so we don't miss anything."

Was there judgment in that tone, as if he'd missed something? He ignored the possibility and focused again. If anybody could hack their investigation, no matter how impossible it seemed, it'd be Abigail Caine. "Agreed."

"Our warrants for the victims' phone dumps were approved." Nester popped into the conference room, papers in his hand. "The application for a warrant to unseal

Tommy Bearing's juvenile record was denied. Judge said we didn't have enough probable cause."

"We don't, but it was worth a try," Laurel muttered. "When will we receive the cell phone extracts?"

"Techs in DC said the phone dumps will take time. We're behind several other requests." Nester slid out of sight.

Huck pivoted. "How about we go interview Morris Lamber about his dead wife? I have Monty reaching out and getting us an appointment." He studied the board, needing to get out of the small space. "You really think these are possible suspects?"

"Everyone is a possible suspect." She stood and fetched a green wool coat off the nearest chair. "I'd like for you to take the lead with Abigail." A light blush suffused her high cheekbones.

"Why?" Curiosity had him halting.

Her gaze slid to the doorway. "I think Abigail is in danger, and if you ask her to go to a safe house, she might do so in an effort to impress you. Or perhaps manipulate you. Either way, she'd be in a safe house."

"I doubt it, but I'll try. For my job. Showing good judgment." Huck didn't think Abigail would let herself be hidden away, but she was probably in danger, so he'd make the effort. "I'll call her on the way to see Morris."

"No." Laurel frowned. "You should call her when I'm not around. Why don't you go to your office and make the call, and then we can meet outside at your truck in fifteen minutes?" She angled her head to look past him to the computer room. "I need to speak with Nester. We should obtain the guest list from that Tempest Ranch charity auction that keeps coming up."

She paused. "Since you're seeing your ex-fiancée again, do you think she would give us her source? If we have proof, any proof, that the mayor was having an affair with his sister-in-law, we might be able to get a warrant for his home."

He was not going to defend himself about Rachel, and he definitely was not seeing her again. "That's shaky," Huck said. "I doubt we have enough to get a warrant for the mayor's home. Besides, Rachel won't give up a source. Not even for me." Definitely not for him. She'd tossed his ass to the wolves for a story before. They weren't even engaged now. "Sorry."

Laurel looked back at the board. "That's okay. Go call Abigail, and I'll meet you outside."

His phone buzzed and he glanced down to read the message from Monty. "Apparently Morris Lamber is in class for the next two hours. We could swing by the station and talk to the officer who took Dr. Rox's complaints. He wasn't on duty when I dropped by earlier." Then he paused. "Is it weird that Morris is back teaching when his wife hasn't even been buried yet?"

"I think so. We'll have to ask him what he thinks. I'll see you outside in a few moments." Laurel moved past him and walked into the computer room without another word.

Huck watched her go. It was impossible to dig into her head and see what she was really thinking. Being back at work was stressful enough; he didn't need to be arguing with his partner on this case.

But he didn't know how to fix things with Laurel. He'd known that sleeping with her during the Snowblood Peak case would be a mistake.

But it had been a hell of a night.


The interview room of the local police station was only minimally heated, making Laurel glad she'd worn a sweater. Huck hadn't been able to reach Abigail, so he'd left a message, and hopefully she'd return the call soon. For now, Laurel needed answers.

Officer Frank Zello was around thirty years old with a wide chest, handlebar mustache, and intense brown eyes. He sat straight at attention in the interview room, his gaze on whomever asked him a question. His uniform was pressed, his fingernails trimmed, and his hair a dark buzz cut. "I spoke with Dr. Rox on three occasions, and each time, she was visibly upset."

Laurel read the reports, appreciating the very neat signature at the bottom of each signed page. Aeneas flopped on her feet and started snoring. "You were detailed in each form."

"Thank you."

Huck kept his focus squarely on the cop. "After three reports, why didn't you offer her protection?"

"I did," Officer Zello said. "But budget constraints made it impossible, according to the sheriff. So I had uniforms drive by Dr. Rox's condominium as often as possible, and I went by several times day and night when I wasn't on duty. Never saw a thing out of place."

"Did you look inside her condominium?" Laurel asked.

The officer bit his lip.

"Officer?" Huck said.

Officer Zello sighed. "Yeah, I did. The sheriff said she was being hysterical or trying to get attention, and maybe that was true, but I did go through her place with her just in case. I didn't see anything out of the ordinary." He scratched his ear. "She was convincing, at least to me. I couldn't get the sheriff on board to dump her phone and find out who was harassing her." He shifted uneasily in his chair. "I was the one who finally advised her to maybe get out of town. Look how that turned out."

Huck lifted his chin. "Even if you had been able to dump her phone, all of the calls came from an untraceable burner. And getting out of town was her only good option if the sheriff wouldn't put someone on her door."

The officer shook his head. "Even so, she came to us for help and now she's dead."

Laurel drew out the photographs of the black dahlias on the porch as well as one of the victim's car with something etched into the snow on the windshield. "She gave these to you?"

"Yes."

"What does that say in snow on her vehicle?"

The officer shrugged. "'Die, bitch, die,' we thought. It was hard to really tell. Also, she thought somebody wiped snow off her car several times in different locations, and that's something odd that she wouldn't have reported without everything else that happened. Her tires were slashed about three weeks before this, but she went and got them fixed without taking a picture. Apparently she had a couple of patients who were known to be violent, and she also worked outside of Seattle where crime has skyrocketed, so she didn't make a proper report, like she should have."

Laurel leaned forward. "Did Dr. Rox say anything else? Anything that didn't make it into your reports or notes?"

Officer Zello breathed out. "I don't think so. I was thorough and even documented the slashed tires, although she didn't want those added to the report. She didn't say anything else about her clients. She had three ex-husbands and said not one of them would've bothered to stalk her. Wasn't dating anybody and hadn't broken up with anybody in years."

The officer had done an admirable job of trying to figure out who'd been stalking Dr. Rox. He scrubbed both hands down his face. "I can't believe this happened. I mean, I felt she was in danger, but not danger like this. And now the mayor's sister-in-law was also murdered by the same psycho? It's crazy. They were both nice women, and now they're dead. We have to catch this guy."

Laurel slid the photographs back into the file folder. "You knew Sharon Lamber?"

Zello's shoulders went back. "Yeah, we all did. Most of the Genesis Valley officers voluntarily worked the charity auction each year, and she made sure we were fed during the event. Then she brought pizzas and cookies the next week as a thank you for us. She was a really nice lady." Zello adjusted his badge on his chest. "I can't figure this out."

Laurel tapped the file folder so all the papers settled inside. "Do you know Abigail Caine? She's a professor at Northern Washington Tech."

"No," Zello said. "Sorry. Is she another victim?"

"No." Laurel stood. "Is it odd that you were the one who took Dr. Rox's report all three times? I assume you're not the only officer on duty here?"

Zello shook his head. "No. After the first time, she asked for me when she came in. I think she knew I believed her and wanted to help."

That made sense. Laurel held the file folder against her chest. "You did a good job on this case, Officer Zello. In fact, I think you did the best you could without any support from the sheriff."

Zello also stood. "Don't tell him that. Besides, if I'd done a good job, Charlene Rox wouldn't be dead." His shoulders went back. "If I can do anything to help you find her killer, call me. Please. I want to help. She was really scared, man. Terrified."

\* \* \*

He meticulously made a notation in his notebook. She'd walked out of her building and down the icy sidewalk to get a yogurt. Why? Had she been hungry or had she needed to get outside, even though the weather was freezing? He'd watched her when he could for weeks, and this was the first time she'd ordered a yogurt.

Though she'd very often walked out of the place she worked to the little shop on the corner, she normally had a latte, muffin, or oatmeal. Not yogurt.

What a mystery she was turning out to be. Oh, she was an uptight and vicious bitch, but at least she was interesting. The satisfaction he'd felt at killing Sharon had disappeared surprisingly quickly. He'd been so aroused, had tried to share his excitement with her, but he'd failed. It had been her fault.

Then the world had gone black.

The rage had been so complete and so raw. He'd come back into himself to find her face gone and his gloves bloody. The darkness of the blood on his gloves had matched the flowers perfectly. The black dahlia flower—the beauty of betrayal.

Every woman was full of betrayal. It was all they knew.

Yet so was he. He'd learned from the best. He could put on a good face. Could mirror their actions and their movements. Even their damn emotions. They thought they were so fucking brilliant, but he was smarter than the smartest of them all.

His hands clenched in the cold. He'd had to destroy the gloves after taking away her beauty with his fists. So much stronger than she'd expected. But the rage had ruled; he hadn't been able to enjoy the moments. Didn't really remember them. But those gloves had told a story . . . a bloody one. So bloody he'd never be able to clean them, so he'd burned them out in the woods. Then he'd scattered the ashes and let her go for good.

She'd deserved to die.

Then the same thing had happened with Charlene. He'd thought she was stronger than Sharon, because she was definitely of stockier build. Like a purebred mare, but even so, he hadn't been able to complete the act. He'd lost it again, and it had been her fault.

She'd ridiculed him. Fought him and then laughed at him. He could still hear the echo of her laugh. Maybe not during their last moments together, but she'd laughed at him from the first second they'd met. Of course, he'd laughed at her, too. The way she looked down at him and thought him harmless, and the unnatural way she thought of herself as so powerful.

Women were not powerful.

His current project held her head high and strode like another prized mare. Proud and intelligent with unearned confidence. She'd probably slept her way to her position, just like the rest.

They all deserved to die.

Bloody.

# Chapter Fifteen

Genesis Valley Community College had been built when the lumber companies of the area were raking in cash, and they had contributed generously to the construction. Lovely wooden buildings made up most of the campus, with a few more recently built residence halls built of off-white stucco.

Faculty offices were housed near a wooded area in a two-story building that blended into the forest.

Laurel strode across the shoveled walk to the door. As she reached it, her boot caught on a chunk of ice and her feet flew out from under her. Just before she struck the ground, Huck caught her up, swinging her against his chest. She hit his muscled torso and let out a pained gasp.

Startled, she looked up into his dark eyes. "You have incredibly fast reflexes."

"Came in handy when I was a sniper." In addition to the impressive reflexes, his strength was something to admire. He held her easily against him. "You okay?"

"Yes. Thank you for catching me." She wasn't a woman who became flustered easily, but heat rose into her face now.

"No problem." His gaze dropped to her mouth.

She caught her breath. They were fighting, weren't they? Was he going to—

The door opened, slamming into his side. He slipped, attempted to right himself, and then fell backward onto the pile of snow edging the walkway.

Laurel yelped as they landed and sank into the berm, struggling to keep from going too deep. Snow fell onto her legs and slid up the arm of one coat sleeve.

"Dude. Sorry." A lanky kid with a backpack slung over one shoulder reached for her hand and hauled her off Huck and to her feet. "You okay?"

"Yes." More snow fell down inside the neck of her coat, and she winced.

Aeneas bounded around, barking in excitement.

"Stop." Huck stood and yanked off his jacket, shaking it out. Snow covered his backside. The dog instantly sat, panting happily as if they'd been playing. "You good, Laurel?"

"Yes." She shimmied to force snow out of her coat, shivering. "Let's go inside." Smiling at the college student, who was now barely holding back a laugh, she hurried inside the still-open doorway, where heat tantalized her skin. "Are you all right?"

"Yeah, but there's snow down my damn pants," Huck muttered. "I'm glad I didn't wear the tactical holster on my thigh today." He reached to the left of his waist and checked his gun. "All good." Then he glanced at a series of worn couches and chairs near the windows. Students were scattered around, reading or taking notes. His gaze scanned a nearby directory. "Morris is on the first floor, probably that way." He pointed down a long hallway with closed office doors.

A small deli was up ahead, and to the left were what looked like study or conference rooms.

Laurel tucked her gloves in her pocket and double-checked that her weapon was safe in her shoulder holster as she glanced at the directory. "Let's see if he's in."

"Sounds good." Huck stomped more snow off his boots onto the rubber mat.

Laurel led the way down the cement hallway, stopping at office 109, where she knocked on the forest-green metal door.

"Come in," a male voice said.

She opened the door. "Dr. Lamber?"

"That's me." Dr. Lamber looked up from the other side of a metal desk, his hair a wild red mass around his pudgy face. His skin was sallow with dark circles beneath his bloodshot eyes. A bulging bookshelf took up the entire left wall and filing cabinets covered the opposite wall of the narrow space. A window showed the forest behind the professor. "What can I do for you?"

Laurel walked inside toward two red plastic chairs and introduced herself and Huck.

The professor motioned for them to sit. He pushed aside the papers in front of him, making his desk, littered with other papers, coffee cups, and fast-food wrappers, even messier. "I already talked to the Genesis Valley sheriff, but I'm happy to help in any way I can." His eyes watered and his hands shook.

Laurel sat, trying not to wince as more snow slid down her freezing spine. "We're very sorry for your loss, Dr. Lamber."

"Thanks, and please call me Morris. My mother was Dr. Lamber." Morris sat back even farther and his chair protested with a squeak. "Do you have any leads yet?"

"Maybe," Laurel said as Aeneas flopped on her boots again. Why did the animal like to lie on her feet all the time? "Morris, do you have any inkling of who could've wanted your wife dead?"

Morris shook his head. "None whatsoever. Well, except maybe the guy she was cheating on me with. I'd love to know that bastard's name." Though the words were angry, no emotion colored his face. Was he in shock? "Have you figured out who it is?"

Huck settled his bulk on the chair. "How do you know she was having an affair?"

Now Morris did pale. "I read a couple of her texts one night. I knew something was going on, but her phone was always locked, so one night I just grabbed it out of her hand."

"What did you read?" Laurel asked.

Morris gulped. "Just plans to meet some asshole she called 'Big Boy.' That was his name. I mean, that's what she named him in her phone contacts. Can you believe that?" He swallowed rapidly as if trying not to vomit. "The two texts I read mentioned what a great time they'd had the weekend before, when she was supposed to have been at a botany conference. Then she kicked me in the nuts and grabbed her phone back." He reached for a soda in a plastic cup. "That was the end, I guess."

"So you have no idea who this man could be?" Laurel asked.

"No."

Huck wiped off his neck. "What about the mayor? Is there a chance your wife was sleeping with her sister's husband?"

Morris blanched. "No. If that's the rumor, I think it's wrong. Sharon didn't really care for Saul Bearing, to be honest. She thought he was a blowhard."

That might've been a good cover. Laurel needed those phone records sooner rather than later. "Where were you the weekend she was killed?" She gave him the appropriate time frame.

"Visiting my brother in Seattle. When things went south with Sharon and she left town, so did I." Morris wrote a name and phone number on a piece of paper and handed it across the desk. "I gave this to the sheriff already. I'm sure there are traffic cameras showing me coming and going, and we also attended a birthday party for a friend at Clopper's Bar on Fifth. There were security cameras everywhere."

"Even so, we'll need a detailed timeline of your activities for the past month," Laurel said. "Also, can you account for your activities last Tuesday night into Wednesday morning?"

"Is that when the other woman died?" Morris asked.

Laurel nodded. "Yes. Where were you?"

Morris shrugged. "At school and then at home. By myself. While there are security cameras here on campus, there aren't any at my house."

So he didn't have an alibi for Charlene's murder. "Have you met Dr. Charlene Rox? Ever seen her?" Huck asked.

"No. I've never heard of her," Morris said. "Sorry."

Why was he sorry? Laurel cleared her throat. Morris didn't seem to hold the kind of mania needed to inflict the damage she'd seen on the victims, but if he were a psychopath, he'd be able to hide it well. That rage couldn't be kept at bay for long, though, and the killer would have to murder again soon. How many women had to die? She had to find this miscreant. "Where are you living now?"

"I rented a house two blocks over and can walk to work." Morris drew a keychain out of his pocket. "You're welcome to search my home, office, vehicles, or person. I just don't care."

"We'll set that up," Huck said quietly. "Thank you for cooperating."

If Morris had been bluffing, he was going to regret his actions. But Laurel didn't envision him as a killer. "When was the last time you saw your wife?"

He looked down at his hands. "She dropped by the office here on her way out of town. I think she was going to have me served with papers that week, but then we talked, and I don't know. Something clicked. She said she'd think about us while on her writer's retreat, and I believed her. In fact, she said it was over with Big Boy." Morris flushed. "She didn't call him that. Just said that she'd made a mistake and had ended it with the man she'd been seeing. I thought maybe we had a chance." Tears filled his eyes. "Now she's dead."

Huck shifted on the plastic seat. "Did she indicate how Big Boy took the breakup?"

"No. Just that it was over, and she'd ended it. Said she'd screwed up." Morris swiped both hands over his eyes, wiping them. "I was just so grateful that they'd ended things that I didn't ask why. Maybe I thought it was because of me. That she wanted to work on our marriage." He looked up, his lips drawn tight. "She said she'd think about it. It was the first hope I'd felt in months."

Huck took the piece of paper with the alibi. "That was very understanding of you. I mean, to want to stay married after she cheated on you."

Morris's gaze dropped again. "I loved her."

Laurel caught movement as his gaze moved to the left. She ran through the conversation. "Did you also commit adultery?"

Morris sniffed. "How did you know that?"

"You're giving visual cues that you're hiding something, and that's the most logical assumption, considering your lack of anger at your wife's adultery," Laurel said. There was some anger but not what she'd expect.

Morris winced. "I really screwed up. Once. Got drunk at a conference for accountancy professors, which is my field, and went to bed with an old girlfriend. It was stupid. I was really drunk, Sharon and I had had a fight before I'd left for the weekend, and I regretted it. Told her about it the second I got home, and I thought we were going to be okay. Four months later, she was dating Big Boy." A snot bubble popped out of his left nostril.

"Who was the woman?" Huck asked.

"Her name is Jennie Smith and she teaches at Seattle University. She's an old friend but that's all. Not married and didn't want anything beyond that night with me." Another tear leaked from Morris's eye, and his face began to puff up. "One stupid night. That's all it takes to ruin everything."

Huck's expression hadn't altered. "What did you and Sharon argue about before you left for your conference and broke your wedding vows?"

Laurel blinked. Was there judgment in that statement?

Morris sniffed again. "I don't remember. It was about something stupid. Something about her dumb nephew. Kid got into trouble, and his folks finally put some restrictions on him, making him pay restitution or whatever. The kid was supposed to weed our lawn and prepare it for winter to make some cash, and he didn't do the job. Yet she wanted to pay the little shit anyway."

Laurel sat up straighter. "Her nephew? Would this be Tommy Bearing?"

Morris nodded. "Yeah. Both those kids are spoiled brats if you ask me. Even the lawyer."

"Do you know why Tommy was in trouble?" Laurel had to acquire his juvenile record.

"No. The mayor had that hushed up fast. If Sharon knew, she didn't tell me." Morris leaned toward them, his gaze intent. "That kid's rotten, I tell you. Sharon hinted that he'd been in trouble before, but that's all I know." He dropped his head into his hands. "We didn't pay him, and the next day, somebody egged our house and slashed my tires. Kid swore up and down it wasn't him, but seriously. Of course, it was him."

Laurel looked at Huck. That was interesting. He nodded.

"We need to get those juvenile records," Huck murmured.

They still didn't have enough for a warrant. "I have an idea for another source of information," Laurel said. "I'll call Kate later tonight and see if she can help. It's a long shot, but we'll see."

# Chapter Sixteen

Laurel finished the dishes after eating dinner with her mother and then joined her in the knitting room, where she sat and let her hands go to work. Her knitting foundation, which supplied booties and hats for premature newborns, was running smoothly, and she'd turned over the finances to a firm in New York. It took her a moment to realize her mother hadn't spoken much during dinner. "Are you all right?"

"Yes." Deidre started knitting and didn't elaborate.

That was odd. While Laurel rarely caught social cues, her mother was not acting as she normally did. "Mom? Is something wrong?"

Deidre paused. "I don't know."

Laurel slowed the movement of her knitting needles. "What don't you know?"

"It's all so silly. Lately I've just felt like somebody is watching me. Today I ran into town because Taber's was supposed to receive a new shipment of yarn, and I could swear I saw somebody take my picture across the street. There was a flash."

Laurel stopped completely. "Are you sure?"

"No."

"Has anything else happened? Any phone calls or anything like that?"

Deidre sighed. "No. Nothing. It's just a feeling, really. The flash could've been anything, but again, it seemed like somebody was watching me in the store and then again later when I grabbed a sandwich from the new deli down the street. I don't know. It's stupid."

"It's not stupid." Laurel searched for soothing words. Her mother's perennial anxiety was so much better lately, but there was a killer stalking the women of Genesis Valley. Deidre didn't fit the profile, though. "Feelings like that are often intuition based on experience. Let's pay attention, okay?"

"Okay."

Laurel made a mental note to keep an eye on the farm. Her phone dinged and she dropped the knitting needles to read the screen.

Her mom started again to knit a light yellow baby's hat. "Anything interesting?"

"Yes." Laurel scrolled through. "Haylee Johnson sent me a contract and requested a retainer. Seems a reasonable amount."

Deidre's needles clacked together rhythmically. "I love the idea of living in an old barn. What a marvelous concept. Plus, if you stay here, you'll be close to me." Her eyes were gentle in the evening light.

Laurel quickly read the contract, which was fairly standard, then signed it with DocuSign. "I'm looking forward to the process. Uncle Blake said he'd help with construction, and I'd like to do some of the work myself." She would take the retainer check by the architectural office after school the following day and perhaps get a chance to talk to the younger Bearing boy again.

Deidre nodded. "That's lovely. Actually creating a home for yourself. I mean, if you stay. Or even if you just use it when you visit." She kicked out her legs and crossed them at the ankles. Her thick blue socks looked fuzzy and warm. "I bet Kate and her girls would love to help with the demolition. Sometimes it's fun to plow a sledgehammer into a wall."

Laurel resumed knitting. That was true. She looked once again at her calm and gentle mother, whose voice was soft even when she was nervous. Who would Laurel be if she'd been raised by somebody else? Somebody cold and unaccepting. Would she be like Abigail? Were her still-fledgling interpersonal skills as developed as they were because of her mother's love? Most likely. "That reminds me." She hit a preprogramed number.

"I am not coming in tonight," Kate said by way of answer as Jon Bon Jovi blared in the background. "Neither should you. Even your big brain needs a break."

Laurel chuckled. "I am taking a break, but I had a thought, if you wouldn't mind. Would you ask your girls if they've heard any rumors about Tommy Bearing, the mayor's kid? I think he's either a junior or a senior at the high school, and you know how rumors abound in institutional settings. He has a juvenile record I can't get to as of yet, and I figured local gossip might help."

"Livin' on a Prayer" faded away—Kate must've turned down the volume. "Oh, the girls will love it. Like they're investigative agents."

"No." Laurel shook her head. "Nothing like that. Just see if they've heard anything—that's all."

"Sure. They're all at different events right now, ranging from cheerleading to orchestra practice, but after they're home, I'll get them on the case." She sneezed. "Excuse me."

"Bless you," Laurel murmured.

Kate coughed. "If Walter gave me a cold, I'm going to kick his butt."

Hopefully the agent was feeling better, because Laurel needed him on legwork for this case. "Take some vitamin C, and I'll see you tomorrow. Thanks, Kate." Laurel ended the call.

Deidre's needles kept clicking. "We should have Kate and the kids over for dinner sometime next week. I've enjoyed getting to know them."

Laurel started knitting again. "Me, too."

"Since I have your full attention, I want to do a ritual over the new tea leaves that just arrived, and the next full moon is on Friday. Will you be available?"

Laurel swallowed. "I don't think so."

Deidre rolled her eyes. "Come on, Laurel. Just because you don't believe in the moon's power doesn't mean she doesn't have some. I have no doubt my work with the moon has helped substantially with my tea subscription business."

As had careful planning as well as Deidre's mastery of mixing different organic and natural ingredients into delicious teas. Laurel shook her head. "Mom, I don't think I'd be an asset."

Deidre waved her hand in the air. "Whatever. I'll handle it with my employees, then. I just thought you'd be interested."

Hardly. "How's it going with your new counsellor?" Her mom had finally told Laurel the truth about her biological father several weeks ago. He'd been a preacher at the local church and Deidre had been seventeen and unwilling. Hopefully now that she had told Laurel the full story, she'd be able to heal from the trauma.

"Good. I like her, and I feel better than I have in years. If I'm imagining this situation with somebody watching me, she'll help. Now that we've talked about it, I feel like I was just being hypersensitive." Deidre ruffled her short blond hair. "In fact, I might even go on a date. I mean, actually see a man."

Laurel coughed. A date? A real date? "That's fantastic. Who's the prospect?"

A pretty blush spread from ear to ear across Deidre's face. "Well, actually, it's Monty Buckley. We met in the hospital visiting you and Huck after, well, you know."

After the Snowblood killer had almost murdered them both.

"Oh. He seems like a nice man." Laurel frowned but kept knitting.

"I know he's ill, but he's a good person, and if nothing else, we can be friends." Deidre sounded more upbeat than she had in a long time. Then she sobered. "I saw your new case featured on the news. Those poor women."

Yes, the story was now on all of the stations as well as online. Huck's ex was already giving interviews as the journalist in the know, and he seemed fine with that fact. "One of the victims is the mayor's sister-in-law, which draws attention."

Deidre set the hat to the side and reached for a peach-colored ball of yarn to begin a pair of booties. "I think it's the creepy flowers left on the snow that's attracting the press."

"The media does love a ritual aspect to a crime."

A knock on the front door had them both jumping. Laurel set aside her knitting. "I'll get it." As her mother continued with the booties, she strode through the kitchen to the front door and opened it. "Huck."

"Hi." He shoved his hands in his jacket pockets in that way he had. Was it to disarm people? To make himself appear as less of a threat? "There's something wrong with this case." In the porch light, his eyes gleamed and tired lines spread out from the corners. "I need to work it through."

Interesting. "All right." She looked at the long, plowed

driveway behind him. The clouds had dispersed, leaving the moon bright and powerful as it glinted off the trees and snow. "Do you mind walking?" It was freezing outside, but walking would help clear her mind. Plus, she didn't want her mother to be bothered by the facts of the case she didn't already know.

"I'd prefer it." His boots were already covered with plenty of snow.

So they were going to continue as if they hadn't had that argument. Good. Laurel reached for the entry closet door and bundled up in a thick parka, snow boots, gloves, scarf, and a hat knitted by her mom. "Mom? I'm going for a walk with Huck and will be back shortly." Without waiting for an answer or a protest, she hustled outside. The frigid air instantly burned her face and she pulled down the hat and more securely wrapped the scarf over her lower jaw. "Let's go."

He turned just as Aeneas bounded out from the trees, happily churning up frozen pinecones.

They walked down the driveway with winter silence all around them. Laurel looked up at the darkened sky with its distant stars. Even they looked frozen.

"This case is all wrong," Huck said, shortening his steps so she didn't have to jog.

"Tell me what's bothering you," Laurel said as Aeneas raced on ahead, his muscles bunching.

Huck stared off into the trees. "Genesis Valley is a small town in a large county. Yet within two months we have two different crazy serial killers leaving bodies for us to find?"

That was an interesting point. "The Snowblood killer had meant to hide the bodies by throwing them off the edge of a cliff." It had only been a UTV accident and an avalanche that had revealed those bodies.

"Even so, two killers right here in *this* town?" Huck

shook his head. "I don't think so. Statistically, I mean." His voice was a low and oddly comforting rumble in the night, despite the macabre subject matter. "Plus, it's the same team working the case. I know it's our job, and crimes like this are specifically your unit's purview, but still. I don't like the coincidence. My gut doesn't like it."

She'd always admired people whose gut made decisions. Of course, it was instinct, which was truly just experience filtered by the subconscious. But she'd learned to trust Huck's subconscious. "The FBI has put out data that there are about fifty active serial killers in the US right now."

"I thought the number was a couple thousand," Huck said.

Laurel grimaced, shoving her gloved hands into her coat pockets. She needed thicker gloves because her fingers were starting to go numb. "That's a statistic from a crime-tracking organization a few years back when we first started tracing kills by new DNA tracking capabilities. Remember that a serial killer is just defined as somebody who kills more than three people. The violent crimes unit is primarily focused on the ritual type of serial killing."

"Okay. But I've heard you use the higher number before," Huck mused.

Laurel nodded. It felt good to be discussing the case in the fresh outdoors, even though she couldn't feel her nose. "Yes. When it's expedient to get something accomplished for a case, I've used the number and might do so again. For the purposes of this discussion, let's agree that there actually are around fifty active serial killers in this country right now." She could guess where Huck was going with the conversation. "So the fact that we have two in Washington State is only twice what we'd expect, but . . ."

"But the fact that we have two right here in small

Genesis Valley is a real statistical anomaly," Huck said, his gaze focused on Aeneas scouting along the tree line.

Laurel hunched her shoulders against the frigid air. "You think there's another factor at play."

"Yeah. Why here and why now?" He looked down at her, his boots breaking leftover ice on the driveway. "You're here. We received a lot of media attention after the Snowblood Peak cases."

Laurel grimaced. "I don't think it's me, Huck." She hadn't seen any sign that the killer had focused on her. "This murderer kills out of rage, not calculation. This isn't a game he's playing. He's not trying to challenge us." The crime scenes flicked through her mind like a slow-motion movie. "He's out of control, except for the flowers. Those are his ritual, which he has to finish. The flowers are a statement, something between him and the victim. It's personal for him."

"So the appearance of a second serial killer in Genesis Valley is just a coincidence?"

"I don't know." It wasn't as if Washington State hadn't had its share of serial killers through the decades. There was something about the remote, wild, icy surroundings that helped hide bodies. But these bodies weren't hidden, were they? "Another element to the profile," she murmured. "He kills them where they are living. Where they've gone to hide." It could be a coincidence, but perhaps not. "It's another way to show he's smarter and stronger than his victims. They can't get away from him, no matter how far they run." She shivered.

"So you don't think the location, here in Genesis Valley, is the key?"

She slipped and quickly regained her balance. "No. I think the real question is *why now*? Why has he started murdering women and leaving black dahlias around their bodies right now? What tipped him into this murderous rage?" She needed those phone extractions from the victims and would have to push Nester on it in the morning.

Huck hunched his shoulders against the cold. "We need to find him to know that, I think. I'm not convinced the timing and location of these kills isn't related to you."

Laurel pivoted to return to the warm home, mulling over the case and Huck's concerns. "Maybe it's all about you, Huck. Have you thought about that?"

"Yeah." He sighed. "I have thought about that."

# Chapter Seventeen

After another fitful night of frightening dreams dripping with aporia, Laurel placed a latte on Kate's pastry case.

"Just a second," Kate said into her phone, holding the device away from her face. "You have somebody in the conference room. She came in, and Walter immediately took her back. That's all I know." She returned to her phone call.

At least Walter was feeling better. Laurel strode around the glass case and through the center door, walking down the hallway and pausing at the computer room.

Nester looked up, today dressed in a blue button-down shirt with a coffee stain already on his right sleeve. "I know, boss. I'm on the Seattle office for the phone dump, and they're messing me around. Well, not messing me around, but I'm definitely not a priority. I've applied for access to the entire system, and I'm just waiting to get it so we don't have to go through this again." He scratched his chin. "I have the warrant, and they have the connections with the carriers, but maybe I should go around them?"

Laurel pushed a latte across his makeshift desk. "Throw in a threat or two and say we need the results within an hour. They probably have the data." She didn't have time for an interoffice agency problem. "Tell them the press is on us and we're going to say something. Or hint at it." She wasn't good with subtext.

"Cool." Nester reached for his phone.

That was probably not the correct plan. Laurel turned back down the hallway to the conference room. A woman sat at the head of the table. She was stunning, with angled features, blond hair to her shoulders, and a slim figure. She flicked through something on her phone, muttering as she did so.

"Hello?" Laurel walked into the room, already feeling warm from the heat blasting from the vents.

"Hello." The woman looked up, and her eyes were a light brown. "You must be Special Agent in Charge Laurel Snow."

Laurel unbuttoned her heavy wool coat and placed it on a seat. "I must be. How can I help you?"

"I'm Dr. Christine Franklin." The doctor had to be in her mid to late thirties. Perhaps early forties.

Walter hurried from the restrooms to the door. "Hi, Laurel. We have a problem." His face was still pale and his complexion wan, but his voice was clear. Yet his gray suit looked rumpled and a size too small. "This is Dr. Franklin, and she saw the news report this morning."

Laurel unwrapped her scarf and tossed it over her coat. "Do you have information for our case, Dr. Franklin?" She pulled out one of the luxurious white chairs and sat.

"Please, call me Christine. I think I'm being stalked by the killer." The doctor slid her phone toward Laurel. "I found those on my front porch three nights ago and thought it odd. But I was exhausted after a fifteen-hour shift and had to return to work shortly, so I just forgot about it. Once I started thinking about the situation, I realized that quite a few odd things have happened lately." Her voice remained controlled, her presentation logical.

Laurel looked at the phone to find a picture of black dahlias in the shape of a heart on a front stoop. "Who did you think did this?"

Christine shrugged. "I didn't think much about it. Just that maybe a delivery person had left them or a secret admirer or something like that. I truly didn't have time to worry about it, so I didn't. Until I saw the news this morning." She wore a light green suit with a white shell, and her jewelry was gold and understated. "Were these flowers left by the killer?"

"Perhaps." Laurel quickly forwarded the photo to herself. "Do you have a security system at your home?"

"No. I've been meaning to get one but just haven't had the chance. I've lived in the same house for ten years, and it's in a nice neighborhood with many five acre lots. There has never been a problem in Forest Ridge, I don't think." Christine brushed her hair away from her face. "I'm concerned. What should I do?"

Laurel thought through the options. Forest Ridge was the same high-end subdivision where Abigail lived in a far corner of Genesis Valley. Now that *wasn't* a coincidence. She needed Huck's team to hurry through the security videos they'd gotten from other residents. "We should get you to a safe house. You mentioned you had a long shift and that you're a doctor. What is your area of practice?"

"I'm the head of cardiology at the Pacific Western Hospital outside of Seattle," Christine said. "My specialty is interventional cardiology, but it seems I spend more time with paperwork now than I did before I was promoted."

Walter's eyebrows lifted. "Pac-Western is one of the best heart hospitals in the country." He took one of the seats.

Christine nodded. "We are, and I'm busy. Apparently

too busy to realize I'm being stalked." She crossed her legs, showing black high heels. How had the woman walked across the parking lot in those shoes? "I did notice that pictures of friends in my office at the hospital had been rearranged, but I figured the cleaning staff had done so."

Laurel stiffened. "How about inside your home? Anything odd?"

Christine chewed on her muted pink lipstick. "Maybe? I couldn't find my light pink bra the other day, but I assumed the dryer had eaten it or something. I should go through the house and check, shouldn't I." She said it as a statement rather than a question.

"Yes." Laurel's heartbeat ticked up. "All the more reason to put you in a safe house, if you wouldn't mind."

Christine blanched. "I'm willing to stay in a safe house, but I'd still need to go to work."

"Can you take a sabbatical?" Walter asked. "This is serious, and you're in danger."

Christine looked down at her phone, which lay innocuously on the table. "Yes, I suppose I could. I wouldn't mind a reprieve, and I have so much paperwork to catch up on. I could do that remotely. In fact, I might like the break from dealing with . . . people."

Walter grinned. "I understand that." His jowls moved as he talked, and it looked like his hair had thinned. How sick had he been?

"Good." Snow melted off Laurel's boots to the floor. "Do you have any sort of relationship with Dr. Sharon Lamber, Dr. Charlene Rox, or Dr. Abigail Caine?"

Christine blew out air. "Sounds like a lot of female doctors." She rubbed her ear. "I do not know Sharon Lamber or Abigail Caine, but Charlene Rox had privileges at our hospital and I met her a few times."

Laurel straightened. Dr. Rox was a psychiatrist, so it made sense she had privileges. "Did she have an office at the hospital?"

Christine shrugged. "I assume so. I could find out for you, if you like. I believe she only consulted periodically at the hospital and actually had her own practice some-where else. As such, she probably shared an office or a workspace at Pac-Western."

"We're still trying to get a feel for her life before she, ah, left work," Walter said.

"Before she fled this killer." Christine paled and her hand shook when she reached for her phone. "I'll make sure you have access to anywhere Dr. Rox worked at the hospital." She fired off a quick text.

Walter patted her arm. "I can see that you're terrified, but you don't need to be. We'll keep you safe." He looked at Laurel, his hangdog eyes earnest. "Right, boss?" At Laurel's nod, he continued. "How about we go to your place and pack a bag, and then I'll drive you to the FBI office in Seattle? We'll arrange for a safe house for you there, and we'll make sure nobody follows us. All right?"

Christine nodded. "That would be nice. Thank you." She wiped off her lipstick. A nervous tic?

Laurel tilted her head. "Dr. Abigail Caine lives in the same subdivision as you."

"Is she dead as well?" Christine whispered.

"No," Laurel said.

Christine exhaled slowly as if trying to control her breathing. "Oh. I'm not home much and I don't know many of the people who live there. Our lots are large and we don't have block parties or anything like that. Most of my life takes place at work."

Laurel had lived many years just like that. In fact, back in DC, she didn't know most of her neighbors. "I understand." She pushed back her chair and stood as the other two did the same. "Walter will take you home to gather your belongings right now, and by the time you two reach Seattle, we'll have a plan in place." She'd make that call herself.

"Thank you." Christine stood.

Laurel paused by the doorway. "Do you know Tommy Bearing, by any chance?"

Christine frowned. "I know Mayor Bearing. Is Tommy one of his kids?"

"Yes. How do you know the mayor?" Laurel asked, her mind drawing quick connections.

Christine stilled. "I can't answer that."

"Personally or professionally?" Laurel asked smoothly.

"Professionally," Christine said, shifting her weight from one foot to another.

So the mayor was probably a patient of the hospital. Tommy had mentioned that the mayor and Harvey Brewerston had been treated by the same cardiologist. Laurel made a mental note to track down more details. "I understand you can't discuss patients, but has the mayor's son ever been present at your hospital with his father? Maybe attended an appointment with his dad?"

"No, sorry," Christine said. "Not to my knowledge. I've never met Tommy Bearing. I don't think I have, anyway."

But perhaps Tommy had seen Christine at some point. "Who does your gardening, lawn work, or landscape maintenance?"

Christine shrugged. "I believe it's the same company who does the snow removal. That's all handled by the homeowner's association."

Another dead end and not Greenfield Architecture. "Have you participated in the charity auction run by the mayor's wife every year?" Laurel asked.

"No. Again, I live at work," Christine said, drawing her beige wool coat off the back of her chair.

"All right. Let's have Walter get you settled, and then we'll talk again. Thank you." Laurel left her coat in place and strode back to the computer center, where Nester was rapidly typing on his keyboard. Once inside the room, she noticed a couple of scratched snowboards mounted on the right wall. One had a two-inch dent in the side. It must've been a heck of a rock he'd hit.

Nester finished typing. "The phone dumps from Charlene Rox and Sharon Lamber are downloading right now." He sat back and stretched. "Yeah, baby."

"I like the snowboards. What are you planning to hang on the wall behind you?" There wasn't a window in the computer hub.

He glanced at the boards. "I thought my diplomas and certificates should go on that wall. I mean, if we stay in this office, which is pretty cool."

That made sense, and no doubt he had many. She needed to make a decision about her job. "Do you snowboard often?"

He nodded, his eyes lighting up. "Yeah. It's my passion and has been since I was like eight years old." He rubbed his hands together. "I have two older brothers who were star athletes in pretty much every sport they tried, and I sucked. I'm much more interested in computers and gaming, except when I'm on a board on the snow, letting gravity take over. Then I'm just as good as they are, if not better." He jerked his head toward the boards. "Have the scars to prove it."

"Is that why you chose to be in this unit?" She'd taken a look at his personnel file, and with his marks, he could've gone anywhere.

"Home is in Tacoma, and this is close to home but with even better ski hills." He glanced at his screen. "Also, I was interested in you and this new unit. You did an amazing job with the Snowblood killer, and I figured this job would keep me on my toes so I wouldn't get bored. If the FBI makes this permanent, I figure we'll be traveling soon as well, since we're specialized, and I like to travel with somebody else footing the bill."

All good points.

He stiffened and then reached for the keyboard. "Here we go. Let me run a quick . . . yeah . . . algorithm . . . just to see . . ." He typed faster than he spoke, his fingers flying. Then he sat back. "Aha."

"Aha?" She moved toward the weathered door that served as a desk for his computer.

"Yeah." He typed again. "There's a number that comes up a lot in Sharon's phone that just stopped showing up three weeks ago. Let me see who this belongs to . . ."

She cocked her head. "You can trace phone numbers now?"

"Yep. Had the techs hook me up, helped them make it better, and figured it was all good. I do have clearance, right?" He leaned forward. "All right. Sharon Lamber spoke with a Dr. Joseph Keyes at least three times a day for a couple of months, often way into the night. Let's see who this guy is." He typed again and then whistled. "A quick Google search shows Dr. Joseph Keyes as a premier cardiac surgeon."

"At Pacific Western Hospital?" Laurel asked.

Nester nodded.

Laurel turned on her snow boot and ran down the hallway, clomping loudly. She barreled into the reception area, ignored Kate's gasp, and leaped down the stairs into the vestibule. She skidded through loose snow as she shoved open the outside door, sliding across ice and scrambling to catch her balance.

It was a crisply clear day with a brilliant blue sky and weak sun. Clouds hovered over the far mountain as if ordered to stay away for the day. She waved her hands wildly. Walter was just pulling out of his parking spot next to a red BMW SUV driven by Christine Franklin.

They both slammed the brakes, opened their doors, and partially stepped out of their vehicles.

"We were just going to her place," Walter said, his gaze sweeping the area.

"Dr. Franklin?" Laurel partially leaned over to catch her breath. "Do you know a Dr. Joseph Keyes?"

Christine's brow furrowed. "Of course. He's the best cardiac surgeon in the country." She held her door for balance. "Why?"

"Are you positive you don't know a Sharon Lamber? She might've known the doctor."

She frowned. "I never met a Sharon Lamber, and I don't pay a lot of attention to Dr. Keyes's personal life."

"Do you have a good relationship with Dr. Keyes?" Laurel asked.

Christine's fingers tightened on the top of the door as her high heels slipped on the ice. "Yes, I do. In fact, that promotion I mentioned? We were both up for it, and I received it."

Laurel's ears heated. "Did that make him angry?"

Christine shook her head. "No. Not at all. In fact, he was

quite gallant about it. Even sent me congratulatory roses—very pretty red ones. He said he was happy for me."

Sure he was. Laurel turned back inside, her heart rate accelerating.

She needed to find Huck.

# Chapter Eighteen

"If we could've waited an hour for Monty to return my rig from the mandatory service appointment, I could be driving," Huck groused, knowing he was being an ass.

Laurel snorted, maneuvering her SUV cautiously down the icy roads. "You should have somebody take a look at that control freak nature of yours."

Did she say freak? Did Laurel Snow just make a joke? "I already have. Several times, in fact." He'd been treated for PTSD, and still was being treated once in a while, although he'd always liked to have control in most situations. He didn't know any snipers who felt differently. "I had to leave my dog back at the office."

"Your dog was sitting on the lap of Officer Ilemoto and seemed to be just fine," Laurel retorted, flicking on the heat. "He can survive without you for a couple of hours."

Yeah, but could Huck survive without Aeneas? He shifted his weight on the leather seat. The dog grounded him.

Laurel's phone dinged and she pressed a button on the dash. "Hi, Nester. You're on speaker and Captain Rivers is here."

"Hi. I've done a really quick background on Dr. Keyes. He's from Minnesota and has an excellent reputation as a cardiac surgeon, according to the medical journals, although he's moved three times. Started in Philly, then went to LA, and then to his current position. I'll need to make phone calls to each place for more information, but I can tell you from a quick search of public records in Washington State that he's had seven malpractice suits against him as well as one civil suit that was settled with a confidentiality clause."

Interesting. Huck leaned toward the dash. "Seven malpractice cases isn't usual for a surgeon of his caliber. Find out what you can about each situation, would you? Who was on the other side of the civil matter?"

"The plaintiff was a woman named Louise Ferranto, and the complaint reads as sexual harassment. For some reason, the hospital wasn't involved—it was a personal suit between the two. She didn't sue the hospital." He was quiet for a moment. "Oh, I see. She was his housekeeper and said he tried to force himself on her. The criminal case was dismissed for lack of evidence, so she sued civilly."

"When?" Laurel asked, driving onto the interstate toward Seattle.

"Criminal case was dismissed six months ago, and the civil case was settled two months ago," Nester said. "The settlement documents are not part of the public record."

Laurel leaned to the side and then merged with the rapidly moving traffic. "If there were other similar complaints that happened at work, the hospital might've settled them outside of the court system. We don't have enough for a warrant yet, but perhaps Christine Franklin could be of assistance there."

Huck watched a small sports car zip by them going too fast. It didn't belong on the roads this time of year. "She might be, but more likely she's under a nondisclosure agreement."

Laurel nodded. "Agreed, but she's scared. She might

make an exception for us if we keep all information confidential." She eyed Huck. "That means no exchanging information with journalists."

Huck stiffened. So they weren't going to play nice.

Nester cleared his throat loudly. "I need to get back to my searches."

Laurel's lips twitched. "Have you been able to reach Dr. Keyes's assistant, Nester?"

"I had to leave a message with her, and a scheduler called me back to say that the assistant is out for the day. She said that the doctor is scheduled with patients all day, as far as she could tell. I didn't ask her to let the doctor know you were coming."

"Good. I'd rather catch him off guard," Laurel murmured. "Let us know when you have more."

"Sure thing, boss." Nester ended the call.

Huck scratched the scruff on his chin. The vehicle smelled like Laurel—pure with a hint of oranges. "Do we need to discuss Rachel again?"

"No."

"Fine. The timeline Nester put together for the cardiac surgeon could make sense for our murderer. He has to pay up in the civil case two months ago, the rage builds, and then he explodes with Sharon Lamber."

Laurel sped up. "Agreed." She cut Huck a look. "You ready for this?"

He frowned. "For what?"

In answer, she pressed a button on her phone, and the sound of dialing came through the speaker.

"Laurel, how lovely," Dr. Abigail Caine answered in her slight British accent. "You caught me just after class, and I'm in my office wondering if I'm safe being here. Have you found the bastard stalking me?"

"Hello, Abigail. You're on speaker with Captain Rivers

and me." Laurel changed lanes to pass a logging truck piled high with snow-covered logs. "Do you know a Dr. Joseph Keyes?"

Silence came over the line for a moment. "Joseph Keyes? Tall guy, forties, graying at the temples? Likes Scotch and drinks too much of it when he shouldn't?" Abigail asked. "That Joseph Keyes?"

"I have no idea. He's a cardiologist," Laurel said.

"Yes, that's him. I met him last year at the charity auction given by the mayor's wife," Abigail said. "I found him to be rather stodgy and full of himself. You know I would much rather talk about me than anybody else. We only spoke for a few moments before I dismissed him. Why do you ask?"

Huck shifted his weapon harness beneath his jacket. It made sense that Sharon Lamber would invite her lover to the auction. "Did you see the doctor interact with Sharon Lamber or the mayor at any time?"

Abigail sighed. "Just a second. Let me run through the night."

Huck glanced at Laurel, who nodded. Could they both do that? Remember sights and scenes with perfect recollection? He wasn't certain that was a gift. Seemed more like a curse.

"I saw Dr. Keyes interact with many people that night, just peripherally, of course. He was not interesting to me. But now that I'm thinking about it, I did see him flirting with Sharon at the bar several times. She wore a light purple Valentino knock-off with decent Gucci heels and jewelry that was beaded and earthy, and she must've appealed to him for some reason. I believe her husband was also there that night. I think she introduced me to him at some point, and I made a quick exit from them."

"The media reported that she was killed before the victim at Witch's Creek?" Abigail sounded irritated.

"Yes. She was the first killed, but the second to be found," Laurel said.

"Then why is this killer stalking me? I have nothing in common with someone so prosaic. Obviously she and Dr. Keyes were shagging, so maybe he's the murderer?" Abigail snapped.

"We have a long suspect list, and Dr. Keyes is interesting to me," Laurel murmured.

Abigail cleared her throat. "Speaking of interesting, Captain Rivers, I was hoping you'd join me for a drink this coming weekend. I owe you one for being so tardy in returning your message. I've been busy."

Had she just asked him out? Though the woman was beautiful, he'd been a Fish and Wildlife officer long enough to recognize a predator when one smiled at him. "It's kind of you to offer, but I'm busy with this case," he said smoothly. "No time for drinks."

"Well, then. Why don't you find this killer so your date-book opens up?" Her chuckle was throaty and charming, yet it made the hair on the back of his neck stand up. "Talk to you both soon." She clicked off.

Laurel reached for the knob near the dash and turned up the heat as if chilled. "She won't relent."

"I know," Huck said. He didn't have time to worry about Abigail Caine right now. Even so. "Does she know that we, ah, that we—"

"Yes. I didn't tell her, but she's remarkably insightful," Laurel said, her brow furrowing. "I admire that in her and in you. I don't have the ability to read people."

Yet Laurel was probably smarter than any of them. The last place in the entire world he wanted to find himself

was caught between those two incredibly brilliant women.
Maybe it was a good thing Laurel was freezing him out.

Damn it.


Agent Walter Smudgeon hitched his belt up over his
belly, wishing he'd worn a different suit this morning. Or
that he'd had a clean and pressed suit to wear. His head still
ached from his cold, and acid rolled up his esophagus from
the burrito he'd eaten for breakfast. One that had tons of
fats and bad shit in it. The stuff his doctor told him he had
to avoid if he wanted to live another ten years.

Sometimes he wasn't sure he did.

But as he stood near the doorway of Dr. Christine
Franklin's surprisingly comfortable home in the ritzy subdivision, he wondered. The place smelled like her. Like
fancy, but subtle, perfume. The kind from Paris that was
spendy and made with organic ingredients.

She made her way efficiently through the home, turning
off appliances and organizing as she went. Now she was in
her bedroom packing her things. What was her bedroom
like?

The living room held a white sofa with calm teal pillows
that invited a guy to flop down and take a nap. The home
was feminine and kind of sweet, attributes the impressive
doctor hid a little bit. Could somebody like her ever be
interested in a guy like him? If he cleaned up his act, lost
some weight, and stood taller again?

He'd gotten divorced a while back and hadn't recovered.
He was punishing himself still. He missed her.

Enough of that crap. He glanced at his trusted watch.
"We need to get a move on, Doctor." His gun felt heavy in
his shoulder holster. They'd leave the subdivision and
he'd impress her with his counter-surveillance maneuvers.

Sure, the experts in Seattle would do the same thing, but it didn't hurt to cut the tail from her now, if the guy was watching.

Christine emerged from the bedroom dressed in jeans and a copper-colored sweater that matched her eyes. She'd placed a bulging laptop bag on top of a suitcase she rolled toward him, efficient and brisk.

Man, she was pretty. He wanted to ask her age but didn't want to be unprofessional. He was probably only five to eight years older than her. Some smart women liked cops.

Did she?

He straightened his shoulders and reached for the rolling suitcase. "I've got this."

"Thank you." She moved to the kitchen counter for her purse, which she tugged over one shoulder. "I just need my winter coat from the closet, and we can go. I think I've taken care of everything." She looked around, for the first time appearing lost. Scared. Vulnerable.

"You have," he assured her. "If not, you give me a call, and I'll come take care of it for you." There were no pets or plants, so he was safe.

Her smile made him feel ten years younger. "That's kind of you, Agent Smudgeon." She'd remembered his name.

His chest expanded two sizes. "You bet. Do you have any lights on timers we should start?"

"No." She moved gracefully to a lamp near the kitchen. "When I'm out of town, I just keep this on. You can't really tell where it's located from outside, and this subdivision is pretty safe and gated, anyway." Then she moved toward him.

He smiled and the movement felt rare. When was the

last time he'd truly been happy? "I think you're being very brave."

She paused and a light flush covered her cheekbones. "I'm scared, to be honest." Then she glanced at the very full laptop bag. "At least now I can finally get some of that paperwork done. Sometimes I can't remember why I fought so hard for this promotion." Her smile now was rueful and yet still beautiful.

He couldn't think of a thing to say. So he opened the door for her, wondering if there was a way he could be put on the protection detail. If they spent time together, he could figure her out. Perhaps show her a card trick or two. When was the last time he'd even done a card trick?

Sound echoed and he halted and focused a second too late. A body rushed straight into him and gunfire popped several times. Confusion blew through his head, fuzzing his vision. That was gunfire. Somebody had shot a gun.

Pain exploded in his abdomen and he fell back, not understanding what had just happened. A woman screamed from far away and then something hard imploded on his cheekbone as he hit the cold tile in the entryway. A figure jumped over him and he caught sight of somebody wearing black socks and boots. Panic rippled through him and he tried to grab the ankle, but his arm wouldn't work.

The woman screamed again and the smell of copper filled his nostrils. His body seized and his nervous system misfired.

Heat and then freezing cold burst through his gut.

Then he felt nothing.

# Chapter Nineteen

Laurel didn't enjoy driving but was feeling warmly amused by Huck's displeasure at being in the passenger seat. The man did have control issues, but he seemed to have them under control. She barely kept back a laugh at her own joke.

Most people didn't think she was funny, and they were probably correct.

His phone buzzed. He pulled it free of his pocket and glanced at the screen before hitting the speaker button. "Hey, Monty. You're on speaker with Laurel and me. You okay?"

"There are reports of shots fired at the Forest Ridge subdivision and units are headed that way right now," Monty said, his voice high and thready.

"Any idea of which house?" Huck asked, motioning for Laurel to turn the vehicle around.

Without questioning him, she took the next exit, pressing the gas pedal. Shots fired?

"No," Monty said. "Just a couple of 911 calls and nothing else."

Huck set the phone on his leg. "Shots fired in Forest Ridge. Call Walter."

Laurel swiftly hit a button on the dash and the phone dialed loudly.

There was no answer.

"We're about twenty minutes away from Forest Ridge if we break all speeding laws," Huck said, glancing at the sign as Laurel drove back down the other lane of the interstate.

She clutched the wheel and drove faster, her mind spinning. "We need a location for those shots."

Huck nodded.

Raised voices sounded in Monty's background. He coughed. "Uniforms are five minutes away from the scene."

"Send everybody," Huck said. "I'm not waiting to find out. I want our team out there and now."

"You've got it. I'll meet you there," Monty said. "I'll phone when the uniforms call in." He disengaged the call.

Laurel swerved around a minivan, her heart racing. "I sent Walter there with Dr. Franklin. Just the two of them. I should've had the local police provide backup." What had she been thinking? Had Walter fired his gun? If so, why wasn't he calling in? He had to be all right.

At least she knew that Abigail was at the school, so she hadn't been shot. "This is my fault," she muttered.

"You sent an armed FBI agent with a witness in the middle of the day," Huck countered. "This killer has struck at night—only victims who were alone and vulnerable. Shooting at people hasn't been his MO." He looked down at his phone as if willing it to ring. "This could be nothing. We get more calls about morons hunting out of season near homes than you can believe."

She wanted to think the shots were unrelated to her case. Yet Walter wasn't answering his phone. Of course, it wouldn't be the first time he'd let the battery on his phone die. The agent seemed to miss the days when cell phones didn't exist. "Huck? I texted a picture from Christine Franklin's phone to mine, so her phone number would be in my received texts."

Huck grabbed her phone off the dash and scrolled through. "Here it is." He pressed a button and then pressed the phone against his ear.

Laurel held her breath.

Nothing. Seconds ticked by as if in slow motion. Finally, Huck spoke. "Dr. Franklin, this is Captain Huck Rivers from Washington Fish and Wildlife. I need you to call me back as soon as you get this message." He rattled off both his and Laurel's numbers. "Please. This is an emergency." He set the phone back in place.

Laurel shook her head. "Her phone might be off. Just in case she thinks the stalker can track her." A hollow feeling dropped into her stomach.

Ten minutes passed. Huck's phone buzzed and he clicked a button. "Monty?"

"Yeah, Huck. We're en route and the uniforms called in an officer down. FBI agent," Monty said, his tone tense.

Laurel's chest compressed. "Status?"

"Don't know yet," Monty said. "Officers are there performing first aid, and the ambulance should arrive any second. I'm just pulling into the subdivision now and will call you." He clicked off.

Laurel floored the gas pedal, already driving beyond the speed limit.

"You need to get a siren for your car." Huck grabbed the handle above his door.

Laurel concentrated on the road. Her ears rang as she took the exit, zipping through a red light and weaving between vehicles toward the subdivision. The gate was open, so she drove through and caught sight of emergency vehicles down the road to the right, on the opposite side from where Abigail lived. She lurched to a stop behind two police cars and jumped out, rushing toward the melee.

Two paramedics were lifting Walter into the ambulance. Blood covered his shirt, and an oxygen mask had been placed over his nose. His eyes were closed and his body unresponsive. Another woman was shouting orders. The second he was loaded, the paramedics continued compressions with one squeezing in breaths on an Ambu bag. His shirt was open so they could monitor his heart.

Huck grasped Laurel's arm and she halted.

Tears welled in her eyes and she sucked in the frigid air, forcing her brain to take control.

Aeneas barked and ran toward them with Monty right behind the dog.

"Status?" Huck asked.

Monty shook his head. "One FBI agent down and no signs of the shooter. I brought your rig and your dog."

"Good." Huck accepted the keys and whistled for the dog. Aeneas immediately calmed and followed Huck toward his truck, nestled against the curb.

The paramedics shut the ambulance doors and it drove off, siren screaming.

Time felt like it slowed. It was shock and adrenaline flooding her body, so she took them in, keeping her mind alert. They had to find Christine Franklin. Laurel's gaze skimmed the two-story white home with its dark blue door. The porch was wide with a swing. A thick puddle of blood showed inside the open doorway on what looked like white tile.

Her senses of sound and smell came rushing back. The cold pierced her skin.

She yanked her phone to her ear.

"Agent Snow. This is my personal phone," Deputy Director McCromby said.

"We have an officer down. Special Agent Walter Smudgeon," she said, her voice crisp even though the blood was rushing through her ears so loudly she could hear it.

Two beats of silence echoed back. "What do you need?"

"I want the FBI crime technicians from the Seattle office here now. I don't care what they have to drop. Get them here. Now." She rattled off the address and then clicked off, striding toward uniformed officers who were securing the scene with crime tape. A quick glance at them confirmed they were Genesis Valley officers.

She paused at seeing Officer Zello. His handlebar mustache looked frozen. "You found the agent?"

"Yes, ma'am," Zello said, his jaw set in a hard line. His partner handed him a wipe, and he tried to remove the blood from his hands. "Found the agent, searched the residence, and then administered first aid until the paramedics got here. Your agent was out the whole time and didn't give us anything."

Laurel nodded. "Thank you for helping him."

"Of course." Zello paused as another patrol car slid to a stop. "You want our officers to start canvassing?"

"Yes." She watched as Huck and Aeneas jogged up. The dog now wore a search and rescue vest, which told him what his job was today.

A Fish and Wildlife officer hurried out of the house to hand over a blouse. "It was in a dirty-clothes basket in the master bathroom," the woman said.

Huck accepted the blouse and leaned down to press it to the dog's nose. "I'm going to try to track Christine." Then he straightened. "Monty? I want everyone on this, including air support. Let's get choppers in the sky. Now."

Monty reached for his radio, quickly calling in orders.

"We'll have the locals canvass, and I've called for FBI crime techs to handle the scene," Laurel said. She nodded at Officer Zello. "Nobody goes in or out until the scene is processed. Except me."

"Understood," Officer Zello said. "I'll take care of it—we'll start going door-to-door."

Monty stood straight in the cold day, his hair starting to turn more white than gray. He had lost weight during the last month, but his eyes were clear. "I called Kate, and she's going to the hospital. She'll keep us updated."

"Thank you," Laurel said softly.

"Hunt, boy," Huck said, taking the dog off the leash.

Aeneas immediately turned and took off between the emergency vehicles with Huck on his heels.

"If the guy kept her on foot, we'll find her," Monty said, glancing at his phone. "Copters are up in fifteen. We'll spot them."

Laurel nodded. "Can you have the state police track down Mayor Bearing and his son Tommy as well as Dr. Joseph Keyes? I want to know where they all are right this second."

"Sure." Monty reached for his radio. "The mayor and his kid should be easy to find. Keyes must be the heart doctor you were on the way to interview?"

"Affirmative." Laurel walked by him. Officers headed in both directions to knock on doors, while Officer Zello remained at post.

He handed her a pair of rubber gloves. "I don't have booties."

"Thanks." She stood next to him and looked beyond the emergency vehicles. The lots were so large she couldn't see another house. Trees were plentiful, even across the street. Meager and weak, the sun nonetheless lit the entire area even as it failed to cut the cold. "Was the subdivision gate open or closed when you arrived?"

"Closed," Officer Zello said. "We used emergency protocol to open it and left it open after we entered."

She scanned the area across the road, seeing large footsteps in the snow. "Did Captain Rivers go that way?"

"Affirmative."

"If the gate was down, either the shooter had the code or came in on foot."

The officer jerked his head toward Huck's footsteps. "The dog went nuts going that way. My guess is the shooter was on foot. He's the Witch Creek Killer?"

"I don't know." She didn't want to make any assumptions. "Is that what the press is calling him? Even though only one victim was found by Witch Creek?"

"It's catchy."

Apparently. She turned and walked into the spacious home, careful to step over the blood. So much blood. "Could you tell how many times he'd been shot?" It was shocking her voice could remain steady.

"No. Sorry."

She moved into the house. A laptop bag and overturned suitcase were next to the back of the sofa. She swallowed and then went room by room, not finding anything interesting. Loud voices had her pausing and hurrying out of the master bedroom to the door, where the Genesis Valley sheriff was yelling at his officer.

"Sheriff York?" She stretched to step over the visible blood and accepted Officer Zello's hand as she did so. Regaining her balance, she looked up at the sheriff. "Why are you yelling?"

"I want inside," he said, his eyes bulging and his bald head gleaming. "My officer just said that the FBI claimed jurisdiction and ordered him to keep everyone out. *My* officer."

A gleaming white FBI technical van pulled into the driveway. The teens must have been nearby already.

Laurel removed her gloves. "The FBI crime scene techs out of Seattle are here. We're using ours for this one. Nobody goes in until they're finished." She nodded at Officer Zello and then moved toward the techs, giving them instructions. Then she caught sight of Huck and Aeneas striding out of the trees. "Thanks." Tucking her chin beneath her collar to warm up, she hurried down the driveway and met them in the middle of the road. "Any luck?"

Huck wiped snow off his shoulder. "Two tracks for about half an acre and then just one, when he must've started carrying her. Man's foot size—I'd guess size eleven but we'll take the techs take a mold. There was blood on the snow where the two tracks became one, which holds deeper imprints from an added weight."

Laurel sucked in freezing air. "How much blood?"

"Just dots. My guess is he knocked her out and carried her to the road on the other side of the gate, where he must've had a vehicle waiting." Huck patted the dog's head. "He's strong enough to carry her."

That didn't exclude any of the suspects in her mind, although she sensed she was missing something.

Huck tugged his phone from his pocket, his jaw tight and his pupils narrowed. "This guy has balls. I'm going up in the Huey to view the scene. You want to come?"

"Yes." She pulled her keys from her jacket and called Nester. "Hi. Would you conduct a search for any real property owned by Dr. Christine Franklin and get right back to me?"

"Sure," Nester said.

Huck nodded. "Smart. Just in case that's part of his pattern. I'll meet you at the Genesis Valley airport, and I'll have the chopper pick us up there. We'll find her, Laurel."

Laurel nodded. "We have to." She'd promised the woman she'd be safe. The wind picked up, scattering snow across her boots. She looked up to see dark clouds over the far mountains. "We'd better hurry."

# Chapter Twenty

They searched the surrounding area from the helicopter until darkness impaired their vision too much. Laurel climbed wearily into her SUV and waved to Huck before driving away. It was only seven at night, but the conditions had worsened, and they couldn't see the ground any longer. According to the pilot, the winds were making it difficult to maneuver. The search team would meet at first light and commence the search again.

She called Nester, her body still vibrating from flying all afternoon into the evening. "Hi. I'm on the ground. What do you know?"

Nester sighed. "Not much. Walter is in a medically induced coma, and if his vitals improve, they want to perform surgery to remove the bullets. He was shot three times and there are two bullets still in his body. Kate has more of the details. I think she went home to see her kids and then is going back to the hospital."

Snow started to dot her windshield, so Laurel flipped on the wipers. "What else?"

"I haven't been able to locate Tommy Bearing. He skipped school today and his parents have no idea where he is right now." Papers rustled. "I ran down to the school and talked to the principal, who was nice enough to call in some of Tommy's friends. Nobody knew where he was. Or rather, nobody would say. I'm not certain." The sound of typing now came over the line. "Dr. Joseph Keyes canceled his appointments today and also disappeared from the grid. He left his cell phone at his office, and his assistant wouldn't tell me where he'd gone. We need a warrant."

They didn't have enough for a warrant. She'd have to think this through. There had to be something she could use. "What about Tommy's phone?"

"It pinged outside of Genesis Valley on the eastern tower, which is not where his home or school are."

Laurel paused. "What about where he works? Is Greenfield Architecture in that direction?"

Nester typed more. "Yes."

Laurel slowed down and flipped a U-turn. "I'll head out there now. Keep trying to find property somehow linked to Christine Franklin."

"I am. She was married for about ten years and her husband died in combat. I haven't found anything under his name, either. She has one brother who lives in Seattle, and he owns one house in the Soft Ridge area. I've been trying to track him down, but he's some sort of hotshot lawyer who hasn't bothered to call me back. I'll keep trying."

"Thanks." Laurel drew connections in her head between the victims. All three victims were currently single, and all three had once been married. Abigail was the outlier, unless she'd been married before. "I'll call you after I check Greenfield." She ended the call and dialed Abigail.

"Twice in one day, sister? This is nice. Why don't you come by for wine and we can dish about the hunky Captain Rivers together?" Just enough sarcasm tilted Abigail's tone to show she was still irritated about Huck refusing her offer of a drink.

Laurel slowed down to scrutinize street signs and then turned, having memorized the route the night before when she thought she'd be popping by to drop off a retainer check. It seemed like a million years ago already. The storm added sleet to the snow, and it froze on her window. "Have you been married before, Abigail?"

Abigail chuckled. "That's a discussion over wine."

"Yes or no?" Laurel didn't have time for wine.

"Yes. Briefly." The sound of a wine cork popping came through the speakers. "For any more information, you'll have to ask me in person." She ended the call.

Laurel sighed and kept driving until she found Greenfield Architecture outside of city limits near a popular community church. Well, approximately eight miles from the church, but that meant near in this rural area. She pulled up to the office, which appeared to have been built decades ago with roughhewn logs and tall eaves. It had withstood the test of time well, although the sign on the arch appeared weathered. Lights shone from inside.

She jumped out of her car, caught her balance on the ice, and hunched her shoulders against the night air. Her breath puffed in visible steam as she crossed the scattered gravel and salt on the sidewalk to reach the heavy-looking wooden door and push it open.

She stepped inside a reception area with rustic, red-cushioned chairs surrounding a square, hand-crafted wooden table strewn with decorating magazines. The counter was also made of wood—this one birch with a barn style doorway to the left. "Hello?"

Davie Tate emerged from a side room that held file cabinets, a donut in his hand. He wore a Genesis Valley High School T-shirt, worn jeans, and scratched snow boots.

His dark hair was ruffled and scratches showed on his bicep. "Whoa. Hi." He jerked to a stop with jelly on his lip that he licked off. "What are you doing here?"

She stepped up to the counter. "I'm looking for Tommy."

Davie shrugged. "You're looking in the wrong place. Sorry." He took another bite of the donut.

Laurel tilted her head. "He wasn't in school today. Were you?"

Davie stared at her and kept chewing. Finally, he shrugged.

She looked him over, and the seventeen-year-old was a couple of inches over six feet with some pudge still around his face and middle, but his arms showed muscle. "Where is Tommy?"

"He's at home, and I think he *was* at school today," Davie said, his mouth full of donut. He met her gaze evenly and didn't look away. She'd clocked him as being shy the other day at the mayor's house but maybe she'd been wrong. So she removed her badge from her back pocket, opened the leather case, and set it on the counter next to flyers for the business. "Do you know what this is?"

He scoffed. "Looks like a badge."

"Good job. It is a badge. Not only that, but it's an FBI badge, which is a federal agency. Did you know that it's actually against the law to lie to a federal agent? Famous people have been sentenced to prison for it." She needed a background check on Davie Tate. "Now how about you tell me where Tommy has been all day and whether or not you were with him."

Davie squinted and his eyes gleamed. "I won't lie to you, lady. But you know what? I don't have to say a fucking thing."

Surprise filtered through her but she kept her face expressionless. "That could be called hindering an investigation. If you just want to live somewhere other than home, say so, Davie. I can make it happen with a criminal charge or two." She zeroed in on his enlarged pupils. "Are you on something?"

"Just life." He laughed at his own joke. Then he sobered. "Speaking of laws, I think you're trespassing. Get the hell out of here." His voice rose several decibels on the last.

She lowered her chin.

"What the heck is going on?" Jason Abbott hustled out of an office with Haylee Johnson on his heels. "Who is yelling?" The architect wore a blue flannel shirt with jeans, and he had a set of plans in his hands. He took in the scene and then put the plans on a table behind the counter, his gaze wary. "What is going on?"

Davie snorted. "Bitch wants to know where Tommy is."

Haylee gasped.

Jason jerked and then moved toward Davie. "What is wrong with you?" He grasped the young man's arm and turned to Laurel. "Sorry about that." Then he focused on Davie again, ducking his head to see the kid's eyes. "Are you on something?" He glanced at Haylee, who lifted her shoulders, her eyes wide.

Davie chuckled. "It's not illegal in Washington State, man."

Jason straightened. "Maybe not, but it's not allowed in this business." He leaned back and scratched his thick hair, his brow furrowing. "I'm fairly certain it's only legal for twenty-one and above. You're seventeen."

Davie shoved his hands into the pockets of his jeans. "Whatever."

Jason exhaled and then partially turned to face Laurel. "He's a good kid but seems to have screwed up. Please don't arrest him."

Laurel held up a hand. "I have no intention of arresting him right now, but he has to answer my questions."

Jason pulled Davie toward the counter. "He will." When Davie turned to him to apparently object, Jason lowered his chin. "He. Will. Now."

Davie looked at Laurel. "Fine," he snapped.

"Where is Tommy?" she asked.

He shrugged. "I really don't know where he is right now. Probably at home or at some chick's house. They all spread their legs for Tommy Bearing, mayor's kid."

Jason groaned. "Stop being a dick."

"Sorry," Davie muttered.

Haylee looked at them all, her head jerking from one to another. "Maybe, I think, maybe we should have his mom here? If he's being interrogated by the FBI?"

Davie snorted. "She's not at home, Haylee. I'm sure she's working for minimum wage in Seattle and won't be home till the wee hours."

"I'm not interrogating anybody," Laurel said, her patience rapidly dwindling. "I merely want to know where you and Tommy were today, Davie. You both missed school." She was just postulating that Davie had skipped school as well. "Where were you?"

Davie kicked the bottom of the counter. "Fine. We skipped because school is boring and went and got a little high. We stayed there for most of the day because Tommy had brought food and his laptop, so we got high and streamed movies for hours. It was great."

"Where?"

Davie closed his eyes and then finally seemed to relax. "At the greenhouse. His aunt has a greenhouse, and she grew some of the good stuff. We sneak in there every once in a while and take some. She never cared. She was cool."

Haylee moved toward him. "There's a usable greenhouse? Why haven't you said anything?"

Davie shrugged. "Because we get our pot there. It's a secret."

This was news. "I take it you're not talking about the small greenhouse near her home?" At his nod, Laurel took her phone out to text Nester. "Where is this greenhouse? There's no record of Sharon Lamber owning a second greenhouse. The one she used at the college didn't have marijuana." Or black dahlias. What was in this new greenhouse? Was it possible the killer had used Lamber's own flowers?

"It's down a private road off Balsam Street," Davie said. "By that old hunting and guiding place that went out of business?"

Laurel typed the message to Nester to trace the owner of the property, noting that there had to be electricity and water service, so somebody was paying the bills and it wasn't Sharon Lamber, or Nester would've known about it.

Jason sighed. "I have a conference call with a colleague in LA about a design I'm bidding for in Seattle but could take all of you out there in an hour or so."

"I'll go now," Haylee said, reaching for her coat on the back of the chair nearest the counter. "I want to see this greenhouse." She chewed her lip. "I could identify any plants for you, if you like."

Laurel shook her head. "We can't enter the structure, and it'll take me until tomorrow morning to obtain a warrant." She eyed Davie. "When I speak with Tommy, is he going to give me the same story?"

"It's not a story," Davie muttered. "It's the truth."

She studied his facial expression but didn't read much. "How well did you know Sharon Lamber?"

"I didn't. She's Tommy's aunt and she had decent pot. That's it." He looked at his hands.

"Okay. How about Charlene Rox? Did you meet her at the charity auction last year? You and Tommy assisted his mom at that, right?"

Haylee hovered closer to Davie. "I think we should stop this now until Davie's mom can be here." She stood slightly in front of the kid. "He's a minor and you're the FBI. This feels like more of an interrogation than a couple of questions."

"I haven't done anything wrong," Davie said, glaring.

Laurel nodded. "Okay. Just curious. What size are your feet?"

He drew back. "That's a stupid question. It depends on the shoe. Eleven to twelve, I guess."

Interesting.

"That's all," Jason said.

"What about you, Jason?" Laurel asked.

He snorted and looked down at his feet. "Size thirteen, and it's tough to find shoes."

She angled her head; he did have large feet.

He met her gaze evenly. "I'm sorry, but we do need Davie's mom here if you want to ask any more questions."

Fair enough. Laurel withdrew a check from her pocket. "The retainer for my barn. Davie? I'll be calling your mom to set up an official interview. Thank you." She turned and walked out the door, her mind drawing connections again. For now, where was Tommy Bearing?

Sighing, she jumped into her SUV. It was time to relieve Kate at the hospital.

Hopefully Walter had regained enough strength to survive a surgery.

# Chapter Twenty-One

After a sleepless night, Huck strode from his office up to Laurel's, finding the reception area empty. Considering it was five in the morning, he wasn't surprised. He continued through the door to locate Laurel in the conference room, butt on the glass tabletop, staring at the two whiteboards. She'd placed pictures and notes about the victims on one and had taped photographs of suspects on the other. Then she'd drawn lines between them, noting all connections.

He looked at the suspects but didn't get a feel for any of them. "The mayor has a verified alibi for Charlene Rox's murder as well as during the time Christine Franklin was taken yesterday."

She stood and yanked the mayor's picture off the glass. "This is all too perfect. Too textbook. The killer might be taunting us."

"I know." Huck rolled his shoulders. "We have to find this guy before he beats another woman to death. Do you think he's speeding up? If so, how soon will he kill Christine?"

"Yes. I think he has a taste for killing and hungers for more. It makes him feel powerful, and he needs that. He craves that. Christine doesn't have long to live unless we find her. Fast." She tossed the mayor's picture onto the table and stared at the remaining suspects.

That left Steve Bearing, Tommy Bearing, Dr. Joseph Keyes, and now Davie Tate. "None of these are good suspects," Huck mused, looking at the connections. "This is a small town and most people are connected. Anybody who attended one auction would be connected to both Sharon and Abigail. Besides, with ritual killings like these, are connections key?"

"No." Laurel retook her seat, her gaze still on the board. "He could have found them all on the Internet. Professional women in the area who have advanced degrees. The word doctor in front of their names. He might not know any of them personally." Stress vibrated from her.

"We'll find him." Huck drew out a chair and sank into it. "All criminals screw up."

"No." She turned those dual-colored eyes on him. "We only *catch* the criminals who screw up. Just think of the ones we don't even know about."

He didn't want to do that. Instead, he glanced at his watch. "The search team is back in the air, but we're flying blind as to where to even look. Canvassing of Forest Ridge and the outlying neighborhood hasn't led to any results, and I went back over the autopsy results for Charlene Rox and Sharon Lamber last night and didn't see anything new."

Laurel placed her stocking-covered feet on a chair. Today she wore gray slacks, a blue cashmere sweater, and cream-colored socks. Sage green stones made up her earrings and her necklace—they looked like they belonged to her mother. Most likely were a gift.

Laurel's stunning dark red hair was up in a ponytail, and she looked young but tired. "Sharon Lamber had a greenhouse, and I'm waiting for a warrant to search it as

well as one for Charlene Rox's work or storage space at
the hospital. Even though Christine Franklin verbally gave
us permission, I want the warrant. We're waking up judges
as we speak. Also, the techs have a result on the shoeprint
mold from the snow. Size eleven and a half Climber Man's
boot. They identified it quick."

"That's a common size and boot," Huck muttered. He
probably had a pair of those, but his feet were a size fourteen. "Well, it's one more element, I guess. Do you want to
drive to the hospital to interview Dr. Keyes now?"

"No. The mayor agreed to bring his son in for a brief interview this morning before his first class, and Davie's
mom agreed to bring Davie in afterward. Apparently
they're all concerned about school suddenly." Her eyes
gleamed. "Do you have an interrogation room in the Fish
and Wildlife office?"

He winced. "We do, but I prefer to use our conference
room. The interrogation room is a closet with no windows
past a bunch of filing cabinets, and it's kind of creepy. I've
only been in there once to look for bottled water, but I'm
not in the office much. More lately because of Monty
slowing down and because of this case, but I prefer to be
quartered at home. As you know."

She tapped her finger against her lips. "That's perfect.
Make sure it's cleared out, would you? I want Tommy in
there."

"Sure." It wouldn't hurt to shake up the kid. "You want
Davie in there next?"

She looked around at the high-end furniture. "No. I
don't think dismal surroundings will intimidate Davie.
Let's bring him here. I want him more relaxed, and he'll
sneer at the white high-end leather. Yes. In here."

"You're the profiler." He knew she didn't like that description, but it was nice to poke her a little. Then he

looked at the neat notations on the boards. "Do you need the boards? All of that is in your head, right?"

"I don't need the boards." Yet she looked back at them. "But seeing everything in one place can spark an idea. I guess."

The boards were really there for other people, but she was too nice to say so. "Give me a profile," he murmured. They hadn't officially created a task force, but they would soon if they didn't catch this guy. "I'd like to hear it."

"The killer is male, white, and younger than fifty," she said, still watching the boards. "He has issues with successful women with advanced degrees. Could be from an overbearing mother or just because he has underperformed. He's organized and methodical in the stalking but then loses control in a rage during the killings. My best guess is he tries to rape them and can't perform the act, then goes berserk."

"Is berserk an official term?"

She shrugged. "It fits. As does he. He can fit into society, and his neighbors or friends will be surprised he's the killer when we catch him. I'm sure he'll have a story to tell that he actually believes. He's a psychopath who is good at mirroring others but only really feels when he's stalking or killing. Or perhaps just afterward when he relives the kill in his head."

"What about the flowers?"

"The dahlias could have something to do with a woman who betrayed him in the past, or just a generalized belief that all women are betrayers. It's also as if . . ." She trailed off, staring into space.

"As if what?"

She returned. "It's a good-bye. A sad gift in the snow from him to her. It's intimate."

Man, her mind was impressive. "How's Walter?"

"The same. He's not strong enough for surgery yet." Dark circles smudged her eyes.

"Were you at the hospital all night?"

She nodded. "Yes. I shouldn't have let him go alone with Dr. Franklin."

"You didn't do anything wrong. Walter was armed and trained. Plus, the gun was a surprise from this killer." Huck wiped both hands down his face, wishing the ice creamery below opened before six. He needed a triple this morning. "I'll get the interrogation room ready for the mayor and his kid." He stood and paused at the doorway, looking back at her. Feeling protective in a way he didn't much enjoy. "I'll bring you a coffee at six."

"Thanks." She looked back at her boards.

He didn't think the answer was there. Hopefully they'd get closer after the interviews today.

Either way, Christine Franklin's time was limited, if she was still alive.

Laurel placed her chai latte on the scratched wooden table as she took her seat in the Fish and Wildlife interrogation room—a cold metal folding chair with worn-out padding. It matched the others in the chilly room. The walls were concrete block, the floor plain cement, and the heat blowing from the one vent near the floor weak. Huck sat next to her.

A sullen-looking Tommy Bearing was flanked by his mother on one side and his brother working as his lawyer on the other side.

"Where's the mayor?" Huck asked after sucking down several gulps of his latte.

"He's away on business," Teri said, dressed for battle in a cream-colored Chanel suit with diamonds at her ears, neck, wrist, and fingers. Her handbag probably cost more than a hand-crafted wooden boat, and her shoes were Louboutins with shiny red bottoms. Her blond hair was cut bluntly to her neck and her makeup was minimal but effective. "Is that what you wished to discuss?"

Apparently mama bear was out in full force.

Laurel sipped her drink, appreciating its warmth. "Where were you yesterday, Tommy?" While his mom was dressed impeccably and his brother wore a silk suit with red power tie, Tommy wore a torn black T-shirt with a marijuana leaf on the front.

Tommy shrugged.

His brother leaned forward. "My client will give you hypotheticals, all right?"

That was just stupid. "If that will move this interview forward," Laurel said. "Hypothetically, where were you yesterday?" She didn't care that the kid had been smoking cannabis.

Tommy rolled his eyes.

His mother jabbed him in the ribs and he jumped. "Now, Tommy. We have to meet with the principal next."

He winced and rubbed his side. "Fine. Mr. Masterson was giving a test yesterday, and I didn't study, so Davie and I decided to ditch school. We went and hung out in Aunt Sharon's greenhouse, smoked some weed, and watched movies on my laptop all day. It was great. Wish I could do that every day."

"My client *hypothetically* smoked weed yesterday," Steve Bearing said helpfully.

Huck rolled his eyes.

"Understood," Laurel interjected. "How did you know about the greenhouse?"

"Me and Davie helped Aunt Sharon out there sometimes when she needed heavy things lifted, and she didn't give a crap if we hung out. Had enough of a stash that she didn't notice when we took some. She was kind of stupid."

"Don't talk that way about your aunt." His mother shook her head. "I had no idea about the drugs. And it's Davie and I."

Tommy again rolled his eyes.

"Who owns the property?" Huck asked.

"Dunno," Tommy replied.

Laurel did. Nester had traced it the night before, and the property was owned by a large corporation with land holdings all over the Pacific Northwest. She'd already spoken with a representative in Seattle, and they'd been leasing the property to Sharon for five years. She paid yearly and that payment covered all expenses, hence nothing was in her name. Laurel would have Nester investigate the corporation further, but so far, it checked out. She'd bring Huck up to date later. "Did you know your aunt was having an affair?"

Tommy looked away.

Teri Bearing sighed. "I did. She was dating a cardiologist on the side but ended the relationship a few weeks before leaving for the cabin." Her eyes widened. "Do you think he killed her?"

"I wonder why you didn't mention this the other day," Laurel said.

Steve leaned forward. "My mother was in shock the other day. She did not intentionally keep facts from an investigating officer."

Sure she had. Most likely to protect her sister's reputation or her family from a vicious news cycle. "That's good, considering it's illegal to hinder an investigation," Laurel said pointedly.

Steve straightened his glasses. "Watch it, Agent Snow. We're here voluntarily and can leave at any minute."

"What size are your feet, Tommy?" Laurel switched topics.

"Twelve." A slight smile played on his lips. "You know what they say about feet."

His mother elbowed him.

Laurel kept his gaze. "No. What do they say about feet?" How would he take to being challenged?

"They say that—"

"Shut up." Steve elbowed him, looking more like a brother than a lawyer for a second.

Huck set down his cup. "Were you and Davie together all day?"

"Yes."

"You're certain?" Laurel asked.

Tommy tugged down his shirt. "Yes. I answered you. We were together all day. Period."

"Did you fall asleep at all?" Huck asked.

Tommy shrugged. "We were really high. Maybe for a bit. Who fucking cares?"

"Tommy!" his mother hissed.

His face turned red and he hunched over. "Are we done yet?"

"Not quite." Laurel watched the interplay. "Do you have access to a gun?"

"No," Tommy said.

His family didn't contradict him. Laurel paused. "How about Davie? Does he have a weapon?"

Tommy snorted. "Where would Davie get a gun? He's on government lunch at school, man. That's just stupid." He laughed. "The guy doesn't even have a car. I drive him everywhere, and sometimes Haylee or Jason have to pick him up at school to go to work. Sometimes he has to borrow their truck. Seriously."

There were a lot of places to get a gun. "Tell me about your previous arrest, Tommy," Laurel said.

His eyes blazed, coming alive. "I didn't do anything. God. I was dating this girl and we got together one night, and I snuck out her window. Then her fucking dad found me and thought I was peering into her window. She was afraid to tell him the truth. So not fair."

"Yet there was enough evidence that you spent time at the youth ranch," Huck said. "We're missing something."

"Whatever." Tommy crossed his arms.

Laurel looked at his brother. "Would you like to expand on that statement?"

"No," Steve said. "All records have been sealed and will be expunged the second Tommy turns eighteen. I will say that he's telling the truth and that the situation wasn't fair to him. But that's all I can say."

She had to get those records opened. "I saw Davie at work last night but he had no idea where you were, and you weren't at home yet. We checked. Where were you?"

"I *was* home. Snuck in through my window, and my folks didn't know." Tommy smirked. It wasn't a good look on him.

"I'll confirm that right now," his mother said.

Right. Laurel kept her focus on the kid.

Teri Bearing tapped perfectly manicured nails on the table. "You are reaching the wrong conclusion about my son. Yes, he got into a little bit of trouble that was not even his fault, and he did his penance. In addition, he has volunteered once a week at the women's center, as well as a local daycare, and he has enjoyed himself. He's learned to give back to the community and to take care of children." She smoothed his hair and he jerked away from her. "Both he and Davie have learned the importance of being responsible and part of a small town."

Sure they had. Laurel purposely didn't look at Teri, thus making Tommy her obvious focus. "Did you know Charlene Rox? The psychiatrist?"

Tommy shifted on his seat. "No."

"Is it possible you mowed her lawn or plowed her drive-way?" Laurel asked.

"I don't know. Me and Davie don't talk to the clients. Well, usually. Davie can bum food off anybody, so he probably would know. But I don't remember that name at all." Tommy glanced at his phone.

Laurel pulled a file folder from her laptop bag on the floor and handed over a picture. "This is Charlene Rox."

Tommy looked at the picture. "Nope. She's kind of hot, though."

Laurel slid pictures of Christine Franklin and Abigail Caine across the table. "How about them?"

He shook his head. "No. Never seen either one of them."

"Mrs. Bearing?" Huck asked.

Teri Bearing looked at the pictures. "As you know, I've worked with Abigail Caine at my yearly charity auction and have not met Charlene Rox. As for Christine Franklin, she was my husband's doctor when he exhibited heart problems and required surgery by a Dr. Keyes to repair a valve. It was a simple surgery."

Laurel's eyebrow lifted. "Dr. Keyes performed that par-ticular surgery?"

"He's the best, and I know of several people Joseph operated on." Teri ducked her head. "That's how Sharon met him. She accompanied me to the surgery and met him when he came to give us the results. I later learned that he asked her out shortly thereafter."

That was unprofessional and slightly unnerving. "Do you know where they'd rendezvous? Did they have a place that was somewhat secluded?" Laurel asked, her heart speeding up.

Teri flattened a perfectly manicured hand on the table. "Our cabin. Where she was killed."

Lines upon lines and connections upon connections snapped together in Laurel's brain.

Yet none of them pointed to a killer.

# Chapter Twenty-Two

Laurel stood in the vestibule that led to Fish and Wildlife as well as the stairs to her office. "I'll call you when Davie arrives."

"Thanks." Huck kept his door open, looking broad and strong in the early light. "What's your take on Tommy? The kid definitely has an overbearing mother."

Laurel grimaced. "Yes, but he seems to be rebelling more than anything else. The killer we're looking for would seem innocuous. He wouldn't be drawing attention to himself like Tommy is, although we need to learn more about his arrest. I'm hoping Kate's kids will be able to help with that."

Huck's phone buzzed and he looked down at it and sighed.

"What?"

"It's Rachel, and she has the story on Christine Franklin. Wants to know if Franklin was in FBI custody when she was attacked." Huck shook his head. "She's trying to make something out of it."

That was all the case needed. "Nobody was in custody," Laurel said. "Not yet, anyway." She needed an update on Walter's status. "I'll call you in a few minutes."

"Wait. I want to see what else Rachel knows."

Laurel turned away. "That's a bad idea, but I'm not your boss."

"I'll do whatever I have to in order to get Christine Franklin back before she's killed," he snapped, his voice lowering.

She swallowed. "We aren't going to agree about this." Trusting the journalist who'd already betrayed him twice seemed illogical, but maybe he still had feelings for the woman. They had been engaged. Laurel strode up the stairs, so tired that the cancan dancers on the faded wallpaper seemed to be moving. Kate wasn't in as of yet, but Nester typed rapidly away on his keyboard in the computer hub. "Hi."

"Hey." Nester grimaced. "Dr. Joseph Keyes still hasn't been found. His assistant doesn't know where he is, but she doesn't seem worried. Said he often takes off for mental health days." He rubbed his bald head. "There was a hint of sarcasm to her voice, but I don't know why. We might need to interview her in person."

That wasn't a bad idea. "Any luck with the warrants?"

"Not yet. Apparently nobody sees the urgency here." He shook his head. "Also, the search team called in and is moving to another quadrant via air. They're just flying around, if you ask me. I'll keep trying to find property where Christine Franklin could be, but I'm not having any luck. Yet."

"Just do your best." Laurel switched her laptop bag to her other shoulder. "Put out a BOLO for Dr. Joseph Keyes, would you? State and federal. I want to find that man."

"Sure thing."

She moved down to her office and focused on paperwork for about an hour before glancing at the clock. Davie Tate was late. She dialed the high school, gave her credentials, and asked if he was in school.

He was not.

The secretary assured her that Tommy Bearing was in attendance.

Laurel set the phone back in the cradle. "Nester?" she called. "Put a BOLO out on Davie Tate, would you? Make sure it includes the local Genesis Valley police." She was so finished with people avoiding her.

"Yep. Working on something right now but will in a sec," he yelled back.

They should probably get an intercom system. Or she could get off her glutes and just walk to his office—that would be healthier. A quick call to the hospital revealed that Walter was now scheduled for surgery later that afternoon. Good. Laurel went back to her paperwork, conducting background checks on everyone she could think of that Nester hadn't already checked out.

A soft knock on her doorway had her jumping. She looked up to see Kate's daughter Viv with a denim backpack in one hand. "Viv. Is everything all right?"

"Yeah." The girl walked inside and looked at the two guest chairs. "These are nice."

"Your mom secured them for the office. Why aren't you in school?" Laurel hadn't heard Kate come in.

Viv pulled out a chair and sat, yanking a notebook from her backpack. "I have a free period and thought I'd come in to work." Her blue eyes sparkled. At sixteen, she was the eldest of the three girls and paradoxically the shortest. Her blond hair was long and straight, and she had her mother's elfin facial features. "This is what I've found."

Laurel held up a hand. "Wait a sec. Does your mom know you're here?"

"Yeah. Just talked to her. She's at the hospital right now

and should be headed this way soon. Agent Smudgeon is having surgery this afternoon, right?"

Laurel nodded. So long as Kate knew where her daughter was right now, she could relax. "Okay. What do you have for me?"

Viv flipped open her notebook.

Nester appeared in the doorway. "Hey. I need a coffee. Want anything?"

"Sure. I'll have another chai. How about you, Viv?" Laurel said and introduced the two.

The girl stared at Nester. "Um. Same thing? Thanks."

Laurel smiled. "We have an account downstairs. Just put it on that and add a tip. Thanks."

Nester nodded and took off quickly.

Viv spun around to face Laurel. "Oh my God. He is so cute. Who is he?"

Laurel paused. Was Nester cute? He did have symmetrical facial features and an athletic build, even though he'd said he wasn't athletic. She'd been more interested in his brain and abilities than his looks. "His name is Nester, and he's our computer expert. He's an FBI agent and is too old for you." The man had to be around twenty-four, and Viv was only sixteen.

"A girl can dream, Laurel." Viv focused on her notebook. "I questioned everybody I could without seeming like a nosy dork, and here's what I have. Apparently Tommy Bearing and Julie Trapper got together one night in her room." Viv looked up. "They did not have sex but did roll around and kiss a lot."

"Was that unusual?" Laurel asked. Maybe Tommy couldn't quite get there, which would cause rage.

Viv shook her head. "No. Julie is a virgin, and Tommy definitely is not. He's slept with a bunch of girls and I think he wanted to with Julie, but she said no. But they did have fun, I guess."

"What then?"

"Tommy climbed out her window and her dad caught him. There was a fight, and Tommy broke Mr. Trapper's nose and wrist. I guess it was bad." Viv's eyes widened. "Mr. Trapper pressed charges, and Tommy got into trouble. Stories vary, but it seems like he was sent to the Tempest Youth Ranch for a two-week course on survival. He passed the course and got to go home. But he and Julie aren't friends anymore."

Laurel digested the information. "Anything else? Anything creepy?"

"Not that I found."

"I'd heard that Tommy was convicted of voyeurism," Laurel said.

Viv shook her head. "All I heard was that Mr. Trapper wanted Tommy charged with everything from trespass to rape to staring in windows, but then Julie said she'd let Tommy inside, so all Mr. Trapper could get him on was battery. It all seems to have gone away now." Viv closed her notebook. "Oh. Also, the Trappers are related to Sheriff York, so that's probably why Tommy was charged."

"Tommy also broke the man's nose and wrist," Laurel murmured. "What's your impression of Tommy?"

Viv blinked. "My impression?"

"Yes. You've seen him in school and have probably noticed how he interacts with others. What do you think of him?"

Viv paused as if giving the question serious thought. "I guess he's okay. I mean, he acts like he's a rebel and all, but then he uses a gold card to buy snacks at the school store. I have an advanced algebra class with him, and he's pretty smart when he wants to be." She shrugged. "He seems like a normal kid in a small town who doesn't want to be known as the mayor's kid all the time."

Laurel smiled. "That's a pretty good profile, Viv."

The girl straightened her light blue coat. "Thanks." She all but hopped on the chair. "I like this kind of work. What else can I do?"

"Have you met a boy named Davie Tate?"

"Yes." She lit up. "He is so hot. You know? He kind of stays in the background but is so cute you can't help but notice him. It's like he's kind of a rebel because he doesn't care what anybody thinks. I mean, he's in my algebra class also, but he doesn't talk or answer questions like Tommy does. But if Ms. Montetro calls on him, he has the right answer. He just doesn't make a big deal about it."

Laurel had pegged him as being intelligent. "What's his general attitude?" The kid had sworn at her.

Viv twisted her lip as she appeared to think it through. "Just kind of cool because he doesn't care. He's nice to everybody, but there's an edge to him that's kind of intriguing." She slipped her notebook back into her bag.

Yet another example of good girls liking bad boys. "Have you ever seen him angry?" Laurel asked.

"He and Tommy goof off a lot in the cafeteria and stuff, but I've never seen him actually mad. Well, except once when Tommy was giving him a hard time about the school lunch. I guess Davie always eats the cafeteria food, while most of us buy cheeseburgers or tacos from the other vendors next to the cafeteria." She sobered. "I didn't think about that. Wouldn't that be in a profile?"

Laurel shrugged. "Who knows. You've done a good job. When Davie became angry, what happened?"

"He slammed his fist on the table, and Tommy stopped bugging him. That was it." She frowned. "But I think that was also the day Tommy got a flat tire. Maybe? I don't know. I can find out."

"No." Laurel held up a hand. "As an investigator, you have to know when to stop asking questions so somebody else can. Otherwise, the subject might become suspicious and refuse to answer anybody's inquiries." She didn't want Viv in either Tommy or Davie's crosshairs, just in case.

"Oh. That makes sense." The girl nodded wisely. "This was awesome. Please let me keep helping." The girls had worked to put the office and computer room together during their winter break.

"Sure. One more question for you about Tommy. Is he dating anybody?"

"No. He was kind of goofing off with Joley Ortega, but I think he's already moved on to a senior named Kallie." She buttoned her coat.

Good. That would please Dr. Ortega. "Thank you for investigating for me."

"Sure. Is there anything else I can do to help? I'd really like to work here," Viv asked.

Laurel's phone buzzed. "I know the FBI has an internship program every summer." Perhaps she could find an after-school position for the girl if the unit was placed in this office. "I can contact my boss in DC and see if we can create an internship position here that runs through the year as a special circumstance since we don't have a full staff yet. It won't hurt to ask, but I also don't want you to give up after-school activities."

"I could do both." She jumped up. "This is awesome. You're going to make this unit permanent, right? I mean, this is where you live, so I'm going to plan like it's happening. When volleyball starts again, I'll have to work around practice, but that's not until spring. Thanks so much." She barreled out the door.

"I don't have permission yet," Laurel called out. Had she ever had that much energy? She glanced at her phone to see a text from her mom just checking in, so she made a quick call. "Hi, Mom," she said when Deidre answered.

"Hi." Deidre sounded tense.

"What's wrong?" Laurel asked.

"I don't know. I went to the specialty spice shop in town, and I could feel somebody watching me again. Then when I went out to the car, there were footsteps in the newly fallen snow right by my driver's side door." Deidre coughed. "I parked by the curb, so somebody had to have walked there on purpose."

Laurel's breath stalled. "Where exactly was your car?"

"The far right parking space by the big oak tree."

Laurel visualized the area. "Don't a lot of people cut around that tree to avoid the fire hydrant and that odd bench with the broken leg?"

"Yes."

"All right, so somebody could've slipped on the snow and stood next to your car. How big were the prints?"

"I don't know," Deidre said. "They were all jumbled together."

Laurel reached for a pencil. "Okay. There's a chance this is nothing, but we want to make sure. I'm going to see if Fish and Wildlife officers will cover you at your house until I get home. Okay?"

"Now I feel dumb," Deidre said. "It was just footprints in the snow. Even so, your aunt and I are taking a three-day trip to Balley's Spa. Uncle Blake said you can stay with him if you're scared."

Laurel sat back. "I'm a trained FBI agent with a gun, Mom. But thanks."

"Okay. I'll text you when we reach the spa. Love you." She ended the call.

Laurel looked at her phone. Her mother was easily spooked, but even so, what if somebody was trying to scare her? Had another of Laurel's cases put her family in danger? Something to think about if she decided to stay in town.

For now, she returned to her computer and paperwork.

An hour or so later, papers rustled and Nester rushed up to her doorway. "I've got it. It was weak, but I've got it."

She looked up and let her eyes focus on him. "What?"

"When I talked to Christine Franklin's brother, he mentioned that she had gone on a date with his friend a while back, a guy named Joe Mush. No criminal record or problems, but I tracked him down to talk to him. He was at a trade show, confirmed by cameras, during the time of death for Sharon Lamber, and out of the country during time of death for Charlene Rox, so he's not a suspect. But I wondered if he knew anything. Spoke to him about half an hour ago, and he did mention that Christine Franklin had just invested in a property. He's an avid fisherman, so he asked her quite a few questions. I think he was hoping for an invite this coming spring."

Laurel was out of her chair and around her desk in a moment. "Property? Why didn't we find it?"

"It hasn't closed yet. But he gave me the fishing stats for the river it's next to, and I dug deep from there. Called two of the local realtors, and one pointed me in the right direction. I'm sending the coordinates to you right now." Nester slapped the doorframe twice and turned to run back to his computer room.

Calling the realtors? That was brilliant. Laurel grabbed her heaviest coat off the hook, shoved her feet in her boots, and ran into the hallway. "Call Huck."

"Already on it," Nester yelled.

Could they find Christine? Laurel bustled down the

stairs while drawing on the parka and yanking the gloves free of the pockets. She nearly collided with Huck as he opened the outside door.

"The Huey is on the ground refueling and will wait for us. Let's go." He ran to his truck while she did the same, and the five-minute drive to the small airport was made in silence.

Laurel was out of the truck before he'd slid to a complete stop, ducking her head and running full bore for the waiting chopper. The pilot was a gray-haired man wearing a Fish and Wildlife uniform, and he opened the back door for her, handing her a set of headphones. She shoved them on, settled into the leather seat, and waited as Huck jumped into the seat in front of her.

Within seconds, they were lifting into the air.

Her stomach dropped as it always did. Flying was not one of her comforts. Even so, she scooted as close to the window as possible, staring outside at the bright day. The sky was clear again, today a cerulean blue with the sun shining below on the sparkling snow. Beautiful and cold.

The pilot banked right, turning toward the mountains beyond the community church. They passed over a river and several creeks as well as summer cabins and picnic spots, all covered in white. All still and deathly silent in their beauty.

Huck showed the pilot his phone screen, and the pilot corrected, flying where the river emerged from the mountains again.

"We should be coming upon the property any second," Huck said through the headphones.

Laurel pressed her nose against the window.

The trees cleared to a wide meadow along the river.

Something red caught her eye, and she nudged Huck, pointing.

The pilot headed in that direction.

Dark red dots became visible in an oval pattern, much akin to the shape of an egg. The dots were faded and buried beneath layers of snow but still showed through from their vantage point high above. They were black dahlias. Laurel squinted to see better and her stomach lurched. In the middle of the flowers, beneath snow and ice, was the shape of a woman.

# Chapter Twenty-Three

Laurel stood up to her knees in snow, feet away from the body. She'd gotten close enough to brush snow off the face, just to be sure.

Christine Franklin's eyes were open in death, the color opaque through the ice. She'd been beaten around the head and face, and bone showed through her left cheek. Even so, she was identifiable.

Revulsion rolled through Laurel along with a rage comparable to the one no doubt experienced by the killer. Any murder was an abomination, but this one was brutal. "He beat her, but not as badly, and I can't see if her hands are still attached." There was a lack of blood around the body, so she hadn't been killed right here. "He carried her out here and left her with the flowers." She squinted to look from their location to the quiet cabin by the river, but too much snow had fallen and covered any footprints.

Huck snapped several photographs with his phone, keeping his distance, just in case there was any sort of clue beneath the snow or ice. "She's really frozen."

Laurel couldn't stop looking at the naked body. Ice had formed over her, along with snow. "Too frozen?"

"Yes." He crouched and leaned over to study the body.

"I think he put her here and then brought water from the river to pour over her." He knocked gently on the ice against the woman's hip with his glove. Then he gently swept more snow away. "The hands aren't here."

Laurel looked back at the Huey, which had landed on the far side of the meadow. "Let's check out the cabin." The crime techs were more than an hour away, but they were coming along with Dr. Ortega. He wanted to see the scene this time as well.

"I'll lead." Huck eyed the distance from the body to the cabin. "Let's walk parallel to where he probably walked, just in case." Then he moved yards away from the body and started kicking a trail with his overlarge boots, his shoulders wide and broad beneath his jacket.

Laurel followed his tracks, listening for any signs of life in the vicinity. There was none. Only the sound of Huck moving. No animals, no rushing water, no wind.

Just silence and death.

She shivered and kept moving, feeling the chill to her soul. She sensed the weight of the body behind her.

Huck kept moving. "This does lead to an interesting question."

Laurel nodded. "If we had a hard time discovering that Christine was purchasing this property, how did the killer know to bring her here?"

Huck ducked beneath the bough of a century-old pine tree. "Unless she told him? He could've held a gun to her head and insisted they go to a place that had meaning for her?"

"Maybe, but I don't think so," Laurel murmured, her hands freezing even in her gloves. "She'd just seen him shoot an FBI agent, and she'd probably been knocked out by him. No woman would lead somebody like that out to a remote location like this. She would've known he'd kill her."

Huck paused at the front of a white clapboard cabin. "People get desperate. She might've told him anything so he didn't shoot her."

"That's true, but she was a logical woman. Like me." Laurel moved up to his side to look at the narrow porch. A snow-covered eave protected the weathered boards and splattered blood. Red coated the porch, the railing, and the front door of the structure. "She was murdered here." There were two larger blood stains that had already sunk into the wood. "He cut off her hands here."

Huck looked around the porch but didn't proceed farther. "No ax. This is the first time he didn't leave the ax."

"This is the first time there wasn't an ax on site," Laurel murmured. "He must've brought his own this time." She looked for any sign of footprints around the cabin, but the snow was too thick. "We'll need to conduct a grid search down the driveway and road for the murder weapon." She looked over at the driveway, and there were subtle indents in the newly fallen snow from thick treads. "He must drive a truck or SUV to have made it here and back. There's no way a smaller car could've gotten through that snow."

"It's not much, but at least it's something," Huck muttered. "You want to go inside?"

She wished she'd remembered her hat back at the office. "We can take a quick look just to make sure it's clear, but I doubt they even went inside."

"I'm looking." Huck stepped up the stairs and over the blood to twist the knob. "Locked." He turned around and kicked back, his boot hitting square by the knob.

The door flew open.

Huck drew a flashlight from his pocket and shone it

inside. "One room, no furniture. There's a bathroom off to the side, door open, vacant." He shut the now-damaged door and sidestepped the blood, jumping down to the snow. "You were right. They didn't go inside."

Even so, the techs could process the scene. "Perhaps the killer has been here, the same way he broke into the other victims' homes. He does like to infiltrate their spaces." Right now, she didn't know. "I promised her she'd be safe."

"Hey." Huck settled a heavy hand on her shoulder, his gaze dark. "This wasn't your fault and you know it. She should've been safe with an FBI agent, and she should've been safe in the middle of the day, according to this killer's pattern. Let it go, Laurel."

He was correct. Her phone rang and she pulled it from her pocket. "Hi, Nester."

"Hi." He sighed. "I have bad news."

Her heart lurched. "Walter?"

"No. Sorry. Not Walter. He's headed into surgery right now. It's Christine Franklin."

Laurel started walking back toward the body, her gaze slashing to each side in case the murder weapon was close. "What about her?"

"The hospital administrator just sent over all the information I requested, including anything Dr. Franklin had written lately. I was thinking articles for medical journals and such, but apparently she contributed lifestyle articles to the hospital newsletter each month as part of her new promotion. It's distributed online and is even accessible to the public."

Laurel stopped walking. "No. Do not tell me—"

"Yep. She wrote about how important it was to take time off and recharge one's batteries, giving her new cabin by the river as an example. Anybody stalking her probably knows about the newsletter, since she's been writing pieces for it for the last six months. She even included a picture of the place she was buying. The cabin is painted white, correct?"

Laurel's head hung. "Correct."

What a completely crappy day. Huck Rivers drew a beer out of the fridge and popped off the top, tipping his head back and finishing the entire bottle in large gulps. The still-wrapped bag of burgers from the Dairy Dumplin' sat on the counter, but he couldn't drum up hunger. He tossed the empty bottle in the trash and fetched another, turning to pad in his hole-riddled socks to the sofa. The fire already burned hot across from him, and he planted his feet on the old coffee table and stretched out.

He and Laurel had waited for the techs while freezing their asses off. Then they'd waited until the scene was clear to actually go through the cabin inch by inch and survey the property down to the river.

Christine Franklin's hands, the talented hands of a cardiologist, had not been found as of yet.

It was a "fuck you" to them all.

Huck half emptied the beer bottle, eyeing Aeneas, who was sleeping soundly on a cushion to the side of the fireplace. At least somebody was content. He had to find this damn killer before another woman was brutally murdered. The killer was speeding up his timeline, and he probably had another woman already in his sights.

Huck's phone buzzed and he fumbled for it on the table behind the sofa. "Rivers."

"Hey. It's Monty."

"Hi." Huck placed the bottle on his thigh. "You okay?"

Monty sighed. "Not really. You're gonna want to get on the Internet and watch the newest podcast from *The Killing Hour*. It's streaming now and the transcript will be in print in the morning. I'll talk to you then." He clicked off.

Huck scrolled through and brought up the website, where there was a new video featuring Rachel. He clicked on it, his gut already churning.

"We end this segment of *The Killing Hour* with an update on the Witch Creek murder case. It appears that Dr. Christine Franklin has been found dead in the middle of a meadow with red flowers all around her, just like the other victims. What makes this murder different is that, apparently, Dr. Franklin was in FBI custody at the time of her kidnapping."

Ah, shit. Huck dropped his feet to the floor. He'd returned her call earlier but hadn't given her any information when she hadn't given him any. Apparently they were now done using each other for facts.

Rachel's eyes glittered. "In addition, there seems to be coordination again between FBI Special Agent in Charge Laurel Snow and Washington Fish and Wildlife Captain Huck Rivers, just like in the Snowblood murder cases. Is it just me, or is there something going on here? I know I'm an opinion host, but I try to get my facts straight for you all. If there's something untoward going on, could that be why poor Dr. Franklin was taken right from under the FBI's noses?"

Huck's head reeled. Why in the world would she even say such a thing? Were ratings that important to her?

Rachel sighed and her face moved into sympathetic lines. "Now, I have to be fully transparent here. I was once engaged to Captain Rivers. We broke up after a particularly difficult case that involved a young boy. I won't go into more detail than that."

Right. She wanted people to dig up the old footage for her. Huck wanted to break something; instead, he set his beer bottle on the table now vacated by his feet.

She sighed. "Captain Rivers went through a difficult time that included counseling for serious PTSD, and then he moved to the middle of nowhere to protect people from bears. But I can tell you that he's the best. When I spoke with him earlier today, he was unusually tight-lipped about the FBI involvement in this case. In fact, he sounded downright angry."

She held a hand to her chest. "To be honest, I think Captain Rivers is brilliant and can outsmart any criminal, so I'm glad he's out there defending us like this. But considering how well I know him, and how upset he seems to be about this case and FBI Agent Snow's behavior regarding this brutal killer, I have to ask. What in the world is the FBI doing, and how many more women need to be brutally murdered?"

The segment ended.

Huck held still for a moment, concentrating on his breathing. This was the last thing Laurel needed right now with Walter in surgery and Christine Franklin's body being autopsied tonight. The woman was feeling guilty enough, and she'd be pissed at him.

His phone rang and he knew who it was before he lifted the device to his ear. "That was a bullshit report," he snapped.

Rachel sighed. "I'm trying to get a new show off the ground, Huck. There was not one thing I said that wasn't true." She was quiet for a couple of moments. "But I'll tell you what. Let me interview you about the Witch Creek Killer, and you can say anything you want about the FBI and Agent Snow. You can defend her and them to your heart's content. Just come on my show."

"No comment." He wasn't going to give her an inch. He knew better.

"Fine. I'll get my news elsewhere." Her voice lost the cajoling tone. "I can't believe you're dating an FBI agent with the emotional range of a potato. I've looked back at the few interviews she gave after the last case—she can't possibly interest you."

He wasn't going there, either. "No comment."

"Whatever. Seriously. She's boring and fake. So much for your liking authenticity in women. There is no way that hair is real. That color doesn't exist," Rachel snapped.

Huck let his chuckle flow through the line. That segment of hers had probably ended any chance he and Laurel had for a romance, if either one of them had wanted one. One night together hadn't done anything but make the situation more confusing. But now Rachel had possibly made it more difficult for him to catch a murderer who bludgeoned women to death.

He cleared his throat. "Don't call me again, Rachel. Stop using me and our unfortunate relationship for your show, because you look like an ass who was dropped by a man, and you don't want that, do you?" Yeah, he knew her as well as she did him. Thank goodness he'd gotten out in time. "We're done, and I have no comment on this or any other case." He let silence hang between them for the last time. "And not for nothin', but the hair color is both unique and genuine. There is nothing unauthentic about Laurel Snow."

He ended the call and threw the phone across the room.

# Chapter Twenty-Four

After midnight, Laurel was shivering violently from both cold and fury as she tried to keep her vehicle on the road after leaving the hospital. She'd shoved her coat in the back seat and the SUV wasn't warm yet. Her phone rang and she pressed the button. "Snow."

"Hi. It's Kate. I couldn't sleep and wanted to check on Walter." Kate had stayed at the hospital until almost ten and then had gone home to check on the girls. Walter had still been in his second surgery of the day, and Laurel had insisted Kate get some rest.

Laurel slowed down at the sight of deer eating at the side of the road. They had a tendency to jump in front of headlights. "Walter is out of surgery and is in the ICU right now. I spoke with his surgeon after the surgery. Apparently, Walter suffered a heart attack and flatlined, but they brought him back." Her throat clogged and she cleared it. "It was a rough go, but the doctor is optimistic." Even her bones felt tired, which was impossible. Only her anger was keeping her alert.

Kate sighed, her voice weary. "Well, I guess that's something. I very rarely miss my jackass of an ex, but nights like this, I wish I wasn't alone. You know what I mean?"

"Sure." Not really. Laurel had never been in a relationship where she leaned on a man. Not in a way to make herself vulnerable. She just didn't know how. Sure, she'd dated, and she had gotten serious with her mouth-breathing ex-boyfriend, but even with Lucas, she hadn't completely trusted. "I doubt my relationships with men are productive." Huck was a case in point.

Kate chuckled. "If you're looking for productive with relationships, then probably not. It's just nice to lean on somebody sometimes."

"Yes, I suppose so." She sped up once the deer were in the rearview mirror. Hers was the only car on the road. "We have each other, correct?"

"Correct. Um, did you see *The Killing Hour*?"

Even the name of the podcast infuriated Laurel. "Yes. I watched it on my phone in the hospital waiting room." How could Huck speak to that viper again?

Kate groaned. "It was terrible, but if you read between the lines, I think Huck probably didn't say anything like she inferred."

"The point is that Huck spoke with her. With a reporter about an ongoing case." Laurel's throat ached from needing to yell. "We don't agree on how to handle this series of murders, and I'm furious he might have hindered our investigation. Women are dying."

"True. On that note, I'm going to bed. Get some sleep, friend. 'Night."

"Good night." Laurel pressed the end button on the dash. Friend? It was nice to have a friend. The sky had cleared but darkness shrouded the trees up ahead. She shivered and drove the freshly plowed Birch Tree Road, knowing she needed to sleep. This anger inside her was new. Logic usually ruled. Yet she took a turn she knew better than to take right now and barreled up a long and windy driveway to park in front of a log house fronting yet another river. This was a mistake.

She slipped out of the car with as minimal movement as possible and ducked her head against the frigid air. The walkway had been shoveled, so she easily made her way to the door. Before she could knock, it opened. "You asshole."

Huck moved to the side. "Hi."

She walked in, noting the fire rumbling in the fireplace and the television showing an old Ingrid Bergman movie.

"How's Walter?" Huck shut the door and warmth surrounded her.

"It was rough, but he made it through." She turned to face him. "You, on the other hand, are about to get kicked in the head. Why in the world would you talk to Rachel again? What's her hold over you?"

"I don't have any feelings left for Rachel, if that's what you mean. I was just trying to do my job." He looked like a solid force in a tumultuous world. Broad chest, long legs, piercing eyes. More than a day's scruff covered his chiseled jaw, and he was utterly and enticingly male. "I didn't say anything that would lead her to make such a report or say such things about you."

"That's not the damn point, Huck." It was shocking how badly she wanted to punch him in the nose and leave a bump there for all eternity. She wasn't a woman who lost control of her emotions. Ever.

"What's the damn point, then?" He towered over her, his eyes flaring.

"The point is that you shouldn't have talked to her at all. She ran with that one little fact. I told you not to talk to her." The words rolled out of her mouth so quickly she had to stop and take a breath.

One of his dark eyebrows rose. "Told me? You *told* me?"

"Yes," she snapped.

"Well now, I guess not everyone jumps when Special Agent Laurel Snow gives an order," he drawled, his facial expression showing anger. "You're not the lead here, either. Many cops use reporters as sources, but that is not what I did today. Not even close."

"No. You just made it more difficult for me to do my job. Period." Why was she so jumbled when it came to him? Or was it this case? It just wasn't making sense to her, and that was driving her crazy.

"That was not my intention," he said, watching her carefully, intense emotion rolling off him.

She threw up her hands, adrenaline shooting through her body. "Your intention is irrelevant. You meant to speak with her, and it backfired." She had to calm down, so she took a deep breath.

He tucked his thumbs in the pockets of his jeans. "Has your boss called?"

"Yes, but I was at the hospital and haven't returned his call yet. It can wait until tomorrow." She sucked in another breath and forced her hands to unclench. "I can repair this with the FBI, and if anything, the killer may relax if he sees the podcast and thinks we're running in circles."

"We are running in circles."

She looked over at the sleeping dog. "The case will be okay. We'll fix it."

"I was more concerned about you," Huck said.

Simple words. True words. She felt them instead of intellectualizing them, and her temper began to calm, even though energy still ripped through her with a frightening intensity. "Huck," she whispered.

He studied her for one beat. "Yeah." Then his hands were at her waist, lifting her, planting her against the side wall.

His mouth was hot and desperate, his body rock hard against her.

She kissed him back, closing her eyes, allowing herself a rare moment to just feel. No thought. No analyzing. No anything but him. Her legs lifted on their own, her thighs pressing against his flanks. He tangled one hand in her hair, drawing her head to the side, deepening the kiss. Flames lashed through her in electric arcs, endorphins and oxytocin flooding her system to create a wild need she'd never experienced before.

He slid a hand beneath her sweater, his body holding her in place. She gyrated against him, her hands gripping the tops of his trapezoid muscles, her nails digging into his T-shirt. His fingers tangled in her bra and he swore, pulling his mouth away.

She gasped in protest.

He had her shirt up to her neck before he paused, his eyes a darker brown than she'd ever seen. "You sure?"

This was a mistake of epic proportions, but she was tired of thinking. Tired of running in circles and being lost, not only in the case but in her life. Where she should live and work and how she could protect her mother. She knew Huck could take her away from reality, and she wanted that right now. Maybe needed it. "Yes." She didn't need to think about it and ducked her head so he could yank the cashmere off. It flew over his head and then his mouth was on her lips, down her jaw and along her clavicle in wild nips and kisses. She ran one hand up his head to clutch his thick hair, surprised at the silkiness of the mass.

He raised his head again, seeking her mouth, taking her under. Her head clunked against the wall.

"Don't stop," she whispered when he halted. Her legs slid down him to find purchase on the wooden floor.

He yanked off his shirt and reached for the button of his

jeans. In a raging and fumbling set of movements, they unzipped and kicked off clothing, leaving her in her bra and him in socks. His hands kneaded her breasts, and he flicked open the bra's center clasp, yanking off the flimsy material. One strap snapped in two.

He lifted her again. "Tell me you're on the pill."

"I am and just had a checkup." Everything inside her ached for him, and she lifted her legs again and pressed against him right where she wanted him. He was hard and ready. She moaned.

"Me, too. All healthy." He smiled. "Although you're the only person I've been with in a year."

"Ditto." She moved against him, more than trusting he wouldn't drop her. "Stop talking, Huck," she whispered.

He lowered his forehead to hers, his eyes blazing, his mouth so close. "All right." Slowly, taking his time, he penetrated her. The muscles in his biceps clenched while he kept her safe against the wall.

She pushed her head back again, heat consuming her. Huck Rivers consuming her. She tilted her hips, and he shoved all the way inside, taking her over.

Pain and pleasure pinpointed in one moment, halting her breath. Then just pleasure.

Primal, frantic, animalistic pleasure ripped through her as he started to move, one hand digging into her glutei and the other holding her in place by the nape of the neck. Her head thunked again, and he swore, moving that hand up to cup and protect her head. But he didn't stop. His body was one long line of muscle and strength as he hammered inside her, as out of control as she.

Sparks of pleasure burned from her breasts to her core, and she gasped in need, sinking her nails into the smooth skin of his chest. It was too much and not enough, a contradiction with no rational explanation.

She tightened herself around him and he groaned, dropping his mouth to her neck and biting.

The erotic nip sent her over, and she cried out, an orgasm blowing through her stronger than any force of nature. She tightened her entire body, strengthening her hold, whispering his name. Waves upon waves rippled through her, exploding again in her center and spinning her through the universe.

He groaned against her, his body jerking with his own climax.

Panting, she released his chest, wincing at the nail marks she'd left. Her mind fuzzed over. Her body went limp.

He still held her, breathing wildly. Then he leaned back, still inside her. "You okay?" His hair was damp and curled beneath his ears, making him look like a sleepy lion.

"Yes." Her voice was soft and her eyelids heavy. "I, ah, I should . . ."

"You're staying the night." He turned and made his way to the bedroom, his hands on her butt, his chest warm against hers. "The storm is worse outside, and you have to be exhausted."

She settled her face against his neck, holding on and for the first time in her life, trusting a man. "All right."

Laurel stretched awake in the big bed by herself with the cozy flannel bedspread, her mind relaxed and her body sore. Wonderfully sore. She blinked several times and turned on her side to see snow falling onto the river outside the sliding glass door. She felt better than she had in weeks; her mind had cleared. Oh, she was still terrified about Walter and could feel the clock ticking down on the killer's next victim, but her brain had kicked back into full gear.

Last time she'd awakened in Huck's bed, he'd told her it was a one-off and that he didn't want a relationship with anybody. Yet she'd driven to his house of her own accord the previous night, and she didn't regret a second, not even the fight. She'd read about angry sex.

She liked it. Of course, she felt safe with Huck, so that probably helped.

Slipping from the bed, she used the master bathroom and then looked for her clothing. It was in the other room. Rare indecision kept her motionless for a moment before she opened a drawer in a worn dresser and tugged out a faded marines T-shirt to pull over her head. The material fell to just above her knees, so she was at least covered enough to fetch her clothing.

Her feet chilling from the wooden floor, she padded out to the living room, where her clothing had been placed on the sofa. Her bra strap was broken.

The sizzle of bacon in the kitchen caught her unaware and she turned to see Huck's bare back as he flipped a piece over. There were scratches down his infraspinatus muscles, disappearing beneath his black sweatpants. He turned, his eyes a tawny brown in the early light. "Morning."

"Good morning." She moved for her clothing. "I won't be long."

He turned and used tongs to place the bacon on a paper towel. "I made breakfast and have coffee on. Come eat."

Coffee? Her mouth watered. She hesitated and then walked to the small round table by another sliding glass door, where he'd already placed scrambled eggs, toast, orange juice, coffee, and plates. "Thank you."

He chuckled and put the tray of bacon in the center of the table. "This is about all I can cook, so enjoy." He reached into the fridge and brought out peppermint-flavored creamer. "I think this is still good." His feet and chest were bare and his hair ruffled, and in the morning light, he looked younger, even with the scruff on his jaw. Perhaps freer. He sat.

The sex had been good for both of them. Mentally as well as physically. She relaxed and reached for the creamer, then sipped her coffee with a small hum of enjoyment. "I was not expecting breakfast." In fact, she wasn't expecting anything.

He paused with a piece of bacon halfway to his mouth and then put it back on his plate. "Are we still fighting?"

"No. I would like to ask you to refrain from speaking with reporters for the remainder of this case." The toast was slightly burned in a way that melted the butter perfectly.

He sat back in his chair, his gaze still lazy with a hint of intent. "Agreed."

"Good." One more obstacle out of the way.

His smile revealed a rarely present dimple in his right cheek. "You know, you're even more beautiful when you're angry."

She liked his dorky side. "That's a lovely cliché," she said, digging into the scrambled eggs covered in cheddar cheese.

"Do we need to talk about this? About last night?" He swept a large hand out. "You're very likeable, but I feel like we should concentrate on finding this killer and not start something up right this second."

Her eyebrows rose. "Most people don't like me." They were intrigued by her, sometimes enjoyed her, but she wasn't accustomed to people actually *liking* her. Oh, they didn't dislike her, but she was difficult to understand or relate to sometimes.

"Most people do like you, but you remain unaware of

that fact if they don't say the words." He took a bite of his eggs.

Interesting. "I am rather literal," she agreed, her heart warming. It was nice to be liked.

"That's why I said the words," he said. "I was a jerk last time, and I don't want to be that this time." He drank half of his coffee in one gulp. "I'm a bad bet. Still have PTSD, don't like being around people, and get obsessed with searching when somebody is lost. I take it personally if I fail, and I'm pissed about losing three women to the psycho we're chasing right now. I'm also generally grumpy, I've been told."

Her feet tingled. Was that a hormonal reaction? How odd. "You are remarkably self-aware."

"Is that a compliment?"

"Most definitely." She chewed thoughtfully and then took a drink of her orange juice. "I agree that we should focus completely on finding this killer and not dwell on last night." Although it had been good for them both. "The dead women deserve that."

Now his face moved into lines she'd learned to recognize as relief.

Her mind drew connections, saw conflicts, possibilities, and pitfalls. This was the intelligent decision, so they could concentrate more fully on the killer before another woman died.

Huck looked down at his food, his brow furrowing. "We're in agreement. Good. I can't get the picture of Christine Franklin in that field out of my mind."

"Me either," Laurel said softly, haunted by those dahlias surrounding the frozen and beaten body.

He glanced back up. "This guy is speeding up, isn't he?"

She set down her glass, no longer hungry. "Yes, and he's probably angry he didn't get the time with Christine that he wanted. The entire situation was out of his pattern. We forced him to make a move and kidnap her."

"How long do you think we have?"

"I think he's already found his next victim, and those urges are going to rule him soon."

# Chapter Twenty-Five

After dropping by her mother's house for a shower and change of clothing, Laurel returned to the office and sat in her conference room looking at the murder board. Connections were everywhere, but they didn't lead to any conclusions. Her phone rang and she lifted it off the glass tabletop. "Snow."

"Laurel? It's George. What the hell is going on there?"

Laurel blew out air. "Hi, Deputy Director McCromby. A reporter was being a reporter, sir. Captain Rivers didn't say anything to the journalist, so she went with supposition."

"What the hell was he doing even speaking with a reporter?" George bellowed.

"He was trying to gain information from her. She has excellent sources and has given us facts before, but I can assure you that he guaranteed me he would not take a call from her again." The board was still bothering her.

"Fine. Make sure of it." George hung up.

Laurel set her phone down and rearranged the pictures and connections in her mind. Once and then again. Her phone rang and she lifted it absently to her ear this time. "Snow."

"Agent Snow? It's Officer Zello. I found Davie Tate

per the BOLO and am outside his place of employment right now. What would you like for me to do?"

Laurel glanced at the clock. "He's missing school, which is truancy. Bring him in for me, would you?"

"Sure thing. He's a minor, so one of us will need to contact his guardian."

"I'm aware of the law. Thank you, Officer Zello." She clicked off and called out. "Nester? I need you to get me Davie Tate's mom on the phone. As soon as possible. Also, we need the search warrant for Sharon Lamber's newly found greenhouse and also the one for Charlene Rox's workspace at the hospital, as well as phone records for any suspects you think we can obtain warrants for. Now." Adrenaline shot into her veins. She was getting closer.

"You've got it. The state crime lab just sent over a report and there were no prints on either of the axes used at the murders," Nester yelled.

"I figured," she muttered.

"Also, Fish and Wildlife just called. They found Christine Franklin's hands a mile away from the crime scene but on the main road. It's like he pulled over and put her hands on a log," Nester bellowed.

Laurel chewed her lip. "Thanks." The killer did seem to want them to search for the hands now.

In less than a minute, Nester called back. "I have Ms. Tate on line two."

Laurel hopped off the conference table and reached for the phone Kate had put on a small glass table in the corner. "Ms. Tate?"

"Yes, hello? Is this really the FBI?" a woman asked, panic in her voice.

"Yes, ma'am. My name is Agent in Charge Laurel Snow, and I'm working on a murder case and need to speak with your son. I think he might have information that could help me." She didn't have to admit that the kid was a possible suspect. "Davie is truant from school today, so I'm having an officer escort him to my office. Could you please meet us here?"

Ms. Tate sighed. "I can't. I'm in Seattle and I have several houses to clean today. Davie couldn't know anything about a murder. Are you sure he's not in school?"

"I'm certain. He's at his place of employment right now but will be here soon. I need parental consent."

The woman's rate of breathing increased audibly. "I can't be there but will ask Jason or Haylee to go with him. I trust them and give permission or consent or whatever for you to talk to Davie while they're with him. I'm sure he'll want to help you. What do you think he could possibly know?"

It was a fair question from a concerned and harried mother. "Davie knew Sharon Lamber, who is one of the victims in this case. He and Tommy Bearing assisted her at her greenhouse with various tasks, and I want to know if he saw or heard anything odd. I need to question him about this case in general, Ms. Tate."

"Oh. Well, okay. I'll call Jason now."

"I appreciate it." Laurel wanted to schedule a time to question Ms. Tate directly but wouldn't make that request until she'd already spoken to Davie. "How about I call you after interviewing Davie to update you?"

Ms. Tate sighed. "That would be wonderful. Thank you."

"You're welcome. I'll speak with you soon." Laurel ended the call. Should she feel guilty about manipulating Davie's mother? She was trying to catch a murderer who beat his victims to death, so her own feelings didn't matter right now.

Her cell phone rang and she reached for it yet again. "Snow."

"Hi. It's Dr. Ortega, and I have a preliminary report for you on Christine Franklin. Blunt force trauma to the head as cause of death. There were signs of a sexual assault but no bodily fluids, and no DNA so far." Papers rustled. "Same as the other victims. You thinking he tries to rape them, can't keep it up, and then goes into a rage?"

"Yes," she said, dropping into a leather chair.

The sound of liquid being poured into a mug came over the line. "I'll email you an official report by the end of the day." He cleared his throat. "I know you're swamped, but have you found out anything about Tommy Bearing? My niece is just head over heels."

Laurel winced. "High school gossip is that he was climbing out of a girl's bedroom, where he'd been invited, and the dad caught him. Tommy assaulted the dad. I haven't been able to get my hands on a juvenile report, but just between us, he's a person of interest in this homicide investigation."

"Are you kidding me?" Ortega snapped.

"No. I don't have anything concrete on the young man. His family has connections to each of the victims, but that's it. I initially put him on the list because of what you'd said about voyeurism, and so far, that hasn't panned out. I don't have enough on Tommy to obtain a warrant for anything. Even so, I want you fully informed."

Without the voyeurism, she might not even be looking at Tommy. Plus, he and Davie alibied each other for the kidnapping of Christine Franklin. One of them could be lying or they could be working together, although that would alter the profile.

"None of this makes me happy."

"I understand. However, high school gossip says that Tommy has already moved on to another girl. If it's true, you might have a broken heart to deal with but no worries of Tommy being around," Laurel said quietly.

"Okay. Thanks. I'll be in touch. Bye."

Laurel made a quick call to the hospital to find that Walter was now listed in serious condition. That was good. She breathed out and then began covering the murder boards with the pull-down screens Kate had had mounted to the wall above them. She had just finished when Officer Zello escorted Davie into the room.

"Here he is," Zello said, his handlebar mustache twitching. "Wanted to stop for breakfast but I told him that wasn't a good idea."

Davie rolled his eyes.

Laurel smiled and gestured to a chair across from her. "Have a seat, Davie. Your mom was going to request Jason or Haylee to be here for your interview, so we'll wait for them."

Officer Zello nodded. "They were behind us, but I think they stopped for coffee downstairs." He shrugged, looking tall and lean in his uniform. "I must not have expressed urgency."

"That's all right." Laurel pulled out a chair and sat across from Davie, whose dark hair looked ruffled. His T-shirt was a worn green, his jeans faded, and his boots covered in snow. "Officer Zello? I appreciate your help with this." The guy would make a better sheriff than the actual sheriff. "Have you ever thought of working for the FBI?"

He nodded. "I have."

"Keep me in the loop, because I'm happy to write you a recommendation," she said.

He smiled, making his eyes twinkle. "Thanks. I'll be in touch." He turned, shoulders back, and walked down the hallway.

Davie rolled his eyes again. "Puke."

Movement sounded and Jason and Haylee crossed in front of the interior windows of the conference room and walked inside, both holding two coffee cups. Jason handed one to Davie and took the seat next to him, while Haylee handed a cup to Laurel and then sat at the end of the table.

Haylee smiled. "The coffee lady downstairs said this is what you like."

Laurel accepted the coffee. "That was kind of you. Thanks."

Jason leaned forward. "Mrs. Tate asked us to sit in, but I need to ask you if Davie should have a lawyer before I go plow. I can't stay long." The architect wore a black down vest over dark jeans, and his beard had been trimmed neatly against his handsome face.

Laurel shook her head. "That's up to Davie, of course, but he's not obligated to be here and can leave any time." She looked at the boy, who was now gulping down his drink. "I just need some help here, Davie. I think you have some answers that may help me find this killer."

Davie wiped off his mouth. "Okay."

Jason cleared his throat.

Davie hunched his shoulders. "I first want to apologize for swearing at you the other night. I was high."

Jason groaned.

"That's all right," Laurel said. "Make it up to me now. Tell me how you found out that Sharon Lamber grew cannabis."

He shrugged. "She hired Tommy and me to move some stuff around for her at the greenhouse, and we saw the plants. It wasn't like she was hiding them or anything." He scratched at a pimple on his neck. "She didn't care if we took some—it was no big deal." He looked at Haylee. "That's all I know."

Haylee patted his arm. "I believe you."

"What about Tommy? He said his aunt was stupid," Laurel said. The kid didn't seem to have much respect for women. Or anybody.

Davie jerked. "Sharon wasn't stupid. She was cool. Was fine with us just hanging out at the place, and she knew we took some of the pot. She didn't care."

She hit him with the next question. "Did you leave the greenhouse the last time you went there to get high? Tommy said he might've fallen asleep and you could've left."

Davie rocked back.

Jason put a hand on the table. "They're both good kids, Agent Snow. You're barking up the wrong tree."

She kept her gaze on the boy.

"No," Davie said. "We were high but watched movies all day. I didn't take a nap and neither did Tommy."

She moved on to asking about the other victims and where he was during times of death.

"I don't know." His face twisted up. "Seriously. I was either at home, at school, hanging with Tommy, or at work. That's pretty much my life."

"Can anybody corroborate the times when you were home?" Laurel asked.

Davie's face colored. "Not usually," he muttered.

Nester popped into the doorway. "We finally got the remaining warrants."

She nodded. "Thanks."

Davie ducked his head. "Warrants for where? Because you don't need one for my house. Feel free."

Haylee perked up. "If one is for Sharon's greenhouse, I'd love to look at it and identify plants for you."

It sounded as if the woman wanted to buy the greenhouse. Nonetheless, her expertise would be beneficial. "Thanks,"

Laurel said. She kept her focus on Davie. "Have you plowed or shoveled any of the homes in the Forest Ridge subdivision?"

Davie shook his head. "I don't think so."

Laurel looked at Jason.

"No," he said, glancing at his phone. "But if you have connections there, I'd love to get that contract. We'd do a good job."

Haylee nodded.

"Davie, did you know that Sharon Lamber was having an affair with a cardiac surgeon?" Laurel asked.

"Yeah. Tommy told me." Davie grimaced. "She was a nice lady, but that probably was a dumb move. Did he kill her?"

So far, Laurel had been unable to find Dr. Keyes, which was rare in this day and age. "Did you ever see them together?"

"No." He drank the rest of his coffee.

Jason stood. "I have to go plow those businesses before it snows again. Hay? Do you have things here?"

Haylee nodded. "Yeah. I'll see you at home."

He clenched Davie's shoulder. "You've got this, Bud. See you later." Then he looked at Laurel. "He didn't do anything wrong and neither did Tommy. I hope they help you with your investigation, but please stop treating them as suspects and don't send uniformed police officers after them again."

Davie nodded.

"You didn't come in when you said you would," she reminded him.

He flushed. "My mom couldn't make it, and I didn't want to come alone."

Haylee grasped his arm again. "You can always ask us. We're here for you."

Laurel pushed a legal notepad across the table along with a pen. "I need you to think back for the last three weeks to where you were every day and night. Sometimes going in chronological order helps with memory."

With a long-suffering sigh, Davie took the pen and started writing, chewing on his lip at the same time.

Jason moved into the hallway, running right into Abigail Caine. He stepped back. "I'm so sorry. Are you all right?"

Abigail wobbled and then nodded, brushing her hair away from her face.

What the heck was she doing at the office?

Jason sidestepped her, waved at Haylee through the window, and hurried down the hallway.

Abigail turned to watch him go, her gaze dropping the distance it would take to check out his butt.

Haylee frowned and partially rose from the chair.

Abigail turned and caught Laurel's gaze through the window before coming to stand in the doorway behind Davie. "Laurel, I need to speak with you. Right now."

Davie jolted and dropped the pen. "Dr. Caine?"

# Chapter Twenty-Six

Laurel stiffened. What in the world?

Davie turned his head to look at the doorway and then shook it. "Oh. Sorry. Your voice, I mean, I thought you were somebody else." He looked back at Laurel. "Sorry."

Abigail walked inside and stood behind Jason's vacated chair, her red-painted nails curling over the white leather. "Mr. Tate? It is me." She paused and then tugged on her hair. "That's right. When I'm at the university, I hide my true colors. The blond wig and blue contact lenses are how I started the school year, so I thought I'd continue. Next year, I'll decide if I want to choose a different color or go natural. Since meeting my sister, I have been tempted to reveal the real me."

Davie's mouth dropped open, and he looked from Abigail to Laurel. "Wow."

Laurel frowned. "How do you two know each other?"

Davie shifted his weight again and seemed to shrink in his chair.

Abigail showed no expression. "Mr. Tate signed up for one of my research projects and participated for two weeks before I discovered that he'd lied on his application and was underage. I was thus forced to remove him from the endeavor."

Haylee leaned toward Davie. "That's her?"

Davie nodded, even his ears turning red. "I said I was sorry." He looked imploringly at Laurel. "I was being paid, man. We don't have much money, and the study looked easy, so I applied. It was really good money."

"I understand." Laurel looked up at Abigail. "As you can see, I'm in the middle of an interview. Please return to the reception area and wait for me."

Abigail smiled; her lipstick matched her fingernails. "There's nobody out there right now, so I'll just go back to your office. Take your time." She tapped Davie on his shoulder with a nail on her way out, and the kid jumped.

Laurel exhaled. Kate had probably gone downstairs in search of food, and Abigail had most likely waited until the receptionist was out. No way would Kate have just let the woman back into the office. "I'm sorry about that." She tilted her head. "Tell me about the study with Dr. Caine."

Davie straightened. "Oh. It was actually kind of fun. Dr. Caine teaches some classes about the brain and behavior, and why we do what we do. The study just involved meeting in her lab a few times a week, and I always signed up for after school, so it was like a job." He picked up the pen again. "She asked me questions about my life and then gave me hypotheticals on how I'd handle situations or problems. Then she'd show me films or have me read something and ask me more questions." He smiled at Haylee. "It was seriously easy money. It sucked when she found out my age." He shook his head. "I wore a high school sweatshirt one day, and I gave myself away."

Laurel nodded. "How did you feel when she removed you from the study?"

"Bummed. I needed the money." He twirled the pen

around in his fingers. "Plus, I was doing good at it. My age shouldn't make a difference, right? I mean, in any scientific study, don't they want the broadest range of subjects? You'd think age wouldn't be part of it. Totally unfair, man."

Not only that, but the study created a direct line from Davie to Abigail, who was a potential victim. "That would've made me angry, Davie."

He nodded. "Yeah. She was all calm like and just dropped me as if I was *nothing*. I told her everything about me. She knows me better than I know me, probably." He stared at Laurel's eyes. "And she's a liar. She looked blond with blue eyes and she really was a redhead with freaky eyes. Who is she to judge anybody?" His throat moved as he swallowed. "No offense."

"None taken." So Davie had a connection to both Sharon and now Abigail. "Did Tommy take part in this study?"

"No. He doesn't need money," Davie muttered.

Was there any connection between the boys and either Charlene Rox or Christine Franklin? "Have you ever seen a psychiatrist?"

"God, no. I'm not crazy," Davie said.

"Has Tommy?" Laurel asked.

Davie shrugged. "Maybe when he was up at the youth ranch, but he didn't say anything about that."

Dr. Rox hadn't worked up at the youth ranch. Laurel opened a file folder from her stack to reveal photographs of Charlene and Christine. "Do you recognize these women?"

"No," Davie said, staring at the victims. "I'm sorry."

Laurel ran Davie through a few more questions and then decided it was time to let him go. "Haylee will drop you off at school. You need to stop being truant, okay?" At his nod, she smiled at Haylee. "I accept your offer to look through the greenhouse this afternoon. Can you meet there around two?"

"Yes." Haylee's smile was wide. "Looking forward to it."

No doubt. Laurel stood and walked them out before returning to her office.

Abigail sat in Laurel's chair on the other side of the makeshift desk, typing into her phone. "You need a decent desk. I have a sliver from touching this old door." She didn't look up.

"Remove yourself from my chair."

Abigail sighed and unfolded herself from the white leather, standing to at least five foot nine in her dark red high heels. She crossed gracefully around the desk to sit in a guest chair.

It shouldn't bother Laurel that her sister was so much taller than her own five foot two, and yet, it did. She hid the discomfort by claiming her chair and looking at her frozen screen. "You tried to hack into my computer."

"If I had tried to hack you, I would've hacked you. I just tried to utilize your computer and used my three tries to guess your password. It wasn't your mother's name or birthday, interestingly enough." Her smile was catlike and now her lipstick had been dimmed by a light pink sparkle.

Laurel opened the laptop bag by her chair to check the lip gloss she kept in there. Pink sparkle. "Did you go through all of my belongings?"

"Of course. It's a pity you don't have a real desk with actual drawers. I was bored within minutes." Abigail crossed her legs beneath a black skirt she'd paired with a matching jacket over a silky white blouse. "Where did you get this gloss? It tastes delicious."

Laurel took control of the situation fast. "Why are you here?"

Abigail lost her amusement. "The FBI contacted me today regarding the search for our father. I've told you, he left the church on his own accord, and that's the end of it. Why are you still looking for him?"

"Because he's missing," Laurel said. She wouldn't stop until she found him. If nothing else, he had to answer for what he'd done to her mother, although the statute of limitations had run out on the rape. "The current pastor of the church filed a missing person's report for Pastor Zeke Caine, and I will find him."

"You don't want to find him. Trust me." Abigail glanced down at her hands, looking vulnerable. Looks could be so deceiving.

Laurel cleared her throat. Their father had forced Abigail to hide her unusual hair color and odd eyes instead of embracing her uniqueness, and then he'd all but given her up when she was a child after her mother died. Abigail appeared to hold an abundance of resentment against their absent and now seemingly missing father, and Laurel couldn't blame her for that. She'd been pretty much forced into college as a young teen without the support that Laurel had received from her own mother. Even so, Laurel needed answers. "What kind of experiments did you perform on Davie Tate?"

Abigail looked from her nails to Laurel's face. She laughed. "Experiments? Come on."

The moment was akin to looking in a mirror but a thousand times more uncomfortable. "Answer the question, Abigail."

Abigail's gaze zeroed in on Laurel's neck. "Oh, little sister. Did a big bad wolf bite you?"

Laurel glanced pointedly at her phone.

"Very well, then. I'll tell you what. We'll go tit for tat." The gleam in Abigail's dual-colored eyes showed no give. The woman would walk right out no matter what Laurel did.

"That's acceptable. You first. Answer my question. I assume the study was performed as part of your doctorate in social and decision neuroscience." Abigail had degrees in computation and neural systems, social and decision neuroscience, game theory, biochemistry, and philosophy with a practical ethics emphasis. The latter was an oddity.

She rubbed at a mark on her boot near her knee. "Of course. My contract with Tech requires me to publish, as I'm sure you're aware. So I've been conducting said research. Davie actually was an interesting subject, and I would've preferred to keep him in the study. However . . . laws and rules and all of that." She waved her hand in the air.

"Your study. Was the focus on simple choices, trial and error, harm or hurt?" Laurel leaned forward. "Or more complex issues such as the way the brain processes information or becomes influenced? Or did you zero in on biology and behavior?" There were so many different avenues of study, and Laurel was fascinated by them all.

Abigail straightened. "Dear sister, you've been looking into my discipline? One of them? I'm honored."

Encouraging the woman would be a mistake. "No. You're not the only person with multiple degrees. Please answer."

"Oh no, not yet. It's my turn. Tell me about the love kiss on your neck." Abigail clasped her hands in her lap. "Is he the animal he appears? He did bite you."

Any information Laurel gave to Abigail could and most likely would be used against her in the future. Even so, she needed answers as well. "I'm not willing to discuss personal matters with you."

Abigail's chin firmed. "It's okay to like it rough. Some of us do." Her voice lowered conspiratorially. "It's not like we're from pure stock. Daddy's heart was black as the devil's and twice as thick, and we do come from him. No matter what your earth-loving, moon-worshiping, mother has told you. Rough can be good. Very good."

"Please focus on the matter at hand." Laurel's ears began to ring and her anxiety clicked up several heated measures.

"I am. If my baby sister is drawn to the dark side, I can only be of help." She winked. "There's a bruise on your left wrist. Did he pin you down?"

She'd gotten the bruise smashing her own arm against the wall when lost in the throes of an orgasm. Laurel flashed back to the passionate night, knowing the hint of violence between her and Huck had only increased her desire for the former soldier. "Do you think Davie could be a killer?" She might as well get down to business.

Abigail's gaze remained on the bite mark. "Of course." She lifted her eyes, nailing Laurel with intensity. "Can't we all? Take you, for instance. You can put yourself right into the mind of a psychopath, and you've convinced yourself it's because of your intelligence and experience. And yet, what if that's not it?"

Laurel decided to play along while ignoring the quickening of her breath. "Meaning what?"

"Meaning . . . perhaps you are a psychopath. You've convinced yourself otherwise and imitate emotion well, but is it real? Do you truly *feel* what you want to feel?" Abigail's lips twitched, and the pink gloss shined in the light. "You think you're awkward with people because you attended university so young and didn't have normal relationships with peers. What if you're awkward because you're truly *different*? You don't feel or think like they do." Her voice lowered even more and the slight British accent emerged. "What if your awkwardness is actually psychopathy?"

Laurel barely kept her interested expression in place. Abigail had zeroed in on her biggest fear. "Are you talking about me or yourself?" Now her own voice lowered.

"We're the same," Abigail countered. "Of course, I would've bitten the good captain back. I don't believe you did so."

How had she lost control of this conversation? "Tell me about Davie or get out of my office."

"Now, now. Let's not get testy," Abigail purred. "I'm here trying to make a connection with you, and girl talk about Huckalishous is one way to do that."

Laurel drew in a heated breath. "You can't connect, Abigail. You know you can't, but that's okay with you. Connections aren't what you want." Anger trilled through her veins, and she didn't push it away. "People mean nothing except for how they intrigue or entrain you, and this is just another game or study for you. That's all. Don't think for one second that I fail to see the real you. You're correct in that I am intelligent and well trained, with experiences that give me nightmares, but I *do* connect with people. I feel to a degree you can't fathom because it's out of that realm where only *you* exist. We are not the same."

Abigail sprang to her feet. "Do you think it's because of your mother? Because she was present during your childhood?"

"Maybe." Laurel could be that honest with her. "I don't know."

"Well. How is Deidre lately? She seems both likeable and lost, if you ask me. Like somebody who'd spook easily." Abigail brushed an invisible piece of lint off her jacket.

Laurel's body chilled as her mind filtered through Deidre's latest fears. "Is that a fact? Have you been harassing my mother to gain my attention?" Or to force Laurel to remain in town?

"Harassing? Of course not." Abigail brushed the air with one hand as if to push the idea away, but her eyes gleamed. "Why would I do that?"

To show that she could? To prove that Laurel needed to stay close to protect her mother? Laurel stood and planted both hands on her desk. "Do not leave footprints around my mother's vehicle again, do not follow her around, and do not try to scare her. Ever." Laurel had feared she'd have to protect her family from this new half sister. "We both may favor logic, but I'll destroy you if you hurt my mother. Hard and fast and with a viciousness even you couldn't match."

Abigail's smile showed too many teeth. "Again, I don't know what you're talking about, but your point is well taken." Her tone was coy. "However, do not for one second consider rejecting me as a sister."

Laurel straightened. "Why not?"

Fire splashed across Abigail's high, smooth cheekbones. "You would not like the result. At all." She grabbed her purse and spun out of the room, clipping rapidly down the hallway and through the door.

Laurel sank back to her chair, her entire body shaking. Heat blasted from the vents pointed at her, but she didn't feel the warmth.

What had she just done?

# Chapter Twenty-Seven

Huck stopped by Monty's office on his way out. "Hey."

Monty looked up from his computer, his eyes bloodshot. "Hey. Where are we with the investigation?"

Nowhere good. "Now with warrants, we're heading out to search the other greenhouse owned by the first victim, and the Seattle FBI is searching Dr. Rox's shared workspace at the hospital." Huck motioned for Aeneas to sit. "You don't have to be here if you'd rather rest." The radiation treatments were obviously taking a toll.

"I don't have anywhere else to be." Monty looked at the framed photo on his desk. "I guess when my sweet wife died, I just stopped meeting people. Dropped friends and only worked. This is all I have."

Huck didn't have any words of comfort.

Monty ran a hand through his rapidly thinning hair. "It's nice having you here in the office. I know you'd rather be called in only when needed, but the office requires strong leadership, and I think you can provide that. You seem more comfortable these days."

"I am." Huck wasn't certain he wanted to be more comfortable, but he did like most of the Fish and Wildlife officers, and they were a strong team. "Though I'm ready for you to be healthy again so you can take over."

Monty's smile looked more like a grimace. "Might take a while. I know we're not friends, but—"

"We're friends." Huck couldn't go through his entire life with just the dog as his friend. "I'm not a great friend, but I consider you one. If you need anything, I'm here. Just name it."

"Okay. Don't waste your life. That's all I ask." When Huck frowned, Monty held up a hand. "I'm just saying. Making friendships and connections matter, and perhaps it's time for you to stop going it alone in the wilderness with the dog. It's nice having you here in the office."

Aeneas barked as if in agreement.

Huck frowned at the dog, whose tongue rolled out. "I'll think about it. For now, I'll call you if we find anything at the greenhouse, and please contact me if the BOLO produces any results for the heart surgeon. His phone was found in his office, but there hasn't been any other trace of him, which I don't like. Dr. Keyes has to be found."

"You've got it. And say hi to Agent Snow for me," Monty said. "Her mama brought me cookies earlier. She's a sweetheart."

"Bye." Huck turned and walked by the rows of file cabinets and out the main entrance to the vestibule, where Laurel was just emerging from her stairwell. "Hi."

"Hi." She buttoned up her wool coat, her gaze sliding past his face to the outside door. "We need to get going."

Huck opened the door for her, noting she didn't meet his eyes. Great. Now what had he done? "I'm driving."

"I assumed." She jerked when he reached the passenger-side door first to open it. "Um, thanks."

"Sure." Amusement caught him unaware and he waited

until she'd sat before shutting her door. How laconic had he been for her to be surprised to see him act as a gentleman? Though he'd never met his mother, his father had taught him better than that. Mostly. He settled the dog in his crate and then jumped inside the truck, starting the engine and letting the cab heat up. They were just a couple of miles away from the greenhouse when he broke the silence. "What's bothering you?"

"Do you think I could be a psychopath?"

He blinked. Once and then again. Yeah, he'd been expecting a "nothing" or a "where are we going" or "last night was a mistake." He should've known better. "No. Do you think you're a psychopath?"

"No." Her stiff shoulders softened. "I know I'm not." Then she chewed on her lip. "Do you think most psychopaths know they're psychopaths?"

"Hell if I know. That's your field." He glanced down at her, trying to track her thoughts. Nope. He had nothing. "Why are you worrying about this?"

She pulled off her black leather gloves. "Abigail dropped by to see me."

"Oh." He nodded. "All right. She got into your head." That was not a good thing. "You let her into your head, Laurel. Why?"

"Because she zeroed in on my biggest fear. I am different and . . ." She looked out the window.

He couldn't imagine what it was like for her to be so different from other people, then find out she had a sister just as unique, and then find out that sister was nuttier than a fucking fruitcake. "Well, considering I was inside you less than twenty-four hours ago, and that you were whispering my name in my ear as you came, I can promise that you are not a psychopath. You are warm and kind and a very safe place for a battered ex-soldier like me to land."

It wasn't a love sonnet, but it was the best he could do. Plus, it was the truth.

"Oh." Pink filtered across her face. "That's sweet, Huck."

"Take that back," he said.

She chuckled. "I won't tell anybody."

"I appreciate that." It was telling how much lighter his chest felt just because he'd made her laugh. "I don't have any advice for you regarding Dr. Caine. The relationship between you is a battle of wits, and when it comes to the two of you, I'm unarmed."

She laughed full out this time. "You're much smarter than you give yourself credit for, I think. Notwithstanding your penchant for trusting ex-girlfriends who are journalists to play by the same rules you do."

"Maybe." He had good instincts and could figure out most people, but there was no way his IQ was the same number as Laurel's. Of course, she'd once told him that an arbitrary number could never give a true measure of intelligence. That was a statement Abigail Caine would never have made. "You and your sister are as different as can be, regardless of hair and eye coloring. Don't ever forget that."

"Half sister," Laurel retorted as he pulled to a stop in front of an expansive greenhouse. "Thanks, Huck."

"Anytime." He actually meant it. Interesting.

Laurel loosened her scarf as she met Haylee at the entrance of the greenhouse with Huck and Aeneas behind her. They'd look around, and the crime techs would finger-print the place the next day, but she didn't hold much hope that they'd find anything. "Thank you for meeting us."

"Sure." Haylee rocked back on her brown boots, her sandy blond hair in a ponytail. "I'm happy to help, and I should be honest. We've been looking for a greenhouse, and if this one is for sale or rent, I want it. That makes me a bad person, but the business is really struggling."

Laurel handed the woman latex gloves. "That doesn't make you a bad person. It's a logical plan."

Haylee perked up as she pulled them over her hands. "Thanks. That's what I thought, too."

Laurel stepped back at seeing a lock on the door, her own hands already covered. "Huck?"

"Yep." He used bolt cutters to slice it. Then he opened the door and walked in first, his gaze sweeping the interior. "Place is hot. Must have heat running. Nobody here. Come on in."

Laurel allowed Haylee in first and then followed her. Had Huck cleared the space for the civilian or for both women?

"Man, there are a lot of flowers in here." Huck lifted a blooming white daffodil to his nose.

Haylee nodded. "Greenhouses can be maintained thirty degrees warmer than the temperature outside, so there's a lot you can grow in the winter. Dr. Lamber was a great botanist. I took a class from her at the community college."

Laurel looked over a feathery fern at the woman. "Did you graduate in botany?"

"Oh, no." Haylee waved her hand. "I didn't graduate. I mean, I want to graduate someday, but right now, we just don't have the money. I'm smart enough, though."

"I'm sure you are," Laurel said.

Haylee ran her fingers over what looked like a witch hazel branch. "Maybe not as smart as you, but I would like to get a degree. Jason has an architecture degree. I'm not good at math, but flowers I understand."

Huck wandered past beds of flowers and plants to the back. "Using electric heat like this must've cost a mint."

Haylee nodded. "Seriously. But it's worth it. Just look

at these flowers. They're beautiful." She pointed to the far end. "You have vegetables over there, roots here, tropical plants there, and different flowers throughout." She walked along one of the three aisles and then stopped. "Ah. Here's the happy stuff."

Laurel walked by the marijuana plants to the far end of the greenhouse, where a desk and small filing cabinet had been set up. Candy and chip wrappers littered the ground along with empty beer cans. No doubt this was where Tommy and Davie had smoked cannabis and skipped school the other day. "We're looking for black dahlias."

They scouted the entire greenhouse but didn't find one black dahlia plant. Laurel's shoulders drooped. "Guess this lead won't pan out. However, why don't you tell me about Davie and Tommy."

Haylee crouched to examine a pot of darker soil. "They're sweethearts who work hard for not a lot of pay." She looked up. "I know Tommy got the job because his parents are making him pay back his lawyer, but Davie really needs the money. He helps his mom out a lot." She stood. "You're wrong about them if you think they could kill anybody."

Laurel nodded. "All right. Who do you think killed Dr. Lamber?"

Haylee stepped back. "Me?"

"Yes."

"Huh." Haylee tugged on her ponytail, her lips pursing. "Well, I don't know. Sharon Lamber was married, and she cheated on her husband, right? How about him? Maybe he got so mad at her, he just started killing all doctors."

It wasn't a bad hypothesis. "He has an alibi," Laurel said.

"Oh." Haylee's face fell. "How about your sister, then?" she conjectured wildly. "Davie told me about some of her

experiments with him, and he thought they were cool.
I'm not so sure. The professor seems . . . predatory."

That was a fairly accurate description. "I don't think
she'd want to spend her precious time setting up crime
scenes like the ones we've seen lately," Laurel said honestly. "If she killed, she'd do it efficiently and then move
on." Without a second thought.

Haylee shivered. "That's creepy."

"You have no idea."

"Hey," Huck called out. "There's something here."

Laurel looked for him but couldn't see beyond a series
of hanging plants. "Just a second." She moved away from
the desk and toward the far corner with Haylee behind her.
"Where are you?"

"Here."

She turned a corner and found Huck ducking down,
brushing dirt from the ground with his glove.

He knocked and something echoed. "My boot hit something hard. What is this?" He tugged and pulled out a
buried metal box.

Laurel crouched to pet Aeneas, who was staring intently
at his master as if waiting for a command.

The box was about one foot wide and two feet long.
Dials on the front lock showed it to be a turn combination.
Huck reached for a gardening shovel and pushed it above
the lock, grunting as he worked it back and forth. Finally, the lock sprang open.

"Whoa." Huck's eyebrows lifted.

Laurel leaned over to see. "Oh." Photographs of Sharon
Lamber in various sexual positions with her husband were
visible on top of many other pictures. She checked to make
sure her gloves were clean and then lifted a stack while
Huck did the same. "Haylee? I need you to go stand by the
door, all right?"

Haylee gulped and nodded, backing away from the photographs as if they were poisonous.

Laurel took a deep breath and flipped quickly through the first half, which were all of Sharon and Morris in various sex acts. She paused at the next picture, which showed an older man kissing Sharon, both of them nude. "I think this might be Dr. Joseph Keyes?" She held up the photograph for Huck.

"Yeah? I don't know who this is." Huck held up a photograph of Sharon engaged in sex with a brown-haired man. "Or this guy." He showed a blond male who looked like he should be surfing.

Laurel filtered through several pictures, finally finding one with the first man's face in focus. It was Dr. Keyes. She recognized him from his photograph on the hospital website. She kept rifling through the pictures, many depicting men who hadn't been identified as of yet. "Our suspect pool might've just exploded."

"Yeah. To an ocean." Huck shook his head. "I have no problem with kink, but tracking down all of these guys is going to take time. I'll need to bring donuts to the office."

"Oh." Laurel paused at seeing a familiar face. She held up the picture. "Officer Frank Zello." His handlebar mustache was unmistakable.

Huck paused. "That's interesting. He was the only point of contact for Dr. Rox, and he might've met Abigail at the auction."

True. Laurel nodded. "He also didn't tell us of his affair with Sharon Lamber. He should have. We'll have to bring him in."

Huck sucked in air, and his nostrils flared as he looked at another picture.

"What?" Laurel asked, her nape itching.

His chin lowered. "Sharon Lamber and Davie Tate." They were definitely engaged in sex. "He's seventeen. Just a kid."

Laurel sat back on her knees, pictures on her lap. "We're going to need to bring him back in as well."

Huck looked at several more pictures. "This isn't his fault. She was the adult."

"No. But if he killed her, he has to answer for it." Laurel felt nauseated.

"Yeah. We'll bring both Zello and Davie in tomorrow morning, and we need to find the cardiac surgeon." Huck looked up, his eyes blazing. "I'm tired of this damn case."

Laurel looked at her watch. "Me, too. And he's going to take another victim soon."

# Chapter Twenty-Eight

He'd been rushed during his time with Dr. Franklin, and it wasn't his fault. Fuck the FBI. He was glad he'd shot the fat guy and wished he could shoot him again. Nobody messed with his timeline. Yet he'd had no choice but to move fast before they could put his Christine somewhere safe.

There was no safety from him.

They should all know that by now.

Kicking snow, he moved between the trees, wanting to howl at the glowing moon. If he were an animal, he'd be a wolf. Primitive and deadly. He punched a tree and the pain grounded him. He'd taken Christine to that stupid cabin during the daytime. Wolves like him hunted at night. He hadn't gotten to spend enough time with her.

She'd been a fighter, but he'd been stronger. It was that simple.

Although he had enjoyed pouring water on her and watching it freeze. That cold bitch deserved to be frozen in a solid block. They all did. They had ice in their veins, and they should see how it felt to be surrounded by it.

Like he very often was. The cold around him, inside him, kept him from being what he needed to be. From experiencing the bliss he deserved.

There were predators and there were prey, and he'd learned which he wanted to be. Oh, he'd been weak once, but now he was powerful. He had studied and he had learned. Yet Christine had let him down like all the others. They'd been joined, so close, and she'd ruined it. It had been her fault. His rage had been so red hot, that the fire had all but blown out of his eyes. When the anger overtook him, it was hotter than any real flame. More out of control. And it wasn't his fault.

She'd failed.

Then the darkness had taken him. When he'd come to, her face was battered and her eyes wide open. The only good thing was that he'd had an ax in his rig so he could remove her hands. None of them deserved to have hands. Hands were for loving, not hitting, and they all hit. His mother had loved to hit him.

Christine had hit him in the nose. Fighting him. He'd crushed her brain and taken her hands, and there wasn't a thing she could do about it. It was unfortunate it took battering a skull to kill the brain, but life was life. This time, he hadn't damaged her face as badly. She'd probably deserved it, but he'd been rushed.

It was her fault.

She'd deserved to die.

Frustration crawled like ants through his veins, and he attacked the trees with each punch, his gloves protecting his hands. When the darkness had overtaken him each time, the gloves had protected him. Not them.

The last one had died too fast. It hadn't been enough. Even though he'd taken her hands, he was restless. Painfully so. To the point that he'd almost forgotten to leave the hands for the authorities to find. They had to be running in circles about that. Hands. Who would take hands only to leave them?

He would. He'd shove them up the women's asses if he could but leaving them for the cops also satisfied him. Unlike the last kill. He didn't get what he wanted.

Not even close to being complete. He hadn't made it again. His thoughts swirled around, and he dropped to his knees, tears streaming down his face to freeze as they hit the ground. It wasn't fair. He was good and right, and they were dirty. They had the balls to look down at him. *At him!*

What was wrong with these successful women? As far as he was concerned, they only had one real job, and it was fulfilling destiny. His destiny. Once again, he hadn't been able to reach bliss. It was their fault, not his. He was special and he was powerful.

Lifting his head, he yelled at the moon. Then he sobered, coming back to himself. All right. He had two more projects now. One of them would be perfect. He never knew who would be next until it happened. Sniffling, he sat in the snow with his back to a tree and pulled his journal out of his coat, then flipped through to review his research on his new projects.

One of them had to be his love. He deserved love, no matter what his mother said so long ago. He was not a loser as she'd said.

Those women were stronger than she was, than she'd ever be, and one of them was going to love him. They were all doctors—smart and beautiful. He read the entries that he'd carefully made in his journal. Those advanced degrees they held up like trophies hadn't taught them to vary their routines, had they?

They were so predictable.

Coffee here, gym there, dry cleaners over there. The same. Get up, work out, go to work, grab dinner, go home. . . . He'd memorized their routines. Well, except for his newest possibility. He hadn't had time to follow her yet.

But he would.

Once in a while they'd go to a spa or on a date, but he could tell their true love was their work.

Until him. He would show them that work was a hollow passion compared to him. Unless they failed to see him. Then they died.

He lovingly caressed each page, wondering which one would be next. Sighing, he closed the book and held it to his chest, the fire burning inside him again. It wouldn't be long. He could feel their meeting happening very soon.

Maybe she would be the one.


Rachel Raprenzi nudged open the door to the condominium with her butt since her hands were full of a pizza box and more research for her newest story. Eating pizza so late at night, or rather, early in the morning, was a mistake, but carbs made her brain work faster, and she had to figure this out. She'd been at the office until around three in the morning when the cleaning crew had gotten so loud she'd decided to go home and get a couple hours of sleep. If she could find the Witch Creek Killer and break the story on *The Killing Hour*, she'd hit the stratosphere with ratings. Plus, she'd beat Laurel Snow to the punch.

A natural redhead, her ass. There wasn't a chance of that. God, Huck was stupid to believe that woman.

Rachel hip checked the door and dropped the box of research on the floor before shrugging off her laptop bag. Switching hands on the unwieldly pizza box, she removed her coat and let it fall as well. Her entire body was tired. She'd been living this case and simultaneously trying to build her brand.

Yeah, she was ambitious, but this case also had to do with Huck.

She missed him. Missed the way he'd looked at her and missed the way he'd taken care of her. Life wasn't safe, but he'd made it feel that way. Why hadn't she appreciated how he protected her from any danger? Kicking off one boot, she hopped until she could get the other one off, and then walked on the hard tile to the kitchen in the darkness, dodging around the boxes she had yet to unpack.

Her phone tinkled, and she tugged it free of her pocket. "Hello."

"Hey. It's Sandy Simpson. We have it on good authority that the FBI has been calling in the Genesis Valley mayor's kid for interviews on the Witch Creek killings. The kid has a juvie record, but we can't get hold of it." Sandy was a researcher for Rachel's station, and she had excellent confidential sources.

Rachel's blood hummed. The mayor's kid? "I want that record. I don't care who you have to bribe."

Sandy snorted. "You're not famous yet. We don't have the kind of budget for bribery. The best I can do is try to interview the kid when he leaves school or maybe talk to some of his friends. You know how kids like to go viral."

"I do. Okay. Get me what you can tomorrow and get some sleep." Rachel ended the call, wide awake again. If the mayor's kid was actually the serial killer, her ratings would rise faster than even she could dream.

This case was absolutely perfect—just like she'd studied in journalism school. A crazy killer who left flowers after stalking victims being chased by a photo-worthy Fish and Wildlife officer working with a brilliant and bizarre FBI agent? She couldn't make this stuff up. The situation was as good as scripted. It was ideal for building her new show.

A rope wrapped around her neck.

She screamed, but the sound was cut off as the rope tightened. A sharp kick to the back of her ankle had her falling onto her knees. Her head jerked back. The pizza box flew away and landed noisily somewhere in the darkness. Gasping, tears filling her eyes, she clawed at the rope.

Her attacker stood above her and slightly loosened the noose. "I won't kill you." The voice was fake and raspy. It sounded like the voice distorter her nephew had worn with a Batman mask for Halloween last year, making it impossible to know anything about the attacker. "Put your hands down." When she didn't comply fast enough, the attacker tightened the rope again.

"Wait," she squawked, forcing her hands down to waist level. "Stop."

The rope loosened.

"What do you want?" she asked, her mouth working independently of her brain.

The chuckle was low and creepy, sending terror through her entire body. "I want to kill you, but I just said I would not. So I guess I'll settle for the next best thing."

A shudder racked her and she almost reached for the rope, stopping herself barely in time. "Please."

"Begging doesn't interest me. You need to solve the Witch Creek murders."

She blinked as the words registered. "You want me to stop investigating?" The roaring of blood through her head was so loud her ears rang.

"No. I want you to figure out who the killer is, and I'm tired of waiting." The rope tightened and then loosened. "Leave Laurel Snow alone. Talk about her again, and I *will* kill you."

Her fingers curled into her palms to keep from reaching

for the rope. The body felt substantial behind her, but she couldn't be sure. The kitchen was in complete darkness, so she couldn't see a shadow. "Laurel Snow?"

The rope snapped taut, and she grabbed for it, frantically scratching her neck.

"Down," the attacker hissed.

Tears streaming down her face, she lowered her shaking hands.

"Don't ever say her name again. Ever. Tell me you understand," the attacker hissed.

"I understand." Terror roared loudly through her head, making her ears ring.

The chuckle was even creepier than before. "I do not think you do. You're still planning on calling the authorities if I let you live. Don't. They can post someone at your door, and your news station can give you security. But for how long? Not forever. I will not forget. If you betray your word, I will watch. I will wait. And I will come and fucking kill you. It doesn't matter when. Do you understand?"

"Yes," she whispered, unable to see through the tears.

"Say it. Say that I will kill you."

She gulped, trying to take a full breath, but the rope was still too tight. "You'll kill me."

"Yes. It doesn't matter how long I have to wait. Say you won't call the authorities."

She sniffed, and the world spun around her. Terror felt like ice sliding beneath her skin. "I won't call the authorities." The room started to tilt in defiance of gravity. "Please." Her mind started to work sluggishly. "Did she send you? Were you hired by her?"

"No. I'm here for you, Rachel. I like the sound of your pain and your fear. Do you understand? Just nod."

She nodded and the rope pulled against her throat. "Tell me why?"

"No."

Even at the edge of unconsciousness, her mind tried to sort out the story. "Why are you doing this?"

"That doesn't matter to you. What matters to you is living and becoming famous by solving the murders, correct?"

"Yes," Rachel whispered, fighting to stay conscious. "Tell me how to find the murderer."

A hard hand, one covered in what felt like a thick glove, descended on her head. She yelped but the rope cut off all sound and prevented her from moving. "That's your job. Follow the story, ask for help, find the leads. But under no circumstances mention Laurel Snow or the FBI again. Do you understand me?"

"Yes."

The hand flattened out, feeling like death. "Say her name again."

Rachel hesitated. "Laurel Snow."

The rope tightened faster than a whip, and she tried to scream but no sound came out. She clawed wildly and the smell of copper filled her senses. Then the darkness pressed in from each corner. She fought it.

The darkness won.

# Chapter Twenty-Nine

Huck's truck screeched to a stop outside of Rachel's new home and he jumped out, running toward the doorway. The police had cordoned off the area with yellow crime tape, and he had to flash his badge to get beyond a burly guy in full uniform. Then he proceeded inside the complex, an older condominium with cream-colored accents and a view of mountains in the distance.

Rachel sat on a sofa with boxes on either side of her. A blanket had been hung over her shoulders and a paramedic was taking her vitals. Her blond hair was a wild mess and a line of bruising was already visible across her neck.

He halted when he saw that she was all right.

She looked up, her eyes vulnerable, and her body shaking despite the blanket around her. "Huck." Tears filled her eyes.

He moved toward her and the two state police detectives who were already taking her statement. They finished and moved on as crime techs milled around, working the scene. "Are you all right?"

"No." Once again, she looked like the sweet reporter he'd fallen for. "I thought he was going to kill me." She shuddered and pulled the blanket more securely around her shoulders. "I called you first but then had to call the state police because I knew they'd get here first. I was so scared."

"It's okay." He moved a box off the sofa and sat, patting her hand. Eons ago, he'd thought he was in love with her, and those feelings were long gone. But he didn't want her to be terrified. "Take a deep breath, hold it, and breathe it out." It was a technique he'd learned from one of his counsellors, and sometimes it could work. "Trust me. Try it."

She did so and soon her breathing grew steady, although she was so pale, she looked like she was about to pass out.

"Tell me everything. You're safe now." He listened to her relate the events of the night, his gut churning.

Finally, Rachel wound down. "Why would Laurel Snow send somebody to threaten me? I'm just doing my job, and if she does hers, it's all as it should be. Why would she do this?"

"She wouldn't," Huck said, running a hand through his mussed hair. He hadn't bothered to brush it when he'd gotten the call. "This doesn't make any sense. It could be the killer messing with us, or it could be some whack job harassing you."

"No." Rachel vigorously shook her head. "He insisted that I not call the police. He didn't want notoriety. His only goal was to frighten me enough to back off Laurel and you." Her hands plucked at the plush blanket over her shoulders. "Would she hire somebody to protect you?"

This was getting out of hand. "Rachel, think about it. Anybody with half a brain would know you'd call the authorities the second you could breathe again. You're also a reporter and an incredibly ambitious one at that. No matter what this person said to you, if you lived through this, you weren't going to be quiet. You were not going to give up on your story."

She swallowed and then winced, putting a shaking hand to the raw skin on her neck. "What does that mean?"

"I don't know. But one thing for sure is that this person wants publicity." If it was the killer, he was looking for more news about himself than he'd been receiving so far. If not, then who could it possibly be? "Are you sure it was a man?"

"I'm not sure of anything. It could've been a man, woman, kid . . . just somebody with a lot of strength and a voice distorting mask or something." A tear leaked down her face but her chin began to firm. "I need to go live in a few minutes. Can I interview you?" There she was. Rachel was back.

He edged away from her as she began to rearrange her hair. "Don't do this. You're giving the guy exactly what he wants if you go public with what happened here tonight." He patted her hand, wanting her to think like a cop and not a reporter for once, even as he knew that wasn't fair. "Don't give this jerk what he wants."

She pushed the blanket off. "This is what I want. Either you stay for the interview, or I'll grab somebody else."

"Grab somebody else and leave me out of it. I'll respond with a full story on another channel, with your competition, if you use me or the FBI this time." He stood and exited the apartment, jogging through the crisp air to his truck. On the way back home, he called Laurel.

"Hi, Huck," she said, her voice clear.

He pulled onto a main thoroughfare. "You sound wide awake."

"I am. More nightmares."

"About what?" He passed a slow-moving shipping truck.

She sighed. "I'm walking in a snowy field and people

I've helped to catch, all killers, are pelting me with frozen black dahlias. I can't get away. I'm sure it's because we're running in circles on this case. The symbols fit."

"Well, it's going to get worse." He updated her on Rachel and her attacker. "This time it isn't my fault."

"No, you're right." Laurel groaned. "If she goes public, that puts the spotlight on me. Not on the case or on the killer, but me. I'm the subject now."

"I couldn't stop her. Do you think that was the killer's goal? Are we closer to somebody than we think?" The move didn't make sense to him, but right now, he was just pissed. All over, from every direction, plain old pissed.

"It could be, or it could be something else." Clothing rustled. "I have a bad feeling I know what this is."

So did he. The hair on the back of his neck rose. "Tell me."

"I angered Abigail yesterday, and this is something she might do in retaliation. It screws up our case, puts you back into protector mode with your ex-fiancée, and shoots me into the limelight. All the actions of a narcissist who thinks she's been wronged."

Huck tilted his head. "I don't know. I do believe your sister could be dangerous, in the right circumstances, but this would be a huge risk. She's a successful professor and entrepreneur, and she wants a relationship with you. What if she got caught? Rachel does know some self-defense and could've gotten a chance to fight back but didn't. Somebody could've seen the attacker. The police are canvassing now and checking any CCTV from the area. This is too much of a risk for Abigail. Do you actually think she would've done something like this?"

"In a heartbeat."

* * *

Early in the morning, Laurel hurried to dress, connections building and breaking in her mind. It was possible the killer had attacked Rachel, or perhaps a nutso fan of hers wanted notoriety and thought a good way to get it was to bring up the current case. Or maybe Rachel was being deceitful, but Huck had seen the bruises. In addition, Laurel couldn't banish that last look on Abigail's face from her mind. Her expression had been both angry and calculating.

She carried her boots into the living room, where her phone rang. Seeing it was her mother, she accepted the video call. "How modern of you to use the video calling. How is the spa?"

"Wonderful." Deidre's eyes were tired but bright. She was knitting. "I had several of my women from the business come up yesterday. We performed the moon ceremony over the new tea, and I was so full of light that I didn't want to sleep. It's going to be a lovely healing gift for so many people." She squinted to see better through the phone. "Where are you going at this hour? It's early."

"I'm on a case." Laurel slipped on her boots.

"Laurel. Where are you going?"

Laurel straightened. "I have a lead and am checking it out. There's no danger. I promise." Even if Abigail had been the attacker, she wouldn't hurt Laurel. Not yet, anyway.

"This doesn't have anything to do with Abigail Caine, does it?"

Laurel jolted. "Why would you ask that?"

Deidre went back to her knitting. "She called my cell phone twice yesterday, offering a partnership in her marijuana growing operation. Says we'd make a fortune adding it to some of our teas. She's correct, but I am not working with that woman. I felt that she was just making herself known, trying to get my attention, since I've already refused her offers before."

"She does enjoy a good mind game," Laurel muttered. It would make sense that, if Abigail were Rachel's attacker, she'd want to be on everyone's mind. Even Laurel's mother.

But had it been Abigail?

"I have to go, Mom. Enjoy your spa appointments." She pulled on a thick parka. The clouds had moved on during the night, leaving the earth unprotected and freezing. "Try to get some sleep by taking a nap later today."

"I will. Be careful, honey." Her mom frowned and pushed several loud keys on her phone. Then the screen finally went blank.

Laurel stepped outside and ran to her SUV, then had to scrape a layer of ice off the windows. She used the drive to practice deep breathing so the oxygen flowed freely through her blood to her brain. Calm and rational thinking would keep her in control of the situation.

The lights were off at Abigail's. The sun was starting to rise over the mountains, but it was still dark. Laurel rang the bell several times, a sliver of impatience filtering through her calm.

Lights flickered on to illuminate the interior of the home. A minute later the door opened to a sleepy-looking Abigail dressed in a black nightie with matching silk robe. "Laurel? What the hell are you doing here?" She stepped back and pulled Laurel through. "What has happened? Are you all right?" She pushed her messy hair over her shoulder.

"I'm fine." Laurel looked down at Abigail's hands, hoping to see rope burn. No burns or bruises were visible. "Was it you?"

Abigail backed up, blinking sleep from her eyes. "Was what me?"

"I'm not playing around. If it was you, we're done. Not only are we done, but I'm going to spend every available second I have looking through CCTV, talking to neighbors, finding dog walkers and kids who'd snuck out of their homes, to catch you. You will regret this like nothing else in your entire life." Laurel let her voice rise.

Abigail took a step back. "Threatening me should be your very last resort, sister." Her eyes cleared and color slipped into her face. "I have no idea why you're here at this ungodly hour, but whatever you think I did, you're wrong."

Laurel looked over to the kitchen, where several bottles of wine stood in the sink. Empty bottles. There was also evidence of a steak dinner with two plates in the overlarge sink. "Did you have a party?"

"No." Abigail tightened her sash. "I think you should leave."

Something was off. Laurel raised her voice. "Hello? Who is here? Show yourself." Her gun was holstered at the back of her waist, and she unzipped her coat in case she needed to reach for it. "Now."

Movement came and a man wearing only a blanket wrapped around his hips stumbled out of the bedroom area. "What is going on?" he groused.

Laurel reared back. "Officer Zello?"

Frank Zello paused and then looked from one woman to the other. "Ah, crap." He scratched his neck and moved toward them, one hand keeping the blanket in place over his obviously nude body. "Hi, Agent Snow."

Laurel stared at him and then looked more closely at her sister. That was whisker burn on Abigail's chin. "Officer? Were you here all night?"

He yawned and then stretched, shaking his head as if to wake himself up. "Yes. Late dinner and then, ah, all night." His gaze moved to Abigail and warmed. "A wonderful night."

Laurel looked at the bottles. "Apparently you drank the wine cellar."

Abigail chuckled. "We did have a nice, intimate little party, didn't we, Frank?"

He grinned and then sobered upon catching Laurel's expression. "We did." He ground a palm into his left eye. "Too much of a party. My head is on fire."

"How did this situation come about?" Laurel asked.

Abigail shrugged. "The kind officer kept performing drive-bys of my house as part of my protection detail, and I invited him in for dinner. One thing led to another. Several anothers." Her chuckle was throaty.

Laurel turned to face the officer more fully. "Rachel Raprenzi was attacked last night."

His eyebrow lifted. "The woman from the podcast? That's too bad, but what does that have to do with us?"

"You drank a lot of wine. Can you verify that Abigail was with you all night?" Laurel asked.

His handlebar mustache twitched. "Of course. We were in bed all night."

"But you were out, right? Slept like a baby?" Laurel pressed.

"Not that out," he retorted, standing up straighter. "I'm a trained officer. If she'd left the bed, I would've known it. You can't honestly be saying that Abigail went and attacked some reporter. That's nuts."

Laurel rezipped her coat. "Very well. Officer Zello, please report to my office to be interviewed at nine AM this morning." At that time, she'd hit him with the fact that she knew he'd slept with Sharon Lamber. So far, she could connect him to all the victims except Christine Franklin, and she hadn't probed deeply yet.

Abigail opened the door, her full lips set in a smirk. "It's always a pleasure, sister."

Laurel left and arctic air froze her nose. As she was driving away, she called Huck and gave him an update.

"Well, that's good, right? Abigail has an alibi, so she wasn't the one who attacked Rachel."

Laurel slowed down as her SUV slid on the ice. "It isn't good. I have absolutely no doubt after seeing her this morning that Abigail was Rachel's attacker."

Without question.

# Chapter Thirty

Huck sucked down a quad-latte like it was water as he sat across from Officer Frank Zello in the dismal Fish and Wildlife interrogation room. It felt as if cold air actually swept across his feet, but he kept his expression as pissed off as he was feeling right now. "So let me get this straight. You're going the extra mile and driving by a possible victim's home, and then you end up getting drunk and engaging in sex with said victim?"

Zello sighed. "Yeah. Believe me, she didn't seem like a victim." He lifted his hands. "It's no defense, I know. But she asked me in, offered me wine, and then we started talking and really connected." His mustache was a distraction and his eyes were seriously bloodshot. Apparently he hadn't slept much. "One thing led to another, as you know, and I spent the night." He leaned forward, one large hand pressed against the table. "She's incredible. Brilliant and beautiful." His gaze moved to Laurel, who sat at Huck's right. "Stunning."

"Okay." Laurel wiped her hands up her face and dug her fingertips into her forehead. Then she sat back. "You're a trained officer. Give me a hypothetical of how she *could have* gotten out of the house to go attack Rachel without your knowing it."

He shook his head. "There's no way. We slept in the same bed, and I would've felt her move. Besides, she's not that kind of a person."

"What?" Laurel asked.

His shoulders hunched and he quickly shot them back. "Abigail is smart, sure. But she's also sweet and just wants a relationship with you. It hurts her that you won't give her a chance."

Huck swore—almost beneath his breath. "You're not thinking with the head on your shoulders."

Laurel visibly attempted to keep the interrogation on track. "You were drunk and passed out. It's okay to admit that."

"I'm also a cop and would've known if the woman in my arms left not only the bed but the house." His chin set at a stubborn angle. "She's right. I'm smart and am not reaching my full potential. I'd make an excellent investigator."

Abigail had apparently really gotten into the man's head. Based on the number of wine bottles Laurel had reported seeing, they'd been severely impaired. Or rather, he had been. But Abigail might've drugged him as well. Though Huck couldn't see any evidence of that in his face.

"Do we have your permission to have your blood tested?" Laurel asked.

The officer stilled and then clenched his teeth. "No."

"Why not?" Huck asked.

"Because we live in the United States, and I don't have to give my blood up to anybody," the officer snapped. "This is bullshit and I'm not playing along."

Huck kicked his chair back. "I don't give a shit if you've smoked pot, Officer. That's not what we're looking for in your blood."

"I don't care. It's my blood and you're totally off base even suspecting Abigail of something like this. I won't be a part of it." He stood.

Laurel's stunning eyes narrowed. "How long did your affair with Sharon Lamber last?"

Zello froze.

Huck motioned for him to retake his seat.

Zello sank back down, his shoulders lowering in defeat, his eyes weary. "It lasted for three weeks and was exciting. Then I discovered that she was married, although separated, and I ended it. When I did so, she laughed at me. Said that I was one of about twenty men she was experimenting with in the sack, boasted that she was in her sexual prime or whatever. I figured I got out in time and thanked the good Lord for that." He frowned. "How did you find out?"

"There are pictures," Huck drawled.

Zello's mouth dropped open. "Pictures of me sleeping with the mayor's sister-in-law?"

"Naked sex pictures," Huck affirmed.

Officer Zello dropped his chin to his chest. "I had no idea. She had a camera set up?"

Laurel cut Huck a look. "You didn't know?"

"Of course I didn't know," Zello snapped. "I don't want sex pictures of me out there. Someday I want to be sheriff and maybe even governor."

Huck coughed. "A charge of hindering an investigation would probably hurt your prospects." He let himself smile. "Or not. These days, in this political climate, who knows? Might help you get those jobs."

"I didn't say anything about Sharon because it's irrelevant to the case, and because I wanted to remain on the case." He tugged at the end of his handlebar mustache.

"Then I saw Abigail and wanted to be able to keep an eye on her. To have an excuse to see her." He shrugged.

Huck kept his bored facade in place. "Sounds like stalking to me. Agent Snow? Is that stalking?"

"That could be considered stalking," Laurel agreed. "Officer Zello, my concern is that you've engaged in sexual relations with two out of the victims of this serial killer. You're also the only person who ever took a police report from Charlene Rox. That leaves Dr. Christine Franklin. Right now, tell us of any connection you had with her. She was a cardiologist."

"I swear, I never met Dr. Franklin and had no connection to her." Zello lifted both hands in the air. "I will voluntarily compile a timeline of my movements for the last month, but it'll take me a little time to go through my calendar."

Huck winced. "I'm not sure we shouldn't book you right now."

"If that's what you want to do, then do it. I should've told you that I'd had a very brief relationship with Sharon Lamber, as did many other men, I believe. But that's all I've done wrong." Zello stood. "Now, I have to get to work. Also, you should watch the accusatory tone, Captain."

Huck's eyebrow lifted. "Excuse me?"

The officer looked from him to Laurel and then back. "I may have started a relationship with a woman on a killer's radar, but at least I'm not sleeping with my partner or the FBI agent in charge of the entire case. Talk about a conflict of interest."

Huck rolled to his feet, menace rushing through his blood.

Laurel stood. "All right. This interview is concluded. Until the case is over, stay away from Abigail, Officer Zello."

"I can't do that." His eyes softened. "She needs protection, and since you won't stay with her until this guy is caught, I will."

"I'm more than happy to put her in a safe house," Laurel countered.

Officer Zello snorted. "You can't cage a beautiful bird like Abigail. She needs to work every day and keep that mind of hers engaged, and I'm going to keep her body safe. It's the least I can do until this is over. But say the word and I'll step aside so you can stay with her. Protect her."

"I don't think that would be a good idea," Laurel said carefully. "I don't know you, and right now you've done nothing but make my job more difficult, but I feel that I should warn you. Abigail is manipulative and dangerous, and she's using you." The words weren't kind, but the motive behind them was honorable. "Be very careful with her, Officer."

He scoffed. "You truly don't know your sister, and that's a travesty, Agent Snow. You have no idea what kind of a brilliant and kind soul she is." He snapped to attention and exited the room.

"Wow," Huck said, exaggerating the word. "One night with Abigail Caine and he's ready to defend her to the death."

Laurel twirled her pencil with two fingers. "He's a good alibi for her last night when Rachel was attacked, and that's all she wants from him." She dropped back into her seat. "She might not have drugged him, and we don't have enough evidence to get a warrant for his blood."

Huck looked down at her. "You've changed your mind? It wasn't Abigail last night?"

"Oh, it was definitely Abigail. But she plied him with

bottles of wine, had sex with him, and then left. That man was out cold for several hours, whether his substantial ego will admit it or not." Laurel tightened her ponytail. "The mere fact that Abigail has an alibi proves to me that she did attack Rachel." There was no way Abigail would be interested in Frank Zello. He'd been too easy to manipulate. "She managed to convince him that she's a kindhearted damsel in distress."

Huck snorted and retook his seat. "Good point. Even so, are you still sure Abigail was the attacker?"

"Yes. Unfortunately." Laurel sat back and stared at the dismal wall. "Do you think it's telling that Officer Zello has had relations with Sharon and now Abigail?"

"Not really. Small town, few single people, he's good looking." Huck shook his head. "My gut says it isn't him. Besides, isn't one of our theories that the killer can't keep it up during the attack and then goes into a rage? Zello obviously can go the distance."

"It isn't the same. A psychopathic rage-driven killer like this one could possibly be married and have a normal life. It's in his fantasy life that he can't keep an erection." Laurel tossed her pencil into her laptop bag and shivered. "Also, Zello didn't know there was a camera capturing shots of them. The techs didn't find a camera, so either Sharon took it with her and we haven't found it, or the killer found it during one of his forays into her house. We need to locate it."

"True." Huck set his hands on his hips to ease the ache in his leg from an old bullet wound. "If Zello didn't know about the pictures, it's possible the other men didn't either. Including Davie."

Laurel nodded. "I know. I'm going to call and have Davie's mother come in and talk to me so I can at least keep her informed. Davie is old enough to consent in

Washington, but he didn't tell us about Sharon, and that's concerning. Maybe. He might be embarrassed. Either way, I'd like to get a read on his mother." Her voice softened. "I don't want Davie to be a suspect."

"Me either. He's just a kid." Huck partially turned toward her. "I'm starving. How about we grab some food? We can talk about the case while we eat a breakfast special at Joe's."

Laurel shifted on her chair. "I wouldn't mind eating and running through this case verbally. I feel like the killer is going to murder again soon."

"Me, too." The whole idea made Huck want to punch a wall.

Her phone rang and she dug it out of her laptop bag. "Hi, Nester. What do you have for us? You're on speaker."

"Hi, boss. Davie Tate lawyered up and has no intention of coming in for an interview unless you arrest him and place him in custody. That message is from his lawyer, one Steve Bearing."

Huck groaned.

Nester chuckled. "I took an earful, believe me. The other item I have for you is a good one. Not only am I printing out all the phone records you want after successfully gaining all necessary warrants, a certain Dr. Joseph Keyes is back in the office today. I have a unit outside the hospital if you want them to go in and secure him."

"Yes," Laurel said. "My patience has ended with the doctor. Have the state police bring him in." She ended the call and looked up to Huck's face. "We have about an hour for breakfast before Dr. Keyes arrives. I need more coffee."

# Chapter Thirty-One

Dr. Keyes managed to put up enough of a stink that he didn't arrive at Laurel's office until early afternoon, accompanied by his attorney. The doctor was in his mid-forties with blondish-gray hair, understanding blue eyes, and a square jaw. He wore a button-down shirt and slacks with a Rolex on one wrist. Laurel measured him to be around six feet tall and two hundred pounds with a lithe physique.

The lawyer appeared to be a decade older with pure gray hair, steel blue eyes, and a five-thousand-dollar suit.

Laurel sat across from the doctor while Huck sat across from the lawyer, file folders in front of them. The two men eyed each other like adversaries in a boxing match, while Dr. Keyes kept his gaze on Laurel.

"Thank you for coming in to speak with us today," Laurel said.

The doctor's smile held amusement. "The state police didn't give me much of a choice." He settled more comfortably in his chair. "Although, now I'm here, I can say that I'm happy about that. I know this is business, but I have to say that you're the most intriguing-looking woman I've ever seen. A heterochromia in already heterochromatic eyes is rare to a degree I'm afraid I can't quantify." He leaned closer, his gaze seeking. "Both the blue and the green shades have an intensity that's rare in and of themselves. Just lovely."

"That's kind of you to say." Laurel waited to see what he'd say next.

"And your hair color. I've never seen any shade like it. Not red, not black, not brown . . ." He palmed the table. "Beautiful."

She smiled and let him continue trying to impress her. "That's kind of you. Most people think I'm strange."

The left side of his mouth lifted. "Not strange. No. Strong. Beauty is power; a smile is its sword."

"John Ray," she murmured.

He sat back, surprise lighting his eyes. "Yes. John Ray. You've read him?"

"Yes."

"I haven't," Huck said. "I doubt he applies to this case."

Dr. Keyes barely cast Huck a glance. "He was an English naturalist who spoke wisdom three hundred years ago. There aren't many FBI agents, I dare say, who would've recognized his words."

"Agent Snow is a unicorn," Huck said dryly. "How about we return to this century and you tell us where you've been the last couple of days, Dr. Keyes." It wasn't posed as a question.

The doctor's gaze wandered over Laurel's face. "I was at my cabin taking some time for myself. Life has been difficult lately."

"Because Sharon Lamber dumped you?" Huck asked. "Or because she was brutally murdered?"

"Both." The doctor clucked his tongue. He shrugged, looking charming again. "I cared very much for her, but I do understand her desire to give her marriage another try. The rejection hurt more than I expected, and then she was killed.

Needless to say, I was having trouble concentrating at work, so I headed up to my cabin to gather my thoughts and read." He leaned forward. "Some Orwell, some Kierkegaard, and some Steve Berry."

Huck drew a photograph from his file folder. "Did you know Sharon set up a camera in her bedroom?"

Dr. Keyes jerked and looked down at the picture that showed the two of them engaged in sex. "Holy— No." He looked closer. "Where was the camera?"

"Based on the angle, it was located in the small book-case by the door," Laurel said, picturing the room in her mind. "It wasn't present when we searched. Do you have any idea where it might be?"

"No." He pushed the picture away. "I'd really appreciate it if you didn't let these get out. How unseemly." Then he turned to his lawyer. "Can we get all of those?"

"No," Huck answered for the man. "Not during an active investigation. Did you know that Sharon was having relations with multiple men?"

The doctor sighed. "No, but it doesn't surprise me. She was carefree and curious, and she had an abundance of energy and life inside her. I don't think she ever meant to settle down with anybody, even her husband." He looked again at Laurel. "I considered her unique. Now I can see that I was wrong."

Laurel didn't smile this time. It was time to change tactics. "I think she rejected you and that infuriated you. That you became almost as angry as you were when Christine Franklin stole the job you wanted."

He reared back at the attack. "I was happy for Christine."

"So she's smarter than you? Or just a better leader?" Laurel pressed.

His smile was slow. "She's neither, but what are you

going to do? She's a woman, and the hospital needed one in a leadership role. Sometimes life is that simple."

"Do you have a problem with women in leadership roles?" Laurel asked.

Huck snickered, playing along. "Does that turn you soft, doc?"

The lawyer slapped his hand on the table. "We're here voluntarily. Insult my client again, and we leave."

Laurel pressed on. "So far, I have three dead in my case. You screwed one of them, and one of them screwed you over. Another, Dr. Charlene Rox, had privileges at your hospital, so no doubt you knew her." She leaned toward him then, giving him the full force of the dual-colored eyes he found so fascinating. "Those three dead women share one basic commonality. You."

"Can anybody verify you were at your cabin these last few days?" Huck asked.

"No." The doctor didn't look away from Laurel. "I was mourning in solitude. Didn't even take my phone."

Laurel tapped her fingers in a pattern on the glass top. "That's odd, isn't it? For anybody to leave their phone behind?"

"Not if one truly wants to unplug. You should try it, Agent Snow. My cabin is yours any time." He rattled off the address. "I'm sure you're already looking through my property records. You won't find the cabin listed. The property was actually owned by my deceased aunt, and she left it to me in her will. I haven't had time to record the deed."

That was possible. "Do you know a Dr. Abigail Caine? She's a professor."

"I'm sorry, but I do not." The doctor glanced at his

watch. "I need to be getting back to prepare for surgeries tomorrow."

"Are you familiar with Davie Tate or Tommy Bearing?" Huck asked.

The doctor paused. "No to Tate, but I have met the mayor's son. I had a patient named Harvey with a heart condition, and the Bearing kid drove him in for appointments once in a while. Seemed like a nice kid who worked for Harvey."

Laurel tapped her fingers on the table. "You also treated Mayor Bearing, correct?"

Keyes smiled. "I can't discuss living patients with you, Agent Snow. Confidentiality rules apply, as you know."

"The mayor already confirmed this to us," Laurel said, waving the thought away. "Yet I don't want to know about him. I just want to know if his son, Tommy, ever accompanied him to his appointments with you. Hypothetically, of course."

"No, he did not." Keyes winked. "Hypothetically."

"Thank you," Laurel said. "I do need to ask you about the sexual harassment case you settled with your house-keeper."

Keyes sighed. "She wanted money. There was no harassment, and a criminal case was dismissed. I gave her some money to go away, and it was a lot less than I would've spent in a lawsuit."

"It was a nuisance payment," the lawyer said smoothly.

That was entirely possible. "How much?" Huck asked.

The lawyer smiled. "That's confidential."

The doctor stood and his lawyer did the same. "Laurel, call me any time. I would very much like to help you find Sharon's killer." He walked out the door with his lawyer following him.

Huck watched them go. "What an ass."

Laurel's brain felt as if had been glued to her skull in a headache of decent proportions. "We have too many suspects."

"All right. Here's the deal. It has been hours since breakfast. Let's go by the hospital to visit Walter and then grab dinner at Raspy's. Their Friday night special usually involves prime rib, and I'm hungry. We can bring notepads and create a mobile murder board with lines and connections and questions. Deal?"

She reached for a couple of legal pads at the end of the table. "Deal. I would like to see Walter." Plus, prime rib sounded good. She was missing a puzzle piece, something just out of her reach. Hopefully they could find it tonight.

After a dinner with too much cheesecake for dessert, Laurel sat back in Huck's truck with the notepads held against her chest. "We didn't narrow the suspect list."

"We will." He glanced her way as he drove through the fat snowflakes dropping on the windshield. Clouds covered the moon, and the night was quiet on the old country road that led away from the long-standing restaurant. They'd closed the place down, working diligently on their notes. "We just have to find him before he takes another woman."

Several rapid shots boomed through the night. Bullets flew through the glass, and Huck jerked back with a pained snarl. A second later, the truck pitched and flew up into the air, hitting an embankment and rolling onto its top. Laurel's seatbelt snapped tight against her chest, and her breath whooshed out of her lungs. Pain seared through her right arm and she cried out, hanging upside down in the hissing metal. Huck smashed into the side of the vehicle and then fell onto the interior of the roof. Metal crunched with the impact.

Then silence.

She blinked. Her mind spun and her stomach ached. Her ribs felt like a hot poker was wedged between them. "Huck?"

No sound came from the downed officer.

More bullets hit the truck in rapid succession.

"Huck!" She released her seatbelt and fell to the crumpled roof, her left hand catching her so she could flip around to her knees. Another volley attacked the truck, and she covered Huck's prone body while reaching for her gun in the laptop bag. Her right arm ached and her fingers wouldn't curl. When the volley stopped, she held her breath and bent down, the gun in her left hand. She was ambidextrous but definitely better with her right hand.

A figure stalked down the vacant road toward them, gun out, moving quickly and barely visible in the darkness.

She lifted her left hand, aimed, and squeezed off several shots through the already damaged windshield. The glass cracked loudly and her ears screamed in pain.

The figure dropped to the ground and fired back.

She crouched to cover Huck and scrambled in her coat pocket for her phone to dial 911.

"911—"

"Officer down on Hourglass Road about five miles from Raspy's Restaurant," she yelled, her voice already hoarse. "Active shooter, FBI agent engaged. Send backup."

When the firing stopped, she peered into the darkness but couldn't see the attacker. He must've been reloading. This was her only chance.

Grunting, she put her back to the seat and kicked the windshield in rapid succession, aiming for the side that was already damaged. It cracked again and fell. Holding her weapon, she rolled out, feeling glass cut into her neck. Then she angled around the truck, staying low, sinking to her thighs in the snow.

Her heart thundered in her head and her lungs seized, but she kept one hand steady on the gun. She took several deep breaths of the glacial air to clear her mind and tried to push the pain away for now.

The shooter stood and fired again.

She ducked to the side, rolled in the snow, and came up shooting at his former position.

He leaped behind a snowbank.

She inched to the front of the truck, searching in the darkness. Slowly, she crept forward, her gun at the ready.

No movement. Then the sound of a branch snapping beyond the snowbank. She raced toward the road, sinking into the thick snow, keeping low and ready to fire. She reached the road and slid to the middle, pointing her weapon at where the shooter had stood. A truck roared to life beyond the trees on the other side, and snow fell off the branches. The vehicle zoomed away down a side road.

Damn it.

The cold had her shaking but she didn't feel it thanks to the adrenaline flooding her system. Wiping blood off her forehead, she turned back and shoved through the heavy snow as fast as she could to the overturned truck. "Huck?" She bent down, trying to avoid the snowy glass. "Huck?"

He lay motionless on the roof, his neck bent at an unnatural angle. Blood covered the side of his face, and his eyes remained closed. Was he breathing?

Panic pushed away the cloudiness in her head.

Sirens trilled in the distance.

She bent to avoid shards of glass and moved back inside the truck, feeling for the pulse at his wrist with her good hand. "Huck?"

# Chapter Thirty-Two

Huck couldn't reach the surface. Ice and water trapped him, sucking the life from him. His lungs compressed, desperate for air. He came to with a gasp, sitting up and punching out. His fist connected with a hand. The echo of the slap penetrated his panicked brain, and he started to fight in earnest.

"Dude. Stop," a male voice said as strong hands grabbed his shoulders and shoved him down.

Down. Back into the water. He couldn't go. With a roar, he struck out, ready to tear the world apart.

"Huck." A soft voice. One he knew. "Stop it."

He stopped. Slowly, he opened his eyes, his breathing ragged. Pain scissored into his brain with sharp blades and he winced, closing his eyes. "Laurel?"

"Yes. I'm here." She placed her hand on his neck, and her skin was freezing. "You're okay. We're in an ambulance."

More slowly this time, he opened his eyes to see the metal roof.

"Hi there." A man leaned over him and looked into his eyes. "How's the head?"

"Bert?" Huck tried to clear the cobwebs from his brain. So many webs. "What happened?"

Bert settled a blanket more securely around him. The burly paramedic was around sixty and built solid, but his touch was gentle. "Just take a deep breath and hold on. You took a bullet to the head."

Huck jerked when the ambulance jolted over a pothole. How fast were they driving? "I was shot in the head?"

Laurel leaned over him, blood on her forehead. She rocked with the movement of the vehicle. "No. Bert, please be serious. Huck, it looks like a bullet hit metal, and a piece of metal ricocheted to your temple. You bled pretty badly, but there's no hole. Only a scrape and some metal imbedded in your skin. The doctor will have to remove it." Her face was tight with pain.

"What's wrong?" He tried to sit up, but Bert shoved him back down.

"I may have fractured my wrist." She held her right arm bent at an angle against her chest.

He tried to sit again. "Then you should lie down. Come here. I'll take the seat." Why was everything so damn fuzzy? "Where's Aeneas?"

Her forehead wrinkled. "You left him with Monty when we went to dinner. I just called, and Monty is going to stay with the dog if you need to remain overnight in the hospital."

"I am not staying the night in the hospital." Not from a freakin' piece of metal. His brain felt like it was wrapped in cotton. "Wait a minute. Did you say a bullet?"

"Yes. We were ambushed about five miles from the restaurant." She leaned her head back against the side of the ambulance and closed her eyes. "One shooter who traversed quickly in the darkness. I couldn't discern size or facial features, but I swear it was a man. He wore all black, and I think he wore a mask. I returned fire and pursued him until I heard a truck take off, but then I needed to see if you required medical assistance from me before the ambulance arrived."

Hold it. She'd been in a firefight while he'd been out cold? "Are you all right?"

"Yes."

They lurched to a stop. Front doors slammed and then the back doors opened. Two paramedics pulled his stretcher out, even though he kept trying to sit up. "Stay down, Huck," Bert muttered. "Just until we get you and Agent Snow inside."

"Laurel?" He tried to turn his head to see her.

"My vitals are good." She walked next to him, her face pale.

Then everything went fuzzy again. He must have passed out, because when he came to, he was in a hospital bed with Laurel sleeping on a chair next to him. Her wrist was in a blue cast and tucked into a sling attached around her neck, and her mouth was parted slightly as she slept. He blinked several times, noting the sound of his heart beating loudly via a monitor above his head.

Frowning, he yanked the leads off his chest.

"Stop that," a woman said.

He jerked and turned to the other side of the bed, where Deidre Snow sat, knitting something yellow. Some sort of hat. "Sorry." He paused. "Wait a minute. What is going on?"

A nurse bustled into the room, her gray hair streaked with green and piled atop her head. She appeared to be about sixty and had wide shoulders. "You did not pull that off your chest."

"I did." He struggled to sit.

"Here." Deidre pushed a button on a large controller

hanging from the metal bed rail, and the head of the bed lifted. "I came back from my spa vacation early, so the least you can do is listen to the nurse." Her tone was more gentle than authoritative.

He settled, noting his chest was bare. "Thank you."

Laurel didn't move. She was really out.

Huck stretched his arms and legs and then spread out his hands. "She should go sleep at home."

"She wouldn't leave you until you awoke," Deidre whispered, her eyes veiled.

His head felt like he'd taken a bowling ball to the skull, and his mouth was drier than his old man's sense of humor had been. Gingerly, he reached up and touched a bandage on his temple.

The nurse gently moved his hand away. "Be careful with that."

He glared at her.

The sound of tennis shoes on tile squeaked outside and then a man strode in. The guy wore a green velour leisure sweat suit beneath an unbuttoned white lab coat, had to be about ninety years old, and carried a tablet in his hands. "It's about time you woke up. I'm Dr. Snoggles, and you're keeping me up."

Huck blinked. Once and then again. "Is this a joke?"

"No." The doctor lifted two fingers. "Follow my hand." He performed several tests and checked Huck's memory, which was fine up until the time his truck had flipped over. "The MRI ruled out other potential injuries, but you most certainly have a concussion. I want to keep you for a day or so to watch you."

"No." Huck would leave now, but he didn't want to wake Laurel.

She stirred anyway, her eyes opening sleepily. "Hi. You're conscious."

"Yeah." He looked at her cast. "How bad?"

"It's a distal radial fracture." She looked down at her arm. "I'm on pain medication and rather enjoy the sensations."

Deidre chuckled. "Good to hear."

"It's a Colles fracture," Laurel said. "I'll have to wear the cast for approximately six weeks."

His head still ached hollowly. "How did you return fire?"

"I'm ambidextrous but just discovered that I need additional practice with my left hand," she said drowsily.

Deidre stood. "All right. Captain Rivers woke up just fine, and now you're coming home with me. It's time to get some rest."

Laurel yawned and stood, her laptop bag falling to the side. "I'll retrieve you when you're discharged tomorrow morning, and we can spend the weekend reading through the phone records of pretty much everybody possibly involved in this case."

The doctor finished making a notation on his tablet. "If you leave tomorrow morning, I'm dismissing you without medical consent."

"That's fine." Huck wasn't staying longer than that.

The doctor shrugged very thin shoulders and walked out of the room, followed by the nurse and Deidre.

"Laurel?" Huck said.

She paused at the doorway and turned, her hair a wild reddish brown. "Yes?"

"Thank you."

Fury felt like needles being jabbed in his balls. He'd made the perfect plan to take out the cop and that bitch FBI agent. He'd followed them to the restaurant and then had found the exact place to wait. So many nights he'd practiced his shooting, and it should've taken only two bullets. But it was harder to shoot at a moving truck than he would've thought.

He jogged through the night, snow falling on him, his breath puffing into the cold air.

The stupid bitch had shot him. He'd had to sew up his own damn arm, and it hurt. Right above the elbow. Sure, she'd just grazed him. Anybody who was a halfway decent shot would've got his head. Of course, she had been falling in the snow.

He needed them dead. They were getting too close, and he couldn't let them stop him from finding the one. The real one.

Keeping his head down, he ran beneath streetlights gathering snow. To anybody watching or any cameras, he would be just a blur. He was careful and smarter than them all.

He had wanted to spend more time with this one, following her, learning everything about her. But he had to try now. Had to be whole. She was calling to him. Hadn't she smiled at him just the other day?

It was true.

He climbed the fence around the subdivision, his pack safely over one shoulder. The one that didn't hurt right now. The stitches in his elbow made his entire left arm ache.

Oh, he'd love to make that FBI agent pay. Maybe he would.

He kept to the tree line and the shadows, finding her house. The woman who was waiting for him so patiently. He paused, listening for any life in the freezing night. There was none. Ducking to make himself smaller, he ran across the road to the side of her house, leaping over her small fence to the backyard, where trees hid him from the neighbors.

Then he took his time, still angry but now beginning to become excited. The sweet thrill of anticipation tasted like sugar on his tongue. He angled toward the back deck and a window that opened to a storage room in the basement. One she apparently never checked. It was unlocked, just like the last time he'd explored her home.

He nudged it open and went in headfirst, just for the challenge. Even with one arm hurting like a sore tooth, he walked his hands down the concrete wall, one by one, until he reached the floor, doing a perfect handstand, even with his injury. Then he flipped over, his boots landing a little too loudly. He stopped cold, listening.

Nothing.

Good.

Adjusting his pack, he strode past boxes of holiday decorations and opened the door, seeing only darkness. He'd memorized the layout of the home but still moved slowly, just in case she'd rearranged the furniture.

It was all the same as last time, when he'd taken a necklace and a pair of her panties. A pretty pair with pink flowers on them.

He moved around stacked lawn furniture to the stairs leading up from the basement and took them two at a time, putting his feet where they wouldn't make a sound. It had taken him a long time to memorize those stairs a week ago, but it was worth it. He emerged into the kitchen, where a small light over the sink illuminated the area.

An open bottle of wine sat about half full on the counter next to an empty wine glass with residue in the bottom. His mouth watered, but he wouldn't take a drink. He was much too smart to leave his DNA. These gloves were new and wouldn't leave a clue as to his identity.

He took a moment to enjoy being in her space without her knowing. There was so much power in the secrets he held. The kitchen smelled like something spicy with a hint of garlic. He frowned. Garlic stank.

Hopefully she slept in the nude. It was so much more fun to drag them out into the snow if they were already naked. It had to happen in the snow.

He crept past the kitchen to the master bedroom, where he could hear her lightly snoring. A small fan on her bed table created white noise by her head, turned toward the window. She slept on her side, her hair messy around her face. For a while, maybe too long, he watched her sleep. Watched her eyes flicker behind her eyelids.

All prey had instincts.

She frowned in her sleep and her feet moved beneath the covers. Then she slowly opened her eyes.

He struck, covering her mouth with his gloved hand.

Nobody heard her scream.

# Chapter Thirty-Three

Laurel hesitated and then stopped inside Walter's hospital room. "Hi."

He was sitting up with tubes crisscrossing all over his body and liquids dripping into a port at his vein. A nasal canula was strung over his ears, and his coloring was that of just-laid cement. "Hi." His hair was mussed and his breathing labored. "I'm so sorry, Laurel."

She put the plant her mother had insisted she bring on the counter. "Just get better. None of this is your fault." It was the killer's fault, and she'd find him.

"What happened to your arm?" Walter's hands trembled on the blanket covering most of his body.

"Colles fracture." At his frown, she moved closer to the bed. "Broken wrist. Huck and I were shot at last night and the truck flipped over." She wanted to look at her phone to see if the lab had any results, but good manners dictated she concentrate on Walter. "The doctor said you're going to be all right."

"Yeah. This is a wakeup call." Walter looked down at his bulging belly. "If I'd been in decent shape—"

Laurel reached for his wrist, patting it. "You still would've been shot three times. This could've happened to any of us." She lowered her head, surprised by how painful it was to stretch her neck. She'd been ignoring her health as well. "I failed to predict how desperate this guy was to shoot an FBI agent and kidnap a suspect from her home in the middle of the day, even with an FBI agent covering her." Christine's kidnapping and murder was on Laurel.

Walter snorted. "Profiling isn't psychic knowledge. This was out of character for the guy, as far as we knew." He wiggled on the bed and then groaned, all the color leeching from his face. "Everything still hurts." Then his gaze caught on her cast again. "You think it was the same guy?"

"We should know shortly," she said. "The techs were able to retrieve several bullets from the truck, and we have the ones removed from your body, so they're making a comparison." She was certain it was the same guy. "He's already proven that shooting people is acceptable to him."

"You think it's a new part of his MO? Using a gun?"

Laurel paused, remembering his movements toward her as he fired. "No. I think we're in the way of what he wants, of what he needs, and it's that simple. We're obstacles that have to be removed and shooting us is the easiest way to do it." She couldn't see the killer gaining any satisfaction or fulfilling his psychotic needs with a gun. The kills had been personal to him. The shootings weren't.

Walter swallowed. "Maybe he's after you now. You fit the profile."

"He hasn't left me any gifts or threats." Well, except for shooting at her, but that wasn't the same. "But you bring up a good point. Why am I not on his radar?" She was professional, had several PhDs, and looked eerily similar to Abigail. Her mind spun with this new puzzle. "Thanks, Walter. I'll check on you when I head home today."

She patted him again and walked out of the room, striding toward Huck's hospital room.

He was already standing in the doorway, filling out a pair of navy blue scrubs. A bandage covered his left temple. "My clothes were ruined." He'd showered, and his unruly hair curled beneath his ears. "The doc released me. Let's get out of here. That nurse keeps coming by to do more tests, and I swear, if I snarl at her again, she's going to order a colonoscopy."

Laurel shook her head. "Then stop snarling at her."

His eyes were a sleepy brown in the morning light. "I can't help it. She keeps trying to poke and prod at me. I think she *likes* it." Was that a glimmer of fear in his expression?

Laurel chuckled and moved back into the hallway. "Fine. I'll take point."

"Good. I expect you to jump her if she makes a move toward me again." He was so close she could feel his breath on her neck.

They safely reached the outside, where the sky was gray and the wind alive after being calm for so long. It slapped them, pushing Laurel back a step. At least it wasn't snowing. They fought the wind to reach the vehicle. "How are you feeling?" she asked.

"Great." He opened the passenger-side door and settled himself in the seat.

She slid behind the wheel and started the engine, hoping the heat would come on quickly. "Great?"

"No. My head hurts and I have a bruise in the shape of Texas on my hip." He sighed and kicked his boots out. "But at least I'm out of there. Where's my dog?"

"Monty said he'd bring Aeneas to the office, but then he's returning home to rest since it's Saturday." She pointed to the back seat. "Your gun, wallet, phone, and coat are in the bag. Officer Zello brought them to the office this morning and said the scene had been processed. He had your truck towed to Zac's Garage but said it looked like it might be totaled."

"Zello? Should he still be on duty?"

Laurel sped up where the road had been partially cleared by a snowplow. "I don't know. He's a good officer, but he did withhold information."

"He's also a suspect."

True. But it was easier to keep an eye on him while he was working. She looked over at Huck. He was pale, but his breathing was normal. "Do you want to swing by and get Aeneas and then have me take you home?"

"No. I want to work this case." He looked out at the misty day. "Why were you at the office so early?"

"I thought I'd start going through the phone records. But then my boss called and I had to update him, and Officer Zello came by to give me your belongings, and then it was time to pick you up."

"Let's go see the records, then."

Laurel's phone rang and she pressed a button on the dash. "Snow."

"Hi. It's Monty. Is Huck with you?" The captain coughed wildly. "Sorry."

"Yes. I thought you were going home to rest?" she asked.

He coughed more. "I will when you get here. We have another body."

Laurel drove into the subdivision with its mature trees and worn wooden fence, winding around to see the emergency vehicles, lights still on, parked by the middle home in a cul-de-sac. The houses in Bluebonnet Field were seventies style, some eighties, but well kept up. They appeared to be located on one-third acres, so there were houses flanking the one with all the activity.

She parked behind a Fish and Wildlife truck and stepped into the cold, skirting a police car to reach the front lawn. The sight in front of her pierced her chest with icy fingers.

"Damn." Huck pulled on his coat over the scrubs, his gaze on the dead woman. Aeneas bounded up, and Huck snapped his fingers. The dog immediately dropped to a sit, his head high and his gaze on his master.

Monty loped more slowly toward them as local officers secured the scene with crime tape that flapped crazily in the wind. "State crime scene techs are already here processing inside the house."

Laurel stood on the sidewalk and squinted to better see the woman. Like all the others, she lay on her back in the snow, her hands removed. Bones poked out of her face, which had been beaten to the point that very little structure remained. Even an eyeball appeared to have dropped next to what used to be her neck. "His rage was amped up many degrees this time. Most likely because he failed to kill us."

Huck's jaw hardened. "There aren't as many flowers around her."

"No. The other scenes held between thirty and forty with an average of thirty-three," she murmured. "There are only twenty here." They were buried beneath an inch of snow, their petals frozen and eerily dark.

"Maybe he's running out," Monty said, turning and coughing.

"Or he's keeping more for his next victim." Laurel looked around. "There's not enough blood here. Was she killed inside?"

Monty shook his head. "No. She was killed in the

backyard, which is hidden from the neighbors by tall trees. The techs are processing now. Want to go back there?"

"After they're finished," Laurel said.

"There are signs of a fight in the master bedroom, and it looks like he went in a basement window. No security system, and so far, none of the gawking neighbors have come forward with any information," Monty said grimly, visibly shaking with cold.

Huck planted a hand on one of his shoulders. "Thanks for this, Monty. I've got it from here."

Laurel nodded. The man needed rest and warmth, not death and arctic air. "We'll call you later with updates."

Officer Zello jogged up, his mustache white with frost. "Morning."

Huck lowered his chin.

Laurel studied the officer, watching for any nuance that could tell her what he was thinking. She didn't have honed instincts or gut reactions to people, but she spent time every chance she found memorizing facial and body-expression studies. "Who was she?"

He flipped open his notebook. "Driver's license inside the purse by the doorway says she's Eleanor Bove with this address as her physical one." He kept reading. "I did a quick look online on my phone and found the same woman, similar picture, listed as the owner of Dr. Bove Dentistry." He looked over his shoulder at the body. "The body is correct height and weight to be Dr. Bove, but we'll need DNA to be positive. Can't tell a thing from her face." Regret seemed to fill his voice. Or was it sorrow? She couldn't get the vibrations of people's emotions that her mother said were possible.

Huck scrubbed a bruised hand through his messy hair. "Why wasn't she on our radar? Did you check police reports?"

Officer Zello nodded. "Yeah. There's nothing on the local or state level."

"Nothing on the federal, either," Laurel murmured. She would've been instantly informed. "So the woman wasn't being stalked?" The deviation from the killer's pattern disturbed her. Or had Dr. Bove just not reported any incidences?

Huck shrugged. "I'll be back." He put an arm over Monty's shoulders and all but forced the captain to a Fish and Wildlife rig, where he ordered an officer to take Monty home. Aeneas remained in place, watching them go.

Officer Zello cleared his throat. "Agent Snow? Your sister said she was busy last night and that she'd call me, but she hasn't. Is that normal or is it the brushoff?" He shuffled his feet.

"My educated guess? She's brushing you off," Laurel said honestly. Abigail used people, and the officer was no longer of use to her.

"Hey. Hey. Let me through," a man bellowed.

Laurel turned to see a round-faced thirty-something man in jeans and a sweater, no coat, trying to shove his way past two officers. His glasses were fogged from the steam of his breath. She turned and strode toward him while Huck approached from the other direction. "Who are you?"

He fought uselessly against the burly officers. "Let me in. That's my wife. Or ex-wife. Whatever. Is it Ellie? What happened? Let go of me." His thin face turned red.

"Stop for a second." Laurel held up a hand and waited until he'd given up fighting and just stood there, panting. "Who are you?"

"I'm Jay Martin. I live just around the corner and woke up to see the police lights out my back window. What happened? Is Ellie okay?" He craned his neck and then went stark white as he apparently spotted the body. "Oh God. Tell me that's not Ellie."

Huck pivoted to block his view. "We don't have an identity yet. But tell us about Ellie."

Jay clamped his hands to his thighs and partially bent over, gasping for air.

Laurel waited until he'd stood, his chest still wheezing. "Mr. Martin, we need help. You said Eleanor was your ex-wife?"

"Yes." Tears gathered in his eyes. "We divorced a year ago because I made a mistake." He gagged. "Had an affair with the gal at the coffee stand on Fourth—it didn't mean anything. She made me feel smart, you know?" He kicked a chunk of ice.

"What do you do?" Laurel asked.

He flushed. "I'm in construction, but I'm between jobs right now."

"I see." Laurel took in his body language. He was embarrassed about that? Was he furious with women who were more successful than he? "Was there any sign your ex-wife was being stalked?"

His eyes widened. "You think that was it?"

"What was it?" Huck interjected.

Jay shuddered. "Somebody left flowers on her porch, and it creeped her out. She thought it was me trying to get back together with her, and she didn't believe me when I said I didn't do it. I did want to get back together but leaving flowers wouldn't impress her." He frowned. "She also kept getting flat tires. Just one at a time. Oh, and she accused me of breaking into the house and doing something with her underwear." He gulped. "Like I'd do that. She was stressed out at her practice, and I figured she was just being dramatic." He looked past Huck to the body. "God, was I wrong." Then he turned and vomited all over his boots.

# Chapter Thirty-Four

Back at the office, Laurel exited her SUV and headed toward the door, jumping when Huck followed closely behind her. Frowning, she moved for the door and opened it with the hulking officer's minty breath stirring her hair. In the vestibule, she stopped and turned to face him. "What are you doing?"

His expression smoothed out. "Nothing. Why?"

She looked beyond him to the parking lot and then back. "You were making yourself big and covering my back."

He didn't respond.

She tilted her head. "You were covering me. Somebody out there has shot at us once, and you were covering me with your body."

Again, no answer.

"Why, Huck?" Snow dripped from her boots onto the tile.

He looked away and then back. "All right. If you're asking if I'm covering your back because you're my partner, the answer is yes. If you're asking if I'm covering your back because you're a woman and half my size, regardless of your job, the answer is yes. And if you're asking if I'm covering your back because I've slept with you, the answer is most emphatically, yes." He rolled his shoulders in a tough guy shrug. "Even if that makes you mad."

Warmth slid through her torso. "Thank you."

His eyebrows lifted. "For covering you?"

"No. For explaining." Life was so much easier when people just told the truth.

"Uh. You're not mad?"

She shrugged. "I know who you are and wouldn't expect you to be anybody else. You're a man who'd protect a woman for all of those reasons, and that's about you, not me. I don't take it as an insult that you don't think I can protect myself as an FBI agent. That instinct is fundamentally who you are, and I'm well aware of what motivates you."

His chin dropped. "Some women would be angry, others would think I'm sweet." He grinned. "I like the way *you* think."

"That's probably a good thing." She didn't know how to think any different. "And you are sweet." She opened the door that led to her office. "Would you like to protect me as I ascend the stairs, or are we good?"

"I also like your sense of humor," he drawled. "It's always unexpected."

She partially turned. "The best humor is."

He snorted. "All right. I'm going to check out my offices and see who's in working on a Saturday and what we have on the books, and then I'll come upstairs and work with you. Deal?"

"That sounds like a good plan." She turned and walked up the stairs, feeling lighter for some reason. Nobody thought she was funny. Except Huck.

Dr. Joseph Keyes was waiting at the top of the stairs, leaning against the display case. He straightened and drew a bouquet of flowers from behind his back.

She stilled and then took inventory of the floor.

Nester poked his head through the doorway. "You have a visitor. He asked to wait in your office, and I said no."

"Thank you," Laurel said, noting that Nester was wearing his gun in a shoulder holster. Was he at the ready because of the shooting the night before, or did he have a dislike for the doctor? "What can I do for you, Dr. Keyes?"

Nester didn't show any sign of leaving but instead stood in the doorway, watching the doctor.

The doctor cleared his throat. "I would like a chance to speak with you alone."

"Why?" Laurel asked.

He rounded his back slightly, lowering his chin much like a challenged gorilla. Apparently the doctor wasn't accustomed to people questioning him. "I know this is awkward, but I was hoping to ask you out." He held out the flowers, which looked like a variety of daisies in plastic paper. From the grocery store?

"No, I don't think so." There were kinder words to use, but she wasn't up to par. Her wrist hurt and the case was not coming together as she'd hoped.

Nester cleared his throat. "We executed a warrant, and your credit card receipts came through this morning, Dr. Keyes. I'm confused why you didn't tell the FBI that you had an alibi for the murder of Christine Franklin."

Dr. Keyes turned the color of a fresh burn. "I . . . for goodness sake."

"What is the alibi?" Laurel asked.

"It isn't what you think," the doctor protested, pulling the flowers back toward his chest.

Laurel nodded for Nester to continue.

"The good doctor spent about ten thousand dollars in the last few days with the North Side Escort service. Man, you must be taking some serious pills." Nester shook his head.

"It's not true—" the doctor protested.

Laurel held up a hand. "It's a crime to lie to the FBI. Just tell me the truth so I can cross you off my list of suspects." The blowhard had seemed like a possible suspect, but she didn't see him wanting to have sex in the snow. A hot tub maybe, but not the freezing snow.

"Fine. I like Candy and Strawberry, and sometimes both at the same time." His eyes sharpened. "They're from a reputable company and they like me, too. So I have an alibi and we can move on from there." He thrust the flowers toward her, and Nester moved out from the doorway.

What was it about men trying to protect her all of a sudden? "As an agent investigating you, I can't accept such a gift." She strode toward the door. "Nester will take the information about Candy and Strawberry, and then we'll follow up with the two ladies." She paused, her mind severing certain connections. "You mentioned before that you'd met Tommy Bearing when he brought in Mr. Brewerston for appointments. Are you sure you have never met a kid named Davie Tate?"

"I don't remember the name," the doctor said, looking at his rapidly wilting flowers. He scrunched up his face. "I guess Tommy had a friend with him once or twice. Dark-haired guy. I honestly didn't pay much attention, since they stayed in the waiting room."

"Thank you. You said you never saw Tommy accompany his father on appointments. What about the dark-haired kid?" Laurel asked, her instincts humming.

The doctor's nose twitched as if he needed to sneeze. "I don't remember, but I doubt it. The mayor came in by himself except for the surgery, when his wife and Sharon accompanied him. That's how I met Sharon."

If either Tommy or Davie had been in the cardiac wing at any time, they could've seen Christine Franklin. "Thank you. Nester will also need you to verify your alibis for the other crimes." She turned and walked toward her office, already forgetting Dr. Joseph Keyes. He most likely suffered from narcissistic personality disorder, like many highly successful people. Plus, he seemed like a jerk. He had served a purpose in the investigation by revealing a possible connection that both Tommy and Davie might have to Christine Franklin.

But he wasn't the killer.

Huck's headache was getting worse by the heartbeat, but he forged on, sifting through Davie Tate's phone records. His weapon felt solid at his hip, and his hands were steady, so it was just a little headache. "So far I haven't found anything interesting."

Laurel looked up from reading through the newest victim's phone records, her eyes unfocused. "Me either." She stretched her neck. "The dentist didn't appear to have a very active social life."

Huck sighed. They didn't have any other leads to pursue right now.

She glanced at her wristwatch. "When is your follow-up appointment with the doctor?"

He shrugged.

"You're going. I need your brain to be working when we finally arrest this maniac." She flipped a page over.

"There's no need to nag me," he drawled, reaching for a yellow highlighter to mark a couple of numbers he didn't recognize. They didn't have names next to them, and they'd called Davie, so they were probably spam.

She read quickly and flipped another page over. "I don't nag. I just shoot."

He turned the page, scanning quickly and then pausing. "Hello."

"What?" She wiped dust off her fingers.

He turned the paper around to show her. "Davie Tate called Dr. Charlene Rox a couple of weeks ago." He scanned the older records. "In fact, he called her office regularly, and he received calls from there. Probably confirmation calls for appointments."

"That's interesting, isn't it." Laurel took a drink of her water. "Davie said he didn't recognize Dr. Rox's picture when I showed it to him."

"Yeah. I'm done screwing around with this kid." Huck grasped his phone and called Ena, who was working the phones this weekend. "Hi. I want a team to go pick up Davie Tate and bring him in. Give him a choice. Either he's charged with a felony and then we talk, or he comes and talks to us without being charged first. Make sure his mother is with him and that he either brings his lawyer or they waive the right to have one. Tell whoever you send to be serious and firm." He clicked off.

Laurel nodded. "Agreed. He ticks all the boxes, but there's still something missing."

"Tommy is what's missing." Huck reached for his soda and took a gulp. Sometimes sugar helped with a headache. "Between the two of them, they're connected to everybody. They don't seem to do anything without each other, even getting after-school jobs. Davie slept with Tommy's aunt, and she dumped him, and they were both probably pissed about the entire situation."

Laurel chewed on her bottom lip. "That's all true. The flowers hint at intimacy." She rubbed her chin and looked at the murder boards. "But where did they acquire them?"

She lifted her head to raise her voice. "Nester? What have you found out about the black dahlias?"

"Not much," he called back. "I've contacted several large growing operations with greenhouses that sell them, but none of those businesses have sold the flowers to anybody in this region. Especially in the amount that the killer would've had to buy. I'll keep looking, but my best bet is that they're homegrown. Somebody has a place around here—we just haven't found it. I've been doing a search of properties owned by everyone in this case, but as you know, sometimes people just rent or don't record deeds. Nothing yet."

Huck glanced at his phone. He had two hours before his checkup at the hospital, and his head actually did hurt, although his vision had remained clear.

Laurel rolled her neck. "I wonder if the Bearings lied to us about Tommy seeing the psychiatrist. Since Davie might've been seeing her, possibly Tommy was as well?"

"Perhaps. Profile Davie for me."

She twirled a pink highlighter through her good hand. "Okay. He's smart and angry about his situation in life, especially compared to his wealthy best friend. Davie was taken advantage of by Sharon Lamber, and he was hurt deeply by Abigail Caine when she tossed him from the study."

"And he was seeing Dr. Rox," Huck murmured.

"Maybe she helped him to focus his anger."

Huck crossed his arms. "Maybe not."

Laurel stared at the table for a moment. "I don't know."

"Go on."

"There's a sophistication to the stalking and the breaking and entering that I don't see in Davie. He might be intelligent, but he's still a kid."

Huck looked at the suspect board. "What about Tommy?"

"Perhaps. He's certainly more worldly and has a sense of entitlement that Davie lacks. Usually when there are partners in a crime, one is the dominant personality. Tommy could be that to Davie." She tugged on the strap of the sling holding her cast. "If so, he's very good at camouflage, which this killer would be."

"We can bring Tommy in as well. Have them see each other?"

Laurel reached for a pencil and made a notation on a sticky note. "Let's interview Davie first. If he sees Tommy, and if Tommy is the dominant personality, then he'll refuse to speak. We need to hit him hard, and if his mother is with him, we'll have a better chance of coaxing him to be honest with us."

"Whoa," Nester called out and the sound of his chair hitting the wall echoed. Clothing rustled and he ran to the door of the conference room. "Just got an email from the lab on the ballistics report. We have a match. The same gun that was used to shoot Walter was used to shoot at your truck the other night."

Huck nodded. "We expected that."

"Yes." Nester's eyes gleamed. "But did you expect the lab to find a fingerprint on a casing left by the shooter when Huck's truck was ambushed?"

Laurel gasped. "No. Whose fingerprint?"

Nester slapped his hand against the doorframe. "The fingerprint belongs to one Mr. Davie Tate."

# Chapter Thirty-Five

Taylor Tate had her son's dark hair and eyes, but her build was petite. Though the woman had to be in her mid-thirties, tops, her eyes looked older. Faded lines already cascaded out from the corners, and her shoulders hunched forward just enough to show exhaustion. Even so, she sat straight and slightly ahead of her son in the white chairs around the thick glass tabletop. "My son has done nothing wrong."

"Good." Laurel held several file folders in front of her while Huck sat like a silent angry sentinel next to her. "Then he should have no problem speaking with us, with your permission."

Taylor nodded and some of her dark hair escaped the bun she'd tamed it in. "He will talk to you."

"So you waive your right to have a lawyer present?" Huck asked.

"Yes," Davie said, staring at the table and hunching his body.

Taylor looked at the now-covered boards behind Laurel and Huck. "We waive a lawyer." Her tone indicated she didn't have a choice.

Laurel watched Davie to discern his motivations. "Are you angry at your mother?"

He jerked. "No." His face flushed.

Taylor's posture softened. "It's okay if you are. I know I spend too much time working in Seattle, but we need the money. Being mad about that doesn't make you a bad person."

Davie looked up and sideways at her before hunching over again, crossing his arms over his stomach. "I'm not mad."

Taylor rubbed her eyes.

Laurel couldn't help but feel sorry for them. It was rare for her heart to overtake her head, but today it did anyway. "Why did you lie to us, Davie?"

"I didn't." He didn't meet her eyes.

"We know you had a sexual relationship with Dr. Sharon Lamber."

Taylor jolted. "You did what?"

Even Davie's ears turned red. "So what?"

Taylor shook her head as if the world had stopped making sense. "Sharon Lamber? Tommy's aunt? When did this happen?" Anger pressed her lips tightly together.

Davie shrugged. "Between Thanksgiving and Christmas, I guess. She was funny and she liked me. And . . . I mean. You know."

"You're a child, Davie," Taylor exploded.

"Ha. I'm as grown up as anybody else," he countered. "She saw me as an adult. I felt like a man with her."

Laurel fought the urge to gag. "She was an adult and you're a minor, and she took advantage of you, Davie. That isn't your fault."

"I'm old enough to consent. She told me," Davie said.

Huck's expression mellowed a little. "If you had to be

told that by her, then you weren't old enough to actually consent."

Legally, he was wrong. Morally, he was definitely correct. Laurel nodded. "Did you talk to Dr. Rox about her during your sessions?"

Davie jerked. "How do you know about Dr. Rox?"

"We have your phone records," Huck said. "Answer the question."

Davie's shoulders slumped. "No. I didn't want Sharon to get in trouble. Plus, I thought we might get back together." He unfolded his arms. "Now we'll never get the chance." He turned to his mother. "I didn't kill her, Mom. I really didn't."

"I know, honey." She reached in and hugged him. "I do."

Laurel watched the interplay.

He turned her way. "How did you find out about me and Sharon?"

"She took pictures," Laurel said gently.

Davie frowned. "Pictures? When?"

"When you were together in her bedroom," Huck said.

Davie's jaw dropped. "There were sex pictures?" Panic had his eyes widening. "Mom, I didn't know. I swear."

"It's true," Laurel said quickly. "She took pictures of herself having sex with other people who were also unaware of the camera."

Taylor slipped an arm over her son's shoulders, fire flashing across her high cheekbones. "I want those pictures destroyed."

"They will be after we finish this case," Huck said. "Why did you lie about not recognizing Dr. Rox when you were shown a picture of her?"

Davie's chin dropped. "I was embarrassed and didn't want you all to think I was crazy."

Laurel's heart hurt for him. "It's smart to seek help if you need it. How did you start seeing Dr. Rox?"

Davie leaned into his mom's side. "I got really angry at one of my teachers after he gave me a C on a paper, and he recommended I see Dr. Rox. She helped me with my anger, and I liked her. A lot."

Laurel watched his facial expressions.

Huck sat back, looking less intimidating. "Did you talk to Dr. Rox about Dr. Caine kicking you out of her study?"

It was smart he was using their titles.

Davie nodded.

"Tell us about that anger, Davie," Laurel said.

He looked like a lost kid for a moment. "Dr. Caine made me feel important. Like she couldn't do her study without me, and then she asked me all about myself. My feelings. What I was afraid of and what I hoped to have. Who I loved, who I hated, and why. She would describe different scenarios, and I'd tell her how I'd react. Then she'd give me a vitamin shot or a drink, we'd watch clips of movies or shows, usually action ones, and then she'd ask me how I felt. We'd talk about what I truly wanted deep down, where the real me lives."

"Vitamin shots?" Huck asked.

"Yeah," Davie said.

Laurel tilted her head. "When, exactly, did you start working with Dr. Caine?"

"The beginning of January when the semester started," he said. "I got paid twenty dollars for each meeting with Dr. Caine, and she decided how many were necessary. I saw her six times before she kicked me out. I went from being interesting to her to useless." There was more than anger in his voice. Hurt?

"Oh, Davie." Taylor hugged him tighter to her side.

"You don't have to work so hard all the time. I'll make more money."

His head hung.

Huck cut Laurel a look.

She opened the top file folder and pushed a picture across the table. "What kind of a flower is this, Davie?" They'd kept that element of the case away from the media so far.

He looked up. "I don't know. A red one?"

Was he playing dumb?

Huck studied him. "Come on. You work part-time for a landscaping business. You have to know what that is."

He squinted and angled his head differently. "Dude, I have no clue. It's a flower."

"Taylor?" Laurel asked.

The woman looked away from her son to study the photograph. "Um, I don't know. A gladiolus or something like that?" She frowned.

Laurel left the picture on the table. "Did you want Sharon Lamber dead?"

"No!" he exploded. "I didn't want Sharon dead at all. I love her. I mean, I loved her. I also didn't want my shrink dead." He turned into his mom's neck. "I'm done talking to you now. Arrest me or not. I don't care anymore."

They were losing him.

"One more question, Davie. How did your fingerprint get on a bullet that nearly killed one of us?" Huck asked.

Davie jerked and turned toward Huck, tears in his eyes. "What?"

"Wait." Taylor held up a hand. "How did you get his prints?"

"He volunteers part-time for a daycare every week," Laurel said, trying to read Davie's emotions. They looked genuine, but she'd been wrong about that before. "He was printed as part of a background check, and those prints are in the state database. Let us help you, Davie."

He gulped. "I never shot at anybody. Ever."

"Okay." Huck gentled his voice. "You touched a bullet, which means you loaded a gun."

Davie scrunched up his face. "Um, yeah. Last summer, I did shoot a gun at a tree. But that was all. I swear."

The hair on Laurel's nape stood up. "Whose gun did you shoot, Davie?"

He looked down and then back up. "It was Tommy's gun. Tommy Bearing."

Laurel shivered in the chilly interrogation room at the rear of the Fish and Wildlife offices as Tommy, Teri, and Steve Bearing finally arrived and sat across from her. She hoped Huck returned soon from his checkup. He'd argued about going, but he did have a concussion, and the doctor wouldn't clear him for duty without the physical. "Thank you for coming in."

Teri Bearing's eyes flared a piercing green. "The two armed officers at our door didn't give us any choice. They *threatened* my son with a felony charge."

Good. Then they'd done their job and even now waited patiently outside in case she needed to arrest Tommy.

Steve Bearing seemed much calmer than his mother, and his gaze was calculating. "We both know you don't have the power to charge anybody, Agent Snow. Even so, we're tired of this nonsense." He leaned over and drew out a case file folder from his leather briefcase. "Here is Tommy's full juvenile record. Have fun with it."

Laurel took the folder, masking her surprise. She scanned the contents, seeing the charging documents, the affidavits, and the plea bargain. It was much as Tommy had claimed.

He'd gone ballistic on the girl's father, but he'd been scared and apparently drunk. "Tommy, did you know that your aunt had an affair with Davie Tate?"

Teri gasped, Steve jerked, and Tommy grimaced.

"Tommy?" Teri asked, what could only be considered shock in her pale expression.

"Yeah. I knew he and Aunt Sharon . . . you know." He looked at his brother. "She told him it wasn't illegal because something about age and consent and being sixteen in Washington State. Davie is seventeen."

Steve looked a little green. "That's true."

"Did that make you angry?" Laurel asked.

Tommy made a loud gagging noise. "I didn't know about it when it was happening, and when he told me afterward, I pretty much wanted to puke. It's all so gross."

"Did you know she took photographs of them engaging in sexual relations?" Laurel asked.

"Oh God." Teri fumbled in her handbag for a tissue to press against her mouth. "I can't believe this. He's a kid. What the hell was she thinking?"

Laurel sat back. It was telling the woman was outraged on Davie's behalf and not worried about scandal. Maybe she wasn't so mercurial.

Steve shook his head. "Aunt Sharon was always a free spirit, but this is way crossing the line." He kept his body at a protective angle toward his brother. "Tommy didn't kill her. I don't know how screwed up Davie might've been after that."

"Did you know that Davie was seeing a psychiatrist?" Laurel asked.

"No." Tommy looked at his brother. "I had no clue. That's not something he would've told me. But how did he get there? Maybe those were some of the days he borrowed my truck? I don't know. Crap. I really didn't know he'd gone nuts."

His mother patted his wrist. "Davie isn't nuts. He just needed help and was smart enough to ask for it." She looked up at Laurel, her body language not as rigid as before. "I don't think Davie would've killed Sharon or anybody else. He might be angry sometimes, but he's a good kid."

Laurel didn't move her focus. "Why did you lie to me, Tommy?"

Steve straightened and put a hand in front of his brother. "Don't answer that. Tell me what you're talking about, Agent Snow."

Laurel waited several seconds until Tommy dropped his gaze from hers. "You said you didn't have a gun. You did have a gun last summer, and you and Davie fired at a tree. Why would you lie about that?"

Steve stilled and looked from Tommy to Laurel. "My client does not own a gun."

"I don't," Tommy said. "Really."

"Did you take Mr. Brewerston to his doctor appointments when he was alive? To that same heart surgeon that helped your dad?" Laurel rapidly switched topics.

Tommy blinked. "Sometimes. I mean, not all the time but once in a while. The old guy was nice enough to give me a job at the architecture firm, and I liked him. I wish he wouldn't have died."

"And Davie went with you, didn't he? Yet here you are, lying to me about a gun, when Davie told me the truth. Why is that, Tommy?" Laurel asked, ignoring Steve's move to grab his briefcase. She couldn't let them leave. "Tell me."

Tommy vigorously shook his head. "No. Davie never

went with me. Nobody did when I was driving Harvey to the heart doctor."

Laurel inclined her head. Something had caught her attention. "Did you ever go to the appointments when you were not the driver?"

"Sure. I went several times, because afterward we'd go by different supply stores and I'd help load the truck." He shrugged. "I liked the old man. He told really great stories."

Laurel's phone buzzed and she tugged it from her back pocket with her good hand. "Agent Snow," she answered.

"It's Abigail." Her sister's tone was stressed. "I've had three hang up calls today, and one just came in. I'm being threatened, and I'm headed your way. This is real, Laurel. You will help me."

Laurel held up a finger to Tommy and stood. "I'll be right back." They weren't finished. She almost had the full story. She hustled outside the doorway. "Where are you?"

# Chapter Thirty-Six

Abigail Caine finished loading the crate of wine in the back of her SUV, her ear pressed to her phone. The vehicle made for a good winter vehicle, although she'd considered purchasing a Nissan Rogue like Laurel was driving right now. She didn't like the way Laurel seemed to be ignoring her again, which made it difficult to sleep. "I'm in the middle of town."

"If you're really being threatened, you need to stop shopping and come to my office." Laurel finally sounded somewhat concerned.

Abigail smiled. Now she didn't have to take some sort of action to make Laurel see that she needed a sister. It was mildly irking that Laurel was willing to let Huck Rivers in, so to speak, but not her own sister. "Why don't you come and fetch me?"

Laurel sighed.

Abigail straightened. The snow dropped lazily onto her nose and she wiped it away. It had been snowing all day, slow and methodically, and the roads were becoming impassable. The wind whistled through the deserted parking lot. Most people had taken refuge inside earlier that day. She'd do so with her sister.

"I'm in the middle of something. Come here, and we'll figure it out together."

A flake landed on Abigail's eye, and she blinked it away. A movement behind her in the parking lot had her pausing. Then a strong arm banded around her waist, partially lifting her, and a rag was pressed against her mouth. She dropped the phone to the snow, gasping in air.

The arm around her was strong.

She shoved an elbow back into a male gut, heard a pained hiss, and then pivoted her hips to gain leverage and kicked down, hitting a thigh. The hand shoved the rag into her mouth, and something acidic burned her tongue. She blew out air, trying to dislodge the rag and not to inhale. She kicked furiously back with both speed and strength.

He snarled like an animal in her ear.

Laurel yelled her name from the phone, now in the dirty snow.

The world spun and Abigail kept fighting, her limbs slowing. Her last thought before the darkness forced her arms and legs to go limp was that she'd left her gun beneath the seat. She should've carried it into the store. Laurel would have taken her weapon.

Would Laurel find her in time?

The world didn't completely go silent around her, and she felt the pain of her body being tossed in the back of a truck. Her cheek and hip hit cold metal, and pain filtered through the fuzziness surrounding her like cotton.

Then they were moving. Driving over bumpy ground. The cold and the pain helped to center her, and soon she could move her fingers again. Then her hands. The feeling began to return to her legs. What had he given her? What had been on that rag?

Not that it mattered. Right now, all that mattered was regaining her strength. Tingles swept up her legs, and she welcomed the return of sensation, even though pain accompanied each awakening nerve. Her head still felt as if a watermelon had taken residence between her ears. Was this how most people felt every day?

The truck finally came to a stop, and she unwillingly rolled to the side. Hands grabbed her ankles and yanked her out, and her nose bumped on the metal. Fury caught her but she remained limp as he flipped her around and hoisted her over his shoulder. She caught a glimpse of his determined face, confirming her suspicions.

He strode across an icy trail and then into a warm, humid building. The feeling began to return to her upper arms and shoulders. Then the area spun as she was flipped back over and landed on a wooden dolly on the floor. She blew hair out of her face and looked up at Jason Abbott.

"Was any of this truly necessary?" she murmured

He crossed his arms, looking down at her. "I think you knew we'd end up here."

She looked around the spacious greenhouse with its rows upon rows of flowering black dahlias. Several other plants grew in a bed in the far corner, one of them with lovely yellow bell-shaped flowers. "You shoved Gelsemium extract in my mouth?" The bastard. "You could have killed me."

"I was willing to take that chance," he drawled. He was dressed in black jeans, shirt, and puffer vest, his dark beard cut short, almost just scruff. His dark hair was also shorter than the last time she'd seen him. He'd always been lean and apparently in good shape, but she'd miscalculated his strength.

"That's quite unkind of you. Don't tell me this is about your hatred for your mother and all of that?" She waved a hand in the air, almost able to raise it to her waist. "I thought we took care of those silly issues."

He crouched so they were eye to eye. "Oh, we did. You taught me, Abigail. Showed me that my strength was in fighting back and taking what I want. Not waiting and seeing. Not turning the other cheek and hoping. You taught me that I was a predator. You were my light."

His mind had been surprisingly easy to infiltrate. But the two weeks away from her had changed him. She'd have to proceed carefully as she sat up fully.

He smiled and looked more like a wolf than a test subject. "But you're just a liar like all of them. At your office at the university, you're a blonde with blue eyes. Yet in real life, you look like this. I didn't even recognize you at your sister's office the other day. Why?"

She shrugged. "I can be whomever I want. Since I started at the university as a blonde, I figured I'd stay that way all year." Or perhaps she was angry with Laurel for ignoring her so she fell back on old comforts. While she now enjoyed her natural coloring when not at work, she hadn't decided to be herself at school. Surely it wasn't cowardice. She was just choosing her own time.

"Your very appearance was a lie." His smile lacked true emotion. "This is when the others started to beg and cry."

Her chuckle moved her shoulders. "I'm not one of them, and deep down, you're smart enough to know that." She leaned toward him, keeping the parts of her body that now worked completely relaxed. "If I remember correctly, we established you have just as high an IQ as any doctor. As your mother."

He lost the smile. "Don't talk about my mother."

Abigail let her smile widen. "We talked about your mother all the time while you volunteered for my study.

How you would like to go back and hit her the way she hit you. How you'd like to smash her face in so that brain she was so proud of would be crushed. Didn't she call you stupid?"

He backhanded her. "You're terrified and hiding it."

Pain crashed through her skull. She welcomed it, letting the hurt sharpen her focus. "I don't feel fear, moron. Not like you want. I'm not afraid of you. You need the fear to fulfill your pathetic fantasy. I'm not scared."

"You will be," he promised. "Or maybe you'll be the one, and you'll live." Hope glimmered in his psychotic eyes.

She unobtrusively took a deep breath, centering herself. Her legs had almost returned to full strength. "You know, it's surprising those flowers don't smell like anything." There were so many. Shouldn't they have even a light scent? "It's like you. You were without light, color, or smell. Until you met me and I helped you tap into your inner strength. What is up with these weird flowers?"

"They're black dahlias. They symbolize betrayal, the specialty of every woman. You're all filthy liars."

She sighed. "That's pedantic. So beneath a true predator. I'm very disappointed in you, Jason."

He reared up.

She tightened her legs, ready to kick when he lunged.

The door opened. A young blonde with unremarkable features walked inside, anger twisting her lips. "I knew it. I knew you were seeing somebody, Jason."

Jason jerked.

Abigail paused. "Well. This is interesting."

Jason started to stand, giving her an opening.

Abigail struck.

* * *

Laurel dodged back into the interrogation room, her phone in her good hand. "Tommy? When you went to the city but didn't drive, who drove the truck on those occasions?" She held her breath.

"Jason did. He was trying to help Mr. Brewerston, and he wanted to take over the business."

Connections and lines. Laurel's mind started to draw links and possible associations. Dr. Keyes had said a dark-haired person had been with Tommy in the waiting room when he'd brought Mr. Brewerston to appointments. He hadn't mentioned age or name. She'd assumed he'd meant Davie. "Tell me right now, or I'm going to arrest you. Did you or did you not have a gun this past summer that you showed to Davie?"

Tommy's head sank. "Yeah. I had a gun, and I told him it was mine. We shot at trees out on Maple River Road." He talked to the table. "I'm sorry. It was just fun. We didn't hurt anybody."

"Tommy?" Laurel whispered. "Whose gun was it?"

He bit his lip. "I just borrowed it. He didn't mind. It's Jason's gun."

Laurel jumped up. "Stay here." She ran through the Fish and Wildlife office and up her stairs, nearly plowing over Nester, who stood guard at the entrance to the conference room.

Davie and his mother looked up, both wide eyed.

"Davie? How did you know about the study at Washington Tech University?" Laurel gulped in air, trying to breathe.

His mouth opened and then closed. "Um, Jason told me. Him and Haylee really needed the money to keep the business afloat, and he was taking any odd job he could. He got to stay in the study, even though I had to leave. I guess I was mad about that, too."

Laurel's ears rang. Oh God.

She turned. "Nester? Get everybody out to find Abigail Caine as well as Jason Abbott. Trace Abigail's phone and call me the second you have her." She barreled out of the office and down the stairs, running to her SUV and speeding out of the parking lot.

Laurel was halfway to the center of town when Nester called. "Did you find her phone?"

"Yeah. It's just coming in. It's on, and the signal is strong from downtown Genesis Valley. Here's the address." He rattled it off. "It's a specialty wine and dessert store. I have everyone actively searching for Jason Abbott now. Units just arrived at his house as well as his place of business, and, so far, nobody has sighted him."

"Keep trying." Laurel spun a U-turn and drove as fast as she dared to the center of town, seeing Abigail's SUV parked in the lot fronting a building that housed several businesses that ranged from a nail salon to a specialty wine store. Abigail's back hatch was open. "Hold on." Laurel stopped and jumped out of her rig, running over to see Abigail's purse next to a box of wine. She looked wildly around and then ran across the icy ground to the wine store, yanking open the door.

A woman jumped back from the shelf where she was rearranging wine bottles.

"Abigail Caine. Where is she?" Laurel snapped, surveying the shelves.

The woman blinked and swallowed. "She left a while ago with wine. Why?"

"Do you have CCTV?" Laurel asked.

The woman nodded. "Yes. Outside the building. The manager has cameras focused on the parking lot. Do you want me to call him?"

"Yes. Call him and tell him that the police will be here to obtain the footage." Laurel turned and raced back to her still-running SUV. "Nester? Send an officer to obtain the footage from CCTV at this location." She put the vehicle in drive and sped away from the parking lot.

"Where are you going?" Nester asked, already typing loudly.

Her mind reeled. "Jason kills at his victim's property. The only other property I know that's owned by Abigail is the land used for Deep Green Grower's Company. I believe the entrance is near where her brother used to live." She sped up, driving dangerously for the conditions on the road. "Call Fish and Wildlife and have them send state troopers out there, and please keep trying Huck." His phone was apparently off while he underwent tests at the hospital. "Tell him where I'm going."

"You should wait for backup. I'll get them out there as soon as I can," Nester said.

"I can't. Just have everyone hurry." She careened around a corner and ended the call, her one good hand tightening on the wheel. Why hadn't she suspected Jason? He was always in the background, charming and kind with a girlfriend. Yet he had the same ties to the victims as Tommy and Davie. He probably even drove Davie to an appointment or two with Dr. Rox for counseling.

And he'd been part of Abigail's study.

That alone made a block of ice drop into Laurel's stomach. Just what behavioral modification had Abigail attempted with Jason?

The thoughts spun around and around in Laurel's head as she drove, finally steering between two tall log columns that supported a sign naming the place. Snow-covered fields stretched to the left with forests to the right of the road. She pressed on, having checked satellite pictures during the Snowblood Peak case to learn that the buildings and operations were straight ahead, along with multiple large, well-equipped commercial greenhouses.

Truck tires had left a good trail in the recently fallen snow, and she drove quickly, pausing when the tire tracks turned onto one of the many side roads through the trees. A quick look ahead confirmed that no other trucks had passed this way recently. Her gun secure on the side of her healthy hand, she turned and followed the tracks.

They led through a large forest, around several bends, and then toward the mountains and a river. A small and dilapidated cabin stood vigil to the side, its walls crumbling and its roof caved in. She kept driving through another grove and then around several more bends, finally heading back toward the river.

A greenhouse lay straight ahead, its lights on inside. A truck and a smaller car were parked beneath a wide tarp.

She pulled over beneath a stand of trees and jumped into the snow. Keeping to the tracks left by the truck, she withdrew her gun and held it in her left hand. That wasn't going to work.

Wincing, she pulled off the sling and tossed it to the side, using her cast to steady her weapon as she trod silently toward the structure, her body bent and her legs freezing.

A scream came from inside, and she moved into a run, reaching the door and pausing.

"You asshole!" a woman screamed. "How could you do this to me?"

A man spoke, his voice a low rumble.

Laurel took a deep breath and then pivoted, kicking in the door and dodging inside.

Jason Abbott immediately grabbed Haylee Johnson and yanked her against his chest, shoving a gun to her neck.

Laurel paused, gun aimed at his head. She glanced

down to where Abigail was sitting up on a wooden dolly, her lip bleeding and her eye rapidly swelling. "Are you okay?"

"Not really." Abigail wiped off her lip. "I made a move too quickly. Just give me about five minutes for my strength and mobility to fully return, and I want another shot at him. Deal?"

# Chapter Thirty-Seven

Laurel kept her gun pointed at Jason and moved cautiously to shield Abigail. "How badly hurt are you?"

"Just drugged and waiting for full feeling to return to my limbs." Abigail groaned, a board creaked, and then she stood next to Laurel. "Good timing, though."

"Get behind me."

Abigail partly obliged.

Haylee's eyes were wide as Jason held her tight against him with the gun shoved into her neck. "I don't understand. Jason? What's happening?"

"Shut up. You're not a part of any of this." He ducked enough to keep Haylee's body partially covering his head. "Agent Snow? I doubt you want to take this shot with your bad hand. Sorry about the wrist, by the way."

Haylee pushed back with her elbow into Jason's ribs. "Jason, what's going on? I don't understand." Tears filled her eyes.

Abigail stepped up beside Laurel. "Your boyfriend is the Witch Creek Killer. He wants an educated woman, a smart one, but he just can't keep it up for one. Can you, Jason?"

Laurel elbowed her. "Shut up. Get back behind me."

"No," Abigail drawled. "Jason doesn't have the balls to kill me. Or you. While the doctors he took on might've been smart, they had nowhere near our intelligence. We're probably smarter than his mama ever was."

Jason's face turned beet red, and he shoved the gun even harder against Haylee's neck. She cried out, her hands lifting in the air.

"What are you doing?" Laurel hissed.

"I'm just explaining to the scared little boy with the gun that his only out is to shoot himself," Abigail said evenly. "You and I each have more doctorates on our own than all the women he's killed combined."

Jason blinked. "You're a doctor, too? Agent Snow?"

Abigail's chuckle lacked amusement. "Several times over, Jason. Are you too dumb to know even that?"

"Stop it." Laurel stepped in front of her sister and hip checked her so she landed back a foot. "Stay behind me and be quiet."

"I can still see over your head," Abigail drawled. "Mostly."

Haylee whimpered. "I told you Dr. Caine's study was bad for you. That she was bad for you." A tear leaked down her face. "This isn't your fault, Jason. None of it. She did this to you, and I'll stand by you. Please let me go."

Jason was staring at Laurel as if he'd never seen her before. His eyes darkened. "Maybe you're the one."

Abigail's cackle stirred Laurel's hair. "There is no one."

"You said there was," he spat. "You told me. You said the darkness is okay and I can let it out. Here in town where I'm safe. Where nobody will know who I am."

Laurel's ears heated. "What else did she tell you?"

"To deal with his anger in a healthy way." Abigail elbowed her in the back. "He's just a loser with mommy issues. I was only trying to help."

"You came to me," Jason roared. "I was in a paid study

last summer that she conducted for people with insomnia. The techniques she suggested helped. Then she came to me before Christmas and told me about a new study. One about treating childhood trauma. She promised to help me become successful and get what I want."

Abigail snorted. "Apparently what you wanted was to kill women in the snow? I'm fairly certain that wasn't my idea."

Laurel needed to get closer to him. She could take the shot, but she wasn't as confident with her left hand, and she couldn't risk Haylee's life. "When did you start killing, Jason?"

He licked spittle off his lip and caught a piece of Haylee's hair. Spitting it out, he grimaced. "I don't know."

"Was Sharon Lamber your first kill?" Laurel strained to hear any sirens. They might be coming in silent if they knew she was already inside.

He gulped. "I thought she was the one. I started tracking her. Learned her every movement and routine just like Abigail and I thought a good predator should." Satisfaction tilted his lips. "Sharon had no idea. Then I decided we should have our date, and she failed. She thought she was so smart, and she failed."

Laurel angled her body to the side for a better line of sight to his brain. "What kind of rage do you have inside you?" she whispered. "To beat a woman's face like that?"

"Her brain was so impressive, she didn't deserve to have it," he countered, sounding almost bored now. "If her body couldn't do it for me, then her brain was useless, right?" He leaned down and kissed Haylee on the top of her head, smiling when she whimpered again. "Dumb girls have their places, but I deserve somebody as smart as I am, and I guess none of them came close. I was even smart enough to wear shoes two sizes too small in the snow."

He laughed. "The second I showed you my size thirteen shoes, you dismissed me as a suspect. My toes were sore for days from those damn boots, but it was worth it."

Laurel should've looked harder at the man, but he just hadn't stood out. "You're going to prison, Jason."

"No, I'm not. I'm better than everyone and smarter than you think. The right woman is just waiting for me," he snarled. "You taught me that, Abigail. That I should never settle."

Abigail snorted. "That's not what I was teaching you."

"Weren't you?" Jason cocked his head. "I don't know. I've always felt the rage, but I've never wanted to act on it until I started working with you. Until we fantasized about how we would've gotten away with the Snowblood Peak murders. On and on and on. God, I was aroused, and you knew it." His gaze grew calculating. "You even offered to rent me this greenhouse when you learned I had a passion for flowers."

"You're psychotic," Abigail muttered. "I thought you were learning to deal with trauma in a healthy way."

"I don't know. Tell me, Dr. Snow. Do you think it odd that, on the heels of the Snowblood murders, there's another ritual serial killer working in your backyard?" Jason's eyes gleamed.

Laurel still couldn't make her shot without putting Haylee in danger. "I do find that odd, Jason."

Jason stretched his neck, his pupils widening. "Your sister sure didn't stop me. We spent so much time talking about perfection and how I could reach it. How I could free the rage inside me, and that it wasn't my fault." His eyes half lowered as if remembering with pleasure. "Now that I see you two together, it does make me wonder—why did you come looking for me, Abigail?"

"Drop the gun, Jason. We'll investigate Abigail, but for

now, you have to let Haylee go," Laurel said, her voice calm. "Let me help you."

Jason tilted his head. "Er, no." He partially lifted Haylee and backed away toward the door. "Make one more move, and I will shoot her through the neck."

Haylee gasped. Her face turned red. Then she panicked, kicking back.

Jason partially dropped her as she fought furiously against him. "Damn it." In a swift move, he pointed the gun at Laurel and fired.

Fire exploded in Laurel's upper arm and she flew back into Abigail, sending them both sprawling to the hard, dirt ground. Abigail rolled to the side and grabbed the gun, coming up on her knees.

"I wouldn't," Jason yelled, shoving Haylee toward them, his gun pointed at Abigail's head.

Haylee fell into them, crying and shrieking.

"Shut up." Abigail brought the gun down on Haylee's head, and the blonde flopped once and then didn't move. Abigail then looked up at Jason, the gun in her hand.

"Put it down," Laurel hissed. There was no way Abigail could get the gun up and shoot before Jason killed her.

Abigail frowned but slowly put the weapon on the wooden dolly. "Take it easy, Jason. I think you're confused. Let's figure it out like we used to."

Laurel tried to sit, her hand going to her wounded shoulder. Blood spurted between her fingers.

"At least it's the same arm," Abigail noted dispassionately.

Laurel panted in air as her body absorbed the pain and adrenaline flowed through her veins.

Jason pointed the gun at Abigail's head. "You are afraid. Stop acting like you're not."

"She really isn't," Laurel breathed out, her arm on fire. "You're wrong about her. No matter what you do, she won't be afraid of you." The man obviously needed fear; they couldn't show any. "The only woman in this greenhouse who's afraid of you is now unconscious." Hopefully not injured too badly. "And she loves you. Don't you feel anything for her?"

"I've tried!" Jason yelled, throwing up his hands and then quickly regaining his focus and pointing the gun at them again. "I really tried, but she just couldn't make me happy. None of them made me happy."

The guy was quickly unraveling.

Abigail set her hand on her thigh at the same level as the gun on the dolly. "Maybe it isn't up to others to make you happy. After studying you for so long, I have to conclude that you can't be happy. You will never be happy. Only you can control your future, Jason." She jerked her head in the direction of his gun, even though the barrel was pointed at her. "Maybe it's time to join your mother."

Laurel fought to remain conscious as the pain increased in intensity. She forced herself up onto her knees. "Just put down the gun and let us help you."

"No," Abigail said, her body stiffening. "I think you know you can't be helped."

"This is your fault!" Jason screamed, jabbing the gun toward her. "I was angry but trying to make a good life before you. Before you jabbed shit in my veins and made me feel invincible. None of those women made me feel like that." He sobered, his face going stony and calm. "Only you." He blinked, his gaze focusing on her as his voice slowed. "This was all practice. They were all dry runs until I could get you here. Abigail." He licked his lips and rolled the sounds around on his tongue, almost sounding like he was humming a low sonnet.

Abigail snorted. "You still won't be able to get it up."

Laurel coughed and struggled to edge toward Abigail. "Don't listen to her, Jason. You were used and you were hurt. I really can help you." She didn't like the way his mood had changed.

"No. You can't." If anything, regret twisted his lips. "You and Haylee are in the way now."

"Wait. You have to at least explain the flowers. I know they symbolize betrayal, but where did you first see them?" Laurel was desperate to keep him talking. Help had to be arriving soon.

He shrugged. "I saw them on an old television show, and I thought they were beautiful. Then I learned more about them, and I figured they're just like women. Lovely and fragile looking but dark at heart. And they freeze so beautifully—just like women do." His gaze cut to Abigail again. "I hope you don't freeze. We're going to have to find a field closer to your home, if you don't mind. We can't stay here." His chin lifted and he breathed out slowly, his body undulating slightly. "You're going to be stunning in the snow."

"Wait, Jason—" Laurel started. She bunched her legs.

"No." He turned and pointed the gun at her head. "If you're around, she can't give her full attention to me. Sorry I didn't know you were a doctor. It's too late now."

Laurel dove for her gun just as the outside door burst open.

Jason turned and Huck kicked the gun out of his hand. Then Jason dove forward and emitted a furious roar, hitting Huck mid-center and half lifting him against the doorframe, which crumpled.

Huck dropped to his feet and punched Jason once in

the face, and then struck him several times in the torso, propelling the killer back toward the flowers. He finished with an uppercut that threw the man up and then down to smash several dahlia plants. His body jerked once and more petals wafted to the dirt floor. Huck brushed snow off his face and then grabbed Jason's shoulder and turned him over, quickly securing him with zip-ties he withdrew from his back pocket.

Laurel sat on the dolly, dropping her now bloody gun to the side to put pressure on her wound.

Sirens echoed in the distance.

Huck scanned the interior of the greenhouse and then hurried to her, crouching. "How bad?"

"I'm uncertain." She let her head loll on her shoulders.

"You're okay." He grasped her good shoulder and leaned over to check for Haylee's pulse. "Was she shot?"

"Just unconscious," Abigail said, dusting off her hands.

State and local police officers came through the door first, and once they'd made sure the scene was secure, they let the paramedics in.

Officer Zello yanked Jason up and shoved him toward the door. The killer was sniffling as he went by.

Laurel lifted her head. "By the way, you are *so* fired from working on my barndominium." She tried to focus on Huck, but her eyes wouldn't cooperate. "I need to find a new architect." She started to pitch sideways.

"I'll start asking around." Huck caught her, holding her upright. Then he lifted her to a gurney and set her down. She grabbed his coat with her good hand and drew his ear to her mouth so she could whisper. "Get a warrant for Abigail's office and lab at the university. I want everything." Then she finally let the bliss of unconsciousness take away the pain.

# Chapter Thirty-Eight

Laurel sat in the hospital bed as her mother once again fluffed her pillows. "I'm fine." The surgery the day before to remove the bullet from her shoulder had been successful, and she'd had a good night with decent sleep. The pain meds were helping, and it was almost lunch time. She'd already seen both her uncles, her aunt, and Kate with her girls. "I'm tiring a mite, Mom."

"Oh." Deidre leaned over and kissed her forehead. "All right. Just keep the radio off, okay? That silly Rachel Raprenzi is all over this story, and she acts like she knows you."

Laurel sighed. "Let's worry about her later."

Deidre nodded. "Fair enough. I'll go home and check on the new teas that came in yesterday. I'll bring you some in a few hours and read to you."

"Thanks." She could actually read to herself, but if that made her mother happy, all right. "Wait a sec, please. You said that the subscription service is going really well and you're swamped. Are you looking to hire more help?"

"Actually, yes. I've been so busy, I haven't even had a chance to place an ad. Why do you ask?" Deidre smoothed the blanket over Laurel's legs.

"I know someone who's looking for a job. She seems kind and she could use the benefits, I think. Her name is Taylor Tate and she has a son who needs a break. What do you think?"

"Fine by me. Text me her information and I'll call her." Deidre patted her knee. "Now get some sleep."

When Deidre left, Laurel settled down for a nap and ended up counting ceiling tiles for about ten minutes instead.

"Hello?" Nester stood in the doorway with a legal notepad in his hand. "Are you up for a visit? I worked all night and have the results from Dr. Caine's office and lab at the university."

"Yes. Definitely yes." It was killing Laurel that she hadn't gotten to help serve the warrant the previous night, but she vaguely remembered Huck talking to her after the surgery and saying he'd take care of it. "Please tell me you found something."

Nester loped inside, wearing jeans and a ratty T-shirt on his day off. Or rather, what should've been his day off.

"I'm sorry I'm having you work weekends during your first month with the team." Just because she worked all the time didn't mean her team shouldn't have some time off.

A nurse rolled Walter in, seated in a wheelchair. "You get used to it," he said, his voice still a little wheezy. "I heard you got shot, too."

Laurel pushed the button to raise the head of her bed. "Yes, but I only took one bullet. You took three."

Walter grinned, his thin hair wispy around his ears. He was still pale, but his eyes were clear. "I guess I win, then." He looked at Nester, who drew up a yellow plastic chair. "Are we having a meeting?"

"Yes," Laurel said. "Hopefully with interesting news."

Nester looked down at the notepad. "I wish. The truth is that Dr. Caine kept meticulous records on each patient in each study, and as far as I can tell, the purpose was to investigate how or why they'd react in certain situations. I found no evidence that she tried to manipulate them or get them to act in any particular way."

Laurel wondered if she'd gotten to the records in time. "She definitely influenced Jason Abbott. Did you find any sort of drugs? Psychedelic, opioids, and so on that could influence the subjects' reactions?"

"No. There were vitamin B shots, which I've already had the lab confirm," Nester said. "She recorded many of the sessions, and I've watched them. Didn't see anything unusual, and all of the scenario videos she has on her computer seem just fine."

"I have no doubt Abigail kept two sets of records," Laurel muttered. Most of the research was probably acceptable.

Nester shook his head. "You can't really think she created a serial killer just to get your attention. Just so you two could work together?"

"I don't know," Laurel admitted. "I think it's possible."

"If she's as smart as I suspect, then we'll never prove it," Walter said.

The nurse returned. "That's long enough, Walter." She appeared to be in her early twenties and had pretty brown eyes.

Walter sighed. "Okay. I'll be back later. Walk out with me, Nester. The boss needs some sleep, whether she agrees or not." He kept talking as Nester took over for the nurse. "I'm thinking I need to get in shape once I'm out of here. How about we create an office health initiative?" Their voices trailed off.

Laurel closed her eyes and counted the stars in their constellations.

"I can tell that you're not sleeping." Abigail said.

Laurel opened her eyes. "I was counting stars."

"Which ones?" Abigail strode into the room in blood-red heels, wearing a black dress.

"The Seven Sisters." The cluster had always interested her.

Abigail smiled, her red-painted lips curving. A mottled bruise on her cheekbone extended to her puffy eye. "How apropos." She switched her clutch to her other hand. "I'm trying not to feel hurt by the fact that you had your goons turn my office and laboratory upside down."

Laurel pushed the button so she was even more upright. "Are you succeeding?"

Abigail pouted. "Somewhat. You were shot, so perhaps you weren't thinking clearly."

Any decision her half sister made would be calculating rather than emotional. "You know what I think."

"I do." Abigail lowered her chin in a conspiratorial way. "You think I'm a sociopath or some other nice label who played with a young man's head just for fun and that my experiment went horribly wrong." She tsked her tongue. "But you're incorrect. I'd never do such a thing. My time is much too valuable."

She looked at a diamond-encrusted watch on her wrist. "I spent two hours this morning being interviewed by the police. I really had no idea Jason Abbott wanted to rent that greenhouse to grow black dahlias. He said he wanted it for plants and his business, and I frankly forgot all about it. The place is miles away from anything else on the property. Who knew he was growing those horrible flowers? I've never even seen a flower like that."

So much for pinning Abigail down. "You're dressed nicely."

"I have a date. Dr. Joseph Keyes invited me to a fundraiser in Seattle, and we both share a mutual interest in you, so I figured I'd go. You're not interested in him, are you?"

"No."

Heavy footsteps sounded and Huck strode inside with a backpack slung over one shoulder. "Hey. I brought—" He stopped at the sight of Abigail in the room. "Dr. Caine." Aeneas ran inside, turned in a circle, and then sat by Huck's ankle.

Abigail chuckled, sliding her hand down his arm. "You did not bring me." She clipped to the door and pivoted. "Feel well, sister. I'll check on you tomorrow." The sound of her heels down the hallway came back clearly and then softened, finally disappearing.

Huck shuddered. "That woman." Then he turned and his brown eyes warmed. "You look better."

"Thanks. The warrants for Abigail's records didn't lead to anything." Her frustration was dulled by the pain meds.

Huck sank onto the yellow chair and placed the backpack on the floor. "Let's start with you for a moment. How are you feeling?"

Oh. Well, she could discuss personal matters before returning to the case. "I'm healing well and I've been thinking." She shifted uneasily.

"That's not unusual."

Amusement ticked through her. "True. But getting shot and seeing you hurt made me think that perhaps life is short." She plucked at a string on the blanket. "I spoke with my boss earlier and put in a request to lead the Violent Crimes Task Force permanently out of Genesis Valley."

Huck leaned back in his chair. "What did he say?"

She sighed. "That he'd take the matter under consideration and give me an answer within the week. In the meantime, I thought, well, I considered, that perhaps we should have dinner together." When Huck didn't answer right away, she hastened to say, "You and me. On a date. Not my boss and I."

Huck grinned and the bandage near his hairline moved. "It's nice to be on the same page with you for once." He opened the bag and whipped out burgers and fries. "I ordered yours loaded except for onions."

She smiled. They had eaten together at a diner once during their previous case. "You remembered."

"Yeah." He set a basket of fries on the bed and then kicked back, the scruff on his hard jaw several days past a five o'clock shadow. A lock of his dark hair fell onto his forehead. In the too-small chair, he looked strong and wide. Very handsome.

"You're good looking," she murmured.

He munched on a fry, watching her carefully. "Thanks. So are you."

"I'm okay." She took a fry with her good hand. It was nice and salty. Her body felt relaxed and warm. The sensations might be from the meds or it could be she enjoyed the captain's company. He was intriguing and so different from anybody she'd ever met. The memory of him rushing in to keep her from getting shot by an armed lunatic kept running through her mind. "You know, we do work well together."

"You make a good partner." He reached over and patted the dog's head. "Although I'd like it if we both stopped getting shot."

She nodded; the room was still nicely fuzzy. "It's a deal.

No more getting shot." She took another fry. "Did you check on Haylee Johnson?"

"Yeah. She was released last night with a little headache and was making noises about suing Abigail, but I don't think she was serious. I think she's freaking out because she was engaged to a serial killer. Poor thing." He shook his head. "The woman had no idea."

"Jason Abbott is a psychopath. He only fakes emotion but is quite convincing." He was also charming and good looking, which were disarming attributes as well. "Has he been charged yet?"

"Not yet, but he's in custody." Huck leaned over and snagged a fry. "We searched his home and found the bloody ax, a journal listing all of his kills, and Sharon Lamber's camera. That guy is nuts."

Laurel settled back against the pillows. "Did you speak with him? About the study with Abigail?"

"I did, and he has a much different tale to tell than what we've found on her computer. There's no way to prove whether any of what he says is true. He said he wasn't violent until he worked with her." Huck chewed thoughtfully and then petted the dog again. "When you're out of here, let's do something fun. Maybe see a movie like normal people."

She opened the burger wrapper. "That sounds lovely to me. Although, I feel I should warn you that I'm terrible at dating."

"Why's that?" He took more of the fries.

She bit into the burger, and it was delicious. "I miss subtext, sarcasm, and subtlety. Also, I become obsessed with my work."

"Ditto, and I like to be left alone usually. Plus, it's just a movie. As partners, even."

She smiled. "That's acceptable."

He cleared his throat. "I also talked to your boss this morning and assured him you were okay, probably before you talked to him because he didn't mention your request. The guy seems to really respect you. He said to ask you how many people have worn red jewelry within three yards of you this last week."

She chewed thoughtfully. "Eleven if you count maroon beads, which he would."

Huck's eyebrow lifted. "Interesting. How many men have worn tennis shoes within three yards of you in the last two weeks?"

"Twenty-seven. Which is an odd number, considering it's winter and only boots make sense." One guy had even been wearing shorts and no socks. People really were crazy.

Huck grinned. "This is a fun game."

"I enjoy it." She cleared her throat. "There's one question that has been bothering me about this case from the beginning, and it's nagging at me, even with the wonderful pain meds in my blood."

Huck ate another fry. "What question?"

"The one you asked when we were walking in the snow. What's the likelihood of two serial killers working in our small Genesis Valley within months of each other?" She took a sip of her water, her chest heavy. "Statistically, I can't compute a number."

Huck nodded. "It seems like Abigail just wants to be your focus. Is she so malignantly narcissistic that she'd push an obviously sick individual into killing, just to gain your attention?"

Laurel looked down at her hands. "I don't know. But the puzzle pieces click together when you consider that possibility."

His eyes sharpened. "I agree. Plus, there's one more thing. I was going to wait until you were out of the hospital to tell you this, but you're already there, of course. It won't lead to any result without proof but does verify what your head and my gut say."

"What's that?" She stopped with a fry half way to her mouth.

"When I talked to Jason Abbott earlier, he did tell me one interesting thing when he stopped sniffling and feeling sorry for himself."

Laurel straightened. "What?"

"He had started to follow Abigail from a distance, but she scared him, so he didn't go near her until this last attack. Also, he swears, and I believe him, that he never left black dahlias on her front lawn. She must've done that herself."

Laurel dropped the fry. "But that means . . ."

"Yeah. It does. She knew everything from the very beginning."

Check out Rebecca Zanetti's
newest Dark Protectors novel, available now!
# GARRETT'S DESTINY
**Pulsing with passion, adventure, and
paranormal suspense and romance,
the latest novel in award-winning
and *New York Times* bestselling author
Rebecca Zanetti's Dark Protectors series delivers an
immortal hero and a dream come true . . .**

### *Love and danger . . .*
For most of his life, Vampire-Demon Garrett Kayrs,
nephew of the King of the Realm, has carried a heavy
mantle of responsibility with ease and control. Fate
declared him heir to the throne, Fortune marked him with
the power of the mysterious circle of Seven, and Chance
promised more surprises to come. Nothing deterred him
from his path. Until the nightmares began—agonizing
dreams of having a female, *the* female, his *mate*, on the
back of his motorcycle—only to have her torn away
from his protection. He feels the menace around her,
the danger she's in, and he can't rest until he finds her . . .

### *Duty and desire . . .*
Destiny Applegate bears the weight of her name with
a respectful balance of fear and purpose. She has been
given some direction, but not nearly enough to truly
understand her duty, what she was born to do. Even as a
child, she had a sense of *him. The* him, her *mate.*
A dream moment or two with him that might have saved
her—or possibly cursed her. So now, when he finds her,
she has no choice but to jump on the back of his bike and
do her best to hold on until she discovers her path—
even if that means ending his.

**"Spicy romantic interplay; highly recommended."**
—*Library Journal* on *Vampire's Faith*

**"Sizzling sex scenes and a memorable cast."**
—*Publishers Weekly* on *Claimed*

Visit our website at
**KensingtonBooks.com**
to sign up for our newsletters, read
more from your favorite authors, see
books by series, view reading group
guides, and more!

Become a Part of Our
**Between the Chapters Book Club**
Community and Join the Conversation